THE AFFAIRS OF STATE

THE AFFAIRS OF STATE

By

TIM STEELE

John —

It ain't
Moby Dick ... but go
to page 206.

Tim
18 Jan 2005

Published in Great Britain by Twenty First Century Publishers Ltd.

A catalogue record of this book is available from the British Library.

ISBN: 1-904433-17-0

Cover design: John and Fred Piechoczek.

To order further copies of this work or other books published by Twenty First Century Publishers visit our website: www.twentyfirstcenturypublishers.com

Acknowledgements

It's entirely possible that without the *Monkey Business* picture of Donna Rice sitting on Gary Hart's lap in 1987 Ken Starr wouldn't have released his Religious-Right approved pornographic tome in 1998. Then I wouldn't have had this idea. So I guess everyone involved in those stories deserves acknowledgement, but not necessarily thanks.

However, I would like to thank Fred Piechoczek and everyone associated with Twenty First Century Publishers. The editing was light-handed but deft. I couldn't ask for more from a publisher, unless it's an all-expenses-paid international book tour and a clean MasterCard.

Mostly, though, I need to thank Drew and Adrienne. Their keen eyes and curiosity make dinner conversation interesting and my life meaningful. They said they'd be mad at me if I didn't even try to get this published.

Of course, they haven't read it yet...

Dedication

For Dottie

who loathes Bill Clinton
as much as I love the guy

Chapter 1 – Prologue

Michael Audray was nearly eighty-nine years old when he died on June 30, 2004. His death, although sudden, was not completely unexpected at his age. He died in his sleep, a seemingly peaceful end to a life that had been anything but ordinary.

The recipient of three Peabodys, two Marconis, countless local awards and a member of the National Museum Radio Hall of Fame for more than 20 years, Michael Audray was familiar to most Americans as the host of The Midday Conversation with Michael Audray on the Betz Radio Network for more than forty-five years.

From its inception in 1939 until his retirement in 1984, Michael Audray conducted more than 20,000 interviews with more than 9,000 guests. Everyone from powerful politicians and regal royals to insufferable actors and trend-setting designers sat across from Michael Audray in the BRN Studio on D Street, Washington DC. But in all that time, he never once had a one-on-one, on-the-record interview with a past or present president of the United States.

That had everything to do with his involvement in the resignation of Franklin Roosevelt on November 7, 1941.

Michael Audray grew up in Carmel, Indiana. The Depression was an overarching experience for everyone in Carmel. His dad had a job selling shoes, which was more than anybody else in their neighborhood could say. Michael was fifteen when things really got tough in 1930. He and his seventeen-year-old brother Pete swept up in the barbershop, delivered groceries, and washed windows. But Michael found his calling when he went to the newspaper office and became a copy boy.

His boss at the newspaper, John Dubosh, was nothing like the newspaper boss from The Front Page. Dubosh was really a kind old guy who saw a spark and encouraged Michael to give newspapers a try.

Dubosh was fond of telling his young employees, "The press is the most powerful tool on Earth, so you needn't be afraid."

Dubosh knew a journalism professor at the University of Michigan and told Michael to send him a letter, and to use his name. Michael won a scholarship and soon was in Ann Arbor.

After graduation, Michael Audray left Michigan for Washington, because that's where all the action was. Europe was in turmoil, the country was slowly coming out of the Depression, there was hope in the air. He left Ann Arbor on a Tuesday, got to Washington on a Thursday, and by the next Wednesday had a job.

He was hired by the Washington Herald to follow the Congressional delegation from six key Midwest states. The Herald had five Congressional reporters, each covering a different region. Because he was from Indiana, they gave him the Midwest.

He got to know all the congressmen from his home state, Michigan, Ohio, Illinois, Wisconsin and Kansas. He learned how to read between all the congressional double talk they'd put into bills and amendments, and, in the tradition of hard-hitting reporters, he learned how to drink. He got his share of stories, an occasional scoop or two, and learned how to write crisp copy on deadline. He was also making enough money to start dressing well.

While working at the Herald, he met Lorena Hickok. She'd been a reporter for AP, but at this point she worked in the White House crafting their policy field reports and helping Eleanor Roosevelt with her newspaper column. He'd see her from time to time at White House functions, where they'd pass the time briefly

In 1938, Peter Betz announced plans to launch a new radio network. He was sixty-two years old and had the energy of a man half that. Peter Betz had not only survived the Depression: he had thrived during it. The word on him was Bootlegger, and though no one ever proved it, he never denied it either. Besides the booze, Peter Betz was a tobacco wholesaler, a textile investor and a Ford automobile dealer. On occasion, he invested in movie productions and was one of the early, silent investors in *Life* magazine. Betz told anyone who would listen that his new network would revolutionize the way people reacted to the radio and electronic news.

He based the Betz Radio Network in Washington and put out the word that he was looking for young bucks to come join his network. Radio experience was not necessary, only a desire to do good work, work long hours, get paid a fair price and come back to do it again. Michael Audray applied, and to his incredible surprise, got a call back the very next day. Peter Betz chose him to host a daily talk show. Peter wanted a show that could cover both government and entertainment issues, featuring interviews with newsmakers and stars. The time slot and the name of the show would be determined. The salary, $30,000, was a huge raise for Michael Audray.

The first person he told was his girlfriend, Sharon Tozzi, a legislative aide to New Hampshire's Senator Paul Buckfield. He didn't know how to tell his editor at The Herald, Stanton Blanchard. Sharon suggested he walk into Blanchard's office reading his last article out loud, then tag it with, "This is Michael Audray reporting for Betz Radio News."

He did. Blanchard threw him out of the office, and threatened to break his legs if he ever came crawling back for a real reporter's job. Michael knew he had made the career choice of a lifetime.

For the next few months Michael studied the craft of radio, came to understand the differences between radio and newspapers, and began to figure out how to get people to pay attention to an upstart network.

Over the years, Michael Audray came to be included on all the A-Lists in official and unofficial Washington. He was recognized as a smart and canny interviewer, able to extract unintended information from his guests. He was a shaper of public opinion in both the political and entertainment spheres, and over the course of his career, he made more than a handful of celebrities simultaneously squirm and squeal.

He was the subject of numerous profiles over the decades, and was generous with his time and comments on any number of topics. But he steadfastly refused to grant any on-the-record interviews related to the FDR resignation, maintaining that history and historians would interpret the events any number of ways.

In 1984, he left his daily one-hour program, but he continued his association with BRN. At seventy-one, he signed a sixteen-year contract with the network to produce a daily five-minute interview segment. Five Minutes with Audray ran each weekday at 12:30 p.m., right in the middle of the time slot he held for those forty-five years. His goal was to continue broadcasting into 2000, and then he'd retire. He reached his goal, and as usual, put BRN in an enviable position. Although the network had over 800 affiliates, not all of them took all the programming offered. But Five Minutes with Audray not only cleared all 800 BRN stations, it also aired on 500 more, making it - and him - the most listened to program on radio. At eighty-five, still spry and sharp of mind, but getting weaker in voice, Michael Audray retired for good on July 4, 2000, exactly sixty-one years after his auspicious network debut.

Tim Steele

Michael Audray was the reason I got into radio. As a high schooler, while everyone else was listening to Duran Duran and early Madonna, I was listening to the last few years of his daily show, and then each five minute segment. If I couldn't hear a particular five-minute show, I'd set up my tape deck to record it. I didn't always agree with what he said, but I was completely taken with how he said it, how he did it, and how he got people to talk.

I went to the University of Missouri and became a Journalism Major. Most of my friends wanted to become TV reporters or anchors, a few wanted to become Woodward and Bernstein, but I just wanted to go into radio and talk with a lot of people. I graduated in 1986 and landed on my feet as a reporter with KMOX, the 50,000 watt giant in St. Louis that gave the world Harry Caray, Jack Buck and Bob Costas, to name a few.

Shortly after I began at KMOX, I began writing letters to Michael Audray. Not fan letters, but letters asking for an on-the-record interview about the one subject he refused to discuss. He always wrote back, always politely declined, and as the letters continued, he replied with more good-natured encouragement for me - but he wouldn't grant me an interview.

I wrote more than fifty letters to him between 1988 and 1993 to no avail. Then, in 1996, he wrote me a letter out of the blue. He told me if I was still interested in discussing FDR with him, he'd talk with me after he retired in 2000. He also laid down three conditions. One, he wanted everything recorded on both audio and video tape. He didn't want final editing control, but he wanted a complete copy of each tape for his family, just in case they didn't like the way I put the story together. Two, if I told anyone at all he had agreed to this interview at any point along the way between 1996 and 2000, the interview was off. No questions asked. And three, he wanted me to wait to air and/or publish the interviews until after his death.

I agreed to all three conditions, although truth be told, it was difficult not telling anyone I had snagged the Interview of the Century…or at least, the Interview About The Story of the Twentieth Century. But I had a few conditions that I asked for as well. I wanted to meet with him soon and often, in order to establish a relationship before the actual interviews began. He agreed. And I didn't want to do these interviews in a studio. I wanted them to be recorded in his home in Georgetown. After thinking about that, he agreed.

We began our discussions on Monday, July 10, 2000, just six days after he officially retired. By this time, I was a correspondent for CBS Radio based in Washington. I took a two-month leave of absence, and met with

4

Michael Audray nearly every day. Some days, we'd talk for hours on end about the FDR Scandal, and on other days, we'd talk about Tiger Woods and drink Molsons while watching The Golf Channel. Most of the time, though, he was focused and anxious to tell his story, a story he had kept inside him for nearly sixty years.

What follows are his words. Shortly after FDR's resignation, he wrote everything down, and kept those notebooks in a safe deposit box in Carmel. He took great pains to keep them private, and although his wife and children knew of their existence, they never read them. In his will, he stipulated that if he hadn't granted an official interview about the FDR story before his death, these notebooks should be published. When we began our interview, he allowed me to read his original notes. In some instances, I have used quotations and cross-checked dates and people from his notebooks to supplement his remarkably few memory lapses. I've also cleaned up some confusing attributions and made it more clear to whom he was referring. And because our conversations stretched over a two-month period, I've put them in a chronological order, but have taken great pains to keep them in context. By and large, though, what you read is what he said in the way he said it about one of the most compelling stories in American history, and his part in it.

And if you don't believe me, both his family and I have a complete set of audio and video recordings. This is Michael Audray's story about what is known as The Affairs of State.

July 4, 1939: Lou Gehrig retires from the Yankees, declaring he's "the luckiest man on the face of the Earth."
July 26, 1939: FDR terminates the 1911 Japanese-American Treaty of Commerce.
September 1, 1939: Hitler invades Poland.
September 3, 1939: England and France declare War on Germany.
September 5, 1939: FDR declares Neutrality and National Emergency.
November 4, 1939: FDR signs Neutrality Act.

Chapter 2 - The Betz Radio Network

BRN began broadcasting coast-to-coast with a loose network of one hundred stations on July 4, 1939. Our studio was on D Street, centrally located in DC's hub. Peter Betz made the fortuitous decision to put our air-studio on the main floor with a picture window looking out on the sidewalk. What we lost in soundproofing we made up for in tourist gawking.

Peter Betz took a very hands-on approach to BRN, and said he would remain the Executive in Charge for at least two years. That was fine with me. It allowed me, and everybody else, to concentrate on putting on interesting stories and programs, while he took the heat for things that went awry and pulled the strings that made things happen.

He put his office on the second floor, directly above the air studio. From that vantage point, he could hear the program by listening through the floorboards or turning on the radio, and he could watch the crowds gather outside the window. He could also see The Capitol. Peter had more friends in higher places than anyone I ever saw, even today. He knew everyone, and everyone, it seemed, wanted to know him.

He took it upon himself to line up the first guest for BRN. He made the decision that BRN would initiate its new network at precisely noon on Independence Day. And he wanted it to be stirring, patriotic and memorable.

With hardly any effort, it seemed, he was able to secure the United States Marine Corps Band to play *Stars and Stripes Forever* at the head of the initial broadcast. He also had the sense to make a recording of that for posterity.

Peter tried mightily to land FDR as the first guest. Roosevelt, though he knew Peter, was hosting a reception for Norway's Prince Olav and Princess Martha, who were visiting the United States to dedicate the Norwegian exhibit at The World's Fair. But FDR told his vice president, John Nance Garner, to fill in.

Garner, who had once told the press that "the Vice Presidency isn't worth a warm bucket of spit," reluctantly agreed to FDR's command. Garner had famously refused to campaign with Roosevelt in both 1932 and 1936, believing that no one cared what the second-in-command said or thought. But Roosevelt suggested Garner utilize this opportunity to draw the distinction that Congress was standing in the way of Roosevelt's initiatives, such as increased funding for the Works Progress Administration and revising the Neutrality Laws. Garner acquiesced.

In this context, Peter Betz handed me the assignment of interviewing the first guest on BRN, the sitting vice president of the United States. But he also handed me something else:

The first question.

Peter told me what he wanted asked. He told me that this was the only question he could think to lead off their network news coverage, and, again playing to the theatrical, told me this would get people talking. Talking about BRN, talking about a new twist to radio news, talking about me.

Although I could see the news value of the question, I thought it was an inappropriate time to ask this of the vice president, and I told that to Peter. He told me that unless I asked Garner this question, and made it my first question, I would have to go groveling back to The Herald, or worse, back to Carmel. He was adamant.

I was twenty-four, figured I had options. I could conduct the interview my way, or I could do it his way. My way meant the highway. His way meant fame. I decided to go with his way.

About 11:45 a.m., Vice President Garner walked into the Betz Radio Network news studio. He was older than my father, taciturn to the hilt. We exchanged pleasantries, as I reminded him that we had met a year before at a State Department function honoring the shah of Iran. He feigned a memory, and gladly accepted the coffee I offered. We sat down and got ready to begin the broadcast when Peter Betz came in. He shook Garner's hand, looked him in the eye, told him thanks for coming. Then he said:

"Mr. Vice President, just relax. Michael's the best we've got."

Then he left. Didn't look at me, didn't turn around, just left the studio. Precisely at noon, Lee Harris, the BRN Staff Announcer, kicked off a new era in radio news and entertainment.

"Live from D Street in Washington DC, this is BRN, the Betz Radio Network. With great pride and humility, we begin broadcasting today, America's Independence Day, on over one hundred radio stations around this country. On behalf of Peter Betz and the entire staff of BRN, we welcome you to what we promise will never be boring, always informing radio news and information. We proudly welcome the United States Marine Corps Band to lead us today!"

While they played, the vice president and I barely spoke. I was going over my notes and trying to keep my heart from beating completely through my chest. Outside our window a crowd of nearly 250 stared in at us. I took a final slug of water, and then I heard the band end. My cue.

"Good afternoon, and welcome to BRN, the Betz Radio Network. My name is Michael Audray. Each day at this time we will feature a prominent person in the news for a live one-hour interview. We call this program the BRN Midday Conversation. Today, as our first guest, we are honored to have the vice president of the United States, Mr. John Nance Garner in our studio. Thank you for joining us, Mr. Vice President."

"It's my pleasure to be here, Michael."

Here we go, I thought. My whole life and career was right here, right now. I glanced out the window at the 250 or so gawkers, front and center, looking in at us, standing immediately underneath the radio speakers. In that instant, I made a conscious decision to go forward, not look back.

"Mr. Vice President, administration insiders tell BRN that you and the president rarely see each other and speak to each other even less. In fact, we're told that the president has made it clear that you will not be a member of the Democratic ticket next year should the president decide to run for a third term. How do you respond to this?"

The crowd gasped. Betz smiled. Garner steamed. I strangely found myself in another zone, almost as if I was looking down on myself.

Garner was clearly off stride. My newspaper side said let him think of his answer. My radio side said he better say something quick. Garner squirmed then said, "Nonsense. The president and I get along fine, and I enjoy his full support."

"Well, when was the last time you and the president spoke privately?"

"Oh, I don't remember exactly."

"Isn't it true, Mr. Vice President, that you and the president haven't seen each other privately in over two years? Isn't it true, Mr. Vice President, that the president thinks so little of you that he hasn't invited you to sit in on any cabinet meetings since early this term?"

Garner was furious. "Mr. Audray, you are young and ill-advised of the way Washington works. If I were you, I would find someone to interview who is more suited to your intellectual capabilities, like perhaps a short-order cook."

With that, Vice President John Nance Garner got up from his chair and walked out of the BRN studios, past the crowd of 250 stunned citizens.

I, however, didn't know what to do. I still had fifty-five minutes to fill, and I had no guest. The thought occurred to me that I also had no future.

Well, somehow I muddled through it with a hodgepodge of well-wishers and on-the-fly staff introductions. When the hour was over, finally, I went right upstairs to Peter's office.

I burst through the door, and before I could say anything, he blurted, "That was the best goddamn thing I ever heard! We're going to shake this town up like no one else ever has! And you, Michael Audray, will soon be the most talked about personality in the country."

That changed what I was going to say. Instead of "What the hell did you make me do?" and "I quit", I heard myself say, "Really?"

"Yes, really. All those other networks are devoted to hard news, the whys and the hows and the whats of things. There's lots of places to hear that information. But people want to hear about other people. They want to know the gossip. They want to feel like they know the people who are in power, or in the movies, or on the radio. They want to feel like an insider. And we're gonna give it to them."

I remember being numb. It was news to me, frankly, that Peter intended BRN to be a personality driven network, who would be more than happy to investigate - and report - the lives of movie stars and politicians. For me, it was a far cry from investigating railroad expansion and the funding for the Tennessee Valley Association.

Then Janine Hart, his secretary, came in and told us that both CBS and NBC wanted to interview me.

"Tell them I don't want to talk with them," I said.

"You'll talk with them," Peter said. "Janine, tell them he'll be with them in a minute. First CBS. Sevareid?" She shook her head, "Collingwood."

He turned to me. "Michael, you'll talk to these networks, and you'll tell them that you were just being a journalist asking a very public figure a legitimate news question. No one has ever run for a third term before, and FDR's gonna. He's gearing up for another campaign, and you're just trying to find out how the second most powerful man in the country feels about his boss. If you do this, and do it with some conviction in your voice, by this time tomorrow you'll have everyone listening to this network." Then he told me something that could've been the mantra for BRN, then and now. He said, "Look, this isn't newspapers. We're in the entertainment business. There's enough ways for people to find out what's going on in the world. All we're doing is taking a different angle than everyone else. Go talk to Collingwood."

I stood there for what seemed like minutes, but was probably only ten seconds. My entire life, past and future, danced in front of me. Then the cloud lifted, and I knew Peter Betz was right. I talked with Charles Collingwood, then Steven Carey from NBC. Then The Washington Post, The New York Times and the Wall Street Journal. And each time, I made sure they had the correct spelling of my name.

Pretty soon, the BRN Midday Conversation was a national sensation. Publicists and agents were drooling to get their movie stars and authors on the show, and they all knew full well that we were going to ask questions about their private lives. Early on, I could tell which stars were simply cultivating an image and which were genuinely wild or madcap. It became important for these celebrities to develop their image on the radio in a way magazines like Screen couldn't provide. And it gave them a chance to be themselves in conversation rather than a guest on a game show.

Errol Flynn, for instance, came across as a legitimate sexaholic. He was charming, debonair, suave, and as randy as they come. He enjoyed our talks, partly because he and Janine would sneak away for a late lunch after the show.

But it was the politicians that I most enjoyed engaging in colloquy. By and large, these were people who came to Washington with an idealized view of helping to shape the world, make history, and do right by others. Those people, those representatives, were really boring. It was the congressmen and senators who understood the personality of politics that made our show swing.

One of our early guests was Senator Paul Buckfield, the New Hampshire Democrat that Sharon worked for. Senator Buckfield agreed to come on the show as a favor to Sharon. He knew that she and I were seeing each other, and he felt relatively secure that he wouldn't be put through the BRN meat-grinder.

We started off easy. Fluff policy questions about tax codes, FDR's Supreme Court nominations, the CCC. Buckfield, an expert in international issues and a member of the Senate Foreign Relations Committee, began talking about the German threat and the officially neutral position of the United States.

"Senator, I know you've been friends for a long time with US Ambassador to England Joseph Kennedy. I know that privately you oppose his views about Adolph Hitler and Germany's intentions. Do you think that Ambassador Kennedy is a Nazi-sympathizer?"

Buckfield fixed a steely gaze at me, and very forcefully answered, "No, I don't."

"Well then, do you think that Ambassador Kennedy is doing a good job in his role in England?"

"Ambassador Kennedy's performance review is strictly up to the president."

"Speaking of Ambassador Kennedy's performance, is it true that his wife Rose asked you to speak with him about the dalliances he's having with any number of British women?"

"This is none of your business."

"Is it true?"

"I'm not going to dignify that with a response. If you want to talk about policy, I'll talk about policy. I'm not going to get into this!"

"But isn't it possible, Senator, that Ambassador Kennedy is being bedded by women who are German operatives in an effort to sway his policy recommendations?"

"That's it! This interview is over." Buckfield stormed out of the studio, but unlike Garner, Buckfield went upstairs. He burst past Janine into Peter Betz's office.

"Paul, come on in. Have a seat."

"Don't give me that shit, Peter. What you're doing with this network is a disgrace! You better clean up your act, or I'll find a way to put the FCC so far up your ass that you only wish it was a hot poker." Out he went, back to his office. Once there, he called Sharon into his office.

"Sharon, you've worked for me for what? Three years? You now have a choice. You either work for me, or you go out with Audray. You're not going to do both anymore. You've got a day to think it over."

Sharon didn't take a day to think it over. She dumped me.

She'd dumped me because she said even she couldn't believe what I had become. She said that I had forsaken my reporter's objective credibility for sensationalism and voyeurism. She said I had become more concerned with my own image than with providing information people could actually use. I tried to defend myself, telling her that none of that was true, that I still believed in giving people all the news, however unvarnished it may be; that in order for people to decide about big issues, they had to understand the people who were in charge of those issues; that the world of 1939 was changing more rapidly than at any other time in our history, and if we didn't pay attention to what those changes were, we were all doomed. Sharon said I was fundamentally wrong, and she could no longer be seen with anyone who believed the things I believed.

It was a quick, clean, complete break. We never went out again socially.

I figured it would be alright, that I'd focus more on my job and spread myself around to other, available women. And that's exactly what I did for a while.

January 8, 1940: Britain introduces ration cards for butter, sugar, bacon, ham.
January 11, 1940: France begins rationing food.

Chapter 3 – The BRN Midday Conversation

One night around Thanksgiving 1939, I spotted the author and activist Dorothy Parker near my table in a restaurant. In 1936 she founded the Anti Nazi League. The next year she won an Academy Award for Best Screenplay for *A Star is Born.* I'd followed her writing career, both prose and poetry, and memorized some of her most pithy comments. When Calvin Coolidge died, she asked, "How could they tell?" I wanted to meet her, so I jotted one of her four-line poems down on a napkin and sent it over to her table along with four martinis. The poem read:

I like to have a martini,
Two at the very most,
After three I'm under the table,
After four I'm under my host.

She nodded in my direction, then jotted a note back:

You'll never be on top of me
Reciting my own poetry.

I sat there with my tail between my legs through the rest of my meal. As I was about to leave, she sauntered over and sat down. She told me she'd love to come on BRN every day for an hour right after my show and dish the gossip she'd been hearing. I politely told her that I didn't deal in gossip. She used her tongue like a samurai sword and told me that's all I dealt in, particularly with the Joe Kennedy story. Although she believed Kennedy was bedding German operatives in England, she had no proof, neither did I, and that made it gossip.

"I want the show," she said. "If I don't get it, I'll expose you for the fraud you apparently are."

Not until that moment did I realize I was in the Major Leagues. Until that time, I thought I was impervious to any fallout or political attacks that might come my way. But when Dorothy Parker, the scion of The Round Table, a noted literary genius and social maven, threatened to expose my weaknesses, I realized I was nowhere near Indiana.

"OK," I heard myself say. "The best I can do is get you a meeting with Peter Betz. After that, you're on your own."

Peter had no trouble dealing with Dorothy Parker. He knew he was a Major Leaguer, and wouldn't be comfortable any other way. He listened to her pitch, then told her, firmly and directly, no. He had no interest in bringing in high profile staff members who would only disrupt the chemistry of the network. He much preferred developing new, malleable talent. For one thing, he told her, they listened better. Then he dared her to write anything negative about me, or any other BRN staffer. He'd be only too happy to turn the tables and make sure everyone knew it was only sour grapes coming from the great Dorothy Parker.

She never wrote one word about me. Ever.

That also told me a lot about Peter Betz. Here was a visionary, a man with a plan for new style presentations, a man who apparently was giving young reporters a break. While all that was true, the method he was using was the experience of a lifetime coupled with employer coercion bordering on intimidation. He knew that once the BRN staff got a taste of the limelight, we would do whatever was necessary to stay there. We were his team. He was the unchallenged coach, calling every single play. And if we varied at all from his plan, we were gone.

When I realized that, I realized that I had changed, that Sharon Tozzi was right.

But I also realized it was OK with me. I was enjoying myself. My celebrity status, although rising, was merely illusionary. I had a fairly benign job of interviewing other celebrities from politics, sports and movies. My ability to actually influence public action was negligible.

By Christmas of '39, the Betz Radio Network had exceeded all expectations. Our list of stations had increased to 112, including two that dropped Mutual Radio News in favor of us. We were constantly sold out, with fifty-seven businesses lined up on an advertiser waiting list. Revenues had exceeded forecast by 622 percent, and Peter Betz was very generous to all his staff in their Christmas paychecks.

Mine even included a hand-written note:

Michael,
Keep doing what you're doing. 1940 will be unforgettable.
PB

And with that, he increased my salary from $30,000 to $65,000.

I couldn't believe my good fortune. And a fortune it was, at least to me. I bought a new car, ten new suits, got a bigger apartment right in the heart of Washington, and still had money left over to send to my mom and dad on occasion.

They couldn't believe it, either. My dad, especially, had trouble understanding how I could get paid so much money for talking on the radio. Here was a man who worked hard his entire life and never made more than $8000 in a year. And that was good money.

But even though he and mom bragged about me to their friends, and even though they reluctantly took the money I'd sometimes send, they each told me to be more respectful of the people I interviewed. I remember dad telling me it was OK to beat up on Clark Gable, because he was only a movie star. But I was to leave Gabby Hartnett of the Cubs alone.

Increasingly, though, everyone who appeared on The BRN Midday Conversation with Michael Audray, as it was now called, expected to answer questions about their lives away from the public. I was getting better at asking, and I was gaining the experience necessary to slide a conversation into those areas. And the listeners, now truly coast-to-coast, wanted to hear Clark Gable talk about intimate rumors regarding Vivien Leigh and him during the making of *Gone With The Wind.*

Early in 1940 I talked with Joe DiMaggio. He was on his way to spring training in Florida with the Yankees, getting ready for his fifth season. He had won the Rookie of the Year Award in 1936, and was willing to come to our studio in Washington. He and I were about the same age, but he was even more focused on his career than I was on mine. I guided our chat to how he would break out of slumps. He said that sometimes he'd just rub his bat up and down with his hand about 30-40 times, trying to put some good energy in his wood.

"Do you ever let girls rub your bat?"

"Oh, sure."

"And…?"

"Well, after they stroke it about 40 times, I pull it away. Sometimes they want to do it again, but generally I say no."

I think it was right then that Joe DiMaggio got his nickname Joltin' Joe. He had no idea what image he had just conjured, but every listener did. And all of them, especially the young women, got a jolt.

The Yankees front office was livid with me. But the public reaction was clearly good, and it helped DiMaggio continue to put the ghosts of Gehrig and Ruth in the background.

Other sports stars were much more likely to play along with the *double entendres*. Ted Williams, the young Boston slugger who was getting ready for his second season, provided his theory on how to hit a home run.

"You dig in and you visualize what you want," he said. He was classically handsome, and both his cadence and his voice were reminiscent of John Wayne. "You spread your legs apart just a little bit, then get into a bit of a crouch. You try to keep your bat up, straight up. Then you size what kind of a pitch it is, and when you see that it's coming right down the middle, you take your bat and swing right through the middle. Always keep your head down, because you don't need to look at your bat to know that it's going to slide right where you want it. Then you sit back and enjoy the motion."

Maybe that's why they called him Teddy Ballgame.

Some movie stars wanted nothing to do with us, but their studios or agents or both made them come on the program to publicize their new movie. Jimmy Stewart and Katharine Hepburn both came on to talk about *The Philadelphia Story*, but neither wanted to be there. They were both scared to death I'd ask about rumors of their on-set fling, but I never got around to it. I actually wanted to ask Katharine Hepburn what she thought of a Dorothy Parker review of a 1933 play called *The Lake*. Dorothy Parker's review contained the classic line, "Miss Hepburn runs the gamut of emotions from A to B." I meant to, but we ended up talking politics most of the time. Stewart was very much aware of Hitler's policies, and was extremely conversant about the invasion of Poland the previous September. He couldn't understand why the United States was not getting more directly involved, especially now that Germany had overrun France and begun air raids on England.

March 18, 1940: Hitler and Mussolini meet. Italy joins the war with Germany.
April 9, 1940: German troops invade Denmark and Norway. Prince Olav flees to London. Princess Martha and the children move into the White House for months.
April 27, 1940: Himmler orders Concentration Camp built at Auschwitz.
May 1, 1940: US Pacific fleet stationed at Pearl Harbor as deterrent.
May 10, 1940: Germany invades the Netherlands, Belgium and Luxembourg.
May 10, 1940: Winston Churchill becomes Britain's Prime Minister.
June 22, 1940: France falls. Vichy government installed.
July 10, 1940: The Battle of Britain begins.
September 7, 1940: The Blitzkrieg of London begins.
September 16, 1940: FDR signs bill reinstating the Draft.
September 26, 1940: FDR imposes scrap iron embargo on Japan.

Chapter 4 – Willkie and Wallace

For the first nine months of our program, we focused about 50/50 on politicians versus sports/movie stars. Now, however, with the drumbeats of war ringing through Europe and no end of politicians willing to marshal public support for either war policies or a continued isolationist stance, our focus became almost exclusively politicians, legislators and operatives.

Our show now had a daily audience of five million. We reached more people than The New York Times, Wall Street Journal and Washington Post put together.

In late 1939, two events set into motion the 1940 presidential election cycle. Vice President John Nance Garner, clearly not going to be invited to join a third FDR ticket, announced in December that he would accept the Democratic presidential nomination if it was offered to him at the convention. He announced that he would not actively campaign for the nomination, but would accept it. Garner joined a growing "Stop

Roosevelt" movement, believing he was the only candidate strong enough to convince FDR to retire. Polls showed Garner to be the lead choice to replace Roosevelt. Roosevelt though, surmised that "Cactus Jack" Garner wouldn't mount a serious challenge and would happily retire to Texas.

Around that same time, Wendell Wilkie switched parties, from Democrat to Republican. Willkie, the legal counsel to the Commonwealth & Southern Corporation, the nation's largest electric utility holding company, had been battling Roosevelt publicly for years. FDR's New Deal initiatives included the Tennessee Valley Authority, which made the case for government, not private, controls of the electric industry. Although Willkie was the darling of many editors around the country, he had never held elective office before, and faced stiff competition for the Republican nomination.

At the Philadelphia Convention, none of the Republican candidates had enough delegates to assure a nomination victory. The two leading contenders, Michigan's Senator Arthur Vandenberg and Ohio's Robert Taft, were rabid isolationists. New York's district attorney, Thomas Dewey, was only slightly less an isolationist. That allowed Willkie, representing the more liberal wing of the Republicans, to speak for the majority who wanted to support the Allies as much as possible without entering the war.

The convention was a bruising fight. Taft and Dewey teamed up to knock out Willkie, but hurt Vandenberg instead. Willkie showed considerable political skill in working behind the scenes at the convention, and on the sixth ballot, the Republicans nominated Wendell Willkie for President.

He needed a running mate, though. His advisers convinced him that he should choose Oregon Senator Charles McNary, despite the fact that McNary had led the "Stop Willkie" convention movement, was an isolationist and a supporter of public ownership of electrical power. Willkie asked McNary, who accepted out of party loyalty.

Roosevelt had no such trouble at the Democratic convention. Because of rules changes he had instituted in 1937, FDR was the first nominee who had absolute final say over who his running mate would be. The president's staff for at least a year had been compiling names of potential running mates. FDR never looked beyond his secretary of agriculture, Henry Wallace, to replace John Nance Garner. In fact, it was a stirring speech by Eleanor Roosevelt at the convention that sealed the deal for Wallace. And FDR said that if Wallace wasn't his running mate, he wouldn't accept the nomination.

Henry Agaard Wallace had been the secretary of agriculture since 1933. It was a perfect fit for him, almost a family tradition. His father, Henry Cantwell Wallace, was secretary of agriculture for President Harding. His grandfather was the editor of the *Iowa Homestead*, a journal of rural and farming life. And as a boy, Henry A. Wallace became friends with one of his father's students, George Washington Carver. Carver was a kind of mentor for Henry, and encouraged him into a scientific direction.

He graduated from college around 1910, and taught himself statistics. He applied that knowledge to agriculture. He came up with this corn-hog ratio chart that helped determine how much a farmer needed to get for his hogs in order to make a profit. While he was a lecturer at Iowa State University, Wallace introduced the concept of econometrics to agriculture.

In 1923, while his dad was Harding's secretary of agriculture, Wallace developed the first commercially successful strain of hybrid corn. This hybrid corn made possible greater yields and agricultural productivity. It took ten years, coincidentally the same year he became FDR's Secretary of Agriculture, for 1% of corn planted in the Corn Belt to be hybrid. By 1943, it was 78%, and by 1965, nearly all the corn planted was hybrid corn. Wallace was a smart guy when it came to farming.

During the '20s, farmers had it really tough. Everybody thinks the Depression started at the end of 1929, but farmers had it rough way before that. All the farmers had planted extra crops to increase yields during World War I, but when the war ended, demand dropped, the foreign countries couldn't afford to import food, and the downward cycle began for the farmers. Henry's dad understood this, and even though Harding was a playboy crook, he might have helped the farm belt. But he died, and Calvin Coolidge took over. Silent Cal was in love with the idea of the unfettered marketplace and refused to help the farmers. Then Henry's dad died right before the 1924 election.

Henry A. Wallace had established a reputation as a philosophic farming economist. He promoted two ideas unheard of at the time: that production costs, and not the free market, ought to determine farm prices; and that farm surpluses were causing the grief in the rural spots of the country. These ideas made so much sense that Charles McNary, who would later be Willkie's running mate, championed a bill that would establish an export marketing corporation to manage farm surpluses and prices. Coolidge, though, vetoed the bill twice, in 1927 and 1928.

But even though the bill didn't pass, it set the tone for agricultural politics, and made farm leaders aware of how much they could accomplish if they stuck together. And these philosophies did not go unnoticed by the then-governor of New York, Franklin Delano Roosevelt.

FDR believed that the only way to solve the massive economic crisis in America was through government intervention in many aspects of everyday life. Since the United States still had a huge farming population, he knew he needed someone to lead the charge for change. Henry A. Wallace was his guy.

Wallace knew that voluntary cooperation among farmers wasn't going to accomplish anything, because the people who cooperated would be undermined by the farmers who didn't. He proposed, and FDR agreed, that the federal government had to step in and support farmers by reducing surpluses. He put this into practice when he became secretary of agriculture in 1933.

Over the next two terms, Wallace kept up his end of the bargain. FDR's New Deal was transforming the American landscape, ending the Depression, and putting confidence back into the American people. Farmers were making more money, selling enough, storing enough, exporting enough, smiling more. Wallace was having a terrific time, and getting great reviews.

His best reviews came from the president. Wallace was able to articulate the goals and philosophies of the New Deal, and FDR loved it. Wallace's background enabled him to become one of the most influential thinkers of progressive politics around Washington. He had the president's ear, and the president had Wallace's mouth.

So when it became clear in his mind that he would go for a third term, Roosevelt knew he wanted to dump Garner and grab Wallace. No president had ever gone for a third straight term, and with war looming, FDR wanted someone other than Garner to be his mouthpiece for certain policies.

FDR's staff, though, wasn't thrilled with Wallace as vice president. They agreed that he was a great agriculture secretary, but Wallace had a kind of rough edge about him. He saw the big picture, knew what the answer should be, and wasn't about to let bureaucracy stand in his way. In short, he didn't have a great deal of diplomatic skills with the members of the House and Senate.

Around 1936, the Supreme Court ruled that the Agricultural Adjustment Act of 1933 was unconstitutional. The AAA, as it was called, encouraged farmers to work together, rather than individually, and to work with the government to set market prices and reduce surpluses. But the Court ruled this was an intrusion on states' rights. Wallace saw this coming, so he set up the Soil Conservation Act of 1935. The goal was to set up a national effort to reduce soil erosion and acreage reduction for conservation purposes. Since this was a national goal, it was constitutional. Wallace carried the day, even though he had a hard time convincing Congress.

He had a hard time convincing Congress because he believed, really believed, that if an idea was right, and met the goals of the project, and helped people, and benefited the country, then there was no basis for argument. He couldn't understand the myopia of some congressmen who didn't see how this would help their particular district. He had no taste for the congressional inquisition about how this would be constitutional while the AAA was unconstitutional. Wallace saw the big picture, knew what needed to be done, and didn't want anyone getting in the way.

He really didn't want to play the game.

But FDR liked him. Wallace was smart, articulate, and a true believer in the New Deal. Domestically, there was no one else around who came even close to the passion and fervor Wallace could bring to the administration's policies.

Internationally, though, Wallace was a little light. He understood there was war on the horizon, but his lack of taste for the diplomatic dance necessary left him unprepared to deal with the British and the French, let alone the Germans and the Italians.

Roosevelt didn't care. He could teach him, if necessary, how to deal with foreign leaders and their minions. What Roosevelt wanted, and what Roosevelt got, was an energetic and believable spokesperson.

At the convention, FDR made it abundantly clear that Wallace was the #2 man on the ticket, or else they had no #1. After Eleanor's rousing speech on his behalf, the party reluctantly nominated Henry Wallace. But the convention had turned so sour he didn't make an acceptance speech.

During the campaign, Wallace's variety of religious beliefs began to emerge as an issue. Technically an Episcopalian, Wallace had abandoned his Calvinist upbringing. Throughout his life, he studied Catholicism, Buddhism, Islam, Zoroastrianism and Christian Science. But during the 1930's, Wallace became influenced by Nicholas Roerich. A native Russian, Roerich and Wallace exchanged a series of letters on a variety of topics, ranging from Wallace's spiritual beliefs to candid observations on the political leaders of the day. These letters somehow landed in the hands of the Republicans, who considered releasing them for the sheer embarrassment. Playing hardball, the Democratic leaders let the

Republicans know that should those letters become public, the Democrats were prepared to release evidence that Wendell Willkie was having an affair. The leaders of both parties decided it wouldn't benefit either candidate, so the letters and the affair never became public knowledge. But Roosevelt never had quite the confidence in Wallace he had before the incident.

Wendell Wilkie did his best to convince the electorate that he was the better presidential candidate. But he was getting nowhere. That's when his campaign manager, Joe Martin, called Peter Betz with a proposal.

Wilkie would sit down with me for a series of five one-hour programs, one a week for five weeks immediately preceding the election. But they would have to be done with a studio audience who would also get to ask questions. Betz thought about it, and came up with an additional idea: the shows would be done in different major cities, and they would be recorded and played back again in their entirety the Saturday before the election. Betz also said, however, that he would make the same offer to Roosevelt.

Martin and Wilkie talked it over for a few days, then agreed. This was to be a completely revolutionary idea in campaigning. The ability to state their views, answer questions directly to voters, and get five hours of national network airtime outweighed the possibility that I would delve into Willkie's personal and professional past.

Peter then lobbied for the president to agree to the same format. He made some concessions to FDR, that it could be recorded in Washington, and the audience size limited, depending on the exact location. But FDR, comfortably ahead in all the opinion polls, said no. Let Wilkie have his say. I'm the president.

Peter had known FDR personally for nearly twenty years. They met when Roosevelt was running for vice president with James Cox at the head of the ticket in 1920. At the time, Peter was just getting into bootlegging, and he'd bend the ear of any politician he could that Prohibition wasn't ever going to work, because guys like him would make a fortune doing whatever they had to do to sell booze to the common man. He was a crook with a conscience then, and gave ten Fords to the Cox/Roosevelt campaign to help them get around and get their message out. FDR had been the undersecretary of the Navy since 1913, and was well versed in international policies. He'd been a big defender of The League of Nations, but everyone, including Roosevelt, knew that Warren Harding was going to win the election. Even though he lost, Roosevelt had gained a national platform. He'd learned how the national game was played.

Peter voted for Harding, because in his heart he knew that he could make more money bootlegging with Harding in office than with Cox. Harding liked to drink and he liked women. Cox was a newspaper publisher who wanted to do good.

Willkie never understood that he couldn't beat FDR, and when this chance to get five hours of network radio time was offered, it was too good to pass up. He prepared for the shows by pouring over statistics and studies and newspaper columns and editorials night and day. He figured that if he could just get people to listen to him, he could carry the day. He never figured that FDR could undermine his five hours of free airtime with five sentences in reply to any reporter's question. And that's exactly what happened.

For me, it was tough to carry this assignment off. First of all, I didn't think Wendell Willkie had five hours of material. He was a dynamic speaker with a great deal of momentum and popular support on his side. He had been campaigning across the country on The Willkie Special, a twelve-car train that carried thirty campaign staffers and forty reporters. He had been literally talking himself hoarse, and smoking three-packs of cigarettes a day didn't help. Aside from his opposition to certain New Deal initiatives, though, he and Roosevelt shared many of the same world views. That first hour, Willkie was most at ease talking about domestic issues, especially the rural electrification policies and how he thought they were wrong-headed. He argued that government had no role in providing electrical hook-ups to rural areas, or even urban areas. It should all be private companies, able to do it quicker, with more efficiency and able to make a profit doing it. By the end of the first hour, Willkie seemed to hit his stride and got a warm reception from the studio audience at the end of the program.

The next day, though, I remember Max Meekin of CBS asked the president if he listened to Willkie and me talk. No, I didn't, FDR said. I was on the phone with Winston Churchill getting an update on England's war effort.

Boom! Just like that, one hour of free airtime zinged by a popular president using the power of incumbency. FDR 1, Willkie 0.

Joe Martin, Willkie's campaign manager, knew right then the entire ballgame was over, but tried desperately not to convey that to Willkie. Willkie was still operating under the assumption that, given the right audience over the next four hours of airtime, and some decent headlines the next day, the public would decide that FDR should be replaced. So Willkie again studied statistics and graphs, came up with interesting though arcane tidbits, even hired a joke writer. He was ready for Free Air Time, Round Two.

This time, we went to Independence Hall in Philadelphia. Peter had pulled some strings to snag the historic location for this "new chapter in history." I went there two days early to make sure that all the tape recording equipment was not only hooked up correctly, but looked good, too. We were expecting a full house, and wanted to make sure that everyone could see well, but noticed our sophisticated equipment, and of course, our network signs.

Peter also had a brilliant idea. Since we were taping the interview with Willkie on Thursday night, he wanted to take short segments of it and use them on our newscasts to promote the full-length airing of the interview on Sunday. No one had ever done anything like that before.

Immediately after our interview was done, I sat with our engineers and told them what parts of Willkie's interview I wanted. I told them we'd only need about fifteen seconds of whatever. I guess this makes me the Father of The Sound Bite.

"The rural electrification policies that Franklin Roosevelt has imposed have crossed the line between what government should do and what private industry does better, faster, cheaper," Willkie said in one bite.

On Saturday, the day before the airing of our Philadelphia interview, NBC's Steven Carey asked FDR if this week he planned to listen to what Willkie had to say.

"No, I don't. Somebody told me that he said our rural electrification policies were wrong-headed. Well, if it wasn't for our rural electrification policies, no one in the rural areas would be able to listen to anything Mr. Willkie has to say."

Boom! Just like that, Willkie was blown out of the water again, only this time even before the program aired. FDR 2, Willkie 0.

Willkie was furious. He felt that releasing bits of what he'd said in the interview had undermined his efforts and given Roosevelt a chance to respond even before the whole story was out.

Willkie told Joe Martin that he wasn't going to allow any more sound bites to be released prior to airtime. Martin told him that it really wasn't all that bad to have two or three days of promotion on coast-to-coast radio with the election coming up soon. But Willkie didn't buy it. He felt swindled, that the free airtime really was costing him quite a bit, mostly in prestige and credibility.

Martin countered, "Look, for Christ sakes, Roosevelt's the master at this. He probably could have come up with that line even without a day to think about it. You can't come off looking childish and petulant. You're the Republican presidential candidate, and you've got to show people that you can take the heat. Let's figure out some things for you to say this week that BRN will choose as their promo spots." Martin had no idea, though, of what those things might be. He knew we'd choose what we wanted. All he wanted was to give Willkie at least a chance of sounding glib.

Willkie's chief speechwriter, Russell Davenport, was chaotically disorganized, even more than Willkie. Davenport would write and rewrite Willkie's speeches right up to the last minute, never giving Willkie a chance to become comfortable with the words he was speaking. Coupled with Willkie's tendency to veer off the script, it made for some rather uncomfortable verbal gaffes.

All week they worked on the key points they wanted to hit. Domestic issues, internationalism vs. isolationism, agriculture, public service companies vs. private industry - all of these were tossed about. But, at the last minute, they settled on baseball.

The third interview was held at The Fisher Theatre in Detroit. The Tigers had just lost the World Series to the Cincinnati Reds a week before in a thrilling seven-game set. Because of injury, the Reds had activated a forty-year-old coach, Jimmie Wilson, to be their back-up catcher during the Series. Wilson ended up hitting .353 and played the lead role in Cincinnati's victory. But Detroit was still in love with their Tigers, and especially the season's Most Valuable Player, Hank Greenberg.

Greenberg was Jewish, the first Jewish superstar. He led the league in homers and RBIs, but was quiet and unassuming. The rumor was that Greenberg was about to enlist in the Army as the war in Europe heated up. The rumors turned out to be true, and Greenberg gave up four years of his career.

Willkie was prepared for this week's interview, armed with more statistics and graphs, but also with some humorous lines and, hopefully, the sound bites he wanted. And they actually were pretty good. We went with:

"The Tigers came close to being champions, but Detroit will show the world that the United States is the real champion!"

"Hank Greenberg is a fine example of how we in the United States don't look at someone's religion, we look at their character. And Hank Greenberg is proving to be not only the American League's Most Valuable Player, but one of the Most Valuable Players for the United States."

"It took a forty-year-old coach to beat the Tigers."

We ran those on our newscasts, and also made some other promotional announcements with them to hype the broadcast. And again, FDR made hay with his own sound bite.

"Maybe it took a forty-year-old coach to beat the Tigers," the president said. "But pitching always wins in baseball. And at fifty-eight, I'm a better pitcher than the other guy."

Laughs from the press corps. FDR 3, Willkie 0.

Again, Willkie blew a gasket. Only this time, he didn't let Joe Martin slow him down. He called Peter Betz directly.

"What the hell are you doing to me, Peter?" Willkie bellowed. "This is bullshit that you're putting parts of my interview on the air even before it's supposed to be on. It just gives Roosevelt the chance..."

"...to blow you out of the water ahead of time. I know, I know. Don't give me that shit, Wendell. What difference does it make if FDR says what he says on Saturday or on Monday? It doesn't."

"It does, too. If the audience hears that line from Roosevelt, they won't even listen to what I have to say."

"Goddammit, Wendell, they're not listening to you now. And if Roosevelt says something about you, then say something about him. We'll air your reply. That's how this game works. This is a new age. People all over the country have radios, and they listen. We're in the business of airing the news, and if we happen to be there when it's created, so much the better for us. In the meantime, don't worry about Roosevelt or us. Concentrate on you. We're not the problem here, Wendell. Your message is. Or more accurately, his message is. People like him, and you haven't convinced them - yet - that we need a change at the top. That's what you've got to do. So stop worrying about what little blips of tape we run about you on our newscasts."

That pretty much shut him up. Willkie became much more calm and more likable over the next two weeks. Instead of cramming for each radio interview with charts and graphs and statistics, Willkie told Martin to schedule him for lots of hand-shaking and whistle-stopping, big groups and little groups.

There were lots of skirmishes inside the Republican Party, mostly because they distrusted Willkie as a turncoat-Democrat. And the party professionals were privately enjoying his slow campaign death. Willkie spent so much time concentrating on winning the nomination he didn't think about a campaign strategy. He never really settled on one or two main themes with which to hammer Roosevelt. He tried the No Third Term idea. Then he tried the FDR Doesn't Know If We Should Enter the

War idea. He often relied on the New Deal Is A Bad Deal idea. He was badly slipping in the polls. In early October, when it looked especially grim, Willkie switched gears completely and appealed to the isolationists. He said that a vote for FDR was a vote for War. Willkie promised to keep the US out of the war. His polls started rising again.

Willkie relaxed for a day before each of the final two hour-long radio interviews. By prior agreement, not his insistence on embargoing any sound bites, the fourth and fifth interviews were done live from New York, then Washington. And both of those were his best performances.

I remember sitting on the stage with him, watching him handle himself effortlessly, and thinking that if he had done this throughout the campaign, and especially during these five hours of radio time, the election might have been different.

Willkie also let Oregon's Senator Charles McNary, the vice presidential candidate, have a bit more of a profile over the last two weeks. McNary was chosen on strictly geographic grounds, to help Willkie in the West, but he was a pretty smart guy. He knew the ins and outs of campaigns, and after the Peter Betz chat, Willkie started to listen to some of the tips McNary gave him. But it was too little, too late. Willkie and McNary really didn't like each other, and by this point of the campaign, there was no real reason for them to become buddies.

Peter Betz had also been trying to get McNary and Wallace to square off in a debate. Willkie OK'd the idea, and McNary was willing to go. Wallace was all set as well, but FDR's people said No Way.

FDR's strategy had been to be presidential, that he was too busy running the country to campaign. Looking at Willkie's rising poll numbers, though, President Roosevelt finally began making campaign speeches. He angrily denied all of Willkie's charges about US involvement in the War.

The final two interviews went very well for Willkie. He came across as knowledgeable, articulate and passionate. He knew why Roosevelt was tip-toeing around the war in Europe. He agreed that the threat to world peace was quite real, and that the US must enter the war.

There were no zingers from Roosevelt to offset the Willkie sound bites we used. My scorecard ended up as Roosevelt 3, Willkie 2.

But to the American public, it wasn't even close. On Election Day, November 5, 1940, Roosevelt carried thirty-eight states to Willkie's ten, winning by more than five million votes.

Almost immediately after the election, Willkie made it clear to the president that he would support the administration's war efforts and do whatever he could to shake the isolationists awake to the real threat posed by the Nazis. FDR accepted the help, and told Willkie that he would gladly use him throughout his third term. The unprecedented third term was seen by many inside the White House as a mandate for the president to do what he thought was best for the country. The American electorate had said, in effect, we like how you guided us through the Depression, now guide us through this war in Europe.

There was some re-shuffling of cabinet members and lower level staffers. But the one major difference was in the vice president's office. John Nance Garner was packing up and leaving. He'd had enough of being vice president, but he wasn't pleased with the way it had been publicly played since our interview. He always harbored some belief that FDR put Peter up to it.

November 10, 1940: Former British Prime Minister Neville
Chamberlain dies.
November 15, 1940: German blitz destroys Coventry and Birmingham,
England.
November 15, 1940: The Ghetto of Warsaw is closed.

Chapter 5 – The Jack Denif Interview

R ight after the 1940 election, Roosevelt sat down for a wide-ranging interview with Jack Denif of NBC. They covered the war, the economy, the new vice president, the uncharted territory of a third term and his reasons for it, Wendell Willkie, the upcoming Army-Navy football game, the continuation of his fireside chats and so on. But what caught my ear was what he said about music.

"I love the swing music," the president said. "I'm a big Benny Goodman fan. That combo he's got with Lionel Hampton, Teddy Wilson and Gene Krupa really plays some fine songs. In fact, the other day I heard it on the radio down the hall, and I went down there, and there was Lucy dancing to it all by herself."

I went to see Peter Betz. "Did you hear the interview between FDR and Denif?" I asked.

"No, I missed it."

"He mentioned Lucy."

"Who? Denif?"

"No. Roosevelt."

"Really?"

"Yeah."

"FDR said that on the air?" Peter was riveted now.

"Yeah. I couldn't believe it. He said he was watching Lucy dance."

"Did he say Lucy Mercer?"

"No, just Lucy."

Peter picked up his phone and called William Doten, the president of NBC. When he wanted something, he started right at the top. He told Doten we were doing a follow-up piece on FDR getting ready for his

29

third term and wanted a transcript of Jack's interview. He said we'd be willing to pay, but we needed it today. Doten said OK.

Then Peter turned to me and said, "When this transcript gets here, Michael, you and I will sit down and go over every word." His eyes were twinkling like a prism reflecting sunlight. "This could be a juicy story."

I left his office thinking only of our late afternoon meeting. But I had a show to prepare. My guest was going to be Herbert Marshall, coming on to promote his new movie, *Foreign Correspondent*.

Directed by Alfred Hitchcock, *Foreign Correspondent* had been getting great reviews in the month since its release. Marshall played the head of a peace organization in the midst of Western Europe's chaotic mess. In the movie, he and his daughter became involved with an American reporter writing about the expanding war.

Clearly, the British-born Hitchcock made this movie to indict the Nazis. Despite its effectiveness, no less than the Nazis chief propaganda minister, Josef Goebbels, said *Foreign Correspondent* was "a first class production, a criminological bang-up hit, which no doubt will make a certain impression upon the broad masses of the people in enemy countries."

While we talked about the political nature of the movie, I was also interested in drawing out information about Herbert Marshall's private life. His twelve-year marriage had recently ended, and I asked if there was another woman.

His eyes narrowed, his voice became a poison arrow. "Mr. Audray, whether or not there is another woman is really none of your business. No matter how I answer that question, it will only lead to other questions and rumors. I don't respond to rumors, and I repeat, it's none of your business."

But I pressed ahead. "Maybe not, but I'll bet you that more people are interested in the stuff that happens off the screen than on it."

"Well, that's too bad. People then should try to have more interesting lives of their own, and not live vicariously through mine. So, I'll say it again: I'm not talking about my personal life."

I moved on to other topics, and the rest of the show went well. But I couldn't stop thinking that more people truly were interested in other people's personal lives than the topics of the day.

The courier arrived at Peter's office at 4:40 p.m. He and I sat down at a small, round table he had in his office, each of us with a cup of coffee. I remember thinking that this was a bit eerie. Here we were poring over a transcript of a presidential interview, looking for any unwitting glimpses into his personal life. We already knew quite a bit about it; we just hadn't ever reported it.

Peter had audience surveys done all the time, and he found out that the highest number of listeners came when we talked about the personal lives of celebrities and public figures. And the more listeners we had, the more money we made from our commercials.

I believed it was not just good radio and good business to delve into the private lives of celebrities: it also provided a public service. I thought if people knew what kind of a scoundrel Errol Flynn really was, they'd stop seeing his movies and he would vanish from the scene, all to the betterment of society.

I was wrong about Errol Flynn, by the way. He was a charming scoundrel, and the worse he was, the better the public liked him.

The press rarely reported certain things about FDR, like the fact he almost exclusively used his wheelchair. The public knew he contracted polio in the '20s. When he stood up for speeches or walked down public steps with the help of aides, the press viewed it not as disingenuous but somewhat courageous. The thinking went here is a guy who refuses to give in to his disease.

There were other, more fascinating things about Roosevelt that we knew but didn't report. His romance with Lucy Mercer Rutherfurd was a widely accepted fact. We collectively didn't report it because there was no mention of it anywhere in the public record, and no way to corroborate the story.

Eleanor was rumored to have dalliances of her own. But she was extremely smart and cagey, and never gave any of us in the press corps even a whiff of anything.

But this, the presidential mention of Lucy in a national radio interview, this was something to jump on. The utter casualness and simplicity of it was most striking.

Peter knew it, too. He sensed The Story, but wanted to have some hard facts before allowing this kind of question on the air. After all, he'd known FDR for twenty years, knew the kind of guy he was, knew that he liked the ladies, but knew also that he was the president of the United States. So if the Betz Radio Network was going to open up this line of questioning, we had to have real evidence.

After about an hour of combing through the transcript, and finding only the one passing comment about Lucy, Peter sat back in his chair.

"This isn't enough, Michael. He'll just say, and possibly truthfully, that he really did just see a staffer dancing in her office because he heard the music and went down there. It is possible that he just heard the music. And he does tend to call a lot of the White House staffers by first name."

I said, "Yeah, you're right. Let's forget about it."

But Peter said, "I'm not willing to forget about it. But we're not the ones in any position to openly investigate this, either." He smiled when he said that, the smile of a boy who had just caught his first foul ball at the stadium. He got up from the small, round table and walked back to his desk, placed his hand on the telephone. "Go on. We'll talk tomorrow."

Tomorrow. Tomorrow, I thought, my guest would be Senator Charles McNary, in his first radio interview since the election.

I got back to my office and found a message from Jack Denif. I returned his call right away. He wanted to know why Peter wanted the transcript of his interview with Roosevelt.

"Oh, we're just doing another profile piece on him, getting ready for the inauguration. Just background stuff."

"Bullshit, Michael. If that was the case, you'd have made the call, not Betz."

Damn, he was good. I smiled and stifled a laugh, tried to keep the ruse going. "No. He just figured he could get the transcript quicker than me."

"Don't give me that line of shit, Michael. That's beneath you. The inauguration is over two months away. Getting the transcript tomorrow morning instead of at 4:30 this afternoon wouldn't make a bit of difference. What are you working on?"

"I told you, Jack. It's just another profile piece on Roosevelt. Peter's got some hot young intern that he's making do all-night research. He wants a report on his desk by nine o'clock tomorrow morning, and wants to see if the kid can do it." Quite a lie, but the best I could come up with that quickly.

"You're lying, Michael. Look," Jack said, breathing slowly, "I'm going to be at The Java Diner in an hour. Stop by. My treat. OK?"

I paused. I knew Jack Denif was a real pro, in many ways a much better reporter than I could ever hope to be. I knew he knew we were up to something, and my guess is that he probably already knew what we were looking at. But I figured, professional courtesy and all, I'd meet him anyway at 6:30.

Jack Denif was older than I, around forty-five. He'd been with NBC for seven years, and had spent time as one of their European correspondents. Fluent in French, he was based in Paris until 1938, when he was reassigned to the White House. He was street-smart, dressed decently, but had a kind of rumpled appearance. His voice was a smooth baritone that he kept in shape by smoking a pack of Luckys each day. It projected intelligence and calmness on the air.

I got to The Java Diner a few minutes early, and he was already there. Sitting at a window booth that overlooked D Street, Jack was drinking a cup of coffee and smoking when I joined him.

"You want some dinner, Michael? I'm hungry, and believe me, it's on NBC."

"Actually, I am hungry. Have you ordered?"

"No, I was waiting for you."

I glanced at the menu, although I don't know why. Every time I'd been there I'd ordered the same thing - a hamburger with American cheese, chopped green olives, a fat slice of tomato and the crispiest lettuce in the world, with fries. I thought about ordering a chocolate milk shake, but got coffee instead.

Jack went for the Day's Special - meatloaf with carrots, a side of applesauce, bread and butter.

"So, Jack, how'd you find out that Peter called Doten?"

"Doten told me."

"He told you?"

"Yeah. He called me up right away. Said that BRN wanted a transcript pronto of my interview with Roosevelt. He wanted to know what the hell could be in there that Betz didn't even try to negotiate the transcript fee."

I laughed. Even I thought that was a little unlike Peter. "How much did he pay?"

"$500."

"You're kidding me, Jack. $500? No, no he didn't."

Jack Denif looked me straight in the eye and got very serious. "Yes he did."

I leaned back in the booth, took the coffee cup in my hands, and took a deep breath.

"What are you working on, Michael?"

I was quiet for a moment, still thinking about how Peter Betz had overplayed his hand by paying $500 for a transcript, when the going rate was $10. "Actually, Jack, I don't think we're working on anything."

"Nice try, Michael. You may not have found what you were hoping to find in that transcript, but you're working on something. You always are. Hey, by the way," he said, in a much brighter tone, "nice job with Herbert Marshall today."

"Thanks," I chuckled. "I thought it went OK. He's pretty good. Have you seen *Foreign Correspondent*?"

"Not yet."

"It's pretty good. Hitchcock did a good job. And George Sanders is great. But, you must have a lot of time on your hands if you can listen to my show in the middle of the day."

"I always listen to your show, Michael," said Jack Denif. "Just like all of America." He drank some coffee and lit another Lucky, then said, "So, if I guess what you're working on, will you tell me?"

"Maybe."

"OK, here goes." Jack inhaled deeply on his Lucky, and as he spoke, the smoke came out of his mouth and nose. "You're looking at the comment he made about Lucy."

He paused. "Go on," I said. "Or is that it?"

"No, but am I right?" I shrugged my shoulders. "You want to look at why the president of the United States is watching his mistress dance to Benny Goodman's music." He took another drag on his Lucky. "Like anybody really cares."

I tried not to change my facial expression. Jack Denif was so on target, but I didn't want to tip my hand. If anybody was going to do this story, I wanted it to be me and us, not him and NBC.

"For Chrissakes, Michael, nobody gives a shit. The guy just got re-elected by taking thirty-eight out of forty-eight states. We're on the brink of a world war, Hitler's a madman, Mussolini's a madman, the French rolled over and England's fighting for their life. That's what people care about."

"Really? So how come my show and our network has the most listeners?"

"People listen to the radio for entertainment. You're an entertainer, Michael, you're not a newsman. That's not bad, understand, that's good. People need to be entertained. They like the escape from the day to day problems of their own lives. But when they want to know about the world, they don't listen to BRN. They listen to NBC or CBS or Mutual. And that's a fact. You've got great shows on BRN, and I like them. But just because you've got a lot of listeners doesn't make you the network of record."

"No, maybe not yet. But soon."

"You think that if you break a story that Roosevelt is wheeling into Lucy's kitchen it'll make BRN more credible? Is that what you're saying?"

"No, because I'm not saying that's what we were looking for in the transcript."

"God, I hate it when you lie. You're such a bad liar, Michael."

"Jack, you are so blunt."

"It's one of my best traits. Look, I picked up on when FDR mentioned Lucy in conversation, but I sure wasn't going to ask him about it. It's not germane."

"Germane to what, Jack?"

"To anything. People want to know what the president - *any president* - is going to do to improve their daily lives, not what he's doing in his private life."

"You really think so, Jack? I'm not sure that people don't care."

Just then, our food came. The meatloaf looked good, but I'm glad I got a cheeseburger. The waitress poured more coffee.

After we each took a few bites, Jack said, "Look at Harding, for Chrissakes. He knocked up Nan Britton when she was about twenty, shtupped her in his office in the White House, then paid to shut her up. People might have found it interesting if they knew, but they were more interested in getting drunk at a speakeasy. All they really wanted from Harding was a blind eye to drinking. Harding gave them that."

"Yeah, but what about Teapot Dome? People cared about that."

"Different deal, Michael. Teapot Dome was official government business that was corrupted by bribes and money. Much different. And we knew that. And when I say we, I mean we in the news business and we as voters."

"I still think people want to know."

Jack was wolfing down his meatloaf and talking at the same time. "They may want to know, but they ultimately don't care. Grover Cleveland, for Chrissakes. During his first run it came out that this unmarried guy had a kid. Don't you remember that from high school Civics class? Remember the slogan his opponents used? 'Ma, Ma, where's my Pa? Went to the White House, ha ha ha.'"

"Yeah, what's your point, Jack?"

"The guy got elected twice, then got married to his best friend's daughter!"

"Well, there wasn't radio back when Cleveland was president. Times are different, Jack. People want different things."

"They may want them, Michael, but they don't need them."

"Who are we to decide what the public does or doesn't need?"

"We're the gatekeepers, for Chrissake. Michael, it's one thing to talk to Errol Flynn about boofing a sixteen-year-old. And the public may find it interesting that Tyrone Power and Charles Laughton like boys…"

"Charles Laughton likes boys?"

"Yeah. What? You didn't know that?"

"But he's married to Elsa Lanchester."

"So? Eleanor's married to Franklin. Doesn't stop the urge."

"What do you mean, 'Eleanor's married to Franklin?' What do you mean?"

I remember very clearly that Jack paused, put down his fork, and looked at me like I was some dumb ass. I felt like a dumb ass at that moment. Then he said, "I like you, Michael, I really do. I think you're very good at what you do. But if you were a newsman, you'd know what I meant. And you'd know it doesn't matter."

In that millisecond, ignoring both the insult and my own momentarily massive insecurity that I was so dense I could be around Washington this long without even suspecting the First Lady was a lesbian and the president was a rolling philanderer, I plunged ahead.

"How do you know it doesn't matter? Don't you think the public would think differently of them if they knew this stuff?"

"Hell, yes, they would. But the public doesn't need to know every little detail of somebody's life. They're doing their jobs, and by an overwhelming margin, people like the job they're doing."

"I think this is more than just a little detail."

"Michael, for Chrissakes," Jack sighed deeply, "do you want all the details of your personal life spilled out in the papers and on the air?"

"That's not the point."

"It sure as hell is. You're a public figure. Why not look at what you do when you're off the air? I mean, you just spent time today asking Herbert Marshall if he was having an affair."

"He didn't tell me anything."

"And I'm glad, because it's none of your business."

"But the public eats that up."

Jack waved that off. "But you haven't said why we shouldn't look at what you do off the air."

"Oh, I'm boring, really. I'm just a radio host."

Jack got serious again. "No. You're an opinion shaper. People listen to you. They *listen* to you. That carries some responsibility. And if you choose to use that leverage in a certain way, then that same leverage will be used on you. That's a fact."

"Well, I've got nothing to hide."

Jack Denif leaned back in the booth and lit another Lucky. "That's too bad, Michael. Everybody else does. I do. Between you and me, Michael, I've had a couple flings that I shouldn't have had. Paris will do that to you. Might make me a lousy husband, but does that make me a lousy reporter? Just because you're a public figure doesn't mean you're not human."

The waitress came by and asked if we wanted anything else. Jack ordered a piece of apple pie. I passed.

"Look, Michael, a lot of us reporters are a little jealous of the success that your network's had. BRN has really made an impact, and most of it's been good. Skewering politicians for their public works, that's good. Getting actors and actresses to kiss and tell, that's fun. And," he said laughing, "when you got Ted Williams to say he let girls stroke his bat, Wow!"

I didn't correct him that it was Joe DiMaggio who said that.

"But you've always got to keep in mind the public good. You do have a responsibility. Don't blur the line between actors and politicians. They're both acting, but only one has a script. The other improvises with life and death issues everyday. As long as they're not screwing the public, it doesn't matter who they're screwing in private."

His pie came. He stubbed out his cigarette and picked up his fork. I sat back in the booth and looked at him.

"Why are you telling me all this, Jack?"

"I told you - I like you. I don't want to see you make a huge mistake. I don't want to see you do anything that's going to make it tougher for guys like me to do my job. But what the hell. You're just working for Peter Betz, who's going to make you do whatever he wants, no matter what I say. But I was hoping, actually, to intercept your story and kill it."

"Well, there is no story, Jack."

"At least none from that $500 transcript."

We both laughed. I threw a $5 bill on the table and stood up. "Dinner's on me, Jack. Thanks."

"Anytime, Michael. I mean it, anytime."

I shook his hand, turned and walked out the door.

He was right, and I knew it. But I was right, and he knew it. We both knew that FDR was having an affair with Lucy Mercer Rutherfurd, and he implied that Eleanor was fooling around, too, maybe with women. Somewhere, there was definitely a story aching to be told.

November 19, 1940: Greek troops defeat the invading Italians.
November 20, 1940: Hungary and Romania declare their allegiance
with Germany and Italy.
December 9, 1940: British offensive begins. Tobruk captured, Italians
retreat.
December 15, 1940: British troops defeat the Italian Army in Egypt.

Chapter 6 – Earl Mercia

When I got to work the next day, Peter asked me to come to his office.

"Michael, I'd like you to meet Earl Mercia."

Earl Mercia was about 5'9, 175 pounds, with nearly-black thinning hair. He stood there in a cocoa-brown suit that hadn't seen the warm side of an iron in way too long. His shirt was pressed, but he had on a canary-yellow tie that fairly announced his arrival. I noticed his overcoat and hat were on the coat rack.

"Earl's a private investigator that I've hired to look into certain aspects of that transcript we reviewed yesterday."

"Really? Peter, can I talk privately with you for a minute?" I whispered in his ear. "Peter, I don't think this is such a good idea. There's no proof. For another thing, how the hell is Earl Mercia going to get close enough to find out any information? And third, this is the president of The United States we're talking about!"

Peter whispered back, but not as quietly. "Well, for one thing, I know who we're talking about, Michael. Earl's a pro. Been through this lots of times. Remember when Senator Hammond was photographed with that almost-naked hooker? Earl. Or when Senator Feathers was caught being drunk and disorderly in Baltimore? Earl. Or when that Georgia congressman admitted to placing bets on football and baseball games? Earl. Or when…"

"OK, OK, I get the point, Peter." I launched into what was basically Jack Denif's argument against going forward with this. "But at the end of the story, all that happened was that those senators' lives and reputations were ruined, despite the fact that they had done well by their states throughout their terms. I'm not sure if we should be dishing this kind of stuff to our listeners. It's different with actors. They ask for it, almost expect it. But politicians, by and large, want to be good public servants. They don't ask for their private lives to be exposed."

"You think their responsibility to the public ends at five o'clock, Michael? Bullshit. These people want everyone to think they are holier than thou, and are good, God-fearing, church-going, morally-upstanding leaders of the community. They're hypocrites, every goddamn one of them. And as long as we have the ability to tell a factual story to let the public decide whether or not they need the information, we're going to tell a factual story. Earl's on retainer. He's got two weeks to find out something, or else we'll call off the dogs. For now. If he can't find anything provable, then we'll move on."

I just kind of stood there.

"Besides, Michael," Peter said slowly and deliberately, "you were the one who came to me with this information."

I sat down at the round table. Earl Mercia sat down next to me, with Peter across from us. "What's first, Earl?" Peter asked.

"First, I cash the retainer," he said, laughing a deep, guttural laugh that he thoroughly enjoyed. "And then I go back to my office and start making phone calls."

"Who're you going to call?" I wondered.

"Just let me handle that, Michael. You go do your radio show." His contempt for me oozed out from behind his lips and hung in the air. We stared at each other for ten seconds or so before Peter said, "Well, then, Earl, go cash the retainer."

We all stood up and Earl walked toward the coat rack. "Don't bother calling me for an update," he said to us both. "I know I've got two weeks to find something. I don't need to be wasting my time talking to you. If I find anything, I'll call you right away." He turned and left.

"Well, Peter, he's a pleasant guy."

"He's an annoying son of a bitch. But he's good. If there's any dirt, he'll find it."

I started to leave his office when Peter stopped me.

"Look, Michael. No other network will touch this story first. But if we break it, they'll all follow, and we'll get the credit. The Betz Radio Network will be the biggest in the business. In the world." I remember just standing there, hands in my pockets. I must've looked flustered.

"Michael, don't worry about it. We won't do anything without hard facts and double corroboration. Promise."

I ran my hands through my hair, muttered, "OK," and went back to my office to prep for Senator McNary.

McNary hadn't talked publicly, at least at length, about his run for the vice presidency with Willkie. Now, back from a vacation with his family, McNary was ready to chat about anything and everything, according to his press secretary.

McNary was the senior senator from Oregon, the Senate minority leader, the first candidate from the Pacific Northwest to be on the national ticket. He'd been in Washington for about twenty years, first as a representative from Portland, then as senator for the past fourteen years. Running with Willkie was safe for him, as he didn't face a re-election challenge until 1942. It gave him a higher profile and made him an instant contender for the Republican nomination in 1944.

He and Henry Wallace had known each other for more than twenty years. They both had interest in farms and farm policy. They were friends, actually, and McNary was one of the few true allies Wallace had in the Senate when he was secretary of agriculture. Had there been a campaign debate between them, it might have more closely resembled a mutual admiration lovefest.

He arrived at the network by himself, twenty-five minutes before air time. He was tanned, looked rested, and was in a jovial mood. I met him in the hallway, and we went into studio to get comfortable. We were talking about football (he was a booster of the Oregon Ducks, although privately he was a big Notre Dame fan), his vacation in the Virgin Islands and *Foreign Correspondent* (which he had seen last night and loved.) Then he offhandedly said something that struck me.

"So, did you hear the interview Roosevelt gave the other night?"

"You mean the one on NBC, Senator?"

"Yeah."

"I heard it. What did you think?"

"Well, it was standard Roosevelt. I couldn't believe he mentioned Lucy Mercer, though."

I stopped making notes and looked right at him. "What do you mean?"

"Well, and this is off-the-record, Michael, OK?" I nodded. "Everybody in Washington knows he and Lucy have a thing going. I don't really care, but it just points to his arrogance. Winning a third term has given him a rather imperial air. He's beginning to think he's not just the president. He thinks he's a ruler."

"You really think so, Senator?"

"Well, again, off the record, yeah, I do. That's one of the things that I was so concerned about. No president has ever gone past two terms. It's tradition. Now, here he is, going for three, and who knows, maybe four or five. I'm not sure that's good for the country."

"What does that have to do with Lucy?"

"Well, by mentioning her on the air, he's almost signaling that he's completely above scrutiny. Look, I know he's got a tough job. And his marriage is one of convenience. But don't flaunt it in public. Keep it private, where it belongs."

"Senator, do you think it's an issue the public should know about?"

"What? His fooling around? No, not really. Unless he continues to make these kind of public statements."

"But as I recall, he only mentioned that he saw her dancing by herself."

"C'mon, Michael. You know there's more to it than that."

"How would I really know that, Senator? Really? Tell me how I'd know, and I'll check it out."

McNary thought about it for a second, and then said, "No. Nice try."

The show went well, as he was forthcoming about a lot of issues and ideas that had been brought up during the campaign. I found it interesting, though, that he and Willkie hadn't spoken since the day after the election. McNary also said that the war in Europe should remain the war in Europe and the US needed to maintain its isolationist policies. When pressed, he admitted his long-time friendship with Henry Wallace had made his defeat a little easier ("at least there's a good guy as vice president") and deflected the notion that he may run for president in four years. "That's a long way off, Michael. I have no idea what will happen. And I have to run for re-election in two years, so there's a lot of decisions to be made."

It was a good, fast hour. McNary agreed to come back another time, and I honestly said I looked forward to it. He was a good guest, able to answer questions in an informational and entertaining way.

When the show was over, we stood up and shook hands across the console. As we shook, he said to me, "Lorena Hickok."

"What?"

"Lorena Hickok. She's a friend of the First Lady's. But don't mention my name."

I already knew Lorena. Why Senator Charles McNary would tell me to ask Lorena Hickok about FDR's affairs was beyond me. But I thanked him for the information and for being a good guest.

I was sitting in my office when it hit me about twenty minutes later. I told Peter to have Earl Mercia look at Lorena Hickok. Lorena Hickok was a fine writer and reporter. She grew up in Wisconsin, and got a job covering University of Minnesota football for the Minneapolis Tribune. She was one of the first women reporters of any kind, let alone sports reporters. Then she moved to New York to work for the Associated Press, and covered some big stories, like the Lindbergh baby kidnapping. Then the AP assigned her to cover Eleanor Roosevelt during the 1932 campaign. They hit it off and became close friends.

Lorena Hickok felt she could no longer objectively cover Roosevelt. She quit the AP and took a job with the White House to write field reports from around the country, to give the new president a sense of what was really taking place before, during and after some of his reform measures were enacted. Her reports were legendary among the staff. Instead of a dry field report, she would write flowing prose that captured the essence of what life was like.

Eleanor and Lorena remained very close friends through the first two terms. Lorena was a stocky woman, not a beauty. Her reporter friends, whom she kept during her years working at the White House, called her Hick, and she fit right in with them, smoking cigars and playing poker whenever she had the chance.

It took less than an hour for Earl Mercia to report back to Peter. He said Lorena Hickok had moved into the White House four days after the election. He said he'd get back when he had more details.

Moving into the White House in and of itself was somewhat newsworthy, but not that unusual. Many staffers lived there. So the big questions were: where was she living; what was she doing; and why did she move in?

I had met the First Lady on a number of occasions, handshaking in reception lines, none of which, to my mind, were outstanding enough to cause her to remember me. The Marion Anderson episode made me, for the first time, reconsider the clout and influence Eleanor Roosevelt had on this country. It was the right thing to do, and she did it with the graceful style of a skilled bulldozer driver

The Affairs of State

One of the great singers of our time, Marion Anderson had been denied the opportunity to sing at a large national event simply because she was black. Eleanor Roosevelt found this untenable, illogical, and completely unjust. So, she invited Marion Anderson to sing at the White House and at The Lincoln Memorial in front of thousands of people in a nationally broadcast event sponsored by the First Lady.

It was said that Lorena was the one who encouraged Eleanor to become more socially outspoken and active. It took awhile for Eleanor to adjust to being First Lady, but once she found her stride she took off. She had been the administration's point person during the first two terms to put a human face on the new policies being enacted. She began a wildly popular weekly newspaper column (which I always thought was ghost-written by Lorena). She traveled constantly, or so it seemed, to promote the administration's policies and her own agendas of social activism, justice and equality for all.

So here I was, in my office by myself, struggling with issues of public policy, private behavior and religious beliefs. But I kept asking myself if the public really needed to know all this. I remember thinking that was different than if the public had a right to know all this. Clearly, I believed the public does have a right to know all this, but they may not need to. I came to call this The Denif Argument. There had to be something else to tip the scales in favor of making this knowledge public.

That night, I went to the movies to relax. I was preparing for tomorrow's show. My guest, Edward G. Robinson, was coming on to talk about his latest movie, *Brother Orchid*. It involved a gangster on the lam, who takes refuge in a monastery and turns his life around. Robinson had already made a series of gangster pictures, and this comedy set him in the role, but played against type.

Robinson came on the show and was one of the best guests I've ever had. We'd never met before, but he was bright, articulate, well read, glib, insightful and funny, and did it all with that distinctive voice that easily transversed good and evil. We talked about *Brother Orchid* and what attracted him to it.

"The character I play, Little John Sarto, is a big-time racketeer who goes to Europe for five years to add culture to his life. He turns over his operation to Jack Buck, Humphrey Bogart's character, expecting to reclaim his lead spot when he comes back. But Buck's got other ideas, and Sarto soon finds himself squeezed out. He ends up hiding in a monastery, where he reclaims more than his racketeering operation. He reclaims his life. I was intrigued with the notion of how a person who does terrible things on a regular basis is, deep down, just a guy looking for some way to be decent."

He also had the glad-handing down pat: "I love your show. I listen all the time." We hit it off, and he agreed to come back and talk about his next movie, the screen adaptation of Jack London's *The Sea Wolf*.

I got off the air and Peter said Earl Mercia had struck paydirt, but wouldn't tell me what. He told me he was meeting with Earl and the network lawyers at 5:30 p.m. He wanted me there, too.

There were six corporate lawyers in the room, one each from Tax, Accounting, Copyright, Civil and Commerce, plus Bart Johnson, the BRN Lead Corporate Counsel, along with Earl, Peter and me. Earl walked over and handed me a piece of paper with a woman's handwriting on it. He told me to read it out loud.

I cleared my voice and began to read:

November 27, 1933
The White House

Hick Dear,
I found two letters and a road map today and did I devour them! I forgot to write you that after 10:30am on December 15, I will be free to meet you and I will have nothing to do so come as early as you can. Why don't we, if the weather is nice, take our lunch and go off each day to neighboring places? If we think we'll be tempted to stay the night we could take a bag and telephone back to the White House what we decided to do. There may be people staying here so I think one night anyway we'll stay away, as otherwise we might have to be polite a while in the evening unless the guests all dine out which is quite unlikely.
There's a bit about you and a picture in the Literary Digest. It's nice! Tommy is mailing it to you.
Press conference at 11 this morning, then two women to see, had five of the girls to lunch and worked all the rest of the time on accumulated mail, but I'm fairly caught up tho' I won't be able to ride tomorrow.
John came in tonight and dined with us. I do like him. They sat on my sofa all evening and seemed to have a swell time while I worked!
Dear One, and so you think they gossip about us. Well, they must at least think we stand separation rather well! I am always so much

more optimistic than you are. I suppose because I care so little what "they" say!

I rather think some of the girls are getting pretty good champions! There have been one or two inaccurate stories and I spoke about them this morning and I trusted the majority of them were with me!

A world of love and my thoughts are always with you,

E.R.

I stopped reading and looked at everyone. "Eleanor Roosevelt?" They all nodded. "Hick Dear? Lorena Hickok?" Again they all nodded.

I sat down, the letter still in my hand. I looked around, my gaze finally settling on Earl Mercia. "Well, this doesn't prove anything. Where'd you get this letter? And how do we know it's real?"

Earl said, "You're right. This doesn't prove anything. But there's lots of them."

"Lots of what? Letters?"

"Yeah, lots of them."

"Where'd you get them? How do we know these are real?"

Peter spoke up. "The handwriting matches known samples of the First Lady's. It's genuine."

"But I'll bet Eleanor writes lots of letters to lots of people," I said.

"Yeah, she does," Earl said, "but she doesn't say she wants to stay the night with any of them." All the lawyers in the room laughed.

"So what are we talking about here, guys?" I said. "What's the point of this meeting? And where did you get this, Earl?"

"I can't tell you where I got it. But I can get more."

I looked at Bart Johnson. "He doesn't have to tell us where he got it?" He shook his head. "So what are we doing here?"

Then Peter took over. "Michael, the lawyers all agree that this looks like the real deal, no forgery, no fakes. We think it's a legitimate news story, and we'd like you to investigate it more, and then prepare a story on it."

"On what? That the First Lady might be having an affair with a woman? What kind of story is that?"

"A big one, Michael. Maybe the biggest."

I immediately started thinking about all the different angles we'd have to cover. First, we'd have to ask the First Lady and Lorena Hickok if there was anything to it. After their denials, we'd have to have back-up documentation to refute their denials. Then we'd have to deal with FDR himself, who was no slouch at bringing the full weight of the Federal Government down on anyone who crossed him. We'd have to talk with religious leaders and community leaders.

I figured this story would go nowhere fast. As I walked back to my office, Earl Mercia approached me.

"Take a look at this, Michael." He handed me a 9x12 envelope. "I didn't show this to anybody else yet."

"Why do you want to show it to me then, Earl?"

"Because you think I'm a contemptible slimeball. You think that uncovering information in this fashion is beneath you. You think that this kind of investigation is low-class. Maybe it is. But I'm just doing my job, and I do it well. Go on. Take a look."

I opened the envelope. It was a picture of the president and Lucy Mercer Rutherfurd. He was sitting in his wheelchair. She was sitting on his lap facing him, her legs spread on either side. There was clearly more going on than cuddling.

"Holy shit," I said. "Where'd you get this? When'd you get this?"

"I took it. Last night."

"Wow." I just kept saying wow.

After a minute, Earl spoke up. "Look, I'm just doing what I do. I've seen a lot of stuff in my time. Betz hired me to find some stuff out, and I'm finding it out. It's all right there. Barely taking me any effort. You just gotta know where to look. Personally, I don't care what they do. They can hump dogs for all I care. But you - well, you gotta decide what to do with this info. I'll see you later, Michael. And when I do, I'll have more stuff."

He left the picture with me. "Hey, Earl, you want this?"

"No," he said without turning, "you figure out what to do with it."

I put it in my briefcase and took it home.

I didn't sleep much that night. I wrestled with the hard, cold facts: the president of the United States and the First Lady were each having affairs with women.

At eight o'clock the next morning, I was waiting in Peter's office. He spotted me as he walked in.

"Michael! Goddamn, I'm glad you're here." He was beaming ear to ear. "Have you seen this yet?" He tossed me the picture of Lucy and the president sharing more than just a wheelchair. That son of a bitch, I thought. Earl Mercia didn't take me into his confidence. He'd already given this picture to who knows how many people. "Yeah, I've seen it, Peter. That's why I'm here."

"Good, good, good. What do you think?"

"If we pursue this story, it'll hurt us. FDR is too powerful. He'll figure out a way to kill us. The public will side with him. And everybody loves Eleanor."

I'll never forget what happened next. Peter Betz leaned back in his chair and took a deep breath. Then he started talking very slowly, very quietly, very deliberately.

"They are big, and they are powerful. But there is freedom of the press. And unless we in the press continue to monitor the big and powerful, the little guys don't stand a chance. Like you." He reached into his desk and pulled out another 9x12 envelope and slid it across to me. "Take a look at this."

I opened the envelope and saw a picture of me with Sharon Tozzi. It was the two of us, making love, naked and in her apartment, shortly after I began at BRN. It was unmistakable that it was the two of us, and I certainly couldn't deny the authenticity.

"Where'd this come from?" I asked

"Earl gave it to me. He took it."

"He took the picture? Why?"

"He was doing his job."

"Somebody hired him to take this picture of me?"

"Well, somebody hired him to take pictures of you, and he got this one. There's others, too."

"There's more?"

"At least a dozen that I've seen. But this is the best one, the one that shows exactly that it's you and Sharon."

"Who hired him?"

"Earl won't say. Client privilege. He's very ethical."

"Ethical my ass. Who hired this son of a bitch?"

"Well, he did say it was a government official, a high-level government official. Judging by the timing of this picture, which was shortly after we went on the air, I have a pretty good idea."

I thought for a moment. "John Nance Garner?"

Peter shrugged his shoulders. "Could be. I don't know for sure. But what I do know is that the government is watching your every move. Shouldn't we watch theirs?"

All of a sudden, this became personal. I hated the idea of being followed, my private life invaded by government snoops.

"If it was Garner," Peter Betz asked, "do you think he didn't show these pictures to anybody? Like his boss?"

For some reason, I started to laugh. "At least you can see my ass. You can't see FDR's."

Peter Betz relaxed. "I've known Roosevelt for years. He covers his ass every chance he gets."

"Who else knows about these pictures, Peter?"

"No one."

"Bull shit. Who knows?"

"Bart Johnson. That's it, really."

"I've got to call Sharon and let her know."

"Be careful, Michael. Then what are you going to do?"

I started to leave his office, when I turned and said, "I don't know. I've got to think about it, Peter."

"Fair enough. Just don't think too long. Other hounds are sniffing this story."

I went back to my office and immediately put in a call to Sharon at Senator Buckfield's office.

Her voice was all business. Even after all this time, she was still mad. "What do you want?"

"I need to see you. Today."

"What about?"

"I can't talk about it over the phone. But we need to see each other today."

She sighed deeply. "OK. Lunch?"

"No. No place public. Either in a conference room over in your area, or a conference room here."

"Conference room? Who else is going to be there?"

"No one, Sharon. Promise. Just you and me."

"I'll come over there. 10?"

When she arrived, I remembered why I had initially fallen for her. She was a gorgeous raven-haired beauty, thin and graceful, with an elegant demeanor about her. But she also had a no-nonsense attitude that permeated everything. She was the package, the total package.

We walked into a small conference room that was just down the hall from my office. I closed the door and we sat across from each other. She still had her coat on.

"Well?" she said impatiently.

I slid across one of the 9x12 envelopes and told her to open it. She looked at me with bewilderment, but did it. She pulled out the picture of the two of us, then slumped back in the chair. "Oh my God," was all she muttered. She slipped off her coat without ever putting the picture down. "Are you - we - being blackmailed?"

"No," I said flatly.

"Then how did you get this? Who took this?"

"A private investigator that BRN hired also was hired to do this, and he shared them with us. But he was hired by a high-level government official to follow me. And he ended up taking a series of pictures of us."

"A private eye took pictures of us? Who's got them? Where are they?"

"Well," I began, "I assume he still has the negatives. Who has the prints, I'm not sure. But I've been told I can assume lots of high level officials have seen these."

"Like Buckfield?"

"No, he's probably not high enough."

Sharon remained slumped in the chair, now with a puzzled look on her face. "Not high enough?" I could see the wheels spinning in her head. "For God's sake, Michael, he's a United States Senator, on the Senate Foreign Relations Committee. There's not many people higher..." Just as she said that, I could tell it clicked. "Roosevelt?"

"I don't think he OK'd it, but he's probably seen them."

For a minute or so, Sharon just sat there, staring at the picture. Every now and then, she'd grunt, shake her head and close her eyes. I put a glass of water in front of her, but she didn't touch it. Then she said, flatly, "Garner."

"Could be," I told her. "I don't know for sure, and the private eye won't say. Client privilege, he says. But that's my guess. He was probably mad over that first-day interview I did with him, and set out to find whatever he could about me." Then I chuckled and said, "But now he's gone, and I'm still here."

"Michael! Don't be so cavalier about this. This is a picture of you and me - me! - and there's others out there floating around. Who knows who's seen them? What are we going to do?"

"Well, that's a good question, Sharon. Here. Look at this." I slid the other 9x12 envelope across the table to her. She grabbed it while never removing her gaze from my eyes.

Slowly she opened it, and pulled out the 8x10 black-and-white photo. Her eyes widened. She whispered the startled whisper of someone whose breath has just been taken away. "That's Roosevelt and, uh, uh..." She continued to stare.

"Lucy Mercer Rutherfurd." Finally, I said, "So, what are we going to do?"

She slipped the photo back into its envelope and said, "Wow. I didn't know you could do that."

"Do what?"

"THAT! I didn't know you could do THAT!"

"Oh. That. I was kind of surprised, too. Anyway, the question is, what are we going to do? What should we do with this information?"

"The information about the pictures of us, or the pictures of Roosevelt? And who took those pictures? The same guy?" I nodded. "The pictures of Roosevelt and Lucy. What should we do?"

Sharon looked at me as if I had lost my mind. "What should we do? You mean, what should you do, or what should BRN do?"

"Both, I guess."

"Nothing. You should do nothing. What's it prove, Michael? That FDR is human? That wheelchair sex is possible? That you're a scumbag for hiring a private eye to spy on the president? It's none of your business. Or, more accurately, it's none of your fucking business." Sharon had regained her power, stood up and took a couple steps toward the door. "I'm not thrilled about the pictures of us. But it's been awhile and nothing has happened, and now that I know about them, I'll be prepared, at least a little bit, for what might happen. But spying on the president of the United States is beneath even you and this network. And the only person to get whacked in this deal will be you." She had her hand on the doorknob when I said, "Eleanor is having an affair with Lorena Hickok."

"WHAT?"

"Eleanor is having an affair with Lorena Hickok."

"Eleanor Roosevelt?" Again, I nodded.

Sharon stood there, stunned. Her mouth drooped open, her coat still draped over her arm. I could see her mind racing. "Eleanor and Lorena?"

"Yeah."

She walked back over to the chair and sat down again. Her coat was draped across her lap and she picked up the glass of water. "Let me get this straight," she said, taking a sip of water. "The vice president hires a private eye to take pictures of us, so you hire a private eye to take pictures of Franklin and Eleanor Roosevelt. And you find out that each is having an affair - with a woman. You have pictures of Eleanor?"

"No, we have hand-written letters."

"Uh-huh." She drank some more water. "So you call me up to show me our pictures and ask my advice. Am I missing anything?"

"Well, you're close enough. We didn't have the pictures of us before we hired this private eye. That was an unexpected development. I just found out about the pictures of us right before I called you this morning."

"And you want to know what you should do. Like, is this a news story? Right? Is that what you're asking me?"

"Basically, yes."

Sharon drank some more water, gently set it on the table. "Paul Buckfield has known FDR for twenty-five or thirty years. He's known that FDR uses a wheelchair almost all the time, but whenever he's in public, he stands, and with help, it looks like he walks. You know that, too, but you don't report it. You don't say he gave a speech today and lied when he walked. You just say he gave a speech today. He's the first president ever to run for and win a third term, and he just carried all but ten states. The American people, by and large, love him. I love him. I voted for him, again. I voted for him because I think he's the man to lead us through whatever is coming up, and because he's done a great job so far. And I'll bet you that if he's been fooling around with Lucy, he's been doing it for a while. And Eleanor, well, people love her more than him. The common person really connects with her. So I guess what I'm saying is this: if you and this network drag them through the mud of a sex scandal, the only ones to get hurt will be you and this network. People will find it interesting, and they'll certainly talk about it. But it won't be front page news for long, and you'll get crushed. And frankly, Michael, I'd help crush you." She took a long drink of water, stood up, walked toward the door and said goodbye without ever looking back.

I understood her point, but I found myself disagreeing with it the more I replayed it in my mind. Slowly, over the better part of an hour by myself in my office, I came to reject her opinion, especially the part about me being the only one crushed.

The more I thought about it, the more I came to believe it was a news story. The public not only had a right to know this, but a need to know it. This kind of behavior is a true barometer of character, of honesty and integrity. If they lie about cheating on their spouses, how can we ever believe them when they talk to us about policies they want to make? It didn't matter that every human being on Earth would probably lie to cover up an affair. I even lied to my high school girlfriend when I went out with another girl. I became convinced that our national leaders needed to set the standard all ordinary citizens should follow. I'll admit, I was pretty mad about the pictures of Sharon and me. I felt violated, hunted, abused, threatened - all of that at the same time. I felt that if the Government would do that to me, what would they do to somebody else? The fact we hadn't been blackmailed by those pictures of Sharon and me did not diminish my feelings of anger and violation.

But what about this notion of spying on the president? Have we crossed the line of fair play and investigation? Is his private life more open for dissection than mine? If I don't like being trailed and photographed, should we expect the president to have a thicker skin about it simply because he's the most photographed person in the world?

And what about Sharon's assertion that the public will care for a moment, but won't want to hear much about it? Could she be right? I doubted it. Just from doing my radio show, I had come to believe the topic that most interested listeners was sex. Doesn't matter if it's Errol Flynn and his reputation, or Ted Williams and an unintentional *double entendre*, people were riveted to the radio when sex was discussed. Her point, though, was that those are fleeting references contained inside a daily one-hour show. The public, she believed, was not interested in a steady diet of sexual chatter, especially about the President and First Lady. That was the easiest point for me to dismiss. I *knew* the public would follow it detail by detail.

Chapter 7 – Congressman Leo Dailey

It was cold in Washington that December. We never got a lot of snow in DC, but that winter seemed to have more than most. I had a relatively high profile list of guests that month. There was Walter Brennan, Glenn Miller, Roy Rogers and Dale Evans, and, of course, Santa Claus. I actually hated interviewing Santa Claus, just because it was so forced and completely made up. But it was a big crowd pleaser, and it made me remember that listeners to my program often just liked to escape.

We also interviewed a few new congressmen, including the Gentleman from the 1st District of Montana, Leo Dailey. He was interesting, very quick witted and completely comfortable on the radio. He knew, intrinsically, radio was the wave to deliver his thoughts and ideas to an audience larger than Montana's 1st District. He understood that his voice and views could be made more powerful by embracing radio rather than merely tolerating it. Leo Dailey was a thirty-six-year-old isolationist Republican Roosevelt-hater with no clear ideology. He won because he was able to use radio more effectively than his opponent. It surely wasn't his intellectual skills. FDR carried Montana easily, but Leo Dailey won in his first race for Congress. Montana State Senator Leo Dailey decided to run for the US Congress in early 1939. On a vacation, he and his wife, Jane Hall Dailey, publicly went to Niagara Falls. Privately, they went to Detroit and met with Rico Tozzi, a bowling alley operator with ties to the trucking industry. Leo told him that he could be counted on to be in the trucker's corner in Congress, but he had to get there first. Leo asked Rico Tozzi for volunteers and money, and got both. For six months or so, Leo planned his campaign strategy. He wanted to be seen as a new breed Republican, who favored both business growth and organized labor. He touted both his youth and his experience. He disagreed with many of Roosevelt's tactics, such as attempting to pack the Supreme Court with extra justices who would rubber stamp his Constitution challenging ideas. And he believed that the United States should stay out of the war in Europe.

Leo had to overcome an entrenched Republican congressman, Landy Bannister. Bannister was seventy-three, had represented Montana in Congress since 1912, and by all accounts had done a good job. But he was no match for Leo.

Leo Dailey announced his candidacy on September 1, 1939, the same day Germany invaded Poland. Although that overshadowed his announcement, it wasn't long before Dailey had Bannister on the ropes through some strategic planning and radio advertising. When the Primary took place in August 1940, Leo Dailey captured the Republican nomination with an astounding 77% of the vote. Bannister pledged his support, but never campaigned for Leo Dailey, who overwhelmed the Democratic nominee in the November elections.

It wasn't often that we booked politicians who called us, but Leo Dailey had a sense of the moment, and it oozed through the phone when I spoke with him. He said he would be in Washington in mid-December and he'd love to be on. I said OK.

When he came to the studio, Leo Dailey was dressed to the nines. The creases in his pants were so sharp you could cut your finger on them. Crisp white shirt, gray suit, black shoes and the most neon-inspired red tie I'd ever seen. And in what would become his trademark, a red pocket kerchief with the Republican elephant prominently showing.

We went on the air and Leo Dailey took over. He said the great state of Montana had some of the most faithful and rabid listeners to BRN and the Michael Audray Show. He said it was a pleasure to be the first native Montanan to be on the show, a point I could neither confirm nor deny. Rookie or not, when he said that he stamped himself as one savvy player.

That hour went very fast, and we stayed mostly with how Leo Dailey came to DC, why he was there and what he hoped to accomplish. His answers basically were: I beat the other guy because I'm younger; I'm here because it's a stepping stone to another higher rung; and I want to make a Big Name for myself.

I filed all this information away in my head and kept his phone number in my book.

All through December, Earl Mercia kept updating Peter on new information he'd learned. I've never known how he found this stuff out, but he did, and he had proof. Eleanor and Lorena had spent a total of thirty-eight nights together in 1939, and sixty-one nights together in 1940. After the Democratic convention in August 1940 they stopped seeing each other. But Lorena moved into the White House right after the election.

FDR and Lucy saw each other regularly. Quite often, according to Earl, FDR and Lucy would dine in his private quarters, and she would stay the night, or leave just early enough to evade the press. From all accounts, Lucy was the love of his life.

The discussions among Peter, the lawyers and me were generally spirited. He always wanted to know how close we were to breaking this story, and I kept hedging.

Our lawyers were concerned that if we broke this story too soon, without all the material possible, FDR would put BRN out of business through tax investigations, FBI checks, police harassment, you name it. We had to be so covered, and so ready to do this, that no matter what FDR did we could weather the storm.

Peter Betz didn't want to hear it, although he agreed with it. For him, it was not about uncovering FDR and Eleanor. It was a big story for his network. He just wanted to make some news.

Earl smelled blood, and he was convinced that something would happen during the Christmas season. He checked and rechecked his sources three times a day, and seemed to develop new leads all the time. Most of them never panned out.

But there was a late afternoon meeting in Peter's office on December 20. Earl came in with a huge grin on his face and a piece of paper in his hand. It was a jewelry store receipt for a $200 emerald pendant purchased on December 13th. Earl then opened his briefcase and brought out a picture he took the night before. It was Lucy wearing the pendant.

"This is good, Earl, but so what? It could be that Lucy bought the pendant for herself. Doesn't prove anything," I said.

"The pendant was designed just for her, and it is engraved 'LM/ HP'."

"HP?"

"Hyde Park. That's what FDR calls himself sometimes when he wants to be anonymous." We looked stunned. No one had ever hinted at that before, but somehow, Earl Mercia knew all this.

"And," he said, "since FDR paid for this, it's taxpayer money."

There was a bit of squirming in the room. Yes, we all thought, it technically is taxpayer money. But trying to get FDR on a tax charge, like the Feds got Al Capone, was stretching it. Thankfully, that's when Bart Johnson spoke.

Bart Johnson, the lead corporate counsel for BRN, had known Peter Betz since high school. Incredibly distinguished looking, with a perfectly coiffed silver mane, Bart Johnson seemed to believe in nothing but the law. He saw the inevitable shades of gray, but chose to see them through the black-and-white prism of legal decisions. Before joining BRN, he was a rich and successful private attorney who brooked no challengers to his legal opinions. Although he was one of five lawyers in the room, no one disputed that Bart Johnson was the first among equals.

"Excuse me," Bart Johnson began, as he rose from his chair and strode across the room toward the wet bar. "I've sat here and listened to all this talk for weeks. I've seen the pictures and I understand the story. Believe it or not, I've had clients who needed protection when faced with similar pictures during their own divorce proceedings. And I'm telling you, you've got nothing. Peter," he said, turning to face his long-time friend, "you can keep having these meetings and coming up with more material than you've got, but what do you hope to find? Some kind of truly illegal activity that Roosevelt is doing? That's not going to happen. We're talking about a guy who is the first person in American history to win a third term as president." Bart Johnson was in courtroom mode now. He turned and faced the rest of the room. "Gentlemen, here are the facts: you've got pictures and love letters, and now a receipt, from both parties; you've obtained these things in underhanded, although technically not illegal, ways. But we are no longer dealing in simply the law. We are dealing now in the arena of public opinion," he continued. "You're never going to have any more damaging material than you have now. The question you should be asking yourselves is not how best to find the President and the First Lady in blatantly illegal activities. No. The question you should be asking yourselves is do you have the stomach to make this information public? Is it really that important? Will the public good be improved through the dissemination of the knowledge you have? If so, release the information in the manner you see fit. If not, drop this and move on to something important."

Bart Johnson turned back toward the wet bar. Just a beat later, he said, "Peter, you're out of gin." Bart Johnson sighed deeply. "Call me when you've made a decision, Peter. I'm interested, but I'm going home."

There was a bunch of nervous shuffling of feet and papers. No one really said anything, but you could hear all the minds working. Finally, Peter spoke.

"Michael," he said softly, "it's your timetable. Just let me know when and how we'll break the story." Then, uncharacteristically, he grabbed his coat and left his own office, still filled with lawyers, Earl and me.

His directive was clear. He still wanted the story broken, and he wanted BRN to break it. But when and how was now up to me. Not if, but when and how.

The lawyers filed out rather quickly. I was slumped in my chair, and Earl was still at the table.

"Michael. C'mon, let's go get a beer."

I was a bit taken back by Earl's friendly offer, but I needed a drink. We went to McGinty's Tavern, almost directly across the street from the studios. I'm not sure exactly, but we tipped back more than a few beers.

I asked Earl if he ever had any compunction about what he did for a living, if he ever stopped to consider the voyeuristic nature of it all. No, he said, it's a living. Pays pretty good, and sometimes there's travel involved. He hadn't always been a political snoop. Like most private eyes, he started out trailing cheating spouses and gamblers with big debts. But it had evolved into a high profile, word-of-mouth business that took him into the top echelons of American political power.

He'd started in 1924, after graduating from Penn State with a degree in business. But he knew he wasn't cut out for a normal nine-to-five job at a bank or a corporation. Earl knew a couple young cops, and they were looking to do some off-duty work to make a few extra bucks. They asked Earl to manage their business, and as he did he became interested in it himself. He knew a little about photography, and as the business grew, he assigned himself a few overflow jobs.

Speakeasies were plentiful at this time, and there was no shortage of people who wanted other people tailed. The business continued to grow, but Earl was soon working by himself when his cop-partners found they could make more money in under-the-table payments from speakeasy owners than they could working extra hours chasing some bookie on the lam.

In 1928, Al Smith was the Democratic nominee for president. He was the first Catholic to run, and as such drew an awful lot of attention from Catholic-haters and other bigots. Earl got a call one day from an anonymous client who was willing to pay $5000 for pictures of Al Smith with another woman at a speakeasy. In the only time he ever asked this question, Earl wanted to know if this was even remotely plausible. The anonymous client didn't answer directly, simply said he wanted the pictures. Earl said, OK, but wanted half the money up front, and the other half if and when he delivered any pictures. Earl got the first half of the money, and tailed Al Smith for three months. He came up completely empty. Al Smith was an honorable and upright guy.

But those three months gave Earl an entry into the world of power politics, and the contacts he made proved financially invaluable to Earl over the course of the next twelve years. He'd investigated the Washington and Hollywood power elite, mixed in with nefarious underworld types. Usually he came up with the goods, as he called them. If not, he still took the money.

And never had any remorse.

He tailed senators and congressmen, judges and lawyers, doctors and university professors. Most of the time it revolved around sex. Sometimes gambling was thrown in, but mostly it was sex. It wasn't always cheating spouses. Sometimes it was just unmarried men and women doing what comes naturally, like Sharon and me.

Generally Earl turned the photos over to the clients and got paid. Occasionally, though, the client wanted Earl to deliver the pictures to the target. Earl didn't like doing this, but when he did, he made sure he got paid extra.

He never saw what he did as blackmail. "That's such a dirty word," he said. "I prefer to think of it as leverage." In his mind, there was a difference, since there was never a demand for money or even a quid pro quo. It was just the fact that the target now knew that there was something exposable, and he should be on his best behavior.

Right as we were leaving, walking back toward our cars, I asked him what he thought I should do about the whole thing.

"I never give advice to my clients," Earl said. "But if you want my opinion, I'll tell you."

"Go ahead."

We were standing next to his car as he stubbed a Camel out with his unpolished wingtip. "OK. With everybody else that I tail, there's always somebody that wants something tangible, something they can put their fingers on. You know, money from a divorce, or a piece of property or the second house or whatever. Here, you're looking for a news story. I don't get it, Michael. I really don't. I mean, what's the most that'll happen? You'll embarrass the president and I'll get a lot of money from your network. But after the story dies down, what have you gotten? Not a whole hell of a lot." He opened his car door, got in, started it up and drove off without a final word. Or maybe that was his final word.

*December 29, 1940: FDR delivers Arsenal of Democracy Speech. 76%
of Americans listen to it on the radio.
January 6, 1941: FDR's State of the Union Speech is dubbed the Four
Freedoms Speech – Freedom of Speech, Freedom to Worship, Freedom from
Want, Freedom from Fear.*

Chapter 8 – The Decision Is Made

The inauguration was less than a month away. Timing on this story was everything, and I had to figure out when the best time would be.

The show had its share of actors and actresses around the holidays. Clark Gable came on one day shortly before Christmas to talk about *Strange Cargo*, his follow-up to *Gone With The Wind*. Gable co-starred with Joan Crawford and Ian Hunter. He and Hunter played escaped convicts, but Hunter had an intense religious fervor. Eventually, Hunter helps Gable realize he must change his ways. The Catholic Legion of Decency condemned this film for its irreverent use of Scripture and its lustful situations. *Strange Cargo* was banned in Detroit and Providence, much to Gable's chagrin and amusement.

But mostly it was politics. We tried to get Henry Wallace to come on the show, but he declined. Wallace had been around Washington for quite a while, but FDR wanted to make sure he stayed in the wings until the president wanted him to do something. We tried to get Senator Paul Buckfield to come back on the show, but he declined. I don't know if Sharon had something to do with that or if he was still upset about his earlier brush with our line of questioning. I also tried to get Joe Kennedy. He'd recently been replaced as US Ambassador to England in response to complaints from Winston Churchill. He never even responded.

Shortly after Christmas, we had Leo Dailey on again. The soon-to-be US representative was glib and available. He had a good handle on how this game was played, and made no bones about being interested in making his name better known.

But when we were done on the air, Dailey asked if he could talk with me in my office. I said sure. We walked down the hall, and he closed the door.

"Michael, I hear you're looking into Eleanor's sex life." My look must have expressed absolute amazement because he barely paused. "Good. That kind of behavior cannot possibly be condoned. What do you need me to do to help you?"

I stammered a little. "I really don't know what you're talking about, Leo."

"Oh, come on, Michael. You know Eleanor and that woman reporter are screwing. Don't kid me. I may look like a rookie, but I've already made lots of friends. And if I know it, you can bet your ass it's on the street. So. How can I help you bring her down?"

"First of all, Leo, I'm not going to confirm or deny what you're talking about. If we are looking into something like this, it's our business at the moment. If we're not, I'm not going to tell you that, either. And even if we are, what makes you think we're interested in, as you say, bringing down the First Lady of the United States?"

"She's a nigger-loving dike, and we don't like them where I come from."

He had taken my breath away. I sat down in my desk chair. "You know what, Leo? I haven't heard anybody say that in quite a long time. And you know what else? You're not in Montana anymore. You're in Washington DC, the center of the major leagues. That stuff will get you crushed pretty quickly. I'd watch what you say and who you say it to. I think we're done, Leo."

Leo Dailey just laughed. "Nice speech, Michael. We're not done, far from it. And when this is all over, you'll thank me for being on your side."

After he left, I realized he was right about one thing: if he knew what we were looking at, lots of other people did, too, both in and out of official Washington. I walked down to Peter's office and told him about my chat with Leo Dailey.

"Yeah, I know, Michael. I was the one who told Dailey."

"What?"

"Look, he's new to town and anxious to make a name for himself. I had Earl check him out. Found out he's married but strays. No kids with his wife, but he's knocked up a couple others. But still no kids, know what I mean? He's got hunger-for-power stamped all over his forehead, but doesn't know how to harness it. He's the perfect new congressman to be out front on this story."

"Are you nuts, Peter? What are you doing telling a Montana hayseed that we're thinking of exposing the private lives of the two most powerful people in the United States?"

"Michael, you're dragging your feet. We need this story. It is a legitimate news story, and if we don't break it, NBC or somebody else will."

"NBC won't," I said, remembering my conversations with Jack Denif.

"The point is, Michael, we needed somebody in Congress who can be the face for our outrage. Leo Dailey, the freshman Congressman from Montana, is the guy. He's young, understands radio, and represents a state where men can screw women and men can screw cows, but women can't screw women."

"You've got a screw loose, Peter. And tell me - what do you think will happen when we break this story? Really. What's going to happen?"

Peter drew a long drag on his cigar. Slowly, with a large grin, he responded. "Roosevelt will get really pissed, Eleanor will get really pissed, Leo Dailey will make his name known, and in about a month, the whole thing will blow over. But in the meantime, we'll be the most-listened to network on the planet. And we'll stay that way. We might even make these bastards more accountable."

I looked at him and for the first time thought he really had gone over the edge. But everything he'd said to me before and all of his other predictions had turned out right, so I just shook my head and left his office.

About an hour later, Peter stopped by my office and dropped off a 9x12 envelope on my desk. "Besides," he said, "they abuse their power." And he walked out.

I was afraid to open the envelope, but I did. Five 8x10 pictures of Sharon Tozzi and me in the backseat of my 1938 Chevrolet in various positions. These were from the same general time as the other pictures of us. I remember not even being angry. But at that moment, I understood what Earl meant when he said it wasn't blackmail, it was leverage. These pictures hadn't been used against me or Sharon. But they were there as a hedge to keep me on my best behavior. It was an abuse of governmental power, and I was in a position to do something about it.

Those pictures made my mind up for me. There was no turning back, not now. I would go forward with the story, but I had to have everything ready and in order.

I spent a lot of time with Earl Mercia and Bart Johnson. I wanted to make sure that what I was going to report was indeed factual and verifiable. That there could be no way for BRN to be accused of misstating facts or reporting falsehoods. I spent a lot of time with our production crew, researching statements the president or First Lady had made in the newspaper or on tape that might possibly be relevant to whatever discussions would come up. I spent a lot of time with the government researchers who helped with information about Franklin and Eleanor's public schedules. And when I wasn't spending time with them, I was spending time with me, making sure that I was comfortable doing what I was about to be doing.

Since the 20th Amendment was ratified in 1933, the presidential inauguration was moved from early March to January 20th. FDR was sworn in for his second term on January 20, 1937, and he'd be sworn in for his third term on January 20, 1941.

We got word that FDR would hold a full-fledged press conference with all the radio networks, major newspapers and wire service reporters on January 15th. Sometimes, he'd hold these press conferences in the Press Room, or sometimes in the Jefferson Room or sometimes in the room where he held his Fireside Chats. But the president's staff decided that this press conference would be held in the Oval Office beginning at 3 p.m.

I checked my schedule for that day and found I could still do my show, have a quick bite to eat, and make it to the White House in plenty of time.

Peter had pioneered the taping of these events. Before BRN came along, the networks would broadcast them live but wouldn't have a copy of it for later. But Peter knew the value of the heard-word, and insisted our equipment would be set up at all press conferences. Peter Betz was, in many ways, a man far ahead of his time. He hired the engineers and bought the equipment necessary to make sure BRN had the edge it needed in the news business. Because he was not afraid to spend the money to get the latest technology, he inspired loyalty among the staff, especially the technical people who just wanted to play with all these new toys. He also encouraged his engineers to make design improvements that would make the job easier, sound better and last longer.

Setting up the recording equipment took a while, and since this press conference was going to be held in the Oval Office, we needed to get special clearance. Normally, we would go through the press office and set up a couple hours early. But this time, we were going into the president's working office.

Our chief engineer, Bob Boot, made the arrangements. He called the president's office and spoke with FDR's secretary, Missy LeHand, about what he wanted to do. Set up would take about ninety minutes, but tear down would only take thirty. Bob Boot said we'd like to be in the Oval Office from 1 p.m. until thirty minutes after the press conference ended.

FDR had to make the decision, though, and it was not high on his list of things to OK. About a week before the press conference, Peter Betz called FDR directly and asked for the time necessary to set up the equipment. FDR at first balked about giving up his office for that amount of time, but when Peter Betz pointed out that the other networks were going to need at least forty-five minutes to set up their microphones and lines, he got FDR to agree to the taping equipment and time frame.

On January 10th, Peter walked into my office and closed the door.

"Michael, at the press conference next week, I want you to ask FDR about Lucy and Eleanor and Lorena. That's the time to do it, the perfect time. It's before the inauguration, and it's in his office. That's the time, Michael." I just sat there with a blank look on my face. "It's a legitimate news story. We've spent the time and the research to back up our questions. We have the First Amendment on our side. And we also have thirty million listeners. I don't care how you do it, but next week at that press conference, you ask him these questions." Then he left my office.

That gave me five days to figure out how to ask the leader of the free world about his sex life. I imagined who would be there, what it would look like, where I'd stand and all the possible responses FDR could give me. I thought about what the other reporters in the room would say, both to the president and to me. I thought about the ramifications for me personally and for BRN. I thought about when I should ask the question, and exactly how I should phrase it. I thought about what life would be like back in Carmel, Indiana.

I spent most of my waking time focusing on this task. I needed to get truly behind the validity of the issue, that the American people really needed to know this. Every time I vacillated, I would look at those 8x10 pictures of Sharon and me. That was the overriding factor. Knowing the government would spy like that on ordinary citizens for an unknown end result not dissimilar to blackmail, I felt it was necessary to expose this kind of hypocrisy.

A couple days before the press conference, I interviewed Frances Farmer. She was a gifted and talented actress, but beset by a whole host of physical and mental problems. Her private life had made great copy for the newspapers and gossip columns because it was so colorful and offbeat. When she was on, she was on. There was no one like her. But when she was off, look out. She came on the show to plug her soon-to-be-released movie, *World Premiere*. It starred John Barrymore as a Hollywood producer whose new movie, *The Earth in Flames*, was about to debut in DC. To hype this anti-Hitler film Barrymore hired three pretend-spies to threaten the premiere. However, three real Nazi spies are actually planning to intercept Barrymore's film and show a real Nazi propaganda piece in its place. The movie was billed as a daft comedy, but Frances Farmer made sure to get her point across that the Nazis were no laughing matter.

"It won't matter," she said, "what people do in their private lives if the Nazis win, because no one - no one - will have private lives. We'll all be controlled by Hitler. Nazism must be stopped, because it is a real threat to people everywhere. I fear the Nazis. People will think what they want about me, but that's OK. At least they can think. People living under the oppression of the Nazis can't think."

Later that afternoon, I ran into Jack Denif. "Nice interview with Frances Farmer today, Michael," he said. "I thought she made some good points about the Nazis. She's probably not as wacko as everybody makes her out to be."

"No, Jack, she's pretty insightful."

"What about you? Are you insightful?"

"What do you mean, Jack?"

"I mean, what's bigger - people's private lives or a story?" I just looked at him. "Are you still looking into what the sleeping arrangements are at the White House?"

"Jack, we look into a lot of stuff, just like you."

"Well let me tell you this, Michael." Jack drew a deep breath on his cigarette. "If you're looking for something different to do, I know for a fact NBC would hire you. If you're uneasy with what Betz is having you look at, come on over to Rockefeller Center. What's more important to you, fame or your integrity? You might be famous, or you might be infamous. Think it over, Michael. Let me know."

We shook hands and then went our separate ways.

January 10, 1941: FDR introduces the Lend-Lease Bill to Congress, suggesting the US supply war materials to Great Britain. "If your neighbor's house is on fire, you don't fight over the price of the hose."

Chapter 9 – The Question

Wednesday, January 15, 1941 was sunny but cold in Washington, DC. I got to work early that morning. I was going to interview Sammy Baugh, the Washington Redskins quarterback, that day. He led the Redskins to the championship just a few weeks earlier, demolishing the Chicago Bears 73-0. It was a phenomenal game, and he was terrific. This was the kind of show, lighthearted and not controversial, I needed.

Peter Betz was there early that day, too. He stopped by my office, even offered me a cup of coffee. "I was just wondering," he said, "if you were going to ask Sammy Baugh about game plans. You know, championship teams all have game plans. I'm sure the Redskins had a game plan for the Bears. You going to ask him about that?"

"Sure, I guess, Peter."

"Do you have a game plan for this afternoon?"

"Yeah. Yeah, I do." Peter nodded and walked down the hall.

Sammy Baugh was a great guest. No big news items, no *double entendres*, just lots of talk about championship football. When I got off the air, I went to my office and went over all my notes and issues once more. I closed my door and rehearsed, something I never did. I wanted to make sure my game plan was solid.

Around 1:45 p.m., I left my office. As I walked out the front door of the building, Sharon Tozzi intercepted me. She'd been waiting for me to come out.

"So?" she asked

"So, what?"

"So...are you going to ask who FDR's boofing?"

I laughed. "What are you talking about, Sharon?"

"I tipped off Buckfield."

"What? What did you say to Buckfield?"

"I told him you were going to ask if FDR was playing pat-a-cake with Lucy."

"What did he say?"

"He said it's common knowledge. What's the big story?"

"He said it's common knowledge? Hmmm."

"So? Are you going to ask?"

"Why do you think I'm going to?"

"I know how Peter Betz works, and I know how you work, and I know who you work for."

"Well, I guess you're just going to have to wait and find out."

"That's a yes. I'll see you. I'm going back to the office, but I'll be listening. With Buckfield."

For some reason, Sharon's ambush relaxed me. It made me laugh. And I looked at her matter-of-factness about FDR and Lucy to mean this really would be a story with no legs.

I got to the White House about 2:20 p.m. I went into the Press Room and saw familiar network faces - Jack Denif, Bill Denton from CBS and Charles Parker from Mutual. There was John Greene of The New York Times and Stephen Sutton of the Washington Herald. These grizzled veterans were all older than I. For the most part, they cleaned themselves up well when they were in the presence of the president. Customarily, though, their shirts were wrinkled and their hair generally needed combing, Sutton particularly. And there was one woman reporter, Ellen Monroe, from AP. I was sure she was there due to the influence of both Eleanor and Lorena.

I ambled over and introduced myself. She was a striking woman, 5'5", 115 pounds, about twenty-five. She was wearing round silver glasses that were nearly invisible against her skin tone and the background of her ocean-sand colored hair.

"Hello, Michael. Nice to meet you. I must admit I listen to your show quite a bit. I like what you do."

"Really? Well, thanks, Ellen. That's quite nice of you. Is this your first presidential press conference?"

"Actually, no. It's my third, but my first at the White House. I've been with AP for about eight months. I've covered Mrs. Roosevelt and done quite a few of her press conferences. She's pretty great. And she's made it a whole lot easier for women to get into this business."

"Do you like the news business?"

"Yeah!"

"Think we'll make any news today?" I asked, in a leading fashion.

"Well, Michael, I guess that's up to us to ask the questions that make the news."

That was a terrific answer, one I hadn't counted on. I muttered something like, "Yeah, you're right" and told her I'd talk with her later.

The press room was filling with reporters, stringers, engineers and White House staffers. The president knew we were there, and promised a prompt start time of 3:00 p.m. The staffers just told us to wait and we'd be ushered in at the appropriate time.

Jack Denif was busy rewriting some questions and prepping his report for NBC. Denton and Parker were kibbitizing, trying to find out what angles were being covered for next week's inauguration. Greene was going over the list of questions he'd prepared. He was famous for coming up with twenty or so questions even though he'd get to ask only one or two. I noticed Sutton had been on the phone for a few minutes, scribbling notes furiously. Ellen Monroe was making sure she had two pens ready, just in case one failed.

I only had one question. But I kept rehearsing it. In my mind, I would ask this near the end of the press conference, after the information about the War in Europe had been conveyed.

At 2:58 p.m., FDR's aide came into the Press Room. "The president is ready to see you," he said, and we all followed.

Bill Denton entered the Oval Office first, followed by Charles Parker, Jack Denif, Stephen Sutton, Ellen Monroe, me and John Greene. FDR was seated behind his desk, and a row of chairs was placed in front of his desk. We all sat down in the order we entered, with Denton on FDR's far left. There were also three engineers in the room, plus the president's aide and press secretary, Steven Early. Everything was set, the recording already underway. FDR was smoking a cigarette in his trademark holder, and grinning broadly.

"I'm glad you could make it to my office today," FDR bellowed. "I'm happy to answer any of your questions." I remember wondering if he knew what my question was going to be, if Senator Buckfield's office had tipped him off. And I remember thinking I didn't want to go first. "Let's start with the Associated Press. Miss Monroe, isn't it?"

"Yes, and thank you, Mr. President. You're the first person in American history to run for a third term as president. The tradition, started by President Washington, has been to serve two terms. Why did you decide to run for a third term?"

"Well, Miss Monroe, first of all it's nice to have you here. I know you've covered some of our goings-on here over the course of the campaign, and I'm glad you're still with us. I'm well aware of the tradition that President Washington began. But these are dangerous times, with dark days looming and our true friends in trouble around the world. When I viewed the field of candidates, I concluded I was still the best choice to lead the United States through whatever may lie ahead. Apparently, the American voter agreed, and I am pleased to serve for another term."

"Do you think, Mr. President," she continued, "that your running for a third term sets a bad precedent for any future president? Should there be a limit to how many terms a president can serve?"

"I believe a president should be able to serve as many terms as he wants to as long as the voters approve. And if, in the future, other presidents want to run for more than two terms, I believe they should be able."

"Mr. President?"

"Yes, Mr. Denton!" FDR and Bill Denton had known each other since he was governor of New York. Despite their friendliness, Denton had been known to get under FDR's skin with his tough questioning.

"Mr. President, you've changed vice presidents. Two questions, sir: have you spoken with Mr. Garner since the election, and what role do you see Vice President Wallace having?"

"Well, Mr. Denton, of course Mr. Garner and I have spoken since the election. And I believe Vice President Henry Wallace will do whatever I tell him to do."

"Well, what will you tell him to do? What do you want Vice President Wallace to do?"

"I expect the vice president to go around the country and articulate the policies that we will set out to accomplish this term. Henry's been around since I first came to Washington, and he has been the most consistent and able public policy salesman we've ever had. Now that we're a country back working, it's important to keep moving forward, while at the same time being ever mindful of the disaster that's unfolding across the Atlantic. We must be prepared to deal with that, and Henry Wallace will help immensely."

"But Mr. President," Denton persisted, "what did you and Vice President Garner talk about?"

FDR smiled broadly, leaned back in his chair, took a deep drag on his cigarette and said, "It was a private conversation, Mr. Denton." All of us laughed out loud.

"Mr. President," began John Greene, "in that same vein, Wendell Willkie came out soon after the election and said that he would be happy to help you and serve your needs in any way he could. Have you spoken with Wendell Willkie since the election?"

"In fact, I have, John. Mr. Willkie graciously made the same offer to me a few weeks ago. I am sure that I will be availing myself of Mr. Willkie's considerable talent and influence in the weeks and months ahead. He and I agree, generally, on the threat enveloping Europe, and he was most anxious to make himself available to me in any capacity I see fit. So, yes, I have spoken with him and plan to use Mr. Willkie whenever and wherever I can."

Jack Denif popped in with his first question. "Mr. President, let's talk about Europe. Prime Minister Churchill is doing everything possible to keep England together under the barrage that Hitler is mounting. Is it safe to say that he is glad you're still the president? And how do you respond to his pleas for American help?"

"Well, Mr. Denif, I would never want to put words in Prime Minister Churchill's mouth. You should ask him if he's glad I'm still here," he said to laughter. "But I will say we have a fine relationship, and I respect the Prime Minister quite a bit. It is true that he has asked for help. But until such time that we deem it necessary to involve ourselves directly in the conflict, we will maintain our distance and provide whatever help we can to assist England and Europe in the fight."

"That sounds like you want to get into the war, Mr. President."

"Mr. Denif, I do not want to get into the war, as you put it. But I will not, and the United States will not, shrink from a fight to protect ourselves. There are many people in this country right now who think we're better off staying neutral at this point, though. As president, I have to take into account what they're saying, too."

"Have you spoken recently with General DeGaulle?" Denif continued.

"Yes. We spoke privately not long ago."

"Would you care to tell us what you and he discussed?"

"No," said FDR firmly but impishly. Again, the reporters chuckled.

"Mr. President, this is Charles Parker from Mutual. A few months before the election, you instituted the draft. Millions of young men have visited the draft boards, and the ranks of the military are swelling. Do you see any scenario where these young men will be sent into front line action?"

"This is a dangerous world we live in, Mr. Parker. There are forces of evil at work in Europe right now, dividing the countries up and re-designing whole sections of geography. As much as I don't want to, there may be a time when I am forced, as Commander in Chief, to send our boys to action. But that time is not here yet."

"Why did you bring the draft back, sir?"

"Well, Mr. Parker, as I mentioned at the time, it is in our long-term national best interest to be prepared for any military eventuality. And a big part of that preparation is having people ready to serve anywhere and at anytime. It takes time to prepare people well, and I must ensure that we are ready to defend ourselves against any possibility."

I glanced over at our engineer Bob Boot. I wanted to make sure our recording equipment was working, that the levels were good, and that everything was set to go. We caught eyes, he nodded. Stephen Sutton and I were the only ones who had not yet asked a question, and Sutton was set to go.

"Mr. President?"

"Yes, Mr. Sutton, how can I help you and the Herald?"

"Well, sir, you can answer this question. In her daily newspaper column, Mrs. Roosevelt has advocated a more integrated approach to the American involvement with the European conflict. She makes some convincing arguments that now is the time for US action, not later. Is she speaking for your Administration, for herself, or is she preparing the country for our inevitable direct involvement?"

"Honestly, Mr. Sutton, asking me a question about the First Lady is something I would have expected from Mr. Audray." FDR looked right at me when he said that, then laughed a hearty laugh, as did all the reporters. I chuckled, although I attempted to keep a poker face all the while wondering if he knew what I was going to ask. The president continued. "Mrs. Roosevelt has strong personal convictions, and her newspaper column is an extension of her beliefs. But the last I looked, I am the president, and I make the decisions as to what we should do and when we should do it. Certainly, I listen to things the First Lady has to say, but you can assume that in her column, she is speaking for herself. By the way," he grinned as he leaned back in his chair and inhaled deeply again, "I read her column everyday."

Jack Denif jumped in again. "Mr. President, what about France? Can you shed any light on what is going on with the Free French movement? And what has General De Gaulle asked for?"

"France is, of course, a huge concern for the United States. Any time a country like France gets overrun by an outrageously large military force, it causes great concern for the United States. General DeGaulle is valiantly leading the Free French fight against Nazism, but make no mistake: it is an uphill battle. The Nazis currently control all the power structures in France. But the Resistance Movement is strong and, I believe, will not be denied."

"Will we help General DeGaulle directly?"

"The United States will do what it can, where it can, when it can."

Bill Denton weighed in again. "Mr. President, have you spoken with Josef Stalin? And if so, what are the possibilities that the United States and Russia will join forces to battle the Hitler-Mussolini faction?"

"I have spoken with Mr. Stalin. What we discussed is not of immediate concern. And I won't comment any further than that."

"But doesn't it surprise you even a little bit, Mr. President, that the United States and Russia might be allies in this fight?"

"First of all, Mr. Denton, nothing surprises me anymore. But Russia has been attacked and betrayed by both Hitler and Mussolini. They must defend themselves as they see fit."

"Mr. President?"

"Yes, Miss Monroe."

"Sir, Mr. Willkie made much of your plan to continue the rural electrification of America during the campaign. What are your plans for electric hook-up now that you've won?"

"They're the same as they were before the election, before I won. It is in our long-term national interest to connect every house in America, in the city and in the country, including the most rural parts of the country, with electric power. This is now 1941. We have the ability and the resources to make this happen. We must also find the will to make it happen sooner rather than later. And as long as I'm president, the electric utilities will be closely regulated and monitored by the government, in much the same way water is."

"Mr. President," asked John Greene of The New York Times, "do you have any special message for the American people that you'll be talking about at the inaugural next week?"

"If I told you now, John, there'd be no need for the ceremony. Join us in five days and find out."

I cleared my throat. "Mr. President?"

"Well, Mr. Audray, I was wondering if you had a question."

This was it. I took a deep breath, centered myself, and followed my game plan.

"Mr. President, is it true that you're having an affair with a woman who was at one time your wife's social secretary, and your wife is having an affair with a woman reporter?"

A hush fell over the Oval Office, as if all the air had just been sucked out of it. All my colleagues glared at me, the engineers stared at me after they all checked their equipment, and Franklin Delano Roosevelt, 33rd president of the United States, glared at me.

FDR stared at me for fifteen or twenty seconds before saying anything. He crushed out his cigarette, leaned forward with his arms on the arms of his chair, and looked directly in my eyes.

"Mr. Audray, I was wrong a few minutes ago when I said that nothing surprises me. This surprises me. It surprises me that you'd even ask such a question, and it surprises me that a fine organization like the Betz Radio Network would be privy to asking this kind of question. What shouldn't surprise you, Mr. Audray, is that I will not even dignify that question with any kind of response. That question is totally out of line, and I hope that if you are ever lucky enough to be invited back to any future press conference, you understand that what we discuss here involves world affairs, not the tawdry kind of affairs you're so famous for on your afternoon radio program. You can all thank Mr. Audray for cutting this press conference short, because it is now over."

With that, he motioned to Steven Early, who immediately conjured up two Marines to escort us out of the Oval Office. As we were being tossed out, the last thing I heard FDR say was "Get these engineers out of here, too."

The Marines ushered us back to the Press Room, and it wasn't until we got there that anybody said anything. Then, everybody said everything at once.

"What the hell was that? What were you thinking? I didn't think you'd do it. Who in the hell do you think you are? You've just blown your career, pal. You're an idiot. Nothing good will come of this, mark my words."

Then, one question pierced the air and created a hush in the room: "Is it Lorena?"

I turned and looked Ellen Monroe in the eyes. "What makes you ask that, Ellen?"

"There's been talk. For a long time."

I recalled what Ellen had said right before the press conference began, that it was up to us to ask the questions that made the news. Suddenly, it began to dawn on all the gathered reporters the only real news from today's press conference was the president's non-denial of my question. True, he refused to answer. But if it wasn't true, he'd have vociferously denied it. The real question for all the other reporters in the room was, what to do with it?

Jack Denif summed up everyone's mood. "Goddamn, I need a drink."

"I really can't believe you did that, Michael," Denton said, shaking his head. "I really just can't."

"Oh, I can," interjected Charles Parker. "You ever listen to his show? Or listen to anything on that network?"

"Sure," John Greene admitted. "I kind of like it, and I like his show. It's entertainment. But this - Jesus, Michael, what were you trying to do?"

"He was trying to get a scoop, John," Jack Denif said, "just like the rest of us."

Greene shot back, "Maybe so, Jack, but we're not looking at a cripples' pecker."

"Hey, John, that's low!" Sutton bellowed.

"It's the truth."

"Well, if we're talking about truth," Jack Denif fairly whispered, "Michael's question hits the truth. I just don't think we're comfortable with it."

"And I know my editors won't be either," Greene yelled. "What's the headline on the Times going to be tomorrow: 'President accused of Infidelity?' Come on. The world's blowing up, and we're asking about *this?* I'm out of here." He continued gathering his notes, grabbed his coat and went toward the door. He stopped in the doorway and turned around.

"Hey, Michael," he called, making sure I looked at him. "Fuck you!" Then he left.

Sutton broke the tension when he said, "I wouldn't expect any help from the Times, Michael."

The furor died down after a few minutes, and the Marines were still there. Other Marines had been dispatched to the Oval Office to help the engineers tear down their equipment, hurriedly. I saw Bob Boot walk briskly past the Press Room. He popped his head in and said, "We got it," and kept moving.

I was ready to go, but waited for Boot. When all were gone except Jack Denif, Ellen Monroe sidled up next to me.

"You didn't answer my question, Michael. Is it Lorena?"

"Why do you want to know, Ellen?"

"I'm a reporter, Michael. And I think this is a story."

"Really?" I paused to take the full measure of Ellen Monroe, AP Reporter, direct descendant of Lorena Hitchcock's trailblazing.

I nodded my head. She said, "Thanks. I'll be in touch." Then she left.

Jack Denif came over. "You got balls, Michael. Lots of balls. I'm not sure what's going to happen, but you've got balls."

When I got back to my office, all hell had broken loose. The switchboard had been flooded with calls, and overwhelmingly the calls were for my head. I had about thirty messages already, including one from Sharon. Her message said, "What are they saying in Carmel?"

In fact, I knew what they were saying in Carmel. I got a message from my mom. Her message said, "How could you talk to the president like that?"

All the major newspapers from around the country had called and wanted a comment or an interview. The other radio networks had made back-door inquiries, because they weren't sure what to do with this.

It seemed the story was really more about the question, rather than the president. It dawned on me I'd been victimized by the same tactic FDR used against Wendell Willkie during our hour-long interviews. One simple ten-second response given by the president had doused the potential sexual wildfire and turned the tables on me. Of all the things I thought might happen, that wasn't one of them.

BRN had two switchboard operators who hadn't heard the press conference. When I walked in, one of them quizzically asked me, "What happened?"

Peter, of course, was grinning ear to ear. "Way to go, Michael, way to go!" He didn't believe I'd go through with it. He loved the hundreds of people who had gathered outside the studio window. He loved the switchboard being swamped. He loved the demands for interviews from all the other media outlets. And, more than anything, he loved the fact that the populace had been stirred up by his network. "Yessir," he said a dozen times, "BRN is on everybody's lips today!"

I agreed, but I wasn't sure if that was a good thing, though I didn't say that to him. I did ask what he thought I should do about all these interview requests. "You're not going to do any of them!" he bellowed.

"Your voice and words will only be heard on the Betz Radio Network! If people want to find out about this, they'll have to listen to us!"

"Unless of course other networks and newspapers pick up the story," I said.

"If and when they do, Michael, we'll own the story. People will know where it came from."

Bob Boot came in to my office and addressed Peter. "You wanted to see me?"

"Yeah. You got Roosevelt on tape, right?" Boot nodded. "Great. Let's go listen. Michael, c'mon." As we walked down the hall, Peter barked, "Janine, get Bart Johnson down to Production."

We walked briskly to the Production Studio. "Let me hear it," Peter said.

The president's voice came on: "Mr. Audray, I was wrong a few minutes ago when I said that nothing surprises me. This surprises me. It surprises me that you'd even ask such a question, and it surprises me that a fine organization like the Betz Radio Network would be privy to asking this kind of question. What shouldn't surprise you, Mr. Audray, is that I will not even dignify that question with any kind of response. That question is totally out of line, and I hope that if you are ever lucky enough to be invited back to any future press conference, you understand that what we discuss here involves world affairs, not the tawdry kind of affairs you're so famous for on your afternoon radio program. You can all thank Mr. Audray for cutting this press conference short, because it is now over."

Peter was listening intently when Bart Johnson walked in. "Bart, listen to this," and told Boot to play it again. When he'd heard it twice more, Peter said, "What do you think, Bart? I want to edit this and play it over and over again."

"Be careful how you edit it, Peter. What's the exact question he's responding to? Can I hear that?" Bob Boot said yes, then cued up the tape to my question:

"Mr. President, is it true that you're having an affair with a woman who was at one time your wife's social secretary, and your wife is having an affair with a woman reporter?"

Bart Johnson took a deep breath. "OK, Peter, how do you want to edit it?"

"Like this," he responded, and handed Johnson a piece of paper with his desired quotation. I looked over Bart's shoulder. It read:

"These tawdry kind of affairs you're talking about shouldn't surprise you. Mr. Audray, I was wrong."

"Be careful, Peter," said Bart Johnson. "These are not direct quotes, and slightly out of context. He's pissed off enough at us right now. We don't need to go out of our way to antagonize him. We've already done that."

Uh-oh, I thought. Our chief lawyer's opinion is that we pissed off and antagonized the president. So I spoke up.

"Look, Peter, if you want to use his answer in an ongoing spot, let's write the spot in such a way where we're using his words verbatim, but not necessarily in sequence."

"What do you mean?" Bart Johnson wondered.

"Well, Peter wants to milk this for all it's worth, and get BRN attached to this. Right, Peter?" He nodded. "So, let's make a thirty second spot with a staff announcer setting it up and attaching the network. Something like, 'Only BRN will ask the tough questions.' Then I ask the question, FDR answers, the announcer comes back on and attaches BRN again, then more from FDR and so on."

Peter nodded. "That might work." Bart Johnson said, "That's better than your edit, Peter. I'm more comfortable with that, legally."

Peter told me to get it written and show him the copy before it got produced. I felt a little more in control of what I thought was a manageable situation. This story would last a week or so and we'd move on. Especially, I thought, if I was in control of what went on the air. After all, it was my ass on the line.

So I went back to my office and wrote the script. I showed it to Peter, who OK'd it and told me to get it produced within the hour. By the time the seven o'clock newscast came on, this spot was ready:

ANNOUNCER: Only the Betz Radio Network will ask the questions no one else dares.
AUDRAY: Mr. President, is it true that you're having an affair with a woman who was at one time your wife's social secretary, and your wife is having an affair with a woman reporter?"
FDR: Mr. Audray, I will not dignify that question with any kind of response.
ANNOUNCER: Despite saying that, the president continued discussing...
FDR: ...the tawdry kind of affairs you're so famous for on your afternoon radio program.
ANNOUNCER: Obviously, he listens to...
FDR: ...a fine organization like the Betz Radio Network

ANNOUNCER: Shouldn't you? The Midday Conversation with Michael Audray, only on BRN.

Peter directed this be the lead story on all the newscasts for twenty-four straight hours. The spot I wrote was scheduled to air once an hour immediately following each top-of-the-hour newscast. I sat with Peter in his office when it aired the first time.

"That's pretty good, Michael. What do you think?"

"Well, I think it's alright. But we've got a tiger on our hands, Peter. Don't make any mistake about that. I'm thinking this is going to take on a life of its own, and we need to be ready. I don't think we are."

Just as I said that, Janine entered the doorway, flanked by two men with no visible sense of humor. "Excuse me..." Janine began.

The man on the left interrupted. "Mr. Betz, the president wants to see you. Now."

Peter shot me a glance, said, "OK," grabbed his coat and walked out. When he got to Janine's desk, he turned to me and said, "Stay here till I get back. Both of you." Then he left, escorted down the hall and into the elevator, flanked by beefy Secret Service agents.

I ran to the news department and told someone to trail Peter to the White House. An intern named Anne Seals jumped up and ran out the door.

I went back to my office, and there was Earl Mercia.

As always, he was blunt. "Jesus, Michael. I didn't think you had the balls."

"That's funny, Earl. Jack Denif thinks that's all I've got. All balls, no brains."

"Yeah, well, you own the story now. So, is Peter still at the White House?"

"He just left, Earl. How'd you know he was going there?"

"C'mon," he scoffed. I shrugged my shoulders. "It's my business to know this stuff."

"Well, then, what's Roosevelt going to say?"

"He's probably going to try to get Peter to back off, try to intimidate him somehow. And if that fails, he'll appeal to their years of friendship."

"What's Peter going to do?"

"My guess is he'll listen, tell Roosevelt to sit tight and it'll all blow over. It's just designed to attract attention to the network."

"Well, Earl, it's already done that," I said sarcastically. "Why are you here, anyway?"

"I came by to drop off more pictures," and he slid a 9x12 envelope onto my desk. "I took these the other night."

I grabbed the envelope and looked inside. There were six pictures, three with FDR, three with Eleanor, each with their paramour. I shook my head and didn't even ask how he got them.

"Oh, they're authentic, alright. Just thought you might need some fresh evidence." He got up to leave when I stopped him for a moment.

"Earl, what's going to happen?"

Earl Mercia scratched his head and said, "I don't know."

Around 9:30 p.m., Anne Seals returned. "The Secret Service took Peter to his house about fifteen minutes ago. He went inside, and they're standing guard outside his house."

Janine and I, still sitting in Peter's office, just looked at each other. Anne said, "And as I was walking past the newsroom, I heard them say Leo Dailey has called a press conference for ten o'clock tomorrow morning."

January 16, 1941: German dive bombers attack British convoys in Malta, creating heavy losses.

Chapter 10 – The Story Has Legs

The next day, Representative Leo Dailey, the freshman Republican from Montana, held a press conference in the hallway of the Congressional office building. Even though he was a freshman, he was a darling among the party leadership. He wasted no time in his opening remarks.

"Good morning. In a press conference with radio and newspaper reporters yesterday, President Roosevelt was asked about his personal behavior, and the personal behavior of the First Lady. While expressing outrage at the question, the president did not deny the accusation. I believe I speak for a great many Americans, and all of my constituents in the great state of Montana, who want to know the truth. And the reason we want to know the truth is simple: in these perilous times, we must have a steady hand on the rudder of state. We must have someone who is morally fit to guide us through these choppy waters, not someone who will be easily distracted by personal shortcomings. We must have a First Family that is a reflection of each American family throughout this great land of ours, not a family that is co-opted by aberrant carnal desires. So today, I stand here willing to lead the investigation into this question about President and Mrs. Roosevelt. I am willing to look into each aspect and report back to the American people with all due haste about this charge. And the sooner we get started, the better. I'd be happy to answer any questions you may have."

Leo Dailey, his suit crisper than a burnt piece of toast, his white shirt starched within an inch of its life, and a red-white-and-blue silk tie knotted perfectly, was just getting warmed up. He took a sip of water and shifted his weight from foot to foot, then began taking questions. He called on Bill Porter of The New York Times.

"Congressman Dailey, have you spoken with any of your party's leaders about what you want to do?"

"Yes, of course I have, Mr. Porter. I spoke with both the minority leader, Representative Martin McKay, and the minority whip, Representative Ken Kerse, and asked their advice."

"And what did they have to say?"

"Well, initially, they wanted me to hold off, if only because I'm new around here. But once I talked with them, I was able to convince them that this is a serious issue that needs addressing. And unless we step up and do it, no one will. I also told them that because I'm new, I'm the perfect person to lead this investigation. I have no ax to grind, no agenda to settle. I can be, I can be..." he struggled to find the right word, "impartial. Yes, Mr. Calloway."

UPI's Herb Calloway had been around Washington since the Wilson administration. In fact, he was the reporter who broke the story about Woodrow Wilson's stroke.

"Congressman Dailey, have you ever met the president?"

"No, I haven't."

"Congressman, it seems from your statement you believe the president, by refusing to answer that question, is lying. Do you believe President Roosevelt is trying to conceal something, and if so, do you have any evidence, or have you seen any evidence, that convinced you and would convince others?"

"Mr. Calloway, if you're asked a direct question and you refuse to answer, I think it's safe to assume you're covering something up. If you have nothing to hide, simply answer the question and be done with it. Yes, over there."

Calloway interrupted before the next reporter could ask his question. "Congressman, you didn't answer if you had any evidence or had seen any evidence that would convince us."

Dailey cleared his throat. "No, I haven't. But that's exactly why we need to look into this matter at once, to determine what kind of man is guiding this ship."

Matt Shaffer from The Chicago Tribune was next. "Congressman, you've been in office for, counting today, thirteen days. Do you really believe that you have enough influence and experience to lead an investigation into the private life of our most public citizen? Furthermore, do you think the American people want an investigation?"

"Absolutely, I do. The American people are hard working, God-fearing citizens who expect their elected officials to represent them honorably and with integrity in all aspects of life, both public and private. I have plenty of experience in investigations from my time in Montana as both a lawyer and a state senator, and as I said before, I'm the perfect person to lead this investigation simply because I am a freshman."

Jack Denif cut in.

"Congressman Dailey, have you ever cheated on your wife?"

Immediately, a complete hush fell over the press conference. Reporters' eyes darted back and forth between Denif and Dailey. Dailey looked a bit stunned, with the look of a person who's mortally wounded but hasn't yet realized it.

"Mr. Denif, I am not the issue."

"But Congressman, the issue you seem to be raising is the private behavior of our elected officials. So: Congressman Dailey, have you ever cheated on your wife?"

Somehow, this story had gained strength overnight. Somehow, reporters now felt it was not only alright but necessary to ask the kind of questions that no one had ever dared ask before I opened my mouth yesterday afternoon. The question hung in the air - Have you ever cheated on your wife - and all the assembled people, both politicos and reporters, held their breath for the answer. The silence became awkward, and Jack Denif knew he had sunk his tenterhooks into the rookie from Montana.

"Congressman, just a minute ago you said that it was important for the American people to know that good, moral people have their hand on the ship of state, and that if you're asked a direct question and refuse to answer, it's safe to assume you're covering something up. So, Congressman, for the third time, have you ever cheated on your wife?"

Leo Dailey did a slow burn. He narrowed his eyes and glared. "No, Mr. Denif," he said slowly and deliberately, "I have never cheated on my wife." He continued to glare right through Denif, and it felt as if Dailey wanted to say something else. But, he held his tongue. After about fifteen seconds of silence, Denif asked, "Can I quote you?"

The reporters chuckled, but Dailey found no humor in it. "I'm sure you will."

Ellen Monroe jumped in. "Congressman, in your opening statement, you mentioned that both the President's and First Lady's private behavior is being questioned, and that only an in-depth investigation can clear this up. Since only the president is an elected official, why do you think it necessary to investigate Mrs. Roosevelt?"

Still off-kilter, Dailey stammered at first. "Mrs. Roosevelt has been an active member of this Administration, and has often made her own views known. It's important that we know what all those views are. She is a mother of children. And her name has been brought into this, not by

81

me. But we must either clear her or find out the truth. And the only way to do that is by investigating."

"But Congressman," Monroe persisted, "Mrs. Roosevelt's office has issued no comment on this question, and the president has refused to answer. Are we to assume you believe them to be guilty until proven innocent?"

"Guilty until proven innocent? Certainly not. That is not the American way. But since they have been accused of morally reprehensible activity, they have a duty to give a straight answer to the public. And I'm not sure the President or the First Lady would ever address this issue unless we force them to address it. And that's what I intend to do."

The Tribune's Matt Shafer spoke again. "Congressman Dailey, I'm a bit confused about your reasoning for the need to investigate these allegations. In light of the fact that President Roosevelt recently was re-elected to an unprecedented third term, carrying thirty-eight of the forty-eight states and winning by more than five million votes, don't you think the American people care more about the quality of public and worldwide leadership than private behavior?"

Dailey didn't miss a beat. "It is precisely because he won by such a large margin that we must investigate. If these allegations are groundless, they will be quickly dispatched. If they are proven true, then we must take steps to ensure that the people we have leading our great country during these perilous times have the moral fiber to direct our actions."

Shafer persisted. "If they are true, Congressman, it doesn't seem to have affected the president's job performance."

That caught Dailey, just a little. The best he could muster was, "Well, no one knew the president was, shall we say, engaged with a woman other than his wife. Let's see if it affects his performance now."

BRN News Director Tim Cullen piped up. "I'd like to return to the question posed to you earlier. You're positive, Congressman Dailey, that you've never cheated on your wife?"

Leo Dailey looked as if the only thing holding him up was his ultra-starched shirt and trademark red kerchief. "Asked and answered. This is not about me. It is about the President and the First Lady."

"So I am correct to assume," Cullen continued, "that you have never, shall we say, strayed?"

"That is correct. I am a faithful public servant, Mr. Cullen."

"I didn't ask you if you were a faithful public servant, Mr. Dailey. I asked if you were a faithful husband."

Once again, Leo Dailey just glared at the assembled reporters. I think it was just occurring to him that these were not the hometown Montana newspaper and radio people he grew up with. These people were all professionals, working the potentially biggest political scandal to hit the public since Teapot Dome, and they smelled blood. Lots of it coming from different directions.

"Ladies and gentlemen," Dailey eventually said, "this press conference is over. I will be conferring with the House leadership and announce our schedule for hearings soon. Thank you very much." He turned sharply and walked back down the hallway, flanked by McKay and Kerse. It appeared there was some animated conversation going on between the three of them.

I watched the whole thing from the background. As everybody was leaving, I ambled over to Tim Cullen and Jack Denif.

"You beat me to the punch, Jack," Cullen said. "I wanted to be the first to ask him about his sleeping habits."

"You gotta be quick, Tim," Denif replied, smiling.

"Just a hunch, Jack, or do you know something?" I wondered. Tim Cullen watched and listened.

"Oh, just a hunch on my part. The loudest squawker generally has the most to hide." Jack looked up from his notebook at both of us. "You guys know something, though, don't you?"

We smiled a bit, then Cullen said, "I think it's safe to say that trail is warm."

"Goddammit, I knew it!" Jack said gleefully. "That son of a bitch can't keep it zipped, can he?" He laughed. "Does he like boys?"

"I don't think so," Cullen said. I shook my head in agreement. "You see the papers yet, Jack?" I asked.

"Oh, yeah, hard to miss those headlines. Is Peter pissed that BRN isn't in bold type across the front of the Times and Herald today?"

"No," I said matter-of-factly, "he's kind of low key today." I didn't mention that Betz had been summoned to the White House last.

"Well, that's surprising. Everybody at NBC is scrambling to figure out what to do and how to play this. We've had lawyers meeting with lawyers, and news people meeting with lawyers." Denif lit a cigarette. "I mean, everyone agrees this is a story, but how in the hell do we play it? Jesus, Michael, this is all your fault." Denif chuckled as he said that.

"So what's NBC going to do?" Cullen wanted to know. Jack shrugged his shoulders. "I don't know. They told me to cover this and then head back to the studio. So, that's where I'm going. What about you?"

Tim Cullen said, "I'm heading back, too." He turned to me and asked, "You coming to that meeting with Johnson and Betz at 11:30?"

"I'll stop in," I said. "I've still got to prep for my show."

"Oh, who's on today?" Jack wondered.

"Ronald Reagan."

"Wasn't he in *Dark Victory*?"

"Yeah, he was, Jack. And in *Knute Rockne, All American*. Should be interesting. I've never met him, but I'm told he's pretty politically aware."

"Really? Reagan?"

"Yeah," I said, "yeah, Ronald Reagan. Well, I gotta go. Ready, Tim?" Cullen nodded and the three of us left the Capitol. We got back to BRN around 10:45 a.m., and as we walked in, we were both told to go straight to Peter's office. When we entered, Peter was sitting at his desk, kind of somber with a cup of coffee in front of him. Bart Johnson was there. Sitting on the sofa were Senator Paul Buckfield and Sharon Tozzi.

Peter told us to come in and sit down. The senator, he said, came by about twenty minutes before with some information that he wanted to share confidentially. Peter assured him that we could keep a confidence, and he stressed to everyone in the room that what would be discussed would remain in his office until he said it was alright to release. We agreed.

I was unsure if Buckfield knew that Peter had been summoned to see the president, or if the senator knew about the pictures of Sharon and me. I was unsure of Sharon's reasons for being there, or if she was just assuming her official position as Buckfield's top aide.

Senator Buckfield began. "As you know, I'm on the Senate Foreign Relations Committee. We have evidence that the Nazis are systematically killing Jews, all the Jews. They're rounding them up and shipping them like cattle into these concentration camps in Auschwitz, Bamberg, Bergen-Belsen, Buchenwald, Chelmno, Jena, Sobibor and Treblinka. Then they're gassing them. Despite the fact we know this, the United States is in no position, not yet anyway, to do anything about it, at least directly. The president is well aware of the gravity of the situation in Europe, and there are plans in place to deal with it the best way we can. But what we don't need is a domestic distraction like what you've caused." Buckfield barely took a breath. "I'm here on my own, but I know I speak for the majority of the Senate, and most of the people in the House. Make this go away. You started this, you end it. Now. You have no idea what you've started. Just look at the Times and the Herald and the Post today. Page 1 is all about who the president might be sleeping with. Meanwhile, Hitler is gassing Jews."

At this point, Buckfield stood up, as did Sharon. "You guys are smart, maybe too smart. Figure out a way to end this story, and figure out a way to shut up that rookie congressman. I don't much like you guys, but I'll do what I can to help you cap this story, because I know - I *know* - it's in the greater interest to see this go away. If you need anything from my office, call me. I've told Sharon to help you in any way she can." Buckfield put on his coat and walked toward the door. "Remember, Peter, not a word of this until I say so. Agreed?"

Peter Betz nodded his head. "We agree. But we didn't cause this domestic distraction, as you call it, Senator. We just investigated news tips and asked the question. Like the guardians of a free press that journalists are."

"Guardians of a free press, my ass. Peter, for Chrissakes, there's bigger stories than extra marital sex. You, of all people, should know better. Again, I'm telling you: make this story go away." Then Buckfield and Sharon left.

Betz sat up straighter in his chair. On cue, Janine walked in. "Janine, set up a meeting with the presidents of NBC, CBS and Mutual. See if you can get the editors of the Times, the Herald and the Post there, too. Tell them to bring their top lawyers. See if you can set it up for later today, or tomorrow at the latest, and tell them it will be here in our Board Room." Janine nodded, turned and left.

We all sat there for a minute, not saying anything. Finally, Tim Cullen asked the question.

"Peter, what do you want us to do about this story? Specifically, Dailey's press conference earlier today? How do you want us to play it?"

Betz leaned back in his chair and sipped his coffee. "Well, you gotta go with it. It's the lead story. Oh, which reminds me..." He leaned into his intercom. "Janine, get Earl on the phone right now. Who's your guest today, Michael?"

"Ronald Reagan," I answered.

"Oh, good. An actor. Keep him away from this story, not that he'll touch it, but don't talk about it."

"Peter," I asked, "what the hell happened last night? What did FDR say to you? What'd he say?"

Peter Betz again leaned back in his chair, and this time swiveled toward the window behind him. "Buckfield's story is only part of it. I can't tell you what Roosevelt told me, I promised him I wouldn't, but he asked me to cap the story, too. He didn't deny it. We go too far back, and we know each other." He stood up, put his hands in his pockets and stared out the window. "We're about to find out if Roosevelt is as good as I think he is."

Janine buzzed. "Earl's on line one."

Peter picked up the phone. "Earl, prove some dirt on Dailey. Don't worry about the cost, and let me know as soon as you've got something. But it's got to be proof. I don't care. Find it. Do it now. And call me, the sooner the better."

Bart Johnson, Tim Cullen and I looked at each other. We knew we had entered a completely different phase of this story. We were treading the line of covering news and making news, shaping the story or being the story. But none of us said anything.

"Bart, I want you and Michael at this meeting with all the network and newspaper heads. Tim, as the News Director, I think it's better if you're not there, to keep your air of objectivity. I'll let you know when Janine sets it up." We all just sat there, nodding. "OK, that's it. Go on back to work." I had only forty-five minutes to prepare for my hour-long interview with Ronald Reagan. In a way, this was comforting. Doing this show had become my haven from all that surrounded me. I felt that, for this one hour a day, I was in control of what happened. I needed a break from the cacophony that was enveloping all of us.

Reagan showed up about fifteen minutes early, which was good. We chatted briefly before the show began, and it gave me the sense that he knew what to do and what to expect. I didn't bring up the scandal, and neither did he.

"Ronald Reagan is our guest today," I began, "who most recently starred as George Gipp in *Knute Rockne, All American*. He's also been in many other films and is currently married to actress Jane Wyman. Ronald Reagan, it's nice to have you here."

"Well, Michael, it's nice to be here."

"Tell me what it's like to play such a variety of characters. This past year, you played a college football player who dies but becomes an inspiration for the team. But a year ago, you played the drunken lout who has eyes for Bette Davis in *Dark Victory*. How do you get your hands around those different personalities?"

"Well, uh, I guess that's why they call it acting." Reagan was relatively soft-spoken and unpretentious, and sometimes I felt the need to get him to embellish his answers. He would often give the shortest answer possible, but he stayed on the subject. Not all actors would.

At one point, I asked him what his other interests were. He said politics, and I wondered if he'd bring up the FDR story. He didn't. He said that he was a full-fledged union member of the Screen Actors Guild, and one day he hoped to run for an executive position with SAG. But he deflected any suggestion that he might run for real political office.

"No, no, I, uh, I see where politics today is heading, and I'm going to stay away from any business that is even screwier than acting."

I laughed. I found him to be an engaging guy, and once he warmed up, a pretty good conversationalist.

"What's next for Ronald Reagan? I hear you've signed on to do another movie. Tell us about that."

"Well, Michael, Ann Sheridan and I were nearly cast opposite each other in a movie about the expanding war in Europe and North Africa. It's going to be called *Casablanca*, but for many reasons, we've both pulled out. I have my reasons and Ann has hers. I'm sure the movie will be made, but I won't be in it. So, at the moment, I don't have any firm prospects, but I'm sure something will turn up."

The hour was over fairly quickly, and I managed to get through it without any direct reference to FDR and Eleanor. There was a note on my desk from Janine. "Meeting with bigwigs 6 p.m., Board Room." I went to Peter's office to find what he hoped to accomplish at this meeting.

"Michael, these are my peers. We've worked with and against each other my whole adult life. I'm going to appeal to them to help contain this story."

"They won't do it, Peter. This cat is out of the bag. Look at the switchboard. Listen to the other networks. Read the papers. Look at all the people gathered outside our window downstairs." Peter peered down, saw a larger than usual crowd, talking to each other and comparing tidbits of information.

"Maybe you're right, Michael. But I have to try."

By six o'clock, everyone was there. The presidents of BRN, NBC, CBS and Mutual, the editors of The New York Times, Washington Herald, Washington Post and the DC Bureau Chief of The Chicago Tribune, each with a corporate lawyer, some with assistants.

"Hello, Michael." It was Stanton Blanchard, my editor from the Washington Herald. This was the first time we'd seen each other since I left for the radio world, since he threw me out of his office. "It appears you've caused a ruckus."

I smiled wanly. "Yeah, it appears that way."

Peter began directly. "Thank you all for coming. I authorized an investigation into the private lives of Franklin and Eleanor Roosevelt which proved fruitful. I believed it would be a small story for our network, that no other radio network or newspaper would run a story so fraught with sexual details. But I believed it was fair game in the world of audience competition. I now feel this story is not in the best interest of the United States, and I believe, together, we can squash this story before it goes much further."

There was a moment of silence while everyone digested what Peter Betz had said. Finally, it was Stanton Blanchard who spoke.

"There is a little something called The First Amendment, Peter. Freedom of the Press. Freedom of Information. Freedom of Speech. It's out there now, Peter. I didn't put it there, but it's there. What? I'm supposed to ignore it? I'm supposed to not give my readers information they can find someplace else? The competition among people in this room is fierce. And what if we agree to cap this story, but the Detroit Free Press or the Baltimore Sun or the Buffalo Daily News follows up with something? Are we supposed to ignore it then?"

Blanchard had real standing amongst his peers. He was Peter's age, had been in newspapers for nearly fifty years, if you count his days as a paper boy. His points were well taken.

"All I'm asking, Stanton, is that you don't do lots of investigations and follow ups of your own. Don't put it on Page One." pleaded Peter Betz. "The people in this room control the most influential newspapers and radio networks in the country. No disrespect to the Buffalo Daily News, but they're not going to spend resources on this. If we don't run with it, neither will they."

"Stanton's got a point, though," said Bruce Wyland of CBS. "We can try to sit on it, but it is out there, and has been now for a full day. And I know it's going to be there tomorrow, too. Right or wrong, people know about this, and they're going to wonder what the hell happened if there's no follow up or logical conclusion. Now, I'm not in favor of going into details - I don't think anyone here *really* wants to do that, but we have to do something with it. We can't ignore what you've brought out, Peter. Besides, if we cap it, and you keep running it, BRN gets to own this story. For good or for bad, you'd own this story. And that's just not going to happen. You know better than that, Peter."

Howard Rivers of The Chicago Tribune punctuated it. "Peter, Peter, Peter. The Tribune's a Hearst Paper. We hate Roosevelt. And don't you remember your history classes about the Spanish-American War? 'You provide the pictures, I'll provide the war.' That's Hearst. We're running with it. Everyday. Count on it."

This was a hot story in the beginning of the news cycle, and it was going to be impossible to cap it.

Peter Betz heard enough. "Alright, gentlemen."

"I hear you've got pictures. What are you going to do with them, Peter?" wondered Stanton Blanchard like the veteran newsman he is.

Without hesitation, Peter Betz replied, "They're ours. They will stay ours. And until I say so, they're not going anywhere."

There were a few throat clearings going on in that room right then. Everyone filed out, one by one shaking hands with Peter Betz. In a free marketplace, competition prevailed.

"This story's not going away, Peter."

"I know, Michael. I know."

January 20, 1941: Franklin Delano Roosevelt inaugurated for his third term.
January 20, 1941: Hitler and Mussolini meet at Berghof.

Chapter 11 – Mary Beth

The next few days went by very fast. The Inauguration quickly regained Top Story status throughout the national press and network radio. FDR himself stayed low and out of the spotlight, preferring to work right up and through his third swearing-in ceremony.

But The Affairs of State, as it had been dubbed by The Chicago Tribune, was not completely off the presses. It wasn't the lead story, but it was a close second to the Inauguration. And more papers were picking up and running the AP stories that Ellen Monroe was filing.

Leo Dailey had put together a schedule for congressional hearings into the allegations about FDR and Eleanor. He ran it by McKay and Kerse, who blessed it for political reasons. They had a decidedly different ideological viewpoint than FDR, and they sensed he was politically vulnerable. They figured if they embarrassed him enough, he'd give in on some of their key legislative points.

Dailey's schedule called for the hearings to begin on the 27th, just one week after the Inauguration. I was afraid I'd be called to testify. I talked with Bart Johnson about that, and he said he'd try to prevent that. But there were no guarantees.

We knew that once the hearings began, the story would bubble back to the top of the news chain. As it was, it had been in the papers and on the radio every day since the 15th, and the public didn't seem to be tiring of it. What's more, they were intrigued and seemed to want the truly intimate, salacious details.

On January 22nd, Peter got a call from Earl, who went to Montana to find out the true stories in Leo Dailey's life. We had reason to believe that Dailey, married without children, had indeed gotten at least two women pregnant and had paid for their abortions. But we didn't have any proof.

Earl told Peter he'd found a woman named Mary Beth Keefer, a thirty-four-year-old waitress who lived in Helena. He talked with her, and in his own way, got her to confide in him that yes, indeed, Leo had gotten her pregnant. But it happened a long time ago, when they were both in college at Montana State. Dailey was prepared to do the honorable thing and marry her, but she miscarried in her third month. Shortly after that, Dailey graduated and left her behind.

Mary Beth Keefer seemed to hold no grudge against Dailey. She had heard the stories about the President and First Lady, and like most Americans, she was curious. She seemed confident that Leo Dailey, "my Leo" as she called him, would do a good job investigating the charges.

Earl told Peter that something didn't seem quite right, though, and he planned on doing some more digging before he came back to DC.

For some reason, I was rooting for Earl. I found him to be a nearly immoral opportunist, willing to smear anyone regardless of political affiliation, as long as the money was green and plentiful. I found Earl Mercia our one big hope.

But Peter had another idea. He wanted me to go to Helena right away and talk directly with Mary Beth Keefer.

The thought crystallized that if we were to discredit Dailey in the same fashion that he was going to discredit FDR, perhaps he'd pull back and whitewash the inquiry. If I was able to go to Helena and get this woman to talk to me, on the record, we'd tell Dailey what we knew. It wasn't blackmail, merely leverage.

Janine made the travel arrangements, getting me from DC to Helena as fast as possible. I flew from Washington to Chicago that night, stayed overnight and flew from Chicago to Des Moines, Des Moines to Butte and Butte to Helena all in increasingly smaller airplanes. Janine told Earl to pick me up at the Butte airstrip and take me to meet Mary Beth Keefer.

It wasn't the easiest trip. When I arrived, Earl said, "You look like shit."

"You should talk," I retorted. "At least I've been traveling all day."

As we drove he filled me in with what he knew.

"Seems Mary Beth and the congressman were coupled up in college. He's two years older, and he'd been kind of a Big Man On Campus. Apparently, he was quite a catch. Don't really know why. I mean, he didn't play football or anything, but lots of people remember him cutting a big swath. Big with the ladies, too, or at least could have been. But he hooked up with Mary Beth. She was an English major looking to get her

M-R-S degree. Apparently, she figured she'd give ol' Leo what he wanted in order to hook him. But she got pregnant. Neither one of them wanted to get married, but Leo said he would. Then, she says, she miscarried right before graduation day. Then Leo split."

"She never saw him again?"

"Oh, no. They saw each other a lot, she says. They've stayed in touch over the years. She's followed his career, and seems to be a big fan of his. But she's never married. Something just doesn't feel right about this."

We pulled in front of Schiavvi's, the Italian restaurant where she waitressed. It seemed to be a nice place, maybe the nicest in Helena. "Does she know we're coming?" I wondered.

"No," Earl said. "But she's here. That's her car over there."

We went in and the host - I hesitate to call him a maitre'd - approached us. I introduced myself, told him that we'd be having dinner, and slipped him a $20 bill. I told him I'd like to have Mary Beth sit down with us for a few minutes. The host looked surprised, but pocketed the $20, and said he'd see what he could do. After he seated us, he went over and talked with Mary Beth. Their conversation lasted half-a-minute or so, and then she ambled over.

I stood up. "Hello, Mary Beth. I'm Michael Audray from BRN."

"Wow. I listen to you all the time. Nice to meet you. What can I do for you?"

"You can sit down and talk with me for a few minutes." She looked a bit leery. "I already talked to your friend the other day."

I glanced at Earl. "Are you my friend?"

Earl sighed and pushed away from the table. "You kids talk. I'm going to the bar."

As Earl walked toward the bar, Mary Beth sat down.

Mary Beth Keefer was an attractive woman, but not beautiful. Petite and fine featured, she had her mousy-brown hair pulled into a ponytail that ended halfway down her back. In her waitress uniform, a black dress and stockings, she looked professional and polished. She had an easygoing manner about her, but her guard was clearly up.

"Mary Beth," I began, "you probably know why I'm here. There's going to be an investigation into whether or not the President and Mrs. Roosevelt are having adulterous affairs. And Leo Dailey is going to be the leader of this Congressional investigation."

"Yeah, I've heard that," she replied. "In fact, I think I heard you ask the president about his fooling around."

"Yes, yes, that was me. But we don't need to talk about me. Let's talk about Congressman Dailey. Seems like you and he have known each other for awhile."

Mary Beth sat up a little straighter in her chair. "I told all of this to your friend," she said tersely.

"Well, I know that, but I'd like to hear it from you. Just tell me about you and Leo."

"Why?"

Why, indeed, I thought. I decided to blurt out as much of the truth as I could and see what happened. "Because, Mary Beth, we've never had this kind of an investigation before, and because Congressman Dailey's on record as saying that he has never cheated on his wife. I can tell you that the mud is going to fly on this story, and what I'm trying to find out is if any mud is going to land on Leo."

"Well, that's a little different from what what's-his-name…"

"Earl"

"Yeah, different from what Earl told me. You're saying it like you want to protect Leo, but he was saying Leo's in trouble."

I didn't think I'd given any indication I was on Leo Dailey's side, but right then, I knew I could get her to talk. "Right," I said. "I just want to know what might be said about him. You know, he's already been on my show twice."

She smiled a big smile. "I heard him both times." The host came by our table, and I asked if I could buy "Miss Keefer" a drink. She looked at him and said it wasn't necessary, but he said it was OK with him. The restaurant was slow at this moment and there was no need to hurry. So she agreed to have a beer, and I joined her.

"Leo and I met in college," she began after the beer arrived. "He's two years older than I am, so I guess you know how old I am, huh?" I nodded. "Anyway, we hit it off right away. We met when I signed up to work on the college newspaper and he was running for president of the Student Senate. He was real good looking, still is, and smart like no one else. I couldn't believe he wasn't seeing someone else, so I kind of made myself available. It wasn't long before we were going steady." Her eyes were looking down at her glass, intently focused on that image from years before. "He got to be the Senate President, and I gave up trying to be a newspaper writer. I decided in my senior year what I really wanted to be." She stopped and took a sip. Then she sat quiet for a bit too long.

"What did you want to be?" I wondered.

She took another sip, then a bigger one. "I wanted to be Mrs. Leo Dailey. He had the whole world in front of him, and I wanted to go along. I figured the best way to convince him was to give him a taste of the pleasures of being married, if you know what I mean." She looked me in the eye. I nodded.

She unleashed a big sigh, and continued. "I got pregnant around the end of February or first part of March. I kind of knew right away, but I didn't know for sure until early May. I went to the school nurse, who I had become friends with, and she checked me out. She told me I was definitely pregnant, and that I should start taking better care of myself now that I was actually eating for two." She fingered the beer glass absentmindedly. "I told Leo right away, and he didn't seem upset or anything like that. In fact, he said it was alright with him, because he was thinking of asking me to marry him anyway."

"So you felt OK?"

"Yeah, I guess I felt as OK as a twenty-year-old college sophomore can feel about being pregnant and not married. I sure wasn't going to tell my parents until after we were married. Leo and I figured we'd wait until right after he graduated in early June. We were looking at getting married around the 15th, and then telling both our parents." She smiled at the memory. Then she looked down and talked a little quieter.

"But right around the end of May, I miscarried. There was no hurry for us to get married right away, and Leo, well, Leo I'm sure felt relieved. We were never the same after that, and about a week after graduation, he told me he was moving to Bozeman to take a job in a law office. He said we'd stay in touch, and that as soon as he had enough money, he'd send for me." She finished her beer. "I guess he never got enough money, huh?"

"I'm sorry that happened to you, Mary Beth. Did you stay in touch at all?"

"Oh, I was able to follow what he was doing. He was always running for something, and his name was in the papers. Montana's a big state, but there's not a lot of action here, so we can keep track of just about everybody. And when he got married, well, that made all the papers around here, because by that time he was a state senator."

"When did he get married?"

"Four years ago," she said without hesitation. "A woman named Jane Hall," she uttered with utter disdain.

"Do you know her?"

"No. But I know her. I know her type. Upper crust, or tries to be. Her daddy's a logger baron, and Jane offered Leo access to all that money so he could get to Congress." Then she said the most confounding thing of the night. "Leo doesn't love her."

"Why do you say that?"

She seemed to stammer, and began choosing her words more carefully. "Oh, just a hunch, I guess. Woman's intuition. Let's leave it at that."

"Would you like another beer, Mary Beth?" I was hoping she'd talk some more, because I felt we were just getting to some juicy stuff. But she declined. "You ever see him or talk to Leo any more?"

She looked at me and paused, started, then paused again. Finally, she said, "Whenever he's in these parts, like campaigning or something, I try to see him."

"When was the last time you saw him?"

"He campaigned here in late October, I guess."

"Did you meet him, or just go to an event?"

Again, she paused, then got careful. "I met him, at an event. Hey, look, it's been nice talking with you, Michael. I hope things go OK for you, but I've got to get back to work. Thanks for the beer." Then Mary Beth Keefer got up, shook my hand and went into the kitchen.

Earl ambled over with a Scotch in his hand.

"Earl, there's something go on there," I said when he sat down. "She's not telling everything she knows."

Earl chuckled. "Hey, if you ever lose your radio job, you might just make a good private dick."

"I don't think Leo Dailey's been keeping his dick so private lately," and we both laughed.

During dinner, we discussed what we wanted to do. I desperately wanted to get back to Washington, but Earl felt there was more work to be done in Montana. I'd leave in the morning, but he decided to drive to Butte and Bozeman to find out more about Leo Dailey's past. Jane Hall Dailey was still living in their house in Helena, packing up for her move to Washington. He wanted to talk directly with his wife. Discreetly, I begged.

"Hey, I can be discreet," Earl said with a touch of disdain.

"That's what worries me," I replied.

"Hey! Who got the pictures of Lucy riding Franklin's pony? I'll be genteel with the esteemed Mrs. Dailey."

Chapter 12 – More Letters

When I got back to the office on Monday morning, the 27th, there was a message Bart Johnson wanted to see me.

"Things have been moving pretty fast over the weekend," he began. "When'd you get in?"

"Last night about 10:30. Got home around 11:30."

"Then you probably haven't heard that Dailey is canceling the hearings into FDR and Eleanor." I was astonished. "He's been welcomed into the Big Leagues."

"What happened?" I stammered.

"Well, I don't know for sure, but all weekend I'd been in contact with Dailey's office trying to make sure he didn't call you as a witness. I'd pretty much gotten him to agree not to, that all you'd do is invoke First Amendment rights - you know, protecting your sources and all that - and he'd be better off trying to get first hand information from people around the White House. Then, last night, I guess around eight, he called and said he was canceling the hearings. As near as I can tell, it was a combination of the Republican and Democratic leadership and the White House putting the pressure on in ways he hadn't even thought about."

"McKay and Kerse were in on this?"

"Well, they hate FDR so much they figured they'd let his pecker twist in the wind for a while. But they also know how it works around here, and FDR has so many favors he can collect they didn't stand a chance of denting him through this. Embarrass him, maybe, but that's about it. So they, I guess, got together with the Democratic guys and went to Roosevelt with a plan. Simple trade-off. McKay and Kerse get some of their pet projects through without White House interference, like some road money and jobs money for their states, they make the hearings go away. And..." Bart Johnson laughed out loud.

96

"What?" I started to laugh, too.

"Dailey's wife was arrested for bootlegging in '33. She wasn't convicted, but McKay and Kerse told Leo that he could count on that coming out if he kept this up. And since Leo gets to use the money that his wife made from booze, he figured it would be better to fold his hand before even anteing up."

I laughed out loud, and laughed very hard. "Have you talked with the good congressman today?"

"No. I figured you might want to."

"Does Peter know?"

"You bet. "

"Earl's still in Montana. Should we…"

"Let him stay and see what he finds," Bart said. "You never know what he'll find, or how it might come in handy around this town. Leverage is always good."

I nodded. Leverage is good. I called Dailey right away but his secretary said he wasn't available. He was, however, going to make a press statement at noon. I told Tim Cullen, who already knew and was set to cover it.

I was on the air when we took a break for the 12:30 newscast. Cullen reported: "Congressman Leo Dailey today cancelled the hearings he had scheduled to begin tomorrow that would look into the allegations of infidelity surrounding the President and Mrs. Roosevelt. Representative Dailey said in a prepared statement he felt the country would be better served at this moment with a less formal investigation, but had no intentions of shying away from this controversial issue. He vowed to press forward with his own look into the allegations, and he promised to make public whatever information he uncovers about what he called 'the moral disintegration that has enveloped the people's home, the home we know as the White House.'"

That statement seemed strange to me. I immediately called the only person I knew who would give me an unvarnished answer.

"What's he doing, Sharon?"

"He's got to say that, Michael. He just had his ass handed to him by his leadership *and the president!* so he's telling the world he'll look into it himself. He's not going to do anything."

"Was Buckfield in on the deal?"

"He knew about it."

"What's he think?"

"He thinks Leo Dailey will remain a very quiet congressman on this issue, unless of course he wants to explain how his wife ran booze for the mob in Montana in '33."

I laughed again at the sheer boldness of how this town worked. I thanked Sharon and had to get back to the second half of my show. It was another lighthearted hour, this time with Carole Lombard.

She arrived at BRN about fifteen minutes before air time, and though we hadn't ever met, we had both done our homework. She was a stunningly beautiful woman with a brain to match. I'd seen her movies, she'd listened to my show.

"Welcome back to the BRN Midday Conversation, I'm Michael Audray. We continue our conversation with Carole Lombard. You and I are both from Indiana. You're from Fort Wayne, and I'm from Carmel."

"I knew you were from Carmel, Michael. Whenever I listen to this show and I hear you get people to say some of those things they say, I knew you had to be a Hoosier."

"Flattery will get you everywhere, Carole. You started acting back in Fort Wayne, didn't you?"

"Yes, I did. I made my first movie when I was twelve..."

"Really?"

"Yeah. It was a silent film, but I was hooked. So when I got a little older, I moved to Hollywood, and here I am today."

The conversation flowed well for long stretches of time. She'd made a string of movies over the past five years, and her two most recent were very different.

"Carole, a year ago you starred in *They Knew What They Wanted* with Charles Laughton. That was a powerful drama. But then you followed it up with a screwball comedy, *Mr. & Mrs. Smith*. Tell us a little bit about how you made those movies, and how you made the choice to make those movies."

"*They Knew What They Wanted* was a picture that I'd wanted to make for a while. I played a lonely waitress who marries an Italian grape-grower, and then it turns from a sweet little romance into a tragic affair. Harry Carey's in it, too, and generally he plays in comedies. But his performance is magnificent. And I'd always heard that Garson Kanin was a director that would draw the best out of you, so that was a selling point as well."

"Garson Kanin has directed a few films in his time, but then you worked with Alfred Hitchcock."

She laughed. "Yes, I did. Hitch wanted to make a screwball comedy. I guess he wants people to know he can direct things other than incredibly suspenseful movies, like *The 39 Steps*, or *Foreign Correspondent*. And I'd heard he wanted to work with me. *Mr. & Mrs. Smith* was the right movie for me to do right then. I wanted to get back to comedy, which I love to do, and Hitch wanted to make a comedy. I think it came off great," she said proudly.

"Well, so do I. We have to take a break, but we'll be back with more of our BRN Midday Conversation with Carole Lombard, right after this."

During the break, I told her that we only had a few minutes left and I wanted to talk about her efforts in encouraging people to join the Army, and a few other things.

"We're back with Carole Lombard. Carole, I know that you're a relative newlywed. How is your husband, Clark Gable?"

"He's just fine, Michael, and he sends his best to you."

"How long have you been married now?"

"A little more than a year, not quite a year-and-a-half."

"How'd you lovebirds meet?"

She smiled at the recollection. "We met at a party at Irving Thalberg's house. He was in the middle of shooting *Gone With The Wind* and he was utterly irresistible," she cooed.

"You're not so bad yourself, Carole."

"Thank you, Michael. Anyway, we met, started seeing each other, and almost immediately fell in love."

"Now I know this is the second marriage for both of you. You were married to William Powell, but divorced him in 1933. How is this marriage different from your first?"

"Well I don't know that you can compare them, actually, and I'm not going to try. I still like Bill a great deal, but we weren't right for each other. Sometimes that happens. After Bill and I divorced, we starred opposite each other in *My Man Godfrey*. We still talk. But with Clark, it's Kismet. We're made for each other. You know, Michael," she said much more seriously, "what two people do in their private lives should really only matter to them. I understand the interest that is generated around people in the spotlight, but ultimately, it isn't really anybody's business what two people do privately. Do you know what I mean?"

I did, indeed, but I wanted her to say more. "Are you thinking of anything currently in the news, Carole?"

"Well, yes," she chuckled. "This whole business about what the President and First Lady did or didn't do with each other or other people - I mean, who cares? I proudly voted for President Roosevelt because I believe he's the man who can lead this country through the perilous times ahead, not because he's my spiritual leader." She laughed out loud again. "Goodness, Michael, you got me to say one of those things I always hear you get other people to say."

"That's my job, Carole. And it's my job to say Thank You for coming by. Will you come visit us again?"

"Absolutely. I'm going to be working on a new film with Jack Benny called *To Be Or Not To Be*. It's a comedy set in Poland against the backdrop of what the Nazis are doing over there right now. That's not a comedic situation, and we definitely need to be aware of what's going on. That's why all this fuss over President Roosevelt is looking in the wrong direction. Anyway, I'd love to come back on when I've got a break in our schedule, or when it's all done."

"We'd love to have you, Carole."

And I meant it. She was a delightful guest, able to banter and hold her own more than most actresses. Unfortunately, she was wrong when she ventured that no one cared about the president's peccadilloes. The stories were breaking. The afternoon edition of The Boston Globe hit the streets with a front-page Associated Press story, written by Ellen Monroe, about Eleanor Roosevelt and an unnamed Lorena Hickok. Although it didn't spell out in detail the allegations, there was no doubt what was implied. The story chronicled Eleanor's trips around the country on "official" business, coupled with "an aide to the First Lady's" travel schedule. It spelled out how their itineraries overlapped, including their stay-overs. The story was relatively short, and if you didn't read it closely enough, you could get the impression it was about Eleanor taking unnecessary trips around the country.

The Chicago Tribune had a front-page story, above the fold, that named Lucy Mercer Rutherfurd, her relationship with the president and the fact that she was at one time the First Lady's social secretary. This story was the first to cite independent and unnamed sources.

And the Wall Street Journal ran an editorial that laid out how this kind of scandal, proven or unproven, could have an "unpleasant effect" on the economy of the United States. "Just as the US is hitting on all cylinders," the WSJ editorial stated, "the market forces will be pulled and tugged in every direction if - and this is a big if - President Roosevelt is distracted from his duties by this potential scandal."

Of these stories, the Tribune's was the most worrisome to Peter Betz. Not only did the Tribune include the Lucy-as-Eleanor's-secretary angle, they had their own sources. That meant they assigned at least one, and probably two reporters, to this story.

Peter wasn't happy.

"Goddammit!," Peter Betz yelled to no one in particular, but in my general direction, "Who are their sources? Why the hell did the goddamn Chicago Tribune get this? Who do they know that we don't? And where's Earl, for Chrissakes?"

"Earl's still in Montana. He's still checking out some deep background on Leo Dailey."

"What the hell for? Dailey's called off the dogs."

"Yeah, Peter, I know. But you know how this town works. Hearings called off this week, but stories like the Tribune's bring it all out again. Bart thinks it's better in the long run to keep Earl there until he's found what he's looking for."

"What's he looking for?"

"Hell, Peter, I don't know. I don't even think Earl knows. But he'll know it when he finds it."

Janine walked in. "Peter, Leo Dailey is here to see you."

Peter and I each did double takes. We shrugged our shoulders, and then Peter said to send him in.

Dailey, his razor-crisp creases and pocket kerchief spelling business, walked in with a swagger that belied the fact he'd just had his ass handed to him by his party's leadership. I noticed for the first time a hint of gangster in him. He didn't seem to have that same disingenuous Montana-hick act he used in our interviews. He spotted me but walked straight toward Peter. He plopped a copy of The Chicago Tribune on Peter's desk and said, "I'm their unnamed source."

Peter didn't even pick up the paper, or miss a beat. "You're a lunatic, Leo."

"Yeah? Well, you're the one that told me about all the dick-dipping." He turned around and walked to the door, then stopped and turned again. "By the way, my wife was a bootlegger for the Mob. We've still got friends. Don't fuck with me anymore." Then he walked out.

Peter and I had just shared the most surreal fifteen seconds of our lives. "Did he just threaten you, Peter?'

"No, he threatened us. That little prick threatened us. Like I don't know mobsters, too? Jesus. What a rookie."

I went back to my office, and found twelve messages, four of them from Ellen Monroe. She wanted to meet to get background on a story she was working on, and wondered if I'd help. I called her and said I could meet her around 5 p.m. at the Java Diner.

Meanwhile, Peter called Thomas Marety, the Editor of the Tribune. He wanted to know if Leo was really one of their unnamed sources. Marety, of course, wouldn't say, but would say that Dailey was certainly a newsmaker these days. Peter told him that Dailey was a loose cannon who wasn't what he purported to be.

"Who in this business is, Peter?" Marety asked sarcastically.

The 4 p.m. NBC newscast mentioned FDR had purchased gifts for a "certain woman acquaintance" on numerous occasions. The New York Daily News was preparing a story for tomorrow's editions that would name that acquaintance as Lucy Mercer Rutherfurd. About a dozen other stories investigating the link between Eleanor, Lucy and Lorena were being prepared for newspapers around the country, all with variations of these details, some more accurate than others.

The White House was trying mightily to ignore all these reports. They outwardly concentrated on pushing their new-term agenda forward. The White House press secretary, Steven Early, announced that Vice President Henry Wallace would be making a speech in Detroit on February 2nd outlining new domestic policy initiatives. That story got reported as a throw-in at the end of the newscasts or buried on page 8.

I ran into Jack at the Java Diner when I went to meet Ellen. "A certain woman acquaintance? Jack, you can do better than that!"

Jack looked a little sheepish. "I know, Michael. It wasn't my idea. It wasn't even my story. But this story has legs. NBC's gonna go with it as far as it goes. We're just going to be discreet in our language, that's all."

"I hear the Daily News is going to name Lucy." Jack shrugged his shoulders and lit another cigarette. "Why didn't you?"

"I feel bad for Lucy," he said.

I told him I'd see him around. Ellen was in a booth about fifteen feet away, and I sat down across from her. We exchanged pleasantries before we really began talking.

"I see you had the lead story in today's Boston Globe. Congratulations. You write very well, and you've obviously done your homework. So, how can I help you, Ellen?"

"You told me Lorena was the one with Eleanor. Right?" I nodded. "Eleanor Roosevelt has been very good not only to me, but to lots of women reporters. But I think she'd want me to do my job. Right?" Again, I nodded. "And I think Lorena would want me to do my job. Do you realize that Lorena was the first woman reporter ever hired by the Associated Press? And here I am almost immediately following in her footsteps." She paused, wistfully sighed, then continued. "So, I came across some letters that I think Lorena wrote to Eleanor, and I wanted to know if, off the record, you could tell me they're authentic."

"Where'd you get these letters?"

"I can't tell you that, Michael. But I trust my source."

"What makes you think I could verify them for you?"

"You know more about this story than anyone, Michael." As she said that, her leg rubbed up against mine under the table. And stayed there. I didn't move my leg.

"I can tell you that I've seen a letter, but I don't know that it's real. Some of the lawyers think it's OK, but I'm only taking their word. I'm not the verifying guy you need."

"What kind of a guy are you?" she asked as she put her other leg around my ankle.

"I'm a guy who likes to explore all possible avenues. And you?"

"I like to explore, too," Ellen said. Her eyes practically melted me.

"Do you have any letters with you?" I wondered.

"No," she said, "I'm keeping them safe in my apartment."

"And why do you think they're safe there?"

"Well, that's the only place I could think of where I have some privacy. I live by myself. Just a few blocks from here."

"Well, let's have dinner," I cooed, "then go explore your, uh, letters." I suggested the Java Diner Special of the Day, roast beef, with potatoes, carrots and gravy, plus blueberry pie and coffee.

The letters certainly seemed real, as genuine as the one I saw from Eleanor to Lorena. I thought only Earl had access to getting this kind of stuff, but apparently I was wrong. Ellen had ways to investigate things I certainly would not have expected from a young AP writer.

Young? I guess it's all relative. I was only twenty-six. She was twenty-five. But I felt older, mainly because I knew my history and my experience. Although she'd been with AP for eight months, I'd only met her a few weeks before.

Ellen Monroe grew up in Ainsworth, Nebraska, the only child of a CPA father and a homemaker mother. Her parents were dyed-in-the-wool Democrats, and voted for Roosevelt in every election possible, including his run as vice president in 1920. She was raised to believe women could do anything, and her parents did everything possible to open doors for her. Ellen was a good student and loved to write. She applied to Pepperdine, received a full journalism scholarship and graduated with honors in 1936. She moved back to Nebraska, briefly working at the

Ainsworth Times before moving on to the Lincoln News in early 1938. She first met Eleanor Roosevelt on an assignment for the News, and, inspired partly by a desire to cover Eleanor Roosevelt more closely, she applied to the Associated Press. The AP liked her writing style and her research abilities, and in April 1940, Ellen moved to Washington to be a wire service political reporter.

I wasn't always aware of my national stature. I spent most of my time in Washington, but Ellen reminded me of my fame. "I've listened to you since you went on the air in '39. You're big in Nebraska." That made me laugh.

She also told me that BRN is a must-listen for almost every political reporter in Washington. Again, as much as I wanted to believe that to be true, it's hard to understand until a peer tells you. And Ellen Monroe was definitely my peer.

How she got these three letters that clearly implied a sexual relationship between Lorena and Eleanor is beyond me. One of them was dated December 5, 1933, coincidentally the same day the 21st Amendment to the Constitution was ratified, repealing Prohibition.

Dear,

Tonight it's Bemidji, away up in the timber country, not a bad hotel and one day nearer you. Only eight more days. Twenty-four hours from now it will be only seven more—just a week! I've been trying today to bring back your face—to remember just how you look. Funny how even the dearest face will fade away in time. Most clearly I remember your eyes, with a kind of teasing smile in them, and the feeling of that soft spot just northeast of the corner of your mouth against my lips. I wonder what we'll do when we meet—what we'll say. Well, I'm rather proud of us, aren't you? I think we've done rather well.

A beautiful drive today—although slippery. I think the president would have got a kick out of it. We drove for miles and miles, it seemed to me, through second-growth pines, a part of the state's reforestation program. Itasca State Park, part of it, at the headwaters of the Mississippi. Lord, they were lovely! But the mere still among them when it got dark, and the road—where the sun hadn't had a chance to melt the ice—was terrible. Almost as bad as the time you and I drove down to New York from Hyde Park the Sunday before March 4. Remember? This is beautiful country, though. I'd forgotten how beautiful it is. We were in one big county today that has within its borders a thousand lakes!

I just got a big kick out of something I overheard. I'm writing this down in the lobby—since I want to hear the President's speech and don't want to climb the two flights to my room twice in one evening—and half a dozen men sitting nearby have been talking politics.

One of them said he'd be willing to bet on the president's reelection in 1936.

"Well, I don't know," another said, "a lot of things can happen in three years."

"Oh, hell," another put in, "he's got more friends now than he had when he went in." And they all agreed on that.

This has been a funny day. They're so damned slow up here. The cold seems to get into their very muscles and brains and makes it impossible for them to do anything rapidly.

(The gang next to me are talking now about recovery.

"I think things will hold just about as they are for a while, " one of them said. They're just getting organized."

"Yeah, we can't expect things to get going in a big way for a few months," another said.

And they all nodded in agreement and seemed perfectly satisfied.)

I was in one village today where not a single man had been put to work under CWA. They just can't seem to get started. I gravely suspect my old friend Governor Floyd Olson of playing politics with relief in Minnesota. I gather that Floyd runs the show himself and is too busy to do a decent job of it. The two states out here where they are dong the best jobs on relief and CWA—South Dakota and Iowa—have the least interference from their governors. North Dakota, Nebraska and Minnesota—all bad. I tell you—Floyd is Floyd. And that's that. And if I were Harry Hopkins or Henry Morgenthau or any of the rest of the boys down in Washington, I'd never forget it—not for a moment. Floyd is for Floyd and, I suspect, a not too scrupulous fighter. He's got brains, too, and that makes him all the more dangerous. There's no point in all this, except that I have the feeling that both Mr. Hopkins and Henry Morgenthau are quite impressed by him. I believe that Floyd would see all the Swedes in Minnesota—except himself—drawn and quartered if it would be to his advantage. He's an ambitious young man, Floyd is.

Darling, I've been thinking about you so much today. What a swell person you are to back me up the way you do on this job! We do do things together, don't we? And it's fun, even though the fact that we both have work to do keeps us apart.

Good night, dear one. I want to put my arms around you and kiss you at the corner of your mouth. And in a little more than a week now—I shall

H

Lorena certainly was connected and had great insights. Morgenthau was secretary of the Treasury and Hopkins was the head of the Federal Emergency Relief Association. And Floyd Olson was, at the time, governor of Minnesota, which is where Lorena was visiting when she wrote this letter.

As we read the letters and discussed their political and professional implications, we both had sex on our brains. I had taken off my coat and tie, and she had slipped off her shoes. She was still wearing a knee-length black skirt and matching blouse. But when she crossed her legs, the skirt seemed to hike up just far enough for me to see the tops of her stockings at her thighs, attached by some wonderfully sinful black garters. The sparks were flying, and though we each had thoughts of taking each other, we didn't. Not that night.

At the end of the evening, I knew two things: one, Ellen Monroe was a first-rate reporter who wouldn't let her personal feelings for Eleanor Roosevelt get in the way of breaking a great story. And two, I wanted to bed her.

January 31, 1941: First US troops arrive in St. John's Newfoundland.
January 31, 1941: Japanese Ambassador Nomura departs for the US.
February 5, 1941: Army General Walter Short, responsible for the fleet
defense, arrives in Pearl Harbor.

Chapter 13 – The Halls of Montana

A few days, maybe a week passed without hearing from Earl. As far as we knew, he was still in Montana. But if anyone could be in two places at once, I would have bet on Earl.

When he did check in, though, he always had news, generally big news. He'd talked with Leo's wife, Jane Hall Dailey, the bootlegging spouse. Bootlegging in and of itself was not that awful, especially since Peter had been a bootlegger in the '20s. But it was her Mob connections and the trail of Mob money to Leo Dailey's congressional campaign that certainly attracted our attention.

Earl said Jane Hall Dailey was a cool customer. She invited him in right away, offered him a drink and was seemingly forthcoming about all his questions. Leo had called her and told her to be prepared for a visit by somebody, so she wasn't surprised. As the wife of a congressman, and the target of a quiet federal trial a few years back, she seemed comfortable answering questions.

She told Earl that her family ran one of the largest logging businesses in Montana, maybe even the entire West. The Halls had been loggers since they moved to Montana after the Civil War. They began not merely logging, but preparing the logs for different applications - paper mills, construction, furniture, and so on, becoming in the process one of the first customizers in the business. Opportunity follows money. The loggers who worked for Hall Timber, as the company was known, liked to have a drink now and again. When Prohibition became law, speakeasies opened across the United States. Montana was no different. John Hall, Jane's father, seized the speakeasy opportunity to recoup some of the money he was paying his employees. But that meant buying booze from nefarious characters.

It wasn't hard to find it, Jane said, as all the big bootleggers were looking to expand their distribution. They had an opportunity to buy the booze from the Capone gang, but opted instead for a slightly lower profile bootlegger from Milwaukee named Lou Martilotta. The beer and booze was cheaper, and the lower profile deflected any unwanted attention from the legitimate logging business that John Hall was operating.

But in 1932, the Feds kept cracking down, and Elliot Ness had The Untouchables winning high-profile battles. They caught Capone for evading taxes in the '20s, and now they went after the littler guys, like Lou Martilotta. They set up a sting operation, and in one of her rare trips to Milwaukee, Jane Hall was trailed by The Untouchables. The Feds arrested her in Helena under The Volstead Act for Transporting Illegal Contraband Across State Lines. She was very forthcoming with this information, as it was all a matter of public record. Her sentence, suspended by a friendly Montana judge who owed his seat on the bench in no small part to contributions from Hall Timber, was six months and a $2000 fine.

What she didn't really want to talk about, though, was how the money funneled from the speakeasy to Leo's various campaigns. She told Earl the accountants were very clean in their details, and any money Leo used for his political career was clean money, that is, money from their own pockets, earned ostensibly from the logging industry. Earl discovered a $200,000 deposit into her and Leo's personal account in September 1932, and asked where it came from. Jane blinked. It was a corporate bonus from Hall Timber for her services, she said. Earl knew better. And he knew that was a trail to follow.

He also asked her if she knew Mary Beth Keefer. At first, Jane Hall Dailey feigned ignorance, but when Earl refreshed her memory, she acknowledged Mary Beth must have been Leo's college girlfriend. When he pressed her if Mary Beth and Leo were still in contact, Jane got tight-lipped and said he'd have to ask them. She quickly regained her composure before politely asking Earl to leave.

Earl had already figured that Mary Beth and Leo were still in contact, and put a tap on her phone. Even before he spoke with Jane Dailey, Earl knew that Mary Beth and Leo had called each other five times since I met her at the restaurant in Bozeman. What's more, he knew what they talked about.

Mary Beth told Leo that two people from BRN came to see her, and that I was one of them. She described Earl to a T, and that's how he told Jane to be ready. Mary Beth told him what kind of questions they were asking, including the pregnancy question. He told her to just shut up and play it cool, and told her not to talk to anybody else from the press, not a radio or newspaper reporter. No one. She wanted to know what was going to happen, and, most intriguingly, when they could see each other again. He told Mary Beth that he probably wouldn't get back to Montana for a little while, not until the Summer recess, but that they'd spend some time together. He promised.

For the next four days, Earl hung out in Helena, just keeping an eye on both Jane Dailey and Mary Beth Keefer. During the day, he'd watch Jane's movements, which mostly centered on packing up for her move to Washington, and at night he'd go to Schiavvi's to keep an eye on Mary Beth. Mostly, he sat at the bar and drank while she worked.

But on his last night in Helena, he slipped the manager a $20 and asked to be seated in Mary Beth's section. He ordered a steak, potatoes, green beans and a salad, along with a double Chivas on the rocks. He was pleasant and quiet, and he could tell that Mary Beth was flustered. It was when she brought him his sundae that he asked her one question.

"Where are you and Leo going this summer?"

"I don't, I don't, uh, I don't know what you're talking about," she stammered.

Earl dropped it right then, but he knew she would call Leo. And he'd listen in.

That's exactly what happened. Mary Beth got home at midnight, and placed a long-distance call directly to Leo's home phone number in Washington. She told him that Earl asked about their summer plans, and that she didn't say anything. At that instant, Leo knew her phone was tapped, and told her he'd get back in touch with her. Then he hung up.

Almost immediately, Earl removed the tap he placed outside Mary Beth's home, and headed toward the airport. He'd gotten what he wanted.

Leverage.

When he got back to Washington the following day, Earl updated Peter, Bart and me. He hadn't called, he said, because he didn't want anyone listening to his conversations. Bart was uneasy about the phone tap, but Peter told him to relax. They wouldn't use it in court or anything. It was information only. Leverage.

Peter told Earl about Leo's veiled threat and asked him to look into Leo's Mob connections. Leo had already made a couple phone calls about Lou Martilotta, who was six years into a fifteen-year federal sentence in Leavenworth. He'd been convicted largely on the testimony of Jane Hall, who in a plea arrangement agreed to testify against Lou in order to stay out of prison herself. He'd already contacted Leavenworth to see if he could talk with Martilotta. Peter smiled. He told Earl to expect a bonus if he came back with really juicy stuff from Leavenworth Lou.

Lou Martilotta was about fifty, medium height, slight build with wiry gray hair and glasses. He looked more like an accountant than a gangster. But he was a career criminal, first getting arrested at eighteen for breaking and entering. He'd also been arrested for fraud, assault, and larceny by the time he was twenty-five. He'd spent nearly four years in jail, but by the time he was thirty, he was out and wanted to become a businessman. The business he chose was booze.

It was just a supply-and-demand thing, he said. People wanted a drink, he'd give it to them. What's the big deal? He prided himself on having high quality alcohol and prices that were better than Capone's. For as ruthless as Capone was, he was also enough of a businessman to understand he couldn't service everybody. So Martilotta and Capone had an arrangement: Al stayed out of Milwaukee and the smaller markets west of Wisconsin, and Lou stayed out of Capone's hair in the bigger markets.

Lou met John Hall in 1926. Other speakeasies had popped up in Montana before then, but the operators didn't understand the police, even in Montana, needed their palms greased to look the other way. When the payoffs didn't come, the arrests did. Soon, Montana was pretty dry. So John Hall, the esteemed president of Hall Timber and one of the largest employers in the state, looked into an alcohol distribution channel for Big Sky Country. He never even approached Capone's group, because even then the Feds were chasing Capone. He was the biggest, the baddest and the strongest. Because of that, he was also the most vulnerable. John Hall opted instead to go with Lou Martilotta, from the city that beer made famous.

They met in Milwaukee. John Hall had written to Lou requesting the meeting, and went there with two other people: his daughter Jane, and her new boyfriend, the recent college graduate with the law degree, Leo Dailey. It was Leo, in fact, who had heard of Lou Martilotta while at Montana State. Apparently, college kids know all the places to find beer, booze and babes. Leo, eager to impress Jane and her wealthy father, tracked down Lou in Milwaukee, wrote the letter that John Hall signed, and sent it off. At the meeting, according to Lou, John Hall was in charge. He wanted it kept simple and quiet. He wanted things run through a company he would set up in Helena, and all the invoices were to be itemized as Logging Materials. If they needed to talk, Lou's secretary would call Jane, and a phone meeting would be arranged.

It was all pretty standard, according to Lou. The first shipment to The Teton Peak Holding Company was delivered in early 1927. The shipments were monthly at first, and as business grew, they became weekly. Jane became his main contact. As the Teton Peak Holding Company business grew, John Hall knew he needed someone to operate it full-time. Lou figured the only person John Hall could trust completely was his daughter Jane. Lou and Jane developed a phone friendship, and he knew she was getting serious with her boyfriend. Lou knew Leo was a lawyer, so he figured—although he never knew for sure - that Leo was covering all the tracks and keeping the books in order.

During the 1932 campaign, Roosevelt said he wanted to repeal Prohibition. While this was wildly popular with the electorate, it was not so popular with the bootleggers. The Untouchables went after every known bootlegger they could in order to rack up as much success as possible before being disbanded.

Once a year, Lou said, Jane Hall would come to Milwaukee to meet with Lou and discuss continuing arrangements. But the Feds followed her on her trip in '32. They took pictures of her meeting with Lou, exchanging envelopes, and going in to a speakeasy at night. They followed her back to Helena, and waited for the next monthly shipment to the Teton Peak Holding Company. And when she was there, signing for the delivery, the Feds burst in and arrested everyone, including Jane.

They put a great deal of pressure on her, and despite the embarrassment it caused John Hall and Hall Timber, she pled guilty. This was, in fact, something they had prepared for, and though John Hall felt badly, he was in a position to take care of his daughter. And Leo, now Jane's husband and a full-fledged lawyer with political aspirations, made sure she wouldn't spend a night in jail.

But the Feds wanted blood, and they didn't care whose it was. So they agreed to go easy on her if she'd testify against her supplier. She did. Lou Martilotta was arrested, and with his previous convictions from years earlier, he was sentenced to fifteen years in a Federal Penitentiary for ignoring Prohibition.

Lou was the last major bootlegger sentenced to prison under the Volstead Act. Capone had gone to Leavenworth in May of '32 on Tax Evasion charges, and then, in September 1933, Lou Martilotta was also sent to Leavenworth. But Lou said he never saw Capone in prison. They were in completely different cellblocks, and word had it that Capone was showing the effects of syphilis.

Lou wanted to know what Earl's interest in all of this was. Earl told him, simply, Leo Dailey. "You mean, The congressman?" Lou asked, laughing. "We get news in here," Lou said. "Leo the Lawyer now Leo the Federal Lawmaker." Lou laughed again. Earl wondered what was so funny, and then Lou gave him his opinion.

"Leo's an arrogant idiot," Lou said, "a bad combination. He looks good, he talks good, he's got that lawyer thing going, but he's pretty empty upstairs. He's got some simple-minded beliefs about how the world should be, and he thinks that getting into politics will give him the ability to change things. Leo doesn't even realize that Jane's pulling his stings. She's the real power, the one with the vision and the money. And she's the one who can't understand how Mr. & Mrs. America couldn't get by during the Depression. I mean, after all, she always had more than enough." Lou said Jane didn't see the irony in making gobs of money from selling illegal alcohol while claiming to be an upstanding citizen.

"She wants power," Lou said. "And Leo's her ticket to ride."

Lou said he didn't hold any grudges against Jane or Leo. In fact, he believed that Jane made a sizable contribution to the sentencing judge's children's college fund to get Lou a lighter sentence. He was facing twenty-five-years-to-life, and wound up getting fifteen-years. With good behavior, he could make parole this year.

Lou described himself as a Gentleman Mobster, a businessman whose business was booming but illegal. He wasn't a Capone-style gangster, who would bash disloyal lieutenant's heads in with a baseball bat at dinner. He was really more of a CEO, paying his staff well, taking care of their families, and staying out of the really nasty side of crime. Lou never did any numbers running or drugs like heroin or shakedowns. Lou Martilotta concentrated on, as he called it, The Two B's - Booze and Broads.

The Broads just went with the Booze, he said. The girls would be there at the speakeasy to show the guys a good time. The girls worked inside the club, never had to go out if they didn't want to, and had enough people around to protect them if the guys ever got too rough. From Lou's point of view, it was like having a Dessert Menu at a nice restaurant.

Lou's main area of influence was in metropolitan Milwaukee. The distribution of the booze to the small towns in Montana, Idaho, North Dakota, South Dakota and Minnesota was just that, distribution. But when you came to Milwaukee, Lou was the man to see for a good time.

One of his best out-of-town customers, Lou said, was Leo Dailey. Leo would come to Milwaukee three or four times a year for long weekends. They'd have a meeting on the morning of his first day in town, then, the rest of the time Leo would drink and have dessert. Lots of desserts. Even though Lou knew Leo was married to Jane, he didn't give it much thought. Leo just wanted to get laid. A lot.

Earl wondered when Lou was up for parole. "First week of June."

Earl gave Lou his business card and wrote some extra phone numbers on it. He told Lou he'd be in touch soon, and asked him to call anytime if he thought of anything else interesting. Lou went back to his cell, Earl went back to Washington.

February 10, 1941: England breaks off diplomatic relations with Romania.
February 12, 1941: Nazi General Erwin Rommel arrives in North Africa to command the Afrika Corps.
February 14, 1941: FDR issues ultimatum to Japan: if you attack Singapore, it means War with the United States.
February 16, 1941: 10,000 Jews in Vienna deported to concentration camps.
March 1, 1941: All Nazi concentration camps are fully operational.
March 1, 1941: Bulgaria joins the Axis.
March 9, 1941: New Italian offensive against Greece begins.

Chapter 14 – Coughlin and Corkman

As Jack Denif said, this story had legs. I now knew people would be listening intently, people who hadn't listened before, people who believed I was a scoundrel who was only interested in the president's sex life.

I had a string of good guests, actors and authors and ballplayers, all well known and uncontroversial. For the most part, they didn't want to talk about The Affairs of State, which was OK with me. But it was easy to put preparing questions for The Andrews Sisters on a lower priority scale than investigating the Executive and Legislative branches of government.

The BRN news staff was working almost exclusively on the details of the story. Tim Cullen began to exercise a heavier editor's hand, much to Peter's chagrin. Cullen issued a directive that sources were double checked, even triple checked, before going with a previously unreported element or angle. Peter thought that was foot dragging, but Cullen eventually prevailed - with Bart Johnson's help. There's nothing like a lawyer to convince you to cover your ass.

But BRN was not the only news organization working double time on this story. All the other major players - AP, UPI, NBC, CBS, Mutual, The New York Times, The Chicago Tribune, all the Washington papers

- had at least two reporters devoted to an investigation. They didn't always report stories everyday, but when they did, they were sure of its authenticity.

Surveys found the public was eating this story up. So far, there was no damage to anyone involved, because the public hadn't made up its mind about The Affairs of State. The American people hadn't come down on the side of Moral Outrage at the First Family or Outright Indignation at the Press for bringing it up. But clearly, they were interested.

The modern Presidency had evolved into a position of celebrity. That is, Americans respected the office, they respected the job, and they believed it to be very difficult. But the person holding the presidency - Franklin Delano Roosevelt - had become a celebrity. He was in the newspapers and on radio everyday for the better part of a decade. There was a belief he had become so good at being president mere distractions like this were interesting sideshows that lightened the mood and made him seem more human.

The Republicans saw it as a way to make political gains for themselves and their districts. After they cut Leo's balls off, Martin McKay, the House minority leader, and Ken Kerse, the House minority whip, publicly stated it might be a "good idea to quietly and at this point unofficially investigate the specter of governmental or ethical violations." In DC speak, they wanted to badly damage FDR domestically at this stage of his third term to set up a better White House match in 1944. They knew if FDR controlled the agenda, and if the War in Europe was at the top of the agenda, the Republicans would get their clocks cleaned again. It was in their best interest to keep this story alive as long as possible.

Jack was one of the reporters NBC assigned to the story. Despite his personal reluctance to pursue this, he took the assignment because "I have mouths to feed." By virtue of his experience and seniority, he was able to cover the angles of the story he thought might pan out. That's why Jack was in Detroit to cover Vice President Henry Wallace's speech.

This was a coming out, of sorts, for Wallace. Elevated to the stature of vice president, he was more than just a mouthpiece for Administration policies. He was The Mouthpiece. Detroit was the lynchpin in Roosevelt's Arsenal of Democracy strategy. Sending his newly minted second-in-command to give a speech at the Detroit Economic Club sent a strong signal that FDR was still counting on the Motor City and Mayor Edward Jeffries for support in every conceivable way.

No one questioned Wallace's vision, his liberalism or his curiosity. But he was relatively shy and introspective, politically insensitive and had no real friends in either house of Congress. Still, this was a chance for Vice President Henry Wallace to put some spit-and-polish on his image.

Instead, the speech broke no new ground while cementing his reputation as a man who could take lyrical, poetic prose and transform it into garbage. Allen Drury, the talented writer who later moved to Hollywood, tarred Wallace's Detroit speech. "A shock of silver-graying hair," he wrote, "sweeps over to the right of his head in a great shaggy arc. He looks like a hayseed, talks like a prophet, and acts like an embarrassed schoolboy." But the event was well attended by Detroit's Who's Who. Mayor Jeffries, Henry Ford, Louis Chevrolet and labor leader Walter Reuther sat near each other. Off to the side were two young men talking animatedly, each pointing fingers in the other's chest. Jack ambled over and introduced himself. He met Jimmy Hoffa and Rico Tozzi. Hoffa was a young labor organizer who at that time was concentrating on the trucking industry. Rico Tozzi described himself as a "bowling alley proprietor with a passion for politics."

Before Jack could ask Hoffa a question, Rico Tozzi grabbed Jack. "What's the big deal about the president getting a little on the side? I mean, I hate the guy, the guy's a prick but who'd want to do it with Eleanor?" But, Rico Tozzi continued, he was surprised that Leo called off the investigation.

Leo?

Rico Tozzi and Leo Dailey met in 1932 in Milwaukee. Rico Tozzi liked Leo Dailey, liked the fact he had plans and ambitions, liked the fact he was from Montana. When Jack asked, Rico Tozzi volunteered that he contributed to all of Leo's campaigns since they met.

So Jack had two stories for NBC - the vice president speaks to the Economic Club of Detroit about the plans and goals of the third Roosevelt term, and in his pocket he had deep background on Leo Dailey from a Detroit bowling alley proprietor.

After the speech, Henry Wallace issued a very firm No Comment on The Affairs of State. Roosevelt let it be known to everyone and anyone in the White House that there was to be No Comment about anything having to do with the private lives of the First Family.

FDR was shrewd enough to know there was interest in it. Although in his eyes reporters were jackals, he knew they wouldn't follow something if there was no public interest or political implication. FDR knew the stakes were high, but figured the story would go away if no one officially talked about it.

Right around this time, Eleanor decided to take a trip. The purported reason for the trip was to marshal support for the Administration's domestic initiatives, and to gather public support if the United States had to enter the War in Europe. The real reason, though, was Eleanor wanted to gauge for herself any early fallout from the scandal.

Eleanor's trip took her from Washington to Atlanta, Nashville, St. Louis, Sioux City, Peoria, South Bend, Cleveland and Altoona. The eighteen-day train trip featured a combination of stopovers, dinners, speeches and whistle-stop handshaking, allowing Eleanor to do what she did best - make the common person feel special.

Almost immediately she noticed something different. The crowds were smaller, less enthusiastic and more reticent than during the election campaign. The reporters noticed it, too, and though they didn't make a big deal of it, it certainly was mentioned in their stories.

The pivotal stop on that trip was Sioux City. It was scheduled to be a three-hour stop at the train station. Eleanor would make remarks from the platform of the caboose, then mingle with the crowd for a while. But as the train pulled in, Eleanor and her staff noticed hundreds of hand-held signs in the crowd.

"Repent, Mrs. Roosevelt". "Eleanor, change your ways. The Bible says so." "God made Man and Woman." "This is Sioux City, not Sin City."

Immediately her public relations staff began debating whether or not to even stop. They figured the reporters would pounce all over the sign-carriers and only add life to the story. But Eleanor was convinced she could defuse the situation.

As soon as the train stopped, she joined the crowd. Shaking hands, posing for pictures, laughing and smiling. But the protesters soon overwhelmed the official welcoming committee. Eleanor Roosevelt, for the first time, found herself face-to-face with a group of women who believed the stories she was in love with another woman. These people weren't happy.

As expected, the traveling press swarmed around the protesters, interviewing them and getting their views. They described themselves as God-fearing Christians who believed the Bible and lived as God expected. They didn't want anyone coming to their town that didn't live as they did. Even a First Lady who had done nothing but champion the common man and civil rights for more than twenty years.

Eleanor climbed back on the platform and tried to deliver her standard speech about the domestic agenda and the evils of Hitler. But her amplified voice could not drown out the protesters' voices: "Eleanor Repent. Eleanor Repent. Eleanor Repent..."

The local police tried to quiet the crowd, even pushing them back by policemen on horseback. That didn't work, and Eleanor didn't want the emotions to escalate. So, after only ninety minutes, Eleanor's train left Sioux City.

The next day, the lead story on radio and in newspapers from coast-to-coast was that Eleanor Roosevelt was heckled out of Iowa.

Similar protesters popped up along the final four stops of the trip, although none of them had the strength or success of the Iowans. Eleanor had gotten the information she wanted. The heartland of America was angry about The Affairs of State. And the anger was fueled by the deeply religious.

The story was out of control, wildly taking on a life of its own. Unless the topic could be changed immediately, Roosevelt's political instincts told him this could get very messy.

Despite the war news - the invasions of North Africa, Yugoslavia, Greece, the island of Crete, with Russia a target - the American press and the American people were fully engaged in the president's hanky-panky. This story gave the loud and legion cadre of Roosevelt Haters a platform to espouse their views to a newly receptive audience.

Beyond the radio and newspapers, there were other voices claiming Moral Superiority and Moral Outrage over the First Family's behavior. Chief among them was Fr. Charles Coughlin.

This Catholic priest from Royal Oak, Michigan had a massive and loyal radio audience for his weekly broadcasts. He mixed Catholic theology and religious fervor with political commentary in a program unlike any other heard on the radio. In the early '30s, Fr. Coughlin supported FDR and his policies. Over the next few years he changed his views completely. Fr. Charles Coughlin became an ultraconservative anti-Semite isolationist who was a pain in the ass to both FDR and the Pope. But he was a fiery orator who inspired his listener followers, and he was determined to stir up Moral Outrage over the infidelities. Fr. Coughlin used FDR's affair as a reason to question his fitness to lead.

"The president dallying with a younger woman who is not his wife is unspeakable," roared Fr. Coughlin one Sunday without acknowledging the slightest trace of irony. "How dare he! If he will lie to his wife, what is to prevent him from lying to us? Where is the line that *the president* will stop at before he realizes he's a liar? And if he's a liar, what do we call his wife? The *First Lady of the United States*! In love with another woman!

A woman who is *living at the White House!* Being a man of the cloth, I can't imagine what actually takes place in their quarters. I don't want to imagine what takes place! I am appalled! I am astonished! I am outraged! But I am not nearly as outraged as Almighty God! If you think that God is not watching this, you are mistaken. If you think God is not concerned about the leadership of this nation, you are mistaken. If you think God is not upset with the United States of America, you are mistaken. God is watching our every move. And He is not happy about what is going on inside our White House. It is up to us, the good and faithful citizens of this great land, to rise up and demand that this lying leader of ours atone for his misdeeds. And the hussy we have as *the First Lady of the United States* must be exposed for the morally repugnant character she is. We must rise up, band together, and demand that these people be held responsible for the continued moral disintegration of this great land of ours!"

It didn't matter if Fr. Coughlin had seen any of the proof we'd seen. He was whipping up a Moral Tornado that would sweep across the country, a storm that began in the fields of Iowa and picked up steam over The Great Lakes.

Once Fr. Coughlin came out so publicly against the Roosevelts, elucidating each allegation so clearly, it became even easier for columnists to weigh in. Up until Coughlin's initial blast, The Affairs of State had remained a factual news story. There were a few editorials, but mostly the opinion makers-and-shapers stayed on the sidelines.

Then B.W. Corkman of The Washington Post filleted Eleanor Roosevelt in his column. He'd hated Eleanor for twenty years or more, and had consistently accused her of being a meddling, nagging wife with Communist leanings and a bleeding liberal heart. He had long ago given up any objectivity regarding her. So when these allegations about Eleanor and Lorena became public, he didn't need to see proof. He just waited until someone else laid them out first.

By B.W. Corkman
Mrs. Roosevelt: No Ordinary Citizen

I'm a sweet, gentle man in my life and in my writing. But I'm told I was rude to Mrs. Roosevelt when I merely stated she was impertinent, cheeky and a schemer, and suggested she remove herself from public life permanently and immediately.

Granted, that is merely my opinion, and others may feel

differently on this subject. Though the meaning may be harsh, the words themselves conveyed my innate decencyand cultured demeanor, and were no more inflammatory than language used to discuss other controversial topics.

Indisputably, Eleanor Roosevelt involves herself in a multitude of issues in which no wife should be involved. However, we are constantly reminded that as the wife of the president, she is not an ordinary citizen.

I agree with that. She is not an ordinary citizen. She is The First Lady of the United States, a woman to whom children, particularly girls, look to for guidance and inspiration. Whether she accepts it or not, she sets a moral tone for this nation, and her actions in her private life reflect her personal beliefs more than any public pronouncements ever can.

If we are to believe that Mrs. Roosevelt is in love with someone other than the president—and make no mistake, I believe this—we must also believe that everything she says and does is a lie. And if we are to believe that the person Mrs. Roosevelt is in love with is another woman—and make no mistake, I believe this—we must also believe that Mrs. Roosevelt has entered a realm of deviancy that all good people can not even imagine.

But our dear First Lady, although married to Our President, has no more rights and no more authority than you or I. Indeed, Mrs. Brown, Mrs. White and Mrs. Joe Collins have the same legal footing as Mrs. Roosevelt. Yet we afford her a special brand of respect because her husband is the highest ranking secular authority in our country. When she abuses that respect, either for profit or by associating with people who crave a different American way, it is not her critics who are to blame. It is she who disrespects the office she holds. And when Mrs. Roosevelt lives in a way that is in direct conflict with traditional American family values, she flaunts her authority in our faces. She has always been a liar, a manipulator and an anti-American sympathizer. Now we must add one more adjective: Discredited.

Mrs. Roosevelt must remove herself from the public immediately. However, even if she does, that will not remove the long shadow of moral doubt hovering over her husband, the president. He must also consider a public retreat.

Even though B.W. Corkman had been attacking Eleanor in print for years, this column resonated throughout the halls of the White House and the houses of the land.

When Peter read that column, he called me into his office and said, simply, "Lead this story wherever it goes. Don't follow it. Lead it."

That wasn't a problem. We had already booked Dick Dayton, the head of the political science department at Georgetown, to come on and give an historical overview of the recent events. Professor Dayton had never before been a guest on any radio program, and though initially reluctant, finally relented after hearing the blast from Fr. Coughlin.

Dayton came to BRN armed with anecdotes from past presidential campaigns, copies of newspaper articles from the 1890s, and an insider's knowledge of how presidential politics has played out over the course of American history. He was a fascinating speaker, articulate and eloquent, and, I must say, evenhanded. He came to neither defend nor skewer FDR.

In a professorial and delicate fashion, Dick Dayton declared, "George Washington may really be the Father of our Country. Although there is no factual proof, stories have persisted, from quite a few sources, that George and Martha's storybook marriage was just that. Storybook. Washington had an eye for the ladies, and they had an eye back. Legend has it that Washington caught his deathly pneumonia while visiting his slaves quarters, if you know what I mean."

Ben Franklin, according to Dick Dayton, had dozens of illegitimate children, many of them born while he was the Ambassador to France. Alexander Hamilton, famous for his duel with Aaron Burr, had survived an ugly blackmail episode regarding his affair with a married woman. Anecdotal evidence suggests the widower Thomas Jefferson became romantically involved with Sally Hemmings, one of his slaves, and in fact had three children together.

More recently, Professor Dayton continued, there was Grover Cleveland. Cleveland overcame acknowledging an illegitimate child and never marrying the mother to win two terms. In his second term, Grover Cleveland married Frances Folsom, the twenty-year-old daughter of his best friend, and had secret cancer surgery. So secret, in fact, not only was the public not told, his vice president wasn't even informed.

Dick Dayton relayed the story of Edith Gault Wilson, "our first woman president." When Woodrow Wilson suffered a crippling stroke, his wife Edith took over control of the White House, making policy decisions she felt her husband would make. She shut out the vice president. Edith

Wilson ran the country, protecting her husband and his image until he was well enough to resume his duties.

But in Dayton's estimation, the most flagrant womanizer in American political history was Warren Harding. Dayton said Harding was a habitual womanizer who was more interested in playing poker than running the government. Great evidence confirmed Warren Harding had a series of affairs before and during his presidency. He fathered at least one child out of wedlock, and paid another woman hush money to keep quiet. Although Mrs. Harding was well aware of the president's proclivities, his conduct infuriated her. On a political trip to San Francisco, Warren Harding died, officially of a rather mysterious case of food poisoning.

It was a fascinating hour. I learned a lot, as I'm sure the listeners did. Then I asked the Georgetown University professor what made The Affairs of State different.

"That's easy," he said. "Franklin Roosevelt is the sitting president. All these other stories I've mentioned, except for the first Cleveland campaign, were not discussed in public at all. The press, rightly or wrongly, chose not to divulge too many details of a public figure's private life. I'm sure many of the people listening today have heard these stories for the very first time. Historians such as I have long known about these flaws, and we use them to put into greater context the accomplishments or failures of our leaders. But for the first time, we have put on display the private life of our two most famous public figures, people who have been in our lives everyday now for the better part of a decade. These are people we think we know. And when we hear something unseemly about someone we know, it shakes our confidence."

"Is this examination a good thing, Professor?"

"I think it's too early to tell, Michael. I make no predictions. I believe we won't know the answer to that question for years, until after the story reaches whatever end it's going to have, and the next bend of world history takes place. Having said that, I do believe we must be careful. We are all human. We all have strong points and weak points."

"How will these revelations affect our standing in the world? Or will they?"

"It's hard to tell on that, either. These revelations, as you call them, about the current president have brought the United States into uncharted territory. The Europeans, particularly the French, have a decidedly more continental attitude about matters like this. But at this moment, I think the French have bigger things on their mind."

March 11, 1941: FDR signs Lend-Lease Act into law.
March 25, 1941: Yugoslavia joins the Axis.
March 30, 1941: The US takes 65 German and Italian merchant ships
into "protective custody".
April 3, 1941: FDR orders 25% of the Pacific fleet to the Atlantic as
part of the Lend-Lease convoys.
April 4, 1941: The British capture Ethiopia.
April 6, 1941: Germany invades Yugoslavia and Greece.
April 10, 1941: Greenland is placed under US control.
April 13, 1941: German troops capture Belgrade.
April 13, 1941: Japan and the Soviet Union sign a non-aggression pact.
April 16, 1941: 460 German bombers attack London.
April 24, 1941: King George of Greece flees.
April 27, 1941: German forces capture Greece.

Chapter 15 – Hunting Leo, Talking Lorena

I ran into Jack Denif at The Java Diner one night in early April. "Whatcha got, Jack?" He was surprised at my directness. Normally, that was his style. To my surprise, he told me.

He said he'd been following Leo Dailey's campaign money trail. Leo wanted to run for the Montana State Senate in 1934, but was concerned his wife's bootlegging arrest would be a hindrance. Shortly before her sentencing in August 1932, her father John Hall made a $20,000 contribution to the presiding judge's re-election fund. Interestingly, John Hall had deposited $20,000 into his personal account just days before his contribution.

Jack had also uncovered the same $200,000 deposit into Leo and Jane's personal account in September 1932 that Earl found. The following month, Leo Dailey formed the Dailey for State Senate Committee. Beginning as an unknown that October, Leo mounted a campaign offensive unlike any Montana had seen to that point. He campaigned for nearly two years, shook every hand in his district, and won the election with 71% of the vote.

For each succeeding election campaign - two for the State Senate, then the Congressional run - Leo Dailey consistently outspent his opponent 6-1. He was media savvy, radio friendly, and always seemed to be able to spend more money than he took in. When Leo left Helena in December to move to Washington, he stopped in Detroit for two days. He spent that time at the Pontchartrain Hotel in downtown Detroit, and had a series of meetings with various labor leaders, all put together by Rico Tozzi. Rico Tozzi and Leo Dailey hit it off for lots of reasons, including their distrust of FDR. Tozzi had called the president "a little prick" within seconds of meeting Jack Denif. Dailey, with the fire, brimstone and now burgeoning confidence of a winner, felt FDR needed to be brought down a notch or two.

Dailey and Tozzi both felt The Affairs of State was the method with which to bring down FDR. Tozzi told Dailey he'd cover his back. He had too much invested in Leo for him to take a back seat. So when the Republican leadership put Leo's nuts in their squirrel teeth and made him drop the official congressional hearings, Tozzi made it clear that McKay and Kerse should go fuck themselves or their contribution river would dry up. And, Jack said with a laugh, McKay and Kerse didn't have to fuck themselves. They had just gotten fucked.

Jack also confirmed that Leo was the source for the story in The Chicago Tribune, and believed him to be the source of leaks to other high profile papers. "I thought you didn't want to have anything to do with this story, Jack."

He shrugged his shoulders, slurped some soup and said, "This angle is like a real news story. I'm not asking about anybody's pecker." Then he looked at me and asked, "Whatcha got, Michael?"

I told him about Lou Martilotta, the Wisconsin bootlegger who received a lighter sentence because the judge had received a large, timely contribution. We suspected that large donation came from Leo and Jane's mysterious cache of $200,000. And I told him Leo was as deeply involved in the bootlegging as anyone, although he made sure to keep his hands clean.

I did not tell him about Mary Beth Keefer.

Earl had friends in Montana who he hired to keep an eye and an ear on Mary Beth. Although Earl had removed the tap from her line when he left town, his friends put on a different one soon after. That tap revealed Leo and Mary Beth talked almost daily. Most of the time, she'd call, though Leo would call about twice a week. These calls, very late at night, would generally last an hour. It was obvious that Leo and Mary Beth had never gotten over each other, but Leo married Jane for her money and connections. Jane knew about Mary Beth, but it didn't bother her. Her real interest was power. She recognized it would be easier to get power through a man and control him than it would be for her to acquire power on her own. In those tapped conversations, Leo Dailey proved to be even more of an ideological zealot than he appeared publicly. He didn't like FDR's policies, inherently distrusted him, remained angry at him for breaking the two-term presidential tradition, and referred to him as "an imperial cripple." But his real disgust lay with Eleanor. "Her Dikeness," as he called her, was completely without moral values and was about to ruin the nation. He honestly felt if he didn't do something to stop these people, the United States would disintegrate.

Leo's mistake was thinking the Washington press corps was as slow and provincial as the Montana press. We were all sharks in search of the story, and we didn't care who was the subject *du jour*. If it wasn't me or BRN, it was Jack Denif and NBC or Ellen Monroe and AP or any of a couple dozen other reporters. Jack said something to me at dinner that night at the Java in between the meatloaf and the pie. "Do you know Hitler likes boys?"

"You mean, Hitler's…?"

"Well, he likes girls, too. He likes boys and girls. He doesn't care who he fucks. Boys, girls, Poland, France, England. He'll fuck anything."

"So what are you saying, Jack? That we should report Hitler's a switch hitter?"

"No. I'm saying there's bigger things that are getting fucked than a socialite and a reporter. I've always said that. I still think the big story, the Really Big Story, is Hitler's plan to invade Russia. But right now, all we can talk about is leg-spreading." The story continued to be big news through April, although nothing new had really transpired. The White House wasn't commenting, Eleanor wasn't traveling (although she did continue to write her column) and the focus was on new domestic initiatives and the War in Europe. Henry Wallace was doing a great deal of traveling and speechmaking, shoring up public support for the Administration. McKay and Kerse had quietly met with Roosevelt in their effort to extract their pound of flesh for Republican-favored legislation, and Roosevelt had given them most of what they wanted. It was widely perceived as a quid pro quo, as long as the quo didn't override the quid. Leo Dailey was, publicly, a quiet congressional freshman, but privately was kicking up all kinds of dust about Eleanor. Earl was still listening to Mary Beth and Leo's phone calls, and kept following the money trail. I continued my show, and that month interviewed Detroit Tigers star Hank Greenberg, ventriloquist Senor Wences, and Joan Crawford.

Greenberg talked about the responsibility of being a Jewish star athlete. He was one of the first to openly mention his Judaism as it related to both baseball and world affairs. He was concerned enough about what Hitler was doing in Europe that he would soon forego the Major Leagues and enlist in the Army for a five-year stint.

Senor Wences, with his staccato "S'alright? S'alright!. OK? OK!", kept me in stitches in the studio with his witty shtick and thick Spanish accent. He was well known to American audiences through movies and various radio appearances. It always struck me as odd, though, a ventriloquist would be popular on radio.

Joan Crawford came across as a no-nonsense movie star, playing the role of a self-sufficient woman. Her most recent role as the title character in *Susan And God,* in which she proselytizes a new religious movement to her family and friends, brought her in to BRN. She was a smart, self-assured businesswoman who steered as far away from politics as possible. She said she let the roles she chose speak for her.

The story really heated up again on April 29th. An above-the-fold, front page story in the Washington Times written by AP Reporter Ellen Monroe contained details of more letters from Lorena Hickok to Eleanor Roosevelt along with a few fresh quotes from Lorena.

Headlined "White House Staffer Talks," Ellen Monroe, through sheer persistence and the network of the sisterhood, managed to get Lorena to say a few things on-the-record. Ellen had followed Lorena for two weeks, and had left dozens of messages for her. The rare times Lorena ventured out these days she was generally with a group of other White House workers. But one afternoon, Lorena soloed across the street to buy some cigars. Ellen approached her as she left the store, and for a few minutes they sat on a bench in view of the White House.

According to the article, Ellen had a copy of another letter with her and read part of it to Lorena.

December 8, 1933
The Androy
Hibbing, Minnesota

My dear,
…Well, here we are at the end of another day, and only six more to go. Darling, I am getting so excited! You're going to be shocked when

you see me. I should be returning to you wan and thin from having lived on a diabetic diet, but I'm afraid I've gained instead of losing weight. Just you or Dr. McIntyre (the White House physician) try to live on green vegetables and fruit, without starch or sugar, in country hotels, where they have nothing but meat, potatoes, pie and cake and see how far you'd go without breaking over. Besides, I feel so perfectly well, and I'm living such an active life, and yet so hungry...

Oh, my dear—I can hardly wait to see you! Day after tomorrow, Minneapolis and letters from you. A week from now—right this minute—I'll be with you!

Good night, my dear. God keep you!

-H

To Ellen's pleasant surprise, Lorena didn't ask to have anything off-the-record. She was smart enough to know that Ellen would be quoting her for attribution. It seemed as if Lorena were glad to be talking about this. The reporter in her felt it important to provide her side to somehow defuse the situation.

"Yes, I wrote that," Lorena admitted to Ellen. "I've written many letters over the years to Mrs. Roosevelt. That's what I do. I'm a writer. That's how I met her. I was a reporter for the Associated Press, just like you are now, covering the campaign of 1932. During the course of that campaign, Mrs. Roosevelt and I became good friends. I felt that our friendship would interfere with my objectivity as a reporter, so when I was offered a job in 1933 to do field reports for the president, I accepted.

"I believed then, as I believe now," Lorena continued, "in the policies that President Roosevelt is crafting. It is my honor to serve him, and I believe, serve my country, in the best way I can. I travel around, I talk with people, I find out what and how the president's policies are affecting average Americans throughout the country, and then I write a report."

Ellen prodded her to explain how she came to write such "intimate" letters to the First Lady. "The word intimate implies certain qualities that I'm not going to talk about. But as I mentioned earlier, Mrs. Roosevelt and I are good friends. On the road, I have a lot of time, and I write a lot of letters to many people."

Do you deny, asked Ellen Monroe, that you and Mrs. Roosevelt enjoy a more physical friendship than most people?

Lorena was nonplussed by the question. "I'm not going to answer that. In this atmosphere, your detractors will make accusations for their own ends, and your supporters will refute whatever accusations come up.

It quickly becomes a finger-pointing, who-can-scream-loudest contest. People will believe what they want to believe."

Ellen asked her what she believed. "I believe there's many more important things to worry about than old letters I admit to writing to Mrs. Roosevelt."

At this point, Ellen wrote in her story, Lorena leaned back on the bench and lit a cigar. "You know, just as Freud said, sometimes a cigar is just a cigar."

The story was explosive, but that line had all the commentators working overtime. B.W. Corkman of The Washington Post strafed Lorena Hickok as "a woman who defends herself through the rantings of a German psychoanalyst whose findings are in complete dispute." Fr. Coughlin spent the bulk of his next broadcast on the implications "of images the cigar conjures that ought not to be conjured in public." They shared the view that a woman who admitted to writing the letters but refused to answer direct questions about the nature of those letters "is quite obviously more than just a friend."

I left a few messages for Ellen, but she was in the eye of Hurricane Media. She finally called back on May 1st, and we agreed to meet on the 4th at her apartment.

Ellen was lovely that night. Her ocean-sand colored hair framed her face, and her green eyes practically twinkled. She was barefoot, wearing brown slacks and an untucked tan blouse. Her apartment was neat and tidy, except for her desk. That was covered with stacks of newspapers, notes, news photos and mail. Lots and lots of mail that she'd received since the story broke, much of it supportive, but not all. Generally the people who didn't sign their letter questioned her lineage, her credentials and her lack of objectivity because she was "just a dumb broad."

I hadn't looked at our meeting as a date, per se, even though it was an evening meeting at her place set up days in advance. But, just to be on the safe side, I brought some flowers and a blueberry pie.

"Do you always bring your colleagues flowers and a pie?" she teased before she let me in.

"I only bring this stuff to Jack," I replied.

She asked me to come in and before I knew it, we were in each other's arms, kissing deeply and passionately. We seemed to fit together, better than I had ever fit with anyone before. It wasn't just physical attraction, although that was certainly part of it. My 6'1" frame had just the right nooks and crannies to envelop her 5'5" totality. More than that, though, we had a mind meld. Ellen and I understood each other. And we understood each other without even having to try.

We made love that night three times. In between lovemaking, we talked about The Story.

I wondered why Lorena had spoken with Ellen. Ellen said, "I think it was purposeful. As much as I was watching Lorena, they were watching me. I believe they - that is, Franklin and Eleanor - decided that they needed to mount some kind of response to the barrage of stories and commentaries. They needed someone who could articulate their position, understood how to play the game, and be willing to take whatever heat came with it. FDR can't do it. Eleanor can't do it. Lucy would be a bad choice, because she's not a public figure. So it came to Lorena. She's experienced, smart, quick, and cagey. In fact, it was probably her idea. She probably said she could figure out a way to talk with me alone. And she did. When I was putting the story together, it struck me that Lorena came out by herself for the first time in weeks. She walked right by me on the way to the store, and almost looked for me on the way out. When I caught up with her, she slowed her pace and we walked right over to the bench and sat down. We sat down. She *wanted* to talk, and she wanted to talk with *me*. Nothing against you, Michael, but you're a man. Lorena wanted to talk with a woman, and who better than the woman who replaced her at AP?"

That night I asked Ellen if she'd be a guest on my show. She laughed, but I persisted. She said she would if her boss said it was OK. I told her I'd call him the next day.

We fell asleep together, but I woke up around 2:30 a.m., kissed her gently, and went home.

May 7, 1941: Josef Stalin becomes the Premier of the Soviet Union.
May 8, 1941: The British RAF attacks Hamburg and Bremen.
May 9, 1941: Great Britain takes control of Iraq.
May 24, 1941: The Bismarck sinks the British battle cruiser HMS Hood.
May 27, 1941: Air and torpedo attacks sink The Bismarck.
May 27, 1941: In a speech, FDR declares an "unlimited national emergency".
June 1, 1941: British forces surrender the island of Crete. Germany captures 17,000 POWs.

Chapter 16 - Parole

Around this time, I was in a meeting in Peter's office with Bart Johnson and Earl. Earl thought it might be somehow helpful if Lou Martilotta was paroled, especially since he'd already done six years for something that was no longer illegal. Earl suggested that Bart represent Lou at his parole hearing in June.

Bart Johnson, the debonair corporate lawyer, immediately declined. Too many conflicts of interest, he said. But he knew some lawyers that might do it, and he could help direct from behind the scenes.

Peter perked up when Bart said this. "Well, I'll be a son of a bitch," Peter Betz roiled. "You can be pretty devious when you want to, Bart."

"Well, it's probably in our best interest, Peter. If he gets out, and we help him, who knows what kind of information he'd be willing to share with us in exchange for his freedom." Bart Johnson paused, then said, "But you didn't hear me say that."

We all laughed. "Hear what?" I asked to another round of guffaws.

Bart said he knew of a young lawyer who was looking to make some money and a name for himself. Hunter Rose, just a few years out of the same law school Bart attended, had declined an offer to join the BRN staff when he graduated. Nothing against BRN, Hunter Rose said, he just wanted his own law firm. But he'd gladly take any cases Bart could throw his way.

Until now, Bart Johnson had never thrown anything Hunter Rose's way. But he kept an eye open, and on those few occasions when he snuck into court to observe Hunter Rose's closing arguments, he was impressed. This seemed like a good job to give to Hunter.

Bart Johnson said that Hunter Rose's fee had to come from Lou Martilotta, without any ties to Bart, BRN, me, anybody. This is how it worked:

Earl went back to Leavenworth to see Lou Martilotta late one mid-May afternoon. Lou didn't expect the visit, but was glad to see Earl.

"How'd that information turn out, Earl? Was it helpful?"

"Yeah, Lou. It was helpful. In fact, I've got something for you." Earl, in full view of the guards, reached into his jacket pocket and pulled out a sealed, letter-sized envelope. There was no writing on the envelope. Earl Mercia slid it over to Lou Martilotta and said, "Lou, if you think of anything else, give me a call. I hope your parole hearing goes well next month. Maybe this will help you get a good lawyer." Earl stood up and said, " Good luck, Lou," as he turned and walked out.

Lou watched Earl leave before he opened the envelope. Inside he found five $1000 bills. Years of poker training allowed him to keep a straight face. But he counted those bills a few times before he quietly folded the envelope, stuck it in his pants pocket, and returned to his cell.

At nine o'clock the next morning, Lou had another unexpected visitor.

"Mr. Martilotta, my name is Hunter Rose. I understand you may need a lawyer for your upcoming parole hearing. I'm quite familiar with your case, and I'd be pleased to represent you, if you'd like."

"Where are you from, Mr. Rose?"

"Washington."

"How do you know about me?"

"I'm a young lawyer with a thirst for justice and an eye on both the news and the future. I make it my business to search for people, like you, who have already paid their debt to society, but can't seem to convince the power brokers of that."

Lou wasn't buying it. "Do you have a card?" Hunter Rose gave him a business card that identified him as Hunter Rose, Counselor At Law, with a Washington DC street address and phone number. "Who are you with, Mr. Rose?"

"I'm an independent lawyer, trying to build up my own firm."

Lou Martilotta thought about this for a minute. "OK, Mr. Rose. I might need some help for my parole hearing. What are your rates?"

Hunter Rose leaned in, then quietly but firmly said, "I've got a deal for you, Mr. Martilotta. If I get you out, you owe me $5000. If you're not paroled, you don't owe me a penny."

Lou sat back in his chair, put his right hand in his right front pants pocket and fingered the folded envelope that still had five $1000 bills in it. Lou burst out laughing. "You got yourself a deal, Mr. Rose."

For the rest of their visit, Lou Martilotta gave Hunter Rose all the details he could think of that might be beneficial to his parole hearing. Hunter Rose told Lou he would be in touch often, and he would be back in Leavenworth at least two days before the parole hearing to go over any last minute details.

Hunter Rose returned to Kansas on June 1st. On the 3rd, he argued successfully on Lou Martilotta's behalf in front of the Parole Board. And on June 4th, Lou Martilotta walked out of Leavenworth side by side with Hunter Rose.

When they got to Hunter Rose's car, Lou Martilotta said, "I'm not exactly sure where you came from. But this is for you." He handed Hunter Rose the envelope with five $1000 bills in it.

"Thank you," Lou said.

The same day Lou Martilotta was paroled, Janine came into the studio shortly before my show was over. She handed me a note that said Peter wanted to see me right away. I figured it was to tell me that Lou was officially out of prison.

Instead, I walked into his office and saw Peter sitting on his couch across from John Nance Garner. Garner's lanky frame draped over the easy chair, his dark blue suit, white shirt and red tie completely in character. My jaw fell quicker than an incompetent high wire performer. John Nance Garner looked me in the eyes and used his best Texas slow drawl, "We meet again."

Peter took over. "Jack and I have been having some discussions over the last few weeks, Michael." It always amazed me that Peter referred to denizens of power by their first names. He did this because, unlike me, he had known these people for decades. "I went down to Texas last week and visited Jack at his home. We talked a lot about what's been going on recently, and I wanted to know what he thought. Can I get you something to drink, Jack?"

"I'll take a whiskey on the rocks."

As Peter Betz got the whiskey for John Nance Garner, he continued briefing me. "Jack's been having a good time at his house. He's been enjoying his retirement with his lovely wife Ettie. How old are you now, Jack?"

"Seventy-three."

"Seventy-three. You've served your country long and well." Turning to me, Peter said, "Jack's thinking that maybe he can do some more for his country. That's why he's made this private trip back to Washington from Texas." He handed the whiskey to Garner.

Garner took a sip and fixed his gaze on me. "You've gotten to be a pretty big deal since we first met. That's all I hear now, wherever I go. Michael Audray, Michael Audray, Michael Audray on," he drawled and dragged, "Bee Are Enn." He took another sip, set the glass down on the coffee table and looked back at me. "That was quite an ambush you laid on me, Michael. I must admit I was ill prepared for those kind of questions. The thing is, though, you had it right." I glanced at Peter but didn't say anything. "Or, I should say, Peter had it right." We all smiled, though I tried to suppress mine.

Garner grabbed the whiskey glass again. "Do you know about my Bureau of Education?" he asked me in that slow drawl.

"I've heard a little bit about it. When you were the minority leader, you and the Speaker, Nick Longworth, hosted informal gatherings inside a little-used room in the Capitol where all the members of the House could meet and have a drink, even though it was Prohibition."

Garner seemed impressed. "That's right, Michael. I see you've done your homework. Nick and I called ours the Bureau of Education, but when Joe Cannon was Speaker, he called his The Boar's Head Club. We'd all get together and get to know one another and get some work done over a drink. That's how I met Peter." I looked quizzically at both of them. "Peter supplied the booze. When was that, Peter?"

"Oh, Jesus, Jack, that must have been around 1919 or 1920."

"Twenty-some years ago. Hmmm," Garner mused. He took another sip and said, "Your whiskey was as good as this stuff, Peter."

Peter chuckled. "Only the best for my friends on The Hill."

Garner adjusted himself in the chair and focused his attention on me. "Peter called me and asked if he could visit me in Texas. I said sure. So he came down last week and we talked about all this sex stuff. He wondered if I knew anything."

His words just hung there. He kept looking at me, glass in hand but not to his lips. Finally, I asked, "Well, do you?"

"Yes." Garner leaned back again, took another sip and waited for me again.

133

"What do you know?" I eventually asked.

Garner paused and said, "Not so fast."

I looked at Peter and asked, "What's going on?"

Peter stood up from the couch and walked over to his desk. "Jack knows a great deal about what goes on inside the White House, having been there every day for the past eight years. And he's willing to talk about all of it - all of it - in an on-air interview with you. But he doesn't want to be ambushed again." Now I leaned back in my chair. "He's willing to do a live interview if we establish certain ground rules."

"Such as?"

"He wants to know what questions you're going to ask"

"What?" I was astounded that Peter was even bringing this up. "Does he want to write the questions, too?"

Garner just sat there and smiled as Peter answered. "Hang on, Michael. Just slow down a second. You can write the questions. Jack just wants to see them before you ask. He doesn't want any questions asked that he doesn't agree to, and he wants us to agree on the order they'll be asked."

"Peter, you're out of your mind," I practically exploded. "This isn't an interview, it's theatre. You were the one who always told me to keep the element of surprise as a weapon. That's what makes for good interviews, when you ask someone something they're not expecting."

"Well, there are exceptions to every rule, Michael. What we're talking about is not a surprise-filled interview. What we're talking about is an in-depth conversation with the man who was at the right hand of power for eight years. We'll get a lot of news out of this, Michael." Peter gave me his grizzled veteran look, the one that alerted me this would enhance both my reputation and the network's.

"Son," Garner drawled, "I'll blow the lid off this goddamn story."

I laughed out loud. "I'm sure you could. Are you sure you want to?"

That's when John Nance Garner, with inside information only he could possibly have, along with a decades-long national reputation and credibility, simply sipped his whiskey, leaned back in his chair, and smiled.

"Here's what Jack and I have agreed to so far, Michael," Peter began. "The interview will be live and last the entire hour. It will be billed as an in-depth conversation with the former vice-president, and will cover his entire career in politics. The questions will go chronologically, and we won't get into the FDR-Lucy thing until there's about fifteen minutes left. We'll get the list of questions to him in about two weeks, and he'll review them. He'll let us know if there's any questions he won't answer, but he won't provide us with questions to ask. He'll honestly answer any approved question we throw at him. And, Michael, this will be the only interview he does. We get the exclusive."

It seemed pretty straightforward. "So I get to ask you any questions at all, and you'll answer them as long as you know ahead of time what those questions are?"

Garner replied, "That's right."

"And you want to see these questions at least two weeks before you come on my show?"

"Yes."

"And you'll do the show live, from our studio?"

"I'd rather do it in Texas."

"It would be easier and sound better, Jack, if you did it here," Peter chimed in. "I'll bring you up to Washington for the interview."

Garner acquiesced.

I picked up a calendar, turned to them and said, "Mr. Garner, how about coming on our network at noon on the 4th of July?" Both Peter Betz and John Nance Garner smiled at the sheer irony. "That'll be our second anniversary, and maybe you'll stay a little longer for an interview this time. Plus, that'll give us time to get the interview prepared and do some promotional announcements."

"That'll be fine," Garner said, sipping his whiskey. "I like that."

"Are you staying in DC tonight?" I wondered. Garner said he was staying at The Knapp, and I suggested a late-evening rendezvous at his hotel room to "get to know each other in our own Bureau of Education."

"Peter," Garner drawled, "you've taught this boy well." Then to me he said, "Come by around 9:30 p.m. Be discreet."

"Absolutely," I said.

We shook hands and I excused myself. Peter Betz and John Nance Garner continued talking privately over a second whiskey, while I went to my office and called Earl.

I told Earl that I was meeting Garner in his hotel room at 9:30 p.m. to discuss a potential interview. I told him I wanted him to somehow get a picture of me with Garner during that meeting. I said I needed Leverage. Earl, amused, told me not to worry.

I'd been to The Knapp enough to know my way around. I walked in the service entrance and said hello to some people I knew who worked there. They didn't bat an eye when I entered the room service elevator and took it to the 10th floor. I walked right up to room 1006, and promptly at 9:30 p.m. I knocked on the door.

John Nance Garner, confident I was alone, opened it. But I did have a friend with me.

"I figured the guy they call Cactus Jack would like Jack Daniels."

"Come on in," Garner motioned, his smile instantly widening.

It was a warm night, and we sat by the open window and talked for a couple hours. He was a much more experienced drinker than I, and we nearly polished off the bottle. But we got to know each other a little, similar to boxers meeting for a rematch.

Generally, we kept to the topic at hand, which was going over areas that we'd cover in our interview. I had done a lot of research on Garner for our initial broadcast, and I reviewed my notes before I went to The Knapp. He'd been in the public eye for more than forty years, and there was a tremendous amount of ground to cover. We only had an hour on the air - about forty-five minutes, really, when you consider the commercials and the news breaks - so this session with Garner would certainly help me prepare the list of questions I needed to submit to him.

I left around midnight. We agreed I would send my list of questions to him by June 20th at a private address in Texas he provided. He'd let me know if anything was out of bounds by June 27th. And he'd arrive in Washington on July 3rd.

John Nance Garner also promised he wouldn't grant any interviews to any competing news organizations until at least January 1st.

I was a happy guy.

June 5, 1941: The US secretly transfers 4000 Marines to Iceland.
June 6, 1941: FDR seized 80 more foreign merchant ships in US ports
to be used for the Lend-Lease convoys.
June 8, 1941: British and Free-French troops invade Lebanon and
Syria.

Chapter 17 – Ellen the Guest

The next few weeks were spent poring over research material for the Garner interview. When I looked over my original notes for our initial broadcast, I was surprised how detailed I was. But I never got to ask any of those questions.

In preparing for this one, though, I had a much better sense of myself, the format, our place in the news chain, and Garner's irascibility. I had no trouble coming up with questions. At one point I had over two hundred questions. But I knew I really only had time for about ten. I planned on sending Garner twenty questions, just in case he wasn't as verbose as I figured he'd be.

I also had to prep for my daily show. Even though it took some considerable arm twisting, I was able to land an interview for June 10th: Ellen Monroe, AP Reporter.

Ellen and I had talked nearly every day since early May and had seen each other a handful of times. Her editors at first refused to let her come on BRN, citing both her hectic schedule, her primary responsibility to the AP, and competitive pressures. Ellen had since written three more articles chronicling the relationship between Eleanor and Lorena, and with each succeeding AP story, more and more papers ran it on their respective front pages.

But I kept after her editors, and eventually they agreed. Or I wore them down. Ellen was fine with the idea of appearing on my show, as long as I promised to keep it on the story and not ask anything personal. I promised.

After I secured her editors' consent, I was flabbergasted to learn I had to convince Peter. To this point, BRN had never interviewed any member of a competing news organization. Peter was concerned that by giving her access, and by association, giving the AP access to our national audience, we were diluting our ownership of the story while simultaneously boosting a competitor. I pointed out Ellen had written four stories on Eleanor and Lorena, all of which ran in the country's biggest newspapers. Almost everyone who would listen to our interview would have also read her articles. We were merely providing another platform for the dissemination of this angle. I agreed it would be different if I wanted to interview Jack Denif from NBC, but Ellen was a newspaper reporter. Peter relented.

He also figured out we were sleeping together.

I was nervous the morning of our interview. I told Ellen I'd have to ask some cursory personal stuff, like her credentials, and then we'd spend the rest of the time talking about her investigation and articles. I told myself to keep relatively dispassionate, so no listener could tell we shared a deepening affection.

"It's my pleasure today to welcome the nationally renowned writer for the Associated Press, Ellen Monroe," I began after the news finished. "Miss Monroe has written a series of articles over the past month detailing the *friendship* of First Lady Eleanor Roosevelt and current White House staffer Lorena Hickok. Miss Monroe, I'm glad to have you here today."

"Please, call me Ellen. And it's nice to be with you, Michael." She winked at me when she said that. Above all, Ellen was constantly very cool and collected.

"Let's start with a little of your background, Ellen. Where are you from, and how did you get interested in journalism?"

"I grew up in Ainsworth, Nebraska," she said. "My parents always encouraged me to do whatever I felt strongly about, and one of the things I loved most of all was writing. My parents really wanted me to be the first person in our entire family to go to college, and they promised they'd help me get wherever I wanted to go. Well, growing up in Nebraska, all you ever see is cornfields and wheat fields. There's really no water to speak of. I wanted to be near the water, and I wanted to learn how to write well, so with the help of some of my high school teachers, I applied to Pepperdine University in southern California. I got a scholarship and graduated in 1936. Then I went back to my hometown and worked for a while on the local paper. I moved to Lincoln and covered the City Beat for the Lincoln News. In fact, that's where I first met Mrs. Roosevelt. She was very inspiring, especially to a young woman like me. I felt the need to cover a larger portion of the world than I could in Lincoln, so I applied to the Associated Press. And, they hired me," she said with a grin in her voice.

"How long have you been with AP?"

"A little more than a year, Michael. About fourteen months."

"You're job title is?"

"My official job title is Associated Press Political Reporter.'"

"Who initially had that position?"

"Well," Ellen said, "if you're asking who I replaced, it was a woman named Dale Elliott. She left when she got married."

"But didn't the Associated Press kind of create this position a while ago, specifically to encourage women reporters?"

"Yes, I guess that's right."

"And who initially had the job that you now have?"

"Lorena Hickok," she said evenly.

"Had you ever met Lorena Hickok before your most recent series of articles?"

"Yes. One of my first assignments for AP was to cover a press conference Mrs. Roosevelt was having. I knew who Lorena Hickok was and her importance in the history of the Associated Press. I went up and introduced myself to her, and actually, I thanked her for cutting the path that I was now following."

"Are you and she friends?" I actually was wondering. This was one of those questions I'd never asked Ellen before. And again, Ellen flashed her cool calmness with her answer.

"I can't say we're friends. We certainly know each other now, and I respect her a great deal for what she's done for women in journalism. But I don't think I'm someone she would call up on a Friday night and ask to go bowling or whatever."

That made me laugh out loud. "Bowling? You'd go bowling on a Friday night?"

"Whatever," Ellen replied, laughing. Then, more seriously, she added, "I hope she respects the work I'm doing. I really don't think I'd be where I am today if it wasn't for the trails made by both Lorena Hickok and Eleanor Roosevelt."

"That's an interesting point, Ellen. So here you are, by your own admission, the beneficiary of the pioneering work done by the First Lady and a former AP reporter, and now you're investigating their behavior."

"I take issue, Michael," Ellen began, "with the notion that I'm investigating their behavior. I'm a reporter who is following leads on a developing story that was put into the public domain by other forces. The stories I've written have dealt with their private behavior, but that's just where the leads have taken me."

"So you're not investigating the private behavior of Mrs. Roosevelt and her ghost writer?"

"No, I don't see it that way. And I also don't believe that Lorena Hickok is Mrs. Roosevelt's ghost writer."

"Really?"

"Really. Lorena is a definite influence on the First Lady's writing style, but I believe Mrs. Roosevelt writes all her own columns for the newspapers."

"Alright. I'll take your word on that. Your articles - and there have now been four published articles since early May - imply that Mrs. Roosevelt and Lorena Hickok have a, shall we say, special friendship. Is that accurate?"

"I can see how you could draw those conclusions, Michael."

"The most explosive parts of each of your articles, Ellen, have been the letters that were written from Lorena to Eleanor. How did you end up with these letters?"

Ellen merely laughed. "Nice try, Michael. But I'm not going to reveal my sources. I am convinced, though, that they are authentic."

"I would guess they're authentic because Lorena Hickok admitted to you, in the first article published, that she did, indeed, write those letters. She said she wrote lots of letters."

"Yes, she did. But she also said she wrote hundreds of letters to many people, as well as the field reports she was filing to the president."

"As I understand it, Lorena has been providing reports to President Roosevelt for years. Explain Lorena's job, and how she came to get it."

"Back in 1932, Lorena Hickok had the same beat I now have. She was covering the presidential campaign between Franklin Roosevelt and Herbert Hoover when she met Eleanor. They became friends during the campaign, and at the end of it, when FDR was elected, Lorena felt that she could no longer objectively cover the Roosevelts. Additionally, she truly believed in the policies that President Roosevelt wanted to enact, and she offered her services as a writer to go around the country to both gauge the mood of the people and to determine if the new president's policies were having the desired effect. She has retained that job to this day, although it has evolved as the Administration is now in its third term."

"So from 1932 through 1940, Lorena provided these reports and traveled around the country on behalf of the president."

"Yes."

"And she still has the same basic job today?"

"Yes."

"So why did she move into the White House shortly after the election last November?"

"I don't really have an answer to that, Michael," she stated. "Anything I say would be mere speculation, and I'm not in the business of speculating."

"I am," I said. "Come on, Ellen, speculate."

We both laughed, but she wouldn't say another word on-the-air. Actually, we had talked about this, and I knew what her thoughts were. I knew she believed that Lorena and Eleanor had reached a point where they wanted to see each other all the time, and moving into the White House under the guise of a senior staffer was the easiest way with the least scrutiny to accomplish that. I was teetering whether or not to keep prodding her, but Ellen shot me a look that told me to simply Move On To The Next Question.

I did.

"How many letters between these two women have you read, Ellen?"

"Have I read? Hmmmm." Ellen paused, mentally counting. "I would guess around fifteen or so."

"What time period do they cover?"

"They start in 1933 and I've seen a few from last year."

"Have you seen any letters from Mrs. Roosevelt to Lorena Hickok?"

"A couple."

"You've seen a couple letters from Mrs. Roosevelt to Lorena?" This was actually news to me. As recently as three days ago, Ellen told me she hadn't seen any.

"Yes."

"I haven't read anything about those letters in any of your articles, though. Why not?"

"Michael, it's because I have not yet been able to secure an interview with the First Lady to get her side, to see what she has to say. And until I do, I don't think there's going to be any way that those letters will make it into print."

"How noble." The sarcasm dripped from my lips.

"I'm just being a good journalist, Michael." Ellen's voice had a touch of anger in it.

I moved on, hoping she wasn't going to stay mad. "According to your articles, Lorena has now spoken with you four separate times, each time privately but in public locations. Why do you think Lorena spoke with you?"

"There's a couple reasons, actually. I believe that as an AP reporter, and especially one that currently holds the position she once held, Lorena had a built-in level of trust. I think she wanted to speak to a woman reporter, and I happened to be it. And I also believe she wanted to get her viewpoint out in the public at least a little bit, in an effort to provide some counterbalance to the chest-thumping that is going on across the country."

"Chest thumping? Do you think there is too much being made about their relationship? Do you think it's not an important issue?"

"At this point, I can't afford to have an opinion. I'm a reporter, looking for facts to fill a story. All I'm doing is reporting the facts as I learn them, and, I might add, as I corroborate them."

"Has Lorena ever contacted you directly and asked to meet with you?"

"No."

"Do you think that you're being used with these private meetings in public places? That is, are you their designated mouthpiece?"

"Well, Michael, I believe that other people see us talking in public. I'm sure that we're being watched. But Lorena Hickok and Eleanor Roosevelt would be extremely disappointed if one of the women they inspired to political journalism by their actions was merely a puppet, or a mouthpiece as you call it, for their particular viewpoint. I am a reporter. I try to be as objective as possible. I try to write as objectively as I can and let the reader decide. And I believe that's what they would want me to do and to be."

"Ellen Monroe, you're a fine reporter. The Associated Press is lucky to have you. Thank you for being my guest today."

"It's been my pleasure."

We sat in the studio for a few minutes and talked. Ellen was relieved that it was over, and astounded at how fast it went. Then she said, "I can understand why people get mad at you."

"Mad at me? Are you mad at me?"

"Well, not really. But I got a little angry when we were talking about the letters from Eleanor. And I get it now."

"Get what now, Ellen?"

"I get why some of your guests sound like they hate you. You're so comfortable in this studio. You're here everyday, you've got the lighting set up just the way you like it, you've got a crowd of people on the street watching you, you know how to play to them. I mean this is your home. This is your turf. Anybody who comes in here is at a disadvantage, because you control all the things that happen in here. And you listen so well, so when you follow up with a question about something somebody just said, you catch them off-guard."

"I do?"

"Yeah, Michael, you do. Like that chest-thumping question. I wasn't even aware I said it. And you came right back at me with a question about chest-thumping. Maybe I'm different because I'm a writer and I have time to re-think what I want to say and how I want to say it before it gets printed. Actors may be used to talking…"

"No, they're used to memorizing dialogue."

"…but this was unnerving. I'm really glad it's over."

"You're not mad at me, though?"

"No, Michael," Ellen's voice sweetened, "I'm not mad."

"Well, would you like to go bowling Friday night?"

June 14, 1941: FDR freezes all German assets. The State Department closes all German consul and propaganda offices in the US. June 16, 1941: FDR expels all German diplomats.

Chapter 18 - Jack's Investigation

The recent spate of articles by Ellen and some others had prompted Leo Dailey to issue a few press releases reminding voters he was "continuing to look into this increasingly scandalous situation." He had a loyal staff that followed up with their media contacts to ensure they'd gotten The Dailey Word.

Jack Denif had been working on his Leo Dailey story for about two months. Jack was competent, thorough, and principled. I admired him quite a bit. He was a first-rate reporter who had seen a lot in his various NBC assignments around the world. Every other reporter was probing The Affairs of State. Jack Denif had been concentrating on the Leo Dailey trail.

One night, soon after Ellen had been on the show, I ran into Jack at the main branch of the DC Library. In his standard directness, Jack didn't say hi, but he grinned and asked, "How long have you and Ellen Monroe been, you know...?"

I was a bit startled. "Was it that obvious?"

Jack shook his head no, but said he actually saw the sparks fly at The Java Diner a couple months ago. I told him we'd started seeing each other shortly after that. "She seems pretty smart," he acknowledged, "and she's a damn good writer. How's she getting those letters and interviews?"

"Honest to God, Jack, I don't know. What are you doing here?"

"I was just about to ask you that, Michael. What's a famous radio star doing at a library in the evening?"

"I'm just doing some background research for an interview I've got coming up." I didn't tell him I was checking details about John Nance Garner. "So, what brings the famous NBC reporter to a library in the evening?"

"I'm still digging up shit on Leo Dailey and his connections with Rico Tozzi."

"Having any luck?'

"Yeah, actually," he said as he lit another cigarette.

"Maybe I can help you, too, Jack." I grabbed a blank piece of paper from him and wrote down Lou Martilotta's name and address. "Lou just got out of prison, and I think this is where he's staying."

Jack looked at it for a moment. "Baltimore? I've been trying to track him down, but the prison didn't have any info, or at least they said they didn't. I tried every place in Milwaukee and Chicago that I could think of, but couldn't find him." He took a deep drag on his cigarette. "Baltimore? How do you know this?"

"I guess my sources are sometimes better than yours." I smiled.

"Yeah, that'll be the day." He stared at the paper some more, then asked, "Why are you giving this to me?"

I looked in his eyes, and I said, "Well, I figure you can soften him up, and I'll knock him out." I meant it, too. I figured if Jack Denif got Lou Martilotta to talk on-the-record about his connection with Leo Dailey, I could really get Lou to blab in a later interview.

Jack called Lou Martilotta from the pay phone at the library. They agreed to meet the next night in the bar at The Knapp.

Jack got there a few minutes before the scheduled rendezvous, and as he told Lou, he'd grab a table in the back corner, facing the door. He ordered a drink from the waitress, but a casually dressed fifty-year-old with a medium build, wiry gray hair and glasses delivered it. "Lou?"

"Jack?"

Lou sat down and told Jack he'd been at the bar for a while. "It feels good to get out and have a drink without worrying that the cops are gonna arrest you."

Jack and Lou hit it off. Jack had a way of getting people to trust him, of getting them to tell him things they didn't think they'd tell anyone. Lou was simply enjoying his new freedom, not quite sure how it happened or how he fit into The Affairs of State. But he wasn't questioning anything.

They talked for hours, the reporter and the bootlegger, each drinking to keep up with the other. Lou found Jack to be a world-class drinker. Jack was up front with Lou, telling him he was investigating Leo Dailey's background because he had thrust himself into the limelight of the current sexcapade.

Lou was open about his involvement with Leo and Jane Dailey. He was willing to go on the record about his bootlegging days, and to a lesser extent, his involvement with the Halls of Montana. Lou's concern, although his operation had long since been dismantled and he vowed to be a legitimate businessman, was more a matter of personal ethics. He believed he still owed it to the Halls - and to all his other customers - to retain an air of silence.

As the night wore on, though, Jack pointed out that in the years since the 18th Amendment was repealed, bootlegging stories had taken on a certain swagger. Hollywood made movies about bootlegging, from Capone to comedies. It was chic to drink, and even more chic to know how to make an extremely dry martini.

Lou eventually agreed to speak on the record about his entire bootlegging career, provided Jack stayed away from his earlier arrests and convictions. Jack had no trouble agreeing to that, since he wasn't interested in Lou as the story. He only wanted Lou Martilotta for part of the story.

They agreed to meet when they weren't drinking. Jack pressed Lou to meet the day after next, with Jack traveling to where Lou was staying.

Jack arrived at the Baltimore row house near the Inner Harbor. Lou was staying with his brother Henry, a little younger, a lot taller, but completely bald. Henry Martilotta had, at one time, been Lou's partner in Milwaukee, but Henry's wife demanded a legitimate life. They moved to where they knew no one, Baltimore, and began a family. Henry got a job as an accountant for Arthur Andersen, specializing in preparing the tax returns and filings for the major corporations in Maryland. Henry's wife died unexpectedly, and he was left to raise two boys. When Lou was released from prison, he offered to come help Henry with the kids for a while. Henry accepted the offer.

Jack Denif arrived right on time, carrying nothing but a reporter's notebook and two pens. Lou was the only one at the house, and offered coffee instead of whiskey. Jack took the coffee, and they began to talk for nearly six hours.

A lot of the information Jack already knew. But there were some nuggets that emerged. On one of her yearly trips to Milwaukee, Jane Hall Dailey was introduced to Thomas Marety, who was then the City Editor for the Milwaukee Journal. Marety took a liking to Jane Hall Dailey, who was most interested in getting this Midwest editor to write a story about her up-and-coming Montana politician-husband. Marety said no one in Wisconsin was at all interested in a Montana lawyer. However, Jane Hall Dailey batted her eyes, licked her lips, and gave Thomas Marety the blowjob of his life in Lou's office. The next month, a profile of Montana political neophyte Leo Dailey appeared in the Milwaukee Journal, a piece that became the focal point in the first Dailey campaign.

A few years later, Thomas Marety became the Editor of The Chicago Tribune, the same paper using Leo Dailey as their unnamed source concerning Eleanor and Lorena.

Lou confirmed the Halls of Montana were steady, regular customers for his alcohol, but they were only middle of the pack players. The Halls would regularly spend $20,000 month, whereas his top customer topped out at nearly $100,000 month. His operation, which included some police, political and newspaper payoffs, was grossing almost $5 million year, with Lou pocketing over a half-million himself.

When he was arrested and convicted, the federal government seized all his equipment, all his property, and all his bank accounts. Today, though he was a free man, Lou was penniless, "but at least I don't have syphilis like Capone."

The interview with Lou Martilotta was the last piece Jack Denif needed to put together his story on Leo Dailey. He was lobbying NBC to air this as a series, but NBC told Jack that the series would air if, and only if, Leo Dailey jumped back into the forefront of The Affairs of State.

Jack knew it wouldn't be long. He diligently put the series together, writing, re-writing, checking sources again and again. He was ready.

June 21, 1941: British and Free-French troops capture Damascus.
June 21, 1941: Hitler orders German subs not to attack US warships.
June 21, 1941: Hitler convinces Mussolini to let Rommel invade Egypt.
June 22, 1941: 3 million German soldiers and 3300 tanks invade
Russia. Russia counters with 3.2 million soldiers and 20,000 tanks.
June 23-24, 1941: The Luftwaffe wipes out most of the Russian Air
Force aircraft, still on the ground.

Chapter 19 – Buckfield's Plea

On Thursday, June 19th, I settled on the twenty questions I wanted to ask John Nance Garner. I showed them to Peter before I mailed them. He said to me, "Don't feel obligated to stick to these questions. Garner wants to feel in control, but we own the microphones. Ask him at least a zinger or two. He won't walk out this time, I guarantee it."

I smiled at Peter. "OK." That's all I said. I had come to believe that Peter would ambush his grandmother if it brought listeners to BRN. For him, there was no other reason to be in radio. If no one was listening, what was the point of even turning on the electricity?

Peter knew all the upper echelon governmental heavyweights. He was their contemporary, and to a varying degree, had managed to learn enough about their personal lives to keep them off-balance and respectful. He had Leverage. So when he guaranteed that Garner wouldn't walk out of the studio if I strayed from the approved questions, I trusted him.

But I'd learned a little about keeping guests off-balance, too. I included a hand-written note with my questions that read:

Mr. Garner,
We may not get to all these questions, but here's what I'd like to talk
about. I'm sure you'll find these acceptable.
Sincerely,
Michael Audray

I paper clipped that note to the typewritten list of questions. The last page, though, was a photograph of John Nance Garner and me talking in his hotel room at The Knapp a few weeks earlier. In the photo, Garner is sitting in an easy chair holding a glass and a bottle of Jack Daniels. I'm just sitting there.

Earl had given me the picture the day after I privately met with Garner. I didn't even ask how he got it, but I knew he would. He actually had taken a few rolls of pictures, but this one, showing Garner holding the whiskey bottle, was clearly our favorite.

As it happened, Earl came by my office that day and laid out a transcript of a phone call from Leo Dailey to Mary Beth Keefer on June 3rd.

Leo told Mary Beth that Lou Martilotta had been paroled. He was worried that I'd interview Lou, and worried more about what Lou would say. He told Mary Beth that Jane was "taking charge" of finding out where Lou was and what his plans were, and that they planned to offer Lou a job. Doing what? Mary Beth asked. Doing nothing, absolutely nothing except keeping quiet.

He also told Mary Beth that Jane was going to stay in DC during July, but he'd be coming back to shake hands and keep his face in the community. He promised he'd spend a great deal of time with Mary Beth at "the cabin in Bozeman." Apparently, Mary Beth knew what and where it was, because all she said was great, she'd get the time off and meet him there.

Earl suggested watching Jane Hall Dailey to see where she went, what she did, who she called while Leo was in Montana. I agreed. Earl said he'd handle the details.

"Thanks for running this by me, Earl, without telling Peter first," I said. "I appreciate it."

"You're OK, Michael. You're catching on."

Earl had been keeping himself busy trying to find Ellen's source for the Lorena Letters, but to no avail. He'd snapped a photo of Ellen and Lorena sitting on a bench near the White House, but I didn't tell Ellen. He was also managing a few phone taps in Montana, tailing Leo around DC, and was now adding Jane Hall Dailey on his to-do list.

Earl excused himself, but invited me to join him for a drink that night around eight o'clock. I met him at his favorite bar, Harrington's, on 8th Street. Earl, rumpled as usual, was sitting at the far end of the bar, drinking a beer. I sat down next to him, and he ordered a beer for me with the simple flick of his left index finger. I'd come to respect Earl. I didn't know how he did what he did, but I knew he was good at it. He knew it, too. We talked about baseball a bit. DiMaggio had his long hitting streak going, and Ted Williams was still hitting around .400. The Senators were having another mediocre season, but Earl Mercia spent more than a few afternoons at the ballpark. It wasn't merely for recreation. Earl often was keeping an eye on a client, either a member of the House or the Senate, or a Cabinet secretary or a Naval officer or some such. Even then, at Harrington's, Earl wasn't totally off-duty. Not only was he talking to me, he was keeping an eye on a woman in the corner booth.

"She knows Lucy," he explained, sipping his beer.

We stayed for a while, and just as I was getting ready to go about 9:30 p.m., Earl asked me to come by his office right around the corner. I'd never been there. It was a small, cluttered office on the second floor, with no sign, just a simple, hand-painted name on the glass door. It was a two-room office, with the outer room a reception area. "I don't have a secretary. I like to keep all the money I make. Besides," he muttered, "I haven't found anybody I can really trust."

His desk was neat and straight, but he had files and photos scattered throughout the office. He sat down at his desk, poured himself a bourbon, offered one to me. I declined. He started skimming through his files, stopping every now and then to hand me one. "Look at this!" he'd say with glee. Each file he handed me contained photos of well-known Washingtonians, a mixture of politicians and celebrity entertainers, in various degrees of compromising acts. I must have been slack-jawed, as Earl got a good laugh at my expense. Few of the pictures were fresh, although they weren't more than two years old. "I should really organize these sometime," Earl said, mostly to himself.

After about ten minutes of searching, Earl found the file he wanted. "Ah," he grunted, set his bourbon down, and walked back to his chair. He sat down, looked at the contents, nodded, then looked inside another file sitting on his desk. He constantly nodded his head, mumbled "Yeah, yeah, yeah" and kept comparing. Finally, he picked out a picture from each and said, "Look at *this!*"

I studied the two pictures side-by-side. Both were photos of Jane Hall Dailey, but taken seven years apart. Both were taken at The Knapp, and in both photos, Jane Hall Dailey was undeniably in the full throes of coital delirium with Arch Hook, Rico Tozzi's lawyer and right-hand man. Earl pointed to the one in my right hand and said, "I took that one two nights ago. It just took me awhile to piece it together. I knew I'd seen them together before, but I couldn't quite place it."

I sat down and asked for that bourbon. As Earl poured, he told me the story in short, succinct Earl-speak. "Back in '34, I was doing some work for GM. They wanted me to get some stuff on the labor organizers who were lobbying Congress. My job was to follow everybody who came to DC. This guy, Arch Hook, was everywhere. But he wasn't an organizer. Turns out he's a lawyer for a Detroit guy who knows all the organizers. I thought he'd met this dame in a bar and they just ended up screwing. Didn't give it much thought. So the other night, after I got the transcript, I decided to keep an eye on ol' Janie. I followed her to The Knapp. She went right up to a room. I found out which room, got in position - just as she was doing," he chuckled, "and took the pictures. All that night, I had the feeling I'd seen the two of them before. But I couldn't place it. Until now."

Arch Hook was in Washington for meetings with the various congressional members, including a private meeting with Leo Dailey. Leo told Jane, who then arranged her tryst with Arch Hook.

I used Earl's phone to call Jack Denif. "There's an interesting twist to your story on Dailey, Jack," I told him. I briefly explained there was proof the Daileys were a tag team using every means necessary to move up the Washington power chain. He wanted to see the pictures. Earl said OK, as long as I promised to bring the pictures back by midnight. I agreed, and told Jack to be at Harrington's at eleven.

Jack and I had a beer together and talked about all the pieces of the Dailey puzzle that we knew. Jack's investigation, coupled with Earl's handy work, revealed the freshman Republican congressman from Montana gained office through the not-so-subtle influence of the Mob and its tentacles in Organized Labor. He was focused on power and influence, and Jane was helping him get it.

I saw Ellen the next morning and updated her on the latest developments. She wasn't surprised we had visual proof of Jane's favors to the powerful. She was in the process of putting another story together about Eleanor and Lorena, this time without letters. The focus of this story, she said, was Eleanor's White House travel records, and the coincidental nature of Lorena's itineraries. Speeches, hotel stays and travel plans were being researched, and she figured it would be ready in about three days. She and I made plans to have dinner that night at an Italian restaurant.

When I got to BRN, I had a message to call Sharon Tozzi. I hadn't talked with Sharon in quite a while and I had no idea what it was about. I called her right away, and she was all business.

"Hi, Michael," she said. "Thanks for returning my call."

"No problem. How are you?"

"Fine. Listen, Sen. Buckfield wants to be a guest on your show next week."

"You're kidding."

"No, I'm not. It's his idea, his request, and he wants to do it as soon as you can get him on next week."

"Uh, let me look at my schedule. What's he want to talk about?"

"Hitler and Mussolini, what they're planning and why we have to get involved."

"OK. Uh, how about Tuesday?"

"Fine."

"Do you need to check?"

"No. He told me to arrange it. He'll be there by 11:30 Tuesday."

"Hey, I've got a question for you, Sharon. Do you know a guy named Rico Tozzi?"

"Yeah." I could hear the disdain in her voice.

"What do you know about him?"

"He's my uncle. He's my dad's brother. He's a small time hood who runs a bowling alley in Detroit. My dad hasn't talked with him in years. I haven't seen him since I was about six. Why?"

"Well, seems the bowling alley has been pretty good to him. Rico Tozzi is unquestionably a key player in Leo Dailey's rise to Congress."

'What?" Sharon Tozzi was completely flummoxed.

"Your Uncle Rico met Leo back in '32, and has been a major, and I mean major contributor to Leo's political campaigns ever since. He's got his fingers in a lot of stuff, Sharon."

"You're kidding me," Sharon spouted. "I had no idea. Honest to God, you gotta believe me, Michael. You're talking about Rico Tozzi, the bowling alley owner?"

"Rico Tozzi, the bowling alley owner from Detroit."

"Oh my God. I've got to call my dad. I'll talk to you later."

That was it. She hung up. Sharon Tozzi, the first woman to be a senator's chief of staff, was young, bright, very intelligent, and focused. She was also the niece of an emerging figure in an ever-widening scandal.

Right before Sharon and Buckfield showed up on Tuesday, I received a telegram from John Nance Garner.

Questions are fine. The picture was clear. Just like the one of you and your girlfriend. JNG

I smiled, folded it up and put it in my pocket. I walked down to the studio when Sharon and the senator arrived. I shook his hand and thanked him for coming. Then I asked Sharon if I could see her for a second. We stepped around the corner and I handed her the telegram.

"What does this mean?" she asked.

"I'm working on an interview with Garner. It's his first interview since he retired. I met with him privately, and arranged to get a couple pictures of us taken without him knowing. I sent him some topics I wanted to cover, and I included a picture of him drinking out of a whiskey bottle. So he sent me this telegram today. Looks like he's admitting he was behind those pictures of us."

Sharon just shook her head. "This town," she muttered. "Hey, you believe me that I don't know Rico, don't you? I mean, he is my uncle, but my dad hates him, hates everything he stands for. I had no idea Rico was into whatever it is he's into."

"I believe you."

I welcomed Senator Buckfield to The BRN Midday Conversation. He said he was glad to be on, and hoped he could provide some substantive news. He did.

Just two days before he appeared, Germany declared war on and began an invasion of Russia. "Operation Barbarossa," as it was called, had been in Hitler's plans for a long time, the senator said. Despite a troop build-up along the German-Russian border over the past year to a level "that is now in excess of 150 divisions," Josef Stalin was not expecting the invasion. Intelligence reports indicated that Italy, Finland and Romania would soon join the German forces in the attack on Russia. Senator Buckfield had already been in contact with FDR and suggested an expansion of the Lend-Lease Agreement to include our new ally, the Soviet Union. Buckfield said the president had already considered that notion, and had been in direct contact with Stalin.

Buckfield was very eloquent and articulate in that hour. He discussed the British surrender of Crete, but also their invasion of Baghdad and Lebanon and their capture of Damascus. He spoke knowledgeably about the Rommel-led invasion of Egypt, and the importance of continued diligence and eventual involvement. Buckfield was convinced the United States needed to enter the fray as soon as possible.

Near the end of the hour, I steered the conversation around to The Affairs of State. Senator Paul Buckfield let it fly.

"For the past hour I have been talking with you and your millions of listeners across this great land of ours about matters of deep national and international significance. I cannot stress how important it is that we pay attention to the spreading lunacy that is enveloping the European and African continents. If we don't pay attention to it, or if we allow ourselves to be distracted, the consequences can and will be enormous. If we as a people choose to focus on the allegedly salacious details from the private lives of public personalities, we do ourselves a disservice. We will play into the hands of our enemies, and we will lay ourselves open to potentially devastating incidents. I believe it is much more important to watch and react to world developments rather than watch and react to titillating and tawdry gossip."

"But don't you think, Senator, the public has a right to know what their leaders are up to? The leaders who could be sending our fighting forces into harm's way? The leaders who need to make decisions that affect the world? Don't you think we have a right to know and decide for ourselves about the people who lead?"

"I do believe the public has a right to know about the public actions of their duly elected leaders. But I draw the line at invading anyone's privacy. There are countries that are being invaded at this very moment, and that is a much bigger national concern. These stories about the First Family are a distraction. They must end, and they must end soon. Otherwise, we are in deep trouble."

June 26, 1941: Finland and Hungary declare War on Russia.
June 28, 1941: The Wehrmarcht captures Minsk.
July 3, 1941: Stalin calls for Scorched Earth Policy.

Chapter 20 – Garner's Interview

John Nance Garner arrived in Washington DC the day before our scheduled interview. He flew in from Texas, checked into a room at the Hilton, and had dinner with Peter. Garner hadn't spoken directly with me since our drinking session at The Knapp.

Garner had lived in Washington for the bulk of his life. A member of Congress for over thirty years before he became vice president, he knew his way around town, had many friends, and was owed countless favors. Although he was a well known, high profile person, he was able to glide in and out of wherever he wanted, whenever he wanted.

July 4, 1941 was a Friday. It was the second anniversary of the Betz Radio Network, and we had come a long way. We were now the most-listened to network with nearly 500 affiliates across the country. Other networks were copying our programming philosophy. In the mornings, we offered The BRN Morning News from 6 a.m. - 8 a.m., immediately followed by The BRN Morning Newsmakers until 10 a.m. From then till 11, The Advice Show offered tips to listeners on any number of things from letters that had been received. The BRN Sports Report aired from 11 till noon, and ran down all the previous day's scores and highlights, plus spotlighted the upcoming sporting events. My show aired from noon till 1 p.m. From 1 p.m. till 4 p.m. The BRN Music Box played the day's top songs. Beginning at 4 p.m., The BRN Newsday Wrap went live and non-stop until 7 p.m. A number of different game shows, quiz shows, music programs and sporting events aired nightly from then until 6 a.m.

In just two years, the Betz Radio Network had outworked, out-hustled and outperformed the established networks. CBS had Edward R. Murrow stationed in Europe. Lowell Thomas and Walter Winchell were Jack Denif's co-workers at NBC. Winchell, in fact, had moved almost exclusively away from gossip and entertainment to political commentary, advocating a US entry into the war. Mutual Radio, which until recently had broadcast mostly dramas and soap operas, now offered a great deal of news with Gabriel Heatter, Wythe Williams and Boake Carter.

But we had more listeners, more loyal affiliates, higher ad rates and bigger profits than any other network in America.

On our second anniversary, we had an incredible line-up of special guests who came by our studios to wish us a Happy Birthday. Gene Autry, Artie Shaw, Benny Goodman, Jimmy Dorsey, Gene Krupa and Glenn Miller stopped by and played some songs. Duke Ellington and Louis Armstrong each came by for a chat. The Andrews Sisters popped in unexpectedly and sang "The Boogie Woogie Bugle Boy" outside in front of our studio window. Cab Calloway came and played his musical quiz with our sidewalk audience. Basil Rathbone and William Boyd, better known at the time as Sherlock Holmes and Hopalong Cassidy, wished us well in person. Humphrey Bogart, Orson Welles, Gary Cooper and Joan Fontaine came by with birthday greetings. But the largest cheer of the entire day was reserved for The Brown Bomber, Joe Louis. The heavyweight champ was still a hero for knocking out Max Schmeling in 1938. And in 1941, he defended his heavyweight title seven times.

The Betz Radio Network was sponsoring the nighttime fireworks over The Capitol. All this really meant was that we paid more than half the cost, put up BRN banners all over the place, and had the prime position from which to broadcast them live to our twenty million listeners coast-to-coast.

The network was buzzing that cloudless and ninety degree day. The heat did not dampen any of the energy inside our building, though. Into all this, John Nance Garner quietly entered through a side door.

He'd been expected around 11:15. At 11:20, I went to Peter's office to see if he'd heard from Garner. He was already there, sitting on Peter's couch. Peter was relaxed, on the phone.

I went back to my office, reviewed my notes again before I entered the studio. I placed a fresh pitcher of water, an ice bucket and a bottle of Jack Daniels near Garner's chair. At 11:58, John Nance Garner walked by himself into my studio.

"Welcome to this special edition of The BRN Midday Conversation. I'm Michael Audray," I began. "Two years ago today, at this very minute, the Betz Radio Network began broadcasting coast-to-coast. We've experienced tremendous growth in that time. We've had our share of missteps, but we've also had our share of successes. I'd like to take this opportunity right now to thank everyone who is listening today, and everyone who has listened over the past two years, for making BRN the most listened to network in the United States. My guest today holds the distinction of being both the first-ever guest on our network, and the first-ever guest to walk out of an interview on our network. Since January of this year, he has been living in his home state of Texas, and this is his first interview since he retired from politics. It is our pleasure, my pleasure, to welcome back a man I never thought would set foot in our network again, the former vice president of the United States, John Nance Garner. Thank you for coming, Mr. Garner."

Garner had moved the bottle of Jack Daniels to the floor, unopened. He had poured himself a glass of water, and had settled himself into his chair. He seemed ready to talk. "It's nice to be here."

"Well, let's see if we can keep you here longer than two minutes today," I quipped. Garner shot back, "It depends on what you ask me."

I laughed. "Well, let's start with your background. You were born in Red River County, Texas on November 22, 1868. You'll turn seventy-three this year, and most of your life was spent living in Washington. But your first elected position was a judge, right?"

"Yes. I was a county judge from 1893 to about 1896, then I went into the Texas state legislature."

"But you had higher aspirations. You wanted to get to Washington. Tell me about that."

"Well, the population of Texas was growing, and in the 1900 census, we got some additional congressional seats. I became the chairman of a redistricting committee, and frankly, I made sure I had a pretty good district for myself. I ran in that district in 1902, and I won."

"And you stayed in Washington ever since."

"That's right."

"So even though you claim to be from Texas, you've lived in Washington for more than half your life."

Garner was slightly perturbed, as this wasn't on the approved list of questions. "What's your point?"

"I don't have a point, I'm merely making an observation. You've lived more than half your life in Washington."

"I guess that's right," Garner said as he glared at me. "I had a job to do in Washington, but I never forgot that I was representing my home district in Texas."

"I'm sure you never forgot where you came from, Mr. Garner." I searched through some of my notes and then said, "So you came to

Washington in early 1903, but it took you a few years before you got some really good committee assignments. It wasn't until the '20s that your seniority made you the ranking Democrat on the Ways and Means Committee, and the chairman of the Committee on Committees. What is that, the Committee on Committees, exactly?"

Garner, ever the parliamentarian, casually explained, "That's the committee that assigns Democrats to each committee. We match up members with their skills and interests, or at least we try to."

"Then, after the 1928 elections, you became House minority leader. Congressman Nicholas Longworth was the Speaker of the House, and all reports were that you two had a great friendship. True?"

"That's true," Garner smiled as he said it. "I was the heathen and Nick was the aristocrat."

"Well, explain a little more of how you and Speaker Longworth would work together. I understand you liked to get together with a number of congressmen at the end of each work day."

"That's true, too. When Joe Cannon was Speaker in my early years in the House, he'd host these get-togethers where everybody would have a drink and shoot the breeze. You'd get to know each other, and the legislation sessions would go easier. So Nick and I decided to put together what we called The Bureau of Education. It was a small room, deep inside the Capitol, where we'd all gather at the end of each session for a drink and a few jokes."

"And this was when?"

"Around 1929, 1930."

"But Prohibition was in effect then."

Garner flashed his legendary unpretentiousness at that very moment. "Prohibition was stupid." We both laughed.

"How did you become Speaker of the House?"

"Well," Garner said seriously, "Nick Longworth died, we had some special elections, and the Democrats came out with a majority. So, I became Speaker, and Bertrand Small became the Republican minority leader."

"You were known, as Speaker, to enforce some pretty strict discipline among the Democrats. You used a slogan, 'You've got to bloody your knuckles!' What did that mean?"

"We didn't have a very big majority, and I needed all of my guys to dig in and vote with the party, to fight together for what we were fighting for individually. So I told them to bloody their knuckles."

"Sam Rayburn called you, quoting here, a terrible, table-thumping Democrat." Again, I was off the script.

But Garner seemed eager to answer. "Sam Rayburn wouldn't know a table to thump if it wasn't for me. He's still using tricks now that he learned from me just by watching."

"Really?"

"Yes, Michael," Garner drawled slowly, "really."

I moved forward. "As Speaker, you tried to work with Herbert Hoover. But you eventually repudiated his economic program…"

"Hoover didn't *have* an economic program," Garner shot.

"…and you proposed your own program in 1932. It was a massive public works program that Hoover vetoed, calling it, and again I'm quoting, the most gigantic pork barrel raid ever proposed to an American Congress."

"A lot of good that did Hoover," Garner quipped. "He was out of a job pretty soon after that."

"That's true. In fact, there was a Garner For President movement that took root in '32."

"I wouldn't really call it a movement."

"Well, William Randolph Hearst and all his newspapers endorsed you for president, even though you didn't encourage any of it. The thinking is that Hearst figured you'd institute a national sales tax and keep the US out of the League of Nations, two things he was interested in."

"I never said anything to Hearst."

"You never talked to Hearst?"

"I didn't say that, Michael. I said I never said anything about those issues to him. That was all in his mind."

I was way off the list of approved questions, but I had him going. "Maybe so, but the drumbeat continued in '32. One of Hearst's writers said that a Garner candidacy is attractive because what the rank and file members of the party want is a Democratic Coolidge."

"Coolidge! I'm not Silent Cal. "

"Maybe, maybe not. But your name was placed into nomination at the 1932 Convention. What happened there?"

Garner took a drink of water, cleared his throat. "Franklin Roosevelt, Al Smith and I were all nominated on the first ballot. But I was in third place. The real battle was between FDR and Smith. After the third ballot, Jim Farley called Sam Rayburn…"

"Farley was FDR's campaign manager, and Sam Rayburn, the same Sam Rayburn who wouldn't know a table to thump without you, was your campaign manager."

"…Right. Farley called Rayburn and suggested that I throw my weight to Roosevelt, and then I'd get the vice presidential nomination. I knew that if I didn't agree to it, the convention would be deadlocked, and who knows what would have happened."

"So you weren't excited about the prospect of becoming vice president?"

"No, not really. I loved the House, and I loved being Speaker."

"We're going to take a short break for some messages and a news update, but when we come back, we'll look at your years as vice president. Our Midday Conversation with John Nance Garner will continue on BRN, in just a moment."

The microphones were barely turned off when Garner bellowed, "What the hell kind of questions are these? I didn't agree to talk about half this stuff!"

I was surprised at my own calmness in the face of this Texas hurricane. "Just relax, Cactus Jack. We're halfway through and it's sounding great."

"You haven't earned the right to call me Cactus Jack, you little impudent son of a bitch."

"Hey!" I yelled. "Leave my mother out of this. You want to call me a prick or an asshole, fine. But you leave my mom out of this!"

That surprised Garner. He smiled. He began to understand that I wasn't scared of him, certainly not like two years earlier. He stood up, stretched, eyed the bottle of Jack Daniels, but didn't touch it. He turned and faced the window, saw about 200 people gathered on the street peering in. He waved, and made a motion that he'd be out to shake hands right after the show.

I motioned to him to sit down, as we were about to come out of the break. "Welcome back to the BRN Midday Conversation. I'm Michael Audray, and we're talking today with John Nance Garner. We've gotten to the point in your career where you've been nominated for vice president in 1932. You had an interesting campaign style. Tell us about that."

"Well," Garner said as he cleared his throat, "I didn't."

"You didn't what?"

"I didn't campaign. See, I tend to look at elections as referendums on the incumbent's performance. In this case, people were going to be voting for anybody but Hoover. Roosevelt was going to win. He didn't need me to campaign for him."

"Well, if you really felt you and Roosevelt were going to win the election of 1932, why did you also simultaneously run for your House seat, which you also won that day?"

"Michael, two reasons. Number 1, you just never know what the voters are actually going to do. I knew that I could win my House seat, and I wanted to make sure that I'd have a strong voice in the government no matter what happened. And two, I knew if FDR and I were elected, and I was also reelected to the House, we could control any special election to make sure it stayed in Democratic control."

"Before the inauguration, you convinced the president-elect to provide government guarantees of banking deposits, eventually creating the Federal Deposit Insurance Corporation."

"Well, that was a good deal. I knew that the federal government had to do something to help spur the economy, and this kind of guarantee would work."

"But despite this kind of early influence on Franklin Roosevelt, you had harsh words for the Office of the Vice President. You called it, quoting here, "the spare tire on the automobile of government," "a no man's land between the legislative and the executive branch," and my personal favorite, "not worth a warm bucket of spit.""

"I didn't mean to say 'spit'," Garner said wryly.

"OK," I laughed. "What's wrong with being vice president?"

"Nothing, by itself. I mean, you're just a step away from being the leader of the United States. But being vice president provides no arsenal from which to draw power. Only when your peers have faith in and respect for a person's judgment can he be influential."

"You found the New Deal to be too liberal. True?"

"I think that's a fair statement."

"You and FDR were often at odds with each other?"

"In the first term, we worked pretty well together. He'd have an idea, I'd tell him how to package it to get it through Congress, then I'd help it through. He was the idea guy. I busied myself with understanding government financing, taxation, tariffs, revenue bills, that kind of stuff."

"But you didn't always agree with him."

"No. He didn't need me to be his Yes Man. He needed me to get the Congress to pass his laws, and I did. It was good politics and good patriotism."

"It's well known, Mr. Garner, that you didn't even make speeches on behalf of the new president and his policies. Why not? Why not go make a speech to promote your administration's agenda?"

"It wasn't my administration, Michael. It was, and is Franklin Roosevelt's. Any speech or statement I made would be searched to find a difference between the president and me. If I was asked for a comment, I told them I was the junior member of the firm. They needed to talk to headquarters."

"Alright. Let's move on to the 1936 election. At the convention, there was a rule changed allowing the delegates to approve both the presidential and vice presidential nominees with a simple majority, instead of a two-thirds vote. Did you feel at all like FDR was going to replace you in '36?"

"No. I knew he wouldn't."

"It didn't take long, though, for some real disagreements to appear. You were adamantly opposed to the sit-down strikes by organized labor in 1936, weren't you?"

"Yes. They're a violation of the business owner's property rights."

"And you were completely opposed to the president's idea of adding justices to the Supreme Court."

"Absolutely. It was a bad idea then, it's a bad idea now."

"Earlier you said FDR didn't need a Yes Man. But he did need a congressional liaison. However, in the middle of the debate about the Supreme Court re-organization, you left town. You went back to Texas. Why?"

"I asked The Boss. He said it was alright for me to go fishing."

"You want us to believe that?"

Garner put a steel glare on me. "Yes. That's the truth. I came back to Washington, and the president gave me the assignment of marshalling that Supreme Court bill through Congress after Joe Robinson, who was the Senate majority leader at the time, died."

"The Supreme Court reorganization didn't go anywhere, then the 1938 mid-term elections turned out not very well for the Democrats."

"That's because Roosevelt wouldn't listen to me. He wanted to get rid of the southern conservative Democrats. I told him that if he tried, he'd end up with southern conservative Republicans. And that's exactly what happened!"

"Consequently, FDR got almost nothing that he wanted between '38 and '40."

"That's right."

"Well, then, Mr. Garner, that takes us to the 1940 election. In December 1939, you stunned almost everyone by announcing that, although you wouldn't actively campaign for it, you would not turn down the 1940 Democratic presidential nomination."

"Uh-huh."

"Why'd you challenge The Boss?"

Garner took a sip of water and cleared his throat. "I wasn't really challenging him so much as I was making myself available. No president had ever run for a third term. George Washington started the two-term tradition. I knew that if Roosevelt really wanted to run, there was no way to prevent him. But I felt there were enough people who wanted a different voice out there after eight years of Roosevelt. I felt he should retire. I figured I was the only candidate out there who could convince him to retire. But I was wrong."

"Obviously, you knew that, if you challenged him, you wouldn't be asked to be on the ticket."

Garner chuckled. "Yes, I knew I would be moving back to Texas."

"Roosevelt was renominated on the first ballot, and you came in third. I know you didn't campaign for him. What did you do on Election Day?"

Garner fingered his water glass, and looked down while he said, "I stayed home. I didn't even vote."

That was a bit of a stunner. I didn't know that. I paused for a moment to let that statement sink in, then I broke for commercials. I looked at him and said, "Jack, this interview is great. We've got fifteen minutes left. You sure you want to go through with this?"

"You're God damn right I do."

"OK." I told him we had two minutes, and then we'd get into it. He nodded his head.

"We're back in our final segment on the BRN Midday Conversation, today with John Nance Garner. Starting with your days as a county judge in Texas, you've been an elected public official for forty-seven years. If you had to, how would you characterize your political and philosophical outlook?"

"That's a good question, Michael." It wasn't on the list. Garner thought for a moment, then he said, "My belief has always been in Executive Leadership, not Executive Rulership."

"Do you think the United States has a ruler now?"

"I believe that Franklin Roosevelt wants power. He craves power. He's changed in office. He does not delegate. His nature is to do everything himself." He paused momentarily, then added, "He wants to control the agenda, too, and I don't think he should. That's the legislative branch's job."

"Well, the president is not able to control everything."

"You mean, like everybody talking about his girlfriend? And Eleanor's girlfriend?" Garner launched right into it. He seemed anxious to get this out. "You don't know the half of it."

"Well, Mr. Garner, would you care to enlighten us with your first-hand insights?"

"Franklin Roosevelt," he began without any hesitation, "has been having an affair with Lucy Mercer Rutherfurd for as long as I've known him. It hasn't been any secret to those of us around him. If you go back and check, you'll find that she's been sitting in the front row for all three of his Inaugurations, and probably when he was sworn in as governor of New York. She's been at the White House probably more than Eleanor."

"Did you see Lucy Mercer Rutherfurd there?"

"Yeah, I'd see her everywhere - in the Oval Office, in the president's private office, in the White House kitchen, in the hallways - and at all times of the day, morning, noon and night. Don't get me wrong, she's a lovely woman, but she's not his wife. And," he said without even taking a breath, "she's not even the only one."

I stammered a bit. This is what he meant when he told me weeks ago that he'd blow the lid off this story. "There's other women?"

"Hell, yes, there's other women." John Nance Garner had just become the first person to swear coast-to-coast. "His secretary, Missy LaHande, does more than take dictation and fill in for Eleanor at parties. She fills in everywhere."

"You've seen Franklin Roosevelt and Missy LaHande together?"

"If you mean, have I seen them in bed together? No, but I know what I know."

"So, you're saying the president of the United States is having an affair with his secretary, too?"

"That's what I'm saying."

"Anybody else?"

"I think he had a fling with Princess Martha of Norway."

"Princess Martha of Norway?" I stammered.

"Yeah. She lived at the White House for months after Norway was invaded in 1940. Shortly before she left, the United States offered aid to the Norwegians and personal shelter for the Prince, which we had never considered doing before."

I was at a loss for words. "Anyone else?"

"Probably, but no one I absolutely know about."

"You said this is common knowledge inside the White House. Do all the Cabinet members know?"

"Sure. So do the kids."

"Whose kids?"

"Franklin and Eleanor's kids. At least Anna does, for sure. Anna has often helped Lucy get into the White House, and has sometimes made travel arrangements for Lucy to meet her dad when he's on the road."

My head was spinning. Garner hadn't mentioned any of this when we met a few weeks back. "You're telling me, Mr. Garner, that Anna Roosevelt, the president's eldest daughter, not only knows about her father's relationships with both Lucy Mercer Rutherfurd and Missy LaHande, but that she actually sets up the rendezvous?"

"Yes, that's what I'm saying. And she also knows about her mother's relationship with Lorena Hickok. Anna is a very bright young woman."

"You know this for a fact?" I needed to double check.

"Yes, Michael. I worked there everyday for eight years, I was there at all hours of the day and night, and I saw many things. I've also been around for, as you made a point of saying, forty-seven years. I have a lot of friends who have a lot of eyes and ears. This is all fact."

"Have you seen Mrs. Roosevelt together with Lorena Hickok?"

"I know what I know."

"If you knew all this, why didn't you say anything before now?"

Garner paused briefly. "No one asked. I've known congressmen and senators for decades, and lots of them have had affairs and failings. But no one asked, until now. I didn't feel it was my place to expose the human underbelly of the people I worked with."

"But now it's alright?"

"You, Michael, asked the question, in public. You have a habit of asking impertinent questions. But once it's asked, I'll give an answer."

"Well, you've worked with the president, in your own words, everyday for eight years, and you've known him for twenty years or so. What does his - and the First Lady's - long-term infidelity say to you about who he is? Does it speak to his character?"

"Absolutely it speaks to his character. And I believe that a person's private behavior is a gauge of his public life. If a person is a liar in private, he'll lie in public."

"Mr. Garner, are you calling President Roosevelt a liar?"

Garner nodded his head. "He has a tendency toward prevarication, sometimes big, sometimes little, but quite often."

"Are you saying he's untrustworthy?"

"I'm saying that President Roosevelt has broken promises to me, the American people and other world leaders. And obviously he and his wife have broken promises to each other and their children."

"Do you think that the private lives of politicians should be this openly discussed?"

"I do. I think it speaks to their character. How they act in private versus how they act in public."

"Well, then, Mr. Garner, you and your wife Ettie have been married over fifty years. Have you ever been unfaithful?'

I thought the veins in Garner's neck would explode. "I am not the focus! I am not going to answer that! How dare you!"

"But you just said that a politician's private behavior is a spotlight on their public life, and you called the president an untrustworthy liar. I just wondered if you had any thing in your past of a similar nature."

"No, I don't."

"Should the press continue to investigate and report on the Roosevelt's private lives?"

"Yes."

"Why?"

"Because they are power-hungry individuals who have had their turn. It is time for someone else to be in charge."

"Like you?"

That caught Garner short. "No. I've had my chance. But presidents shouldn't run for third terms, and they can't control the agenda."

"Well, we can't control the time. John Nance Garner, it's been an eye-popping hour of discussion. We thank you for coming by and sharing your stories and your insight into recent history and current events. Best of luck to you in your retirement from public life, but, we hope, not from public view."

"Thank you, Michael."

As the microphones were turned off, Garner stood up. I could tell he was wondering if he should shake my hand. I had strayed so far from the question list, but he stayed in the studio. Just like Peter said he would. John Nance Garner reached down, grabbed the bottle of Jack Daniels, and walked out the studio door, and through the back entrance of BRN, avoiding the crowd who had watched him this past hour.

July 7, 1941: American Troops join British troops in the occupation of Iceland.
July 7, 1941: At a secret meeting in Berlin, Himmler orders the development of a large scale killing center at Auschwitz.

Chapter 21 – The Garner Aftermath

The reaction to Garner's bombshells was swift and ubiquitous. The wire services and the other networks began reporting it immediately. All the newspaper accounts credited BRN with snagging the interview, while the other networks attributed "a radio interview earlier today." All of this made Peter Betz very happy. "Tonight's fireworks won't compare to what we had here this afternoon!" is all he said to me while he practically skipped down the hall.

The interview's aftermath took on a life of its own. As with the first Garner chat, I was again besieged by other media outlets. Only this time, I didn't do any of them. The Betz Radio Network was now quite capable of manufacturing its own publicity.

Everywhere we went that afternoon and evening, *the* topic of conversation was The Garner Interview. The part that had the most tongues wagging was Garner's assertion that Anna Roosevelt encouraged her father's dalliances. The public was almost becoming used to the idea that FDR was seeing another woman. They were less comfortable with the thought of the First Lady with Another Lady. But they were absolutely apoplectic with the revelation that the First Daughter was a co-conspirator.

The cacophony only got louder. On Sunday, Fr. Charles Coughlin devoted his entire broadcast to the "immorality, deceit, obfuscation and societal breakdown being advanced by this so-called leader of ours. If Franklin Roosevelt believes that we will be willing to let our boys fight and die on his say-so, he's sorely mistaken. The President and the First Lady - or, I should say, the Cheater and the Deviant - have relinquished their authority over anyone in this land we call America. When Franklin Roosevelt tells us that the War in Europe is a threat to our safety and security, how can we believe him? He has lied to us everyday of his public life! How do we know he is not lying to us about the threat that Hitler poses?"

Coughlin demanded a protest march in front of the White House for later in the week, "just as soon as I can get to Washington and protest with you."

On Monday, B.W. Corkman took the entire Roosevelt family to task in his Washington Post column.

> Never before in the history of the Republic have we been forced to face our own failings in the manner we must face them now. Never before have we been saddled with a man in the White House who has been laid bare as a power-hungry, philandering, lying, cheating human being who has obviously been a failure not only as a husband, but as a father. Never before have we been saddled with a woman in the White House whose own libidinous inclinations make the most stout-hearted amongst us shiver, who has proven herself to be as much of a liar, cheat and failed mother as her so-called husband. And never before have we been confronted with a family whose values are so skewed they would take their own children into confidence about so deviant a lifestyle, and encourage their participation in it.
> Corkman continued, For the first time in our history, a man has been elected to a third term as president. Perhaps, for the good of our country, it may be time for that person to do something else that's never been done in our history. Resign.

The Chicago Tribune ran a package of front-page articles that day. One included a transcript of what Garner had said in the final segment of our interview. One was a brief synopsis of the chronology of The Affairs of State to this point. And one was an opinion column by Thomas Marety, essentially agreeing with B.W. Corkman. Although he didn't come out and demand FDR's resignation, he did question "whether or not the president has the effectiveness, the ability or the moral fortitude to lead us in whatever struggles may lie ahead. We call for the president to think long and hard, and do what's ultimately best for the country."

The Tribune, though, did something that no other paper to that point had. These wrap-around articles bordered two side-by-side file photos. On the left was a picture of the president and Anna Roosevelt, but in the lower-left hand corner of the picture was the unmistakable, and

Tribune-identified, visage of Lucy Mercer Rutherfurd. On the right was a picture of Eleanor and Lorena standing next to each other on a bridge overlooking a stream.

Peter Betz saw this front-page and called Thomas Marety directly. Peter wanted to know why they decided to publish these old file photos around fresh articles.

Marety said, "These are the only photos we've got. Remember, Peter, this is a Hearst Newspaper. In this case, you supplied the war. We supplied the pictures. But if you've got other pictures, let us know."

From every corner of the country, columnists and editorial writers were demanding an investigation into the allegations, even FDR's resignation. For most people, the boiling point was Anna's involvement. That spoke volumes for the level of deceit employed by the Roosevelt family to gain and maintain power.

The White House continued to keep a closed mouth. Both Franklin and Eleanor cancelled their public appearances for the week, citing pressures of the war. FDR's advisers were split on what he should do. Some were advocating a Fireside Chat, others a press conference, others maintained silence was the best policy. Still others thought a strongly-worded denial in a press release would do the trick, and even others thought that continuing to get the message out about the war in Europe and Hitler's plans would eventually overwhelm the salacious details.

FDR opted for the silent treatment. Press secretary Steven Early continued to release information about the War and new domestic initiatives. But the press briefings began to center almost exclusively on The Affairs of State.

On Thursday of that week, Fr. Charles Coughlin was in DC to lead a protest march in front of the White House. Nearly 8000 people, chanting "FDR Must Go," lined Pennsylvania Avenue directly in front of the White House. Protesters carried signs invoking "Moral Leadership for Immoral Times." The White House asked the DC Police to disperse the crowd, but Coughlin's group had a protest permit. The Secret Service formed a human wall between the protesters and the Rose Garden. An AP photographer took the shot of the Secret Service blocking the protesters from marching closer, and it ran on front pages everywhere.

The elitism and imperiousness that had served FDR so well for so long was now seen as arrogance and aloofness. Suddenly, Franklin Roosevelt had gone from the Emperor to the Emperor with No Clothes.

Janine told me to go to Peter's office. When I walked in, he handed me the phone. "Somebody wants to talk with you," he smiled.

I put the phone to my ear. "We gave 'em a pretty goddamn good show, didn't we, Michael?" It was John Nance Garner, calling from his home in Texas. "My phone hasn't stopped ringing. If it's not reporters, it's my old friends. If it's not friends, it's strangers who got my number somehow. I'll tell you, that interview was the goddamndest thing I've ever been part of. Ol' Roosevelt's got his shorts in a vice. He doesn't know what to do. He even called me!"

My ears perked up. "Roosevelt called you?" Peter sat up straighter, too. "When?"

"A couple days ago. Asked me why I said all that."

"What'd you tell him?"

"I told him I wanted to set the record straight about a lot of things. I told him none of this would've happened if he'd just retired after two terms like he should have. And I told him he only had himself to blame."

"What did he say?"

"He said he was just sorry that I brought Anna into this. He said he thought that was unnecessary. That was it. That's all we talked about. It was pretty short."

"Did he sound mad?"

"At first he did, but then at the end he kind of sounded sad."

"Do you have any regrets, Jack?"

"Not one. Not a goddamn bit. I'd do it again."

When the phone call wrapped, Peter told me it was all off-the-record. " I gave Jack my word. We can use it as background."

Tim Cullen was waiting in my office with news. Leo Dailey had called a Press Conference for the next morning to announce he was going to officially open the once-cancelled hearings into the conduct of the Roosevelts.

At precisely 10 a.m. on Friday, July 11, 1941, Congressman Leo Dailey, flanked on the Capitol steps by House minority leader Martin McKay and House minority whip Ken Kerse, began his press conference. As usual, Dailey's suit, starched white shirt and red tie with a blue pocket kerchief were unnaturally crisp in the hot and humid air of a Washington summer. "Let me say at the outset we will not be answering any questions today. We will be happy to answer any and all of your questions another time. But today we are here to announce that next Monday we will open hearings into the truth and conduct of the President and Mrs. Roosevelt. We will investigate whether any laws were broken - other than the laws of God - whether any official government documents were maliciously obscured in an attempt to suppress the truth, whether any taxpayer dollars were used to promote or maintain a conspiracy involving malfeasance and subterfuge, and whether any government employees participated in this conspiracy against their will. These are serious charges and allegations, and we will treat them as such. We will be seeking the truth by hearing testimony from those involved, and if necessary, we will subpoena witnesses. These hearings will seek to uncover the truth, and we will look wherever these hearings take us. These are unusual times for our democracy, and we must maintain a diligent defense of truth, in all its forms. I have asked for, and received, the chairmanship of this committee, and I have the full support of the Republican House leadership. I do not relish this task. But as an elected public servant who loves my country and cares about the truth, I will do my best to carry out this assignment with both haste and care. We must move quickly in these dangerous times, but we must also be careful that we search for the truth wherever it lies. I look forward to the conclusion of these hearings, because that will mean we have found the truth. And it is the truth that will ultimately allow our great country to prevail. Thank you very much."

With that, Dailey, McKay and Kerse turned and walked back inside the Capitol, without taking any questions.

The crowd of reporters was already beginning to disperse when I sidled up to Jack Denif. He was counting something in his note pad.

"He said 'truth' nine times. He ain't looking for truth. He's looking for headlines."

"How's your story, Jack?"

"It's good. Ready to go."

"Look over there." I nodded my head toward the lower steps of the Capitol, about Thirty feet from where the microphones had been set up. It was Jane Hall Dailey and Arch Hook standing side by side, chatting. Fifty feet behind them and to their right, Earl was nonchalantly snapping photos.

As Jack approached them they separated their stance by a foot or two. "Mind if I ask you a question or two, Mrs. Dailey?"

"Actually, I do," I overheard her say. "I was just here to support my husband. He's the one who should be answering questions."

"Oh, I'm sure he'll be doing that soon enough," Jack said, with more than a hint of insouciance. Turning to her companion, he said, "I'm Jack Denif from NBC. And you are...?"

"I am not important," Arch Hook said. "I'm just in town on some business, and happened to be walking by."

"I see," Jack said as he closed up his notebook and stuffed it in his pocket. "You two know each other?"

Jane Hall Dailey and Arch Hook looked quickly at each other and simultaneously stammered that they'd met briefly before, but just ran into each other.

Jack gave them a knowing eye, then winked at them. "Mmm-hmm. Good to see you, Mrs. Dailey." Then, as he walked away, he turned and said, "You, too, Arch."

That completely unnerved them both. Jane Hall Dailey and Arch Hook seemingly went their separate ways. They were so interested in getting away from Jack they didn't notice that Earl Mercia was following them. But Earl had a way of not being noticed.

I walked back toward Jack. "When do you think your Dailey story will air?"

"Soon," he said as he lit a cigarette. "Real soon."

July 17, 1941: Joe DiMaggio's 56-game hitting streak ends.
July 17, 1941: FDR proposes doubling the number of night baseball
games to keep war workers on the job.
July 21, 1941: The Luftwaffe begins attacking Moscow.
July 21, 1941: FDR asks Congress to extend the draft.
July 26, 1941: FDR freezes all Japanese assets, suspends all trade with
Japan and places an embargo on oil to Japan.
July 31, 1941: Goerring signs the order for The Final Solution.
August 9, 1941: FDR and Churchill meet off the coast of
Newfoundland, sign the Atlantic Charter.
August 9, 1941: Poll shows 74% of Americans still oppose the War.

Chapter 22 – The Leo Dailey Series

McKay and Kerse knew these hearings would be nothing more than show for headline writers. They knew anybody they subpoenaed would either be uncooperative or plead The Fifth Amendment. They knew anybody who willingly testified in front of the committee would not have any, shall we say, intimate knowledge of the details. But Leo Dailey convinced them these hearings had to go forward for political reasons. Dailey was pretty good with a calendar, and he suggested these hearings could drag on for the better part of a year, rendering the Democrats vulnerable in the 1942 mid-term elections.

When McKay and Kerse looked at the House and Senate make-up, they presumed any political damage they could inflict on Roosevelt now would come back in their favor. They'd also been talking with John Nance Garner.

Garner told them he would refuse to speak in front of the committee. If subpoenaed, he told them, he would refuse to testify by publicly labeling it a partisan grandstanding gesture. He also didn't want to go under oath. But Garner told McKay and Kerse who would testify, people in the White House who had first-hand knowledge, but didn't have enough clout to refuse a subpoena.

The hearings began with great fanfare and more than a fair amount of bluster from Leo Dailey. The all-Republican four-member committee each took turns bashing FDR for "moral degeneration," which was "leading our nation down the road to ruin" during these "dangerous and perilous times." The opening day only lasted twenty-seven minutes, as no witnesses were called. But the stage was set for the following days.

Dailey made a point to note "this committee will attempt to interview people of interest who have first-hand knowledge of the actions we're investigating." He listed a number of job positions inside the White House - cooks, cleaning staff, maintenance personnel, gardeners and so on - that would be called to cooperate.

But the White House made it abundantly clear they would not allow these people to testify under any circumstances. They argued these were federal employees working directly for the president, and therefore covered by executive privilege. "If this minority-party snitch-fest progresses to the point where these employees, or any White House employee, is called to testify," the White House press secretary Steven Early said, "we will actively pursue all legal means to prevent their appearance."

Dailey used this to his advantage. "It seems to me President Roosevelt has something to hide," Dailey said at a hearing soon after the press release. "If he's got nothing to hide, then let these people testify and tell us their stories."

The White House countered it has nothing to do with FDR hiding anything. It has everything to do with the confidentiality associated with the White House. If these people are compelled to testify, they said, the entire scope of what can be freely discussed inside the White House now and in the future will be completely compromised.

Newspapers and the networks bandied these competing arguments around for quite a while. These were not arcane discussions of non-essential legal matters. This was a weighty constitutional decision. The public, though, clearly wanted to hear the testimony.

The Executive Privilege Issue wormed its way through the courts, with each side winning on appeal. Although the hearings weren't providing any testimony, Leo Dailey managed to keep his mug on the front page for more than a month. By the third week of August, Dailey had only that initial twenty-seven minutes of Congressional inquiry. As the issue was winding its way up to the United States Supreme Court, Leo Dailey came in for some scrutiny.

Jack Denif had taken a little extra time to revise and update his investigation. His five-part series began on Monday, August 18, 1941.

"Congressman Leo Dailey, a Republican freshman from Montana, is chairing the investigation into the personal conduct of President and Mrs. Roosevelt," Jack began. "Congressman Dailey has been an outspoken critic of the alleged infidelities of the First Family. He's been quoted as saying the Roosevelts are leading this country into moral disrepute, that they are purveyors of a deviant lifestyle and have relinquished any authority they may have had in leading this country during times of war. In announcing the congressional investigation, Congressman Dailey called for finding out the truth not once, not twice, but nine times in a brief announcement."

Jack continued, "We at NBC felt it was a good idea to find out more about Leo Dailey. Who he is, where he came from, what he stands for. He's young, good looking, articulate, and always dressed impeccably. Beyond that, we didn't know much - until now. Over the next five days, we will reveal what we've learned about Congressman Leo Dailey, from discussions we've had with him, his friends and family, his supporters and his detractors. We expect to provide a well-rounded picture of the man who is investigating the president, and we hope you find it informative. Our five part series will look at his youth and upbringing in Montana, his college years, his first forays into elective office, his family and his rise to the United States Congress."

Jack Denif had spoken with Dailey on-the-record for this series, which Dailey thought would be a puff-piece. The interviews had taken place over the course of two months, and though Jack had asked tough questions, Dailey believed the finished product would be flattering and complimentary.

So when Dailey heard that the five-part series would focus on those topics, he felt secure that his national profile would rise.

Each five-minute segment aired three times daily on NBC. Part one dealt with Leo's youth. Leo had a younger brother, Clark. His parents, Benjamin and Martha Dailey worked long hours in a grocery store, saving their money so Leo and Clark could go to college. He was a Boy Scout, a mostly-A student, a high school baseball player and an insatiable reader. He worked hard at everything he did, and took an interest in government at a young age, reading with interest the newspaper accounts of the World War I battles. He wanted to know what governments did, how they worked, what effect they had on people, and how they could work better and more efficiently. As a high school sophomore, he made up his mind that Woodrow Wilson's League of Nations was a bad idea.

Leo and his staff were pleased with the first segment. In fact, they all agreed to listen to the next report together, in Leo's office.

At Montana State University, Jack's second report related, Leo Dailey continued to excel through hard work and a curious mind. He eventually became student body president, but had also developed a reputation as a ladies man who liked to drink. He became engaged to Mary Beth Keefer, the report continued, but broke off the engagement shortly after she miscarried. He moved to Bozeman after graduation, joining a law firm as a junior member. This report marked the first time Mary Beth Keefer's name had been mentioned publicly.

Dailey's staffers, crowded around his desk, were aghast and silent. An awkward uneasiness filled the room. Dailey hit the roof. "That son of a bitch!" he yelled at the radio. "Somebody find me the phone number for the president of NBC. I'll put a stop to this bullshit!"

His staff had tiptoed out of his office when one of them noticed a delivery man standing in the waiting area. "I have a Special Delivery package for Congressman Dailey," he said. A staff member tried to sign for it, but Earl Mercia, dressed in a delivery uniform, said, "I'm sorry, but I have to have the Congressman sign for this directly." The staffer gingerly led Earl Mercia into Leo Dailey's office. "Please sign here," Earl said. Dailey did. Earl thanked him and left.

Dailey opened the envelope and found six 8x10 pictures taken just last month of Leo Dailey and Mary Beth Keefer at a cabin in Montana. The Congressman and Mary Beth were engaged in various sex acts, all different, yet with both parties completely identifiable. Dailey sat stunned for a moment, then yelled to a staffer to "grab that delivery guy." But Earl was long gone.

"I've got NBC on the line," his secretary said. Dailey just shook his head and said he'd have to call them back later. He sat there, looked at each picture again and again, and wondered what else was coming. But he didn't say a word to anybody.

That night, Jane Hall Dailey told Leo she was going back to Montana until the effects of this series passed. Leo told her it would be better politically if she stayed, but she was adamant. She knew what lied ahead. She remembered Jack Denif approaching her at the Capitol Steps press conference, knowing who Arch Hook was without an introduction and figured the rest of the week was going to be really ugly. She'd already packed, and she quietly left DC in a cab to the airport. The Wednesday report chronicled Dailey's involvement with Lou Martilotta, bootleggers, and his decision to run for the Montana legislature immediately after the mysterious appearance of $200,000 in his and Jane's personal bank account.

Using Lou Martilotta's quotes, Jack Denif painted a word picture of how Leo Dailey had been providing the legal cover for his wife's and father-in-law's speakeasies. Regarding Leo's Milwaukee junkets, Lou Martilotta said, "We had booze and broads at our place. If we'd been a restaurant, the booze were the entrées, and the broads were the dessert. Leo liked dessert. A lot of dessert." The story touched on his friendship with Rico Tozzi. It drew a circumstantial link to their initial meeting in 1932 and the $200,000 bank account deposit that had always been officially explained as a bonus from the Hall Timber Company.

Dailey listened to this report at his apartment, delaying his customary early arrival. What he didn't expect, though, was the crush of reporters waiting for him when he did arrive at his office. Literally fighting through the crowd, Dailey kept issuing terse No Comments before he got into his office's protective custody.

McKay and Kerse were all over Dailey on Wednesday. They'd cancelled whatever public appearances they had, and they met privately for two hours. McKay and Kerse wanted to know what else was going to come out. Better to hear it now, they told Leo, than to hear it with the rest of America tomorrow morning. Leo told them he wasn't sure, but felt confident the worst was over.

"It damn well better be," Kerse demanded.

It wasn't. Jack Denif's Thursday report was explosive. For the first time publicly, he revealed that even before Leo and Jane were married, they were the officers of the Teton Peak Holding Company, a sham cover for the distribution of booze during Prohibition. He revealed Jane was arrested and tried on felony charges related to the Volstead Act, and only avoided prison when she agreed to testify against Lou Martilotta. Jack revealed Jane had developed close friendships with newspaper editors and Mob lawyers, implicating both sexual favors and a money trail that financed campaigns. He also tagged the story with the fact Jane Hall Dailey left town earlier in the week.

The rest of the press corps was beating down the doors of Dailey, McKay and Kerse. McKay bravely faced them, saying over and over "these allegations are merely that - allegations - and they will be investigated. To this point, I am not aware of any enforced laws that have been broken…", which was his way of saying the booze running was a non-issue because now it's legal, "…and we will be diligent in getting to the bottom of this."

Around five o'clock that afternoon, Earl Mercia, dressed once again in his Delivery Man outfit, arrived at Leo Dailey's office. He knew Leo wasn't there, didn't want him to be there. Earl pretended to have instructions that only Dailey could sign for the envelope, but agreed to let Dailey's secretary sign if she promised that the Congressman would get it. She promised.

Leo walked in to his office about 5:45 p.m. and was handed the envelope. He looked at it, went into his office, and closed the door. He slowly opened the manila package, and pulled out a dozen 8x10 pictures. All featured Jane. The first half-dozen were with Thomas Marety. The next half-dozen were with Arch Hook. And all of them were well-taken photographs of Jane in a variety of sexual acts with each man, naked and clearly enjoying it.

Leo set the pictures down, picked up the pictures of him and Mary Beth, then grabbed a bottle of Scotch and poured himself a tall drink.

The final report focused on Leo's run for Congress against Landy Bannister. It detailed how the young and energetic Leo Dailey's campaign was fueled in large part from Rico Tozzi's organization in Detroit. Jack Denif was clear that there was no election fraud. Leo won fair and square. But he also made it clear most of Leo's campaign money came from an out-of-state source who had ties with some pretty shady characters.

"It seems," his report concluded, "that Congressman Leo Dailey is not the morally upstanding public servant he is demanding our president to be. He is not a bad man. He is just a man, a man with many flaws. Jack Denif, NBC News, Washington."

Dailey's phone rang. It was Kerse. "You're toast, Leo. We need to talk."

That afternoon, Friday, August 22, 1941, the United States Supreme Court handed down its emergency opinion in the matter of the Executive Privilege Issue. The Court ruled the White House did, indeed, have the ability to exercise Executive Privilege, preventing any of its employees from testifying in front of Congress about the inner workings of the White House.

August 19, 1941: German troops surround Leningrad.
August 22, 1941: Hitler orders his generals in Russia to drive south,
away from Moscow.
August 25, 1941: British and Soviet troops invade Persia.
September 3, 1941: General deportation of German Jews begins.
September 4, 1941: FDR closes Panama Canal to Japanese shipping.

Chapter 23 – Dailey Fights Back

L eo Dailey refused to stay on the canvas. The following Monday
morning, he held a press conference in the lobby of the Capitol,
in front of the statues of the Founding Fathers. Flanked by McKay
and Kerse, plus the members of his House Committee investigating the
Roosevelts, Dailey insisted the investigation would continue.

"Good morning," he began. "I'll be happy to answer any questions,
but first I have a statement to make. The decision by the United States
Supreme Court last Friday in the matter of Executive Privilege is, in our
view, wrong and rendered in a highly partisan atmosphere. However, it is
the final decision from the highest court in our land, and we must abide by
that decision. It does not, however, end our investigation into the actions
of the President and First Lady. It merely hampers it. Although we will
not be allowed to subpoena anybody who currently or previously worked
in the Roosevelt White House, we will be able to hear testimony from
others with direct knowledge related to the incidents under investigation.
Those people, who have never been in the employ of the White House,
will be asked to voluntarily testify before our Committee. Should they
refuse to comply voluntarily, we are prepared to issue subpoenas forcing
them to do so. We expect to begin hearing testimony, beginning two
weeks from today, September 8th. During these next two weeks, we will
be drawing up a list of people we would like to speak with, and we will be
contacting them directly. The people we contact need to understand that
this is an official investigation by the United States Congress, and is to
be treated with seriousness and respect. The goal of our Committee is to
discover the truth and make it known in a timely manner. We would like

to conclude our investigation rather quickly, but we are not in control of how compliant our witnesses will be. We would hope that, for the sake of the country, the individuals called to testify before our House Committee would meet with us speedily, answer questions directly and honestly, and provide the information we are seeking. My colleagues and I would be happy to answer any questions you may have at this time."

The crush of reporters from all the networks, newspapers and wire services began shouting simultaneously. Like a seasoned pro, Leo picked the reporters by both pointing and calling out their names. First was The Chicago Tribune's Matt Shafer.

"Congressman, last week you were the subject of a profile on NBC that described a pattern of illegal activity, connections with underworld characters and infidelity. You have yet to make a public statement about that. What do you have to say about those reports?"

It was here Leo Dailey showed the consummate political skill that had helped him rise to the United States Congress. He understood the changing times of the media, and knew exactly how to get his message across to the people that mattered - the voters in his home state of Montana. He also folded in the Republican leadership with his answers and his demeanor.

"The NBC series of reports on me by Jack Denif - by the way, is Jack here? I don't see him - is a collection of unsubstantiated hoo-ha, circumstantial evidence, mixed with a smidgen of fact, and all old tales. It was nothing but a week-long character assassination authorized by a media outlet that has consistently shown its liberal bias. After listening to the reports, and subsequently reading their transcripts, I will only say that a tiny, tiny fraction of what was reported could even be remotely considered true." Leo then pointed to another reporter, but heard a voice from the back. "By the way, Congressman, I am here," Jack Denif yelled. "Answer this question…"

"I don't think so, Jack," snapped Dailey. "I've answered enough of your questions to last a lifetime." Then he called on Stephen Sutton of the Washington Herald.

Sutton took a half-step forward. "You said a minute ago, Congressman, that only a small fraction of the NBC reports are true. Which fraction is true, and what isn't true?" Sutton stepped back and tossed a knowing glance at Jack.

Dailey didn't miss a beat. "It is true that my wife was arrested and tried for being involved in providing alcohol when it was illegal. Her involvement, as it came out at her trial, was limited in both time and scope. The fact that the prosecutors were clearly more interested in the supplier is underscored by the fact they reduced the charges against her in return for her testimony against Mr. Martilotta. Let me remind you that Mr. Martilotta is a career criminal who has been in and out of prison for the bulk of his adult life. I would not treat anything Mr. Martilotta says as gospel. Let's face it - he went to prison based largely on testimony provided by my dear wife Jane, who I think should be considered a hero in this matter. It doesn't surprise me that he is providing the kind of vicious character smears that are merely an attempt to paint both my wife and me as anything but clean-living Americans. Charles."

Mutual's Charles Parker directed his question elsewhere. "Congressman McKay, in light of the revelation about Congressman Dailey in last week's report, did you or the other Party leaders ever discuss a replacement for the Committee Chair?"

McKay, not expecting any questions, was a little slow to answer. "I think it would be not completely truthful if I stood here and said the Party leadership had no concerns," he began. Pausing to collect his thoughts, he moved forward. "But I do take issue with the wording of your question, Mr. Parker. The story last week about Congressman Dailey related to allegations, not revelations. Nothing has been proven, and you've heard Mr. Dailey this morning refute much of the report." He nodded in Leo's direction. "After a weekend of discussing the big picture, all of the various facets of what is going on in Washington and the world, we feel comfortable we have the right man at the right time guiding this Committee."

"Congressman Dailey!" It was Ellen Monroe, not even waiting to be officially recognized. "In that NBC story, Lou Martilotta made it very clear you not only visited his operation in Milwaukee, you partook of all of the delights available. Do you deny his account?"

"Well, Miss Monroe, I'm not surprised that you have asked for comment about that aspect of these ill-researched reports," Dailey retorted sarcastically. "Again, may I remind you that Mr. Martilotta is a convicted felon, a career criminal, whose motives in smearing my name should be investigated."

Ellen persisted. "But you didn't answer the question. Do you deny the accuracy of the statements by Lou Martilotta?"

"Let me say this again, because you obviously don't understand me." At this point, Dailey was glowering at Ellen. "Mr. Martilotta, a career criminal, should have his motives checked as to why he said what he said."

Ellen kept after him. "Do you know Lou Martilotta?"

"Do I know Lou Martilotta?" Dailey repeated. "I can't say that I *know* him. We may have met once or twice, but I don't really know him."

BRN's Tim Cullen interjected. "Congressman…"

"I'm sorry, Tim," Dailey interrupted. "I've already answered Miss Monroe's questions. I'm sure that will get back to BRN." This thinly veiled slap at Ellen's professionalism and integrity was greeted by a chorus of groans from the reporters, and snickers from the politicians. "One more question. Bill?"

"Are you comfortable, Congressman," began CBS's Bill Denton, "investigating the president and his family while you are under virtually the same cloud of character suspicion? Don't you find it a bit unseemly and untenable?"

Dailey had been waiting all weekend for this question, and he was ready. "No, I don't find it even remotely the same. First of all, I'm not the president of the United States. I do not have the power over hundreds or thousands of government employees, I do not control the federal budget, I do not have the same influence over the average American's life and I do not have the ability to send our troops into harm's way in any part of the world. The report about my wife and me was fueled by convicted felons and political foes. These are not the same type of stories about character and leadership. Not by a long shot. Thank…"

Denton interrupted quickly. "Congressman, you're a Republican. The president is a Democrat. Are you a political foe of the president's?"

"In a general sense, yes," Dailey quickly answered. "But the fact we are of different political parties is of no mind. We are merely truth-seeking Americans trying to make sure our leaders live the kind of life that makes us proud. Thank you all very much."

Dailey, clearly the ringleader of this gang, turned and walked away from the podium. The other Republicans followed.

Ellen was seething when both Jack Denif and Tim Cullen walked up to her. "Asshole," she said.

"Yeah," Jack said, "but you noticed he didn't really deny anything. He just sent up some smoke about Martilotta's background."

"I'm sure that will buy him some time," said Tim Cullen. "But it won't play long."

"Yeah, well, we'll see how he survives more scrutiny from the written word," Ellen said in a not thinly veiled threat as she left.

Ellen had been working the various angles of The Affairs of State for several months. Most of her time was spent examining the relationship between Eleanor and Lorena. She developed quite a few leads and contacts, but more importantly, she'd cultivated a certain kind of friendship with Lorena. Ellen had written a total of ten articles detailing the letters written, the trips taken and the time Eleanor and Lorena had spent together. She somehow managed to get nearly fifty letters the women had written to each other between 1935 and 1938. Ellen Monroe was the only reporter that had actually spoken with Lorena during this entire investigation. Lorena had remained on the White House staff and continued to provide her field reports to FDR. Despite hundreds of interview requests from every conceivable news organization, Lorena ignored them all. Whenever she wanted to talk, which was rarely, she would meet Ellen on the bench near the White House. Ellen kept those meeting signals secret.

Ellen had written, and Lorena tacitly confirmed, that Eleanor spent a great deal of time at a stone cottage in Hyde Park, New York, with her close friends Nancy Cook and Marion Dickerman. She also spent time in Greenwich Village with Esther Lape and Elizabeth Read, who were quite politically active.

Ellen had also been researching and writing background profiles on Lucy Mercer Rutherfurd. The four articles that appeared under her byline in July had provided the public with the first detailed look at, as the articles were titled, The President's Paramour. The articles laid out the basic facts: Lucy had been hired in 1914 as Eleanor's social secretary; she and Franklin began an affair, which Eleanor demanded be terminated in 1918 when she discovered love letters between the two; Lucy married Winthrop Rutherfurd, a wealthy South Carolina businessman, in 1920, and they stayed married until he died in 1940.

But Ellen's articles did more than lay out the known facts. Her research showed FDR and Lucy never stopped being together. The couple traded love letters of their own over the years, and often saw each other surreptitiously. She published the long-known press secret of FDR's presidential train dallying for hours in a small town New Jersey railway station, the same small town where Lucy lived. She also detailed the times when the presidential train parked at Bernard Baruch's South Carolina estate for half-days, near where Lucy's summer home was. And Ellen found the pictures that proved Lucy Mercer Rutherfurd was indeed in the front row at each of FDR's inaugurations, beginning with his governorship of New York. These articles were printed on the front pages of every major and minor newspaper in the country. Although they provided topics of conversation among the public, they did not make lips flap in the same way the articles about Eleanor and Lorena did.

On September 4th, Leo Dailey sent out a press release.

In the past ten days, The House Committee investigating the conduct of The president has contacted more than thirty people to testify in this matter. To date, twenty-nine of them have agreed to appear before our Committee, some of them reluctantly. Only one has refused her voluntary cooperation. So today, the House Committee has issued a subpoena to Lucy Mercer Rutherfurd of Allamuchy, New Jersey to testify on Tuesday, September 16, 1941. If she fails to appear before our committee, she will be held in contempt of Congress, and will face the full measure of the law. We sincerely hope Mrs. Rutherfurd will cooperate with our Committee.

September 7, 1941: FDR's mother, Sara, dies at age 87.
September 7-8, 1941: British air raids on Berlin begin.
September 11, 1941: In a Fireside Chat, FDR reveals a shoot-on-sight
order against all German and Italian shipping.

Chapter 24 – Tozzi and Doones

For months, FDR's strategy had been to remain silent about this imbroglio. When he did make public statements, they dealt with the widening war in Europe, other foreign matters, and new domestic initiatives. His public appearances had been dramatically curtailed. When the Supreme Court ruled the White House employees were protected by executive privilege, FDR believed it was only a matter of time before this story wound down and out of the public eye.

But the House Republican leadership's decision to allow Leo Dailey to proceed caught the White House off guard. Still, they believed there was no way anyone who would testify in front of the Committee would have any embarrassing knowledge.

Nor did the White House believe the Committee would actually subpoena Lucy. When she was, FDR was livid. He wanted to hold a press conference and denounce this entire investigation as impossibly partisan and without merit. He decided instead to call J. Edgar Hoover.

FDR ordered Hoover to provide embarrassing material that would force Dailey to back off. Within an hour, Hoover was in the Oval Office with Dailey's dossier and photos. They included pictures similar to the ones Earl Mercia had delivered to Dailey, only more of them and over a longer period of time. The dossier detailed Leo's involvement with Lou Martilotta and Rico Tozzi. It completely confirmed Jane Hall Dailey as a knowing bootlegger who was more than friendly with Thomas Marety, Arch Hook and Rico Tozzi. It even included the little known fact that Leo Dailey failed the Montana State Bar Exam twice. Hoover told FDR there was plenty more where this came from, especially if added to the inch-thick file on Rico Tozzi.

FDR sent two FBI agents to Leo Dailey's office, with instructions to deliver Dailey to the president immediately. When Dailey was ushered into the Oval Office, FDR was sitting at his desk with his head down, doing paperwork. Dailey twice said "Mr. President" before FDR even acknowledged him. He never looked up, but told Dailey to sit down at a chair near the desk. When Dailey did, FDR tossed him an envelope, told him to open it.

In it, Leo Dailey saw a series of photographs of British and Soviet troops invading Persia, destroying the dam on the Dnieper River, and Jews being stuffed onto trains in Germany. They were graphic and grizzly, chilling. Dailey studied them for a few minutes, said nothing.

Then FDR tossed him another envelope. This envelope contained dozens of pictures taken over the past three years of Leo Dailey with Mary Beth Keefer, and Jane Hall Dailey in a threesome with Arch Hook and Rico Tozzi.

FDR, finally looking up from his paperwork, said, "The first envelope is the real world. The second envelope is the Washington world. Don't confuse the two. Back off on your investigation, because there are things taking place in the real world about which you have no idea." Then he grabbed a cigarette and his holder, lit it, and went back to his paperwork. After a minute or so, he looked at Dailey still sitting there, and said, "We're done."

Dailey stood up and said, "Mr. President, you believe you're the only person in the world who can deal with what's happening in Europe. You're wrong. Other elected leaders can deal with it, probably better. We're in a new world, and you're using old tactics." Dailey disgustedly tossed both envelopes on the desk, turned and walked out of the Oval Office.

When Dailey reconvened the hearings on Monday, September 8th, he opened with a statement.

"Last Thursday, this Committee announced we were issuing a subpoena to hear the testimony of Lucy Mercer Rutherfurd. Later that day, I was escorted into the Oval Office for a meeting with the president. In that meeting, he threatened me, my career and my family, and instructed me to curtail this investigation. Let it be known right here and right now I will not bow to the power-hungry, will not break in the face of threats, and will not bend in search of the truth. Many things may be said about me in the coming weeks, and I'm sure most of them will be lies. If you want the truth, just listen to the testimony you will hear throughout the next few weeks."

Dailey knew the lead story in all the papers and on the networks would be his contention the president threatened him. The public was getting increasingly concerned about FDR's attempts to hush up whatever stories were going to come out, and were mystified by Roosevelt's refusal to be brought into a discussion of the matter. Even now, FDR made no comment. The closest he came was when the press secretary, Steven Early, issued a flat denial the president ever threatened the congressman, his career or his family. The official line was, "The president met with the congressman to update him on a matter of national security."

The hearings that Monday were short. No testimony, just a list of twelve people who had agreed to appear before the Committee that week to provide whatever information they knew. There were two surprises on that list, Rico Tozzi and Warren Doones. When we got the list, we scrambled to book those people on BRN.

We knew where and how to find Rico Tozzi. We didn't know why he would be testifying in front of this particular committee, but we knew who he was. We had no idea who Warren Doones was. Dailey's office was not cooperating with us, and McKay and Kerse's offices weren't any help, either. They wanted to keep the big surprise for themselves.

I called Sharon Tozzi wondering what her uncle was going to testify about. "Honest to God, Michael, I don't know."

Through a series of phone calls, we found out that Rico Tozzi was already checked in at The Washington Hilton. However, he had his own security detail with him, plus two guards stationed outside his door. I called Earl and asked him to see what he could do about getting a message directly to Rico Tozzi.

Our entire news department was trying to track down Warren Doones. We had sent a closed circuit message to our local affiliates to aid in the search. Within hours, we found him.

Warren Doones was a mechanical engineer from Flagstaff, Arizona. Forty-seven, married with four kids, a member of the First Flagstaff Baptist Church, a Republican member of the Flagstaff school board, and a veteran of World War I. More importantly, he had boarded a train for Washington by himself on Saturday. He was due to arrive in DC early Wednesday evening.

I desperately wanted to interview both Rico Tozzi and Warren Doones before they testified. If I couldn't get that, then I wanted an exclusive with them immediately after their appearance in front of the House Committee.

I sat down with a map and a train schedule. At this point, Warren Doones was coming up on St. Louis. I called our affiliate in St. Louis and told them he was on the train that would soon be pulling in to the station for a ninety minute layover. I told them to send someone to the depot to talk with Warren Doones, to tell him I wanted to interview him coast-to-coast prior to his testimony. And I said I would call the train station thirty minutes after their arrival so I could speak with him directly.

I had also given a note to Earl for Rico Tozzi. In it, I included ten $100 Monopoly bills. The note, on BRN letterhead, read:

> *Mr. Tozzi,*
> *If you agree to appear on my show prior to your testimony in front of the House Committee, I will gladly exchange these Monopoly dollars for real dollars. If you appear on my show immediately after your testimony, and do not grant any other radio interviews, I will gladly exchange these Monopoly dollars for half their face value. Please call me at this number with your answer: Twinbrook 2-8684.*
> *Michael Audray*

I had no idea how Earl was going to get this to him, but I knew he would.

I had our switchboard connect me to the Depot Manager's office at the St. Louis train station precisely thirty minutes after Warren Doones' train arrived. After about five minutes, I was speaking with a quiet, reserved but confident-sounding man.

"Mr. Doones, this is Michael Audray. It's a pleasure talking with you."

"No, Mr. Audray, it's my pleasure to be speaking with you. I listen to you all the time."

"Thank you, Mr. Doones, we know you're coming to Washington to testify in front of the House Committee investigating the president's conduct. We just don't know why. I'd like to talk with you on the air about your involvement in this matter, and I'd like to do it before your testimony."

Warren Doones was hesitant. "I don't know, Mr. Audray. I promised Congressman Dailey I wouldn't talk with any reporters. I kind of feel like I'm breaking that promise right now."

"Mr. Doones, I assure you," I said, with so much sincerity in my voice it surprised even me, "Congressman Dailey and I are very close. His concern is that you would speak with reporters before you even arrived in

Washington, tipping your hand about what you're going to say. I'm sure he wouldn't mind if you spoke with me immediately before you appear at his Committee."

He'd had just enough political experience to know he shouldn't trust anyone. But I could tell he was interested. "Can I think about it for just a bit, Mr. Audray?"

"Well, sure, just not too long. Why don't you call me from your next stop?"

"Let me see," he said, checking his schedule. "Our next big stop is in Louisville, Kentucky, around 7:30 tonight. Would that be alright if I called you then?"

"Yes, Mr. Doones. That'll be fine. Just don't talk with any other reporters between now and then, alright?"

"Alright."

I gave him my phone number and told him to call collect. "I think you'll actually feel more comfortable testifying in front of the House if you speak with me first. I'm friendlier than the Congress, and I'm a good place to warm up."

Warren Doones laughed. "I'll think about it, Mr. Audray, and I'll call you tonight."

Meanwhile, Earl had been working the Rico Tozzi angle. He'd called his friends at the Hilton, discovered Rico Tozzi was the only one in the room, but that he had six security men with him, two guarding the doors at all times, while the other four took turns sleeping in a separate room. Earl called the Food Service Manager. He offered the manager $50 if he let Earl deliver the room service dinner whenever Rico Tozzi ordered.

At 6:30 Earl got a call that Rico Tozzi had ordered room service. Changing quickly into the Hilton bellman's outfit, Earl went to the service entrance. He slipped the manager $50, then took the tray of food to Room 974. The guards demanded to see the food, and Earl uncovered the steak and potatoes meal. They told Earl they'd take it from here, but Earl protested. "C'mon, guys, I live on tips." They looked at each other, frisked Earl then let him in.

Earl entered and closed the door behind him. "Your dinner's here, sir," he called out. Rico Tozzi sauntered over to the table where Earl was plating the food. He sat down and put a napkin into his shirt collar, slipped a fiver to Earl who slipped my note to Rico Tozzi.

Rico Tozzi looked quizzically at the envelope, but opened and read the note. He laughed. "Son of a bitch," he chortled. "Tell Audray he's got balls."

"Should I tell him that, or do you want to tell him that yourself?"

Rico Tozzi thought about it for a minute. "I'll tell him myself. Now, gimme back my five bucks."

"C'mon, Rico," Earl said, "I live on tips."

Warren Doones never called me from Louisville. I had some of our other affiliates along the train route check to make sure he was still on board. He was. He was just not talking to anyone.

We had called every hotel we knew to see where Warren Doones was booked. He had no reservation, at least under his own name. We planned on meeting the train when it pulled into DC around 6 p.m. Wednesday. But so did every other news organization.

On Tuesday, Leo Dailey started taking testimony about the President and First Lady's conduct from a variety of people who really didn't have any clue about anything. Tim Cullen covered the hearings and managed to finagle the testimony schedule. Rico Tozzi was the only witness scheduled on Thursday, and Warren Doones was the lone witness Friday.

Late Tuesday afternoon, our reception desk called my office. There were five men demanding to see me. Although not belligerent, they were firmly insistent. "Who are they," I asked over the intercom. "We're with Mr. Tozzi," came the reply. I told them I'd be right there. Immediately, I called Janine and told her to have Peter and Bart in my office in five minutes. I straightened up my desk a bit, put away some files I didn't want seen, tightened my tie and went to the reception desk. I introduced myself to the first guy I saw when I turned the corner. He shook my hand but didn't say a word. He turned his head, nodded toward the door, and a few seconds later two more men walked in. One of them was Rico Tozzi.

"Nice to meet you, Mr. Tozzi," I said. "Please come back to my office." I led the way for Tozzi and all six of his bodyguards. We got there just as Peter and Bart arrived. Like the well-trained soldiers I believed them to be, the original five bodyguards stayed outside my office as Tozzi and his one guard entered.

"Who are these guys?" Tozzi barked.

"Rico Tozzi, I'd like you to meet Peter Betz, the owner and founder of the Betz Radio Network, and Bart Johnson, the BRN Corporate Counsel."

"I don't want no fucking lawyers in here!"

Peter stepped in. "Mr. Tozzi, Bart's been involved in all of our most intricate negotiations and investigations. He's..."

"Goddammit! I said I don't want no fucking lawyers in here." Tozzi lit a cigarette. "Either the lawyer goes or I go."

I walked over to the door and opened it. "Well, thank you for coming, Mr. Tozzi." I stood there and motioned for him to leave.

Tozzi drew deeply on his cigarette, eyed both Peter and Bart. "Close the fucking door, smartass. Fine. He can stay."

I closed the door and everyone but the bodyguard sat down. "What brings you to our studio unannounced, Mr. Tozzi?" I asked.

"You said you'd give me a thousand dollars to talk on the radio."

I had written that note, but I never told Peter or Bart about it. I hadn't really thought he'd take the bait. I glanced at both of them, and Peter, to his credit, backed me up.

"That's my money, Mr. Tozzi," Peter answered. "You won't see a cent of it unless you agree to answer all of Michael's questions. All of them."

"What the fuck is this? The fucking Spanish Inquisition? You told me that if I talked on the radio before I went to Congress you'd give me a G."

"Well, yes," I said, "but you've got to answer our questions. That's how my show works.""

"What kind of questions?"

Bart jumped in. "Anything we ask. Your background. Your business. Who you know. What you know. And why you've been called to testify in front of this House Committee."

"Well, I'll tell you why I'm talking to Congressman Dailey," he said without even attempting to disguise the disdain in his voice. "But that other stuff..." His voice trailed off.

"As I understand it, Mr. Tozzi," I said, "you feel you've been painted unfairly in the Detroit press, that your name and reputation have been tarnished."

"That's right."

"What better way to get your own views across than talking to twenty million people coast-to-coast? You answer my questions the way you want to, and then all of America can decide what they think of you." Peter tried desperately to suppress a smile.

"Yeah. All I gotta do is answer your fucking questions, then everybody will know I'm just a regular guy."

"Exactly," I said. "You're a regular guy."

"So, why are you talking to Leo Dailey?" Bart wondered.

"Ah, he's a fucking putz!" snapped Tozzi. "He couldn't hit water if he fell out of a boat. But he sure does think a lot of himself." He lit another smoke. "He wants me to talk about the FBI and how they keep checking me out."

Peter, Bart and I just looked at each other. Finally, I asked, "What does that have to do with the president's conduct?"

"He told me he's trying to develop this pattern of conduct, like Roosevelt abuses his authority and has people he doesn't like investigated for no reason."

Bart Johnson leaned back in his chair and ran his hand across his forehead. "Really?" he muttered.

"Yeah, really," Tozzi shot back at him. "What? You think I'm just making this fucking stuff up?"

"No, no," Bart replied. "Just a little surprised, that's all."

"The FBI checks up on me all the fucking time. I swear, I should just give them offices at the bowling alley. I know all the fucking FBI agents in Detroit."

"How long has this been going on?" I wondered.

"As long as that prick's been in the White House. I mean, things were fine when Hoover was there. Then Roosevelt comes in and boom! I'm fucking living with the G-Men."

"Hoover?" Peter wanted clarified. "Herbert Hoover or J. Edgar Hoover?"

"Herbert Fucking Hoover!" Tozzi snapped. "That's a pretty dumb fucking question for a guy who owns the fucking network."

Peter didn't like being dressed down. "Maybe so, but this dumb fucking guy has the cash that you won't see if you don't answer our dumb fucking questions."

"OK, OK, Herbert Hoover. J. Edgar Hoover's the queer ruining my life."

"Excuse me?" I said. "Run that by me again."

Tozzi looked at me like I was from a different planet, and he spoke slower. "Hoover the FBI guy is a queer. And he's ruining my life."

"You're saying Hoover's homosexual?"

"What? Like you didn't know?" Tozzi was surprised, especially when he looked around and saw that Peter and Bart had the same looks I did. "Yeah, the guy's a fruitcake. He's got this guy Clive that he likes to hump. Christ, I've got a file on Hoover as thick as the one he's got on me. Hey, you guys got anything to drink?"

Peter called Janine, told her to bring a bottle of Scotch to my office.

"So, what else you guys wanna know? Is that it?"

"No, Mr. Tozzi," I said. "We've got plenty of questions. I guess the most important is making sure that you definitely want to be interviewed on the radio, and you're willing to do it before you testify in front of Leo Dailey."

"Yeah. I want the G. And I'll tell you everything you want to know, unless of course I don't want to."

"It doesn't work that way," I reminded him. "You answer all the questions, then you get the money. Besides, if you don't answer everything, people across America are going to have an incomplete view of who you are."

Tozzi shrugged his shoulders, as Janine entered with the Scotch and glasses. Tozzi was the only one who had a drink, and we all got comfortable. For the next ninety minutes, we sat in my office and talked about Rico Tozzi's life, career, his connections to Leo Dailey, the Mob and his involvement with the FDR investigation. What we felt at the end of our chat was no motive to help Dailey, only a motive to hurt FDR for having the FBI investigate him.

Peter, Bart and I huddled for a few minutes near the end of our discussion, with Rico Tozzi still sitting there drinking Scotch. "OK, Mr. Tozzi," I said, "you've got a deal. Tomorrow at noon, you'll be in our studio and we'll talk about everything we've talked about here today. But you've got to answer all the questions I ask. At the end of the hour, we'll give you the money. Deal?"

Rico Tozzi stood up, smacked down his Scotch glass, took his cigarette out of his mouth and shook my hand. "Deal." He turned to leave my office.

"We'll send a car for you," I said.

"No you fucking won't," he retorted. "I'll be here in time. This is what you call trust. You gotta trust me that I'll show up. I gotta trust you you're going to pay me." Then he opened the door and walked out, surrounded by his security detail.

We watched him walk out. Then Peter looked at me and said, "Two years ago you never would have handled that like you did today. Paying him a thousand dollars to talk…." He let the sentence dangle. "Nice job, Michael."

About thirty minutes later, after I'd re-scheduled tomorrow's original guest, Sydney Greenstreet, my phone rang.

"Mr. Audray, this is Warren Doones."

"Mr. Doones! Where are you?"

"I'm in Hagerstown, Maryland. I got off the train here. I'm not going to take it into Washington. I've been reading the newspapers along the way, and every paper I pick up has a story about me. I figure if you were smart enough to send somebody to meet me in St. Louis, there'd be a hundred people in Washington. I don't want to have to look at all those flashbulbs. Maybe I'm wrong, but I'm guessing there's going to be a lot of reporters meeting that train. So, I got off."

I had to think fast. "What are you going to do, Mr. Doones? Do you want me to meet you?"

"I'm not sure what I want, Mr. Audray. Part of me wants to talk with you, and part of me just wants to go home."

"You don't want to talk with Congressman Dailey anymore?"

"I think I have to. He told me he'd subpoena me if I didn't come to Washington. I told him I couldn't afford to take the train right now, so he paid for it."

I could hear some confusion and ambivalence in his voice. "Look, Warren. May I call you Warren?"

"Sure."

"Warren, I can be in Hagerstown in about two hours. I'll drive there by myself. I'll drive you to your hotel. Or, if you want to, you can stay at my apartment for a couple days."

Warren Doones thought about it for a minute. Finally, he said OK. He said he'd be sitting at the Hagerstown train depot, wearing a black pin-stripe suit, a black fedora, round glasses and traveling with a dark green valise.

Before I left, I called Tim Cullen. "What have you found out about Warren Doones?"

"Not much," he said. "About the only personal thing we've been able to dig up is that he's an amateur photographer."

On the drive to Hagerstown, my mind was racing. Formulating questions for Rico Tozzi, how to continue gaining the trust of Warren Doones. All the while, I kept thinking about the power of the radio network. Through a combination of hard work, luck and tenacity, I'd been able to snag the most sought-after interviews in America, back-to-back. And one of the interviewees was going to stay at my place.

The Hagerstown train depot was nearly empty when I arrived. It wasn't difficult to spot Warren Doones, and we greeted each other warmly. I put his valise in the trunk of my car as we headed back toward DC. Over the next two hours, I learned a lot about him: where he grew up, what his favorite sport was, how he met his wife, the names and ages of his four kids, what it's like to have a teenage daughter who wants to date, his reluctant but successful run for the Flagstaff school board, what a mechanical engineer does on a daily basis, his favorite recipes to make, and his photography hobby. But when I tried to steer the conversation around to why he would be testifying, what he would say and how he came to Leo Dailey's attention, he remained tight-lipped.

"I'm just not sure I should say anything right now."

"Warren, if you tell your story to Congress, people are only going to be able to read your words. They'll get reported all over, and you'll be quoted, that's for sure. But if you agree to talk with me on the radio, people will be able to hear your words in your own voice and in your own style. It'll be a much more complete picture of what you know. Whatever that is."

Still, Warren Doones wasn't convinced he should talk on the air. I told him I was going to interview Rico Tozzi tomorrow at noon, "and he needed to be convinced, just like you," I said. "He decided it was a good thing to do."

As we pulled into my apartment building, Warren told me he'd think about it overnight and let me know in the morning.

"Michael, I just want you to know I appreciate you helping me like this."

"Like what?"

"Oh, picking me up and keeping me away from all the other reporters. I mean, I know you're a reporter, too, and you want me to talk with you about what I know. I'll make you this promise: I won't talk to any other reporters but you. My wife and I think you're fair and we like your style. We listen to you all the time. If I'm going to talk with anybody, I'll talk with you."

Chapter 25 – Rico, Warren and Anne

The next morning I awoke around 5:30. I showered and dressed before Warren woke up. I called the network and spoke with Tim Cullen.

"Tim, you've got to send one of your interns to the Sheraton and check in under the name Edward Dunwoody. Make sure he takes a suitcase with him, and pays in cash up front for three days."

"What the hell's going on, Michael?"

"You've got to trust me, Tim. You've got to do this right away. The Sheraton. Edward Dunwoody. Now. I'll explain when I get in."

"Fine." I could tell Tim Cullen was exasperated, but he knew this was important.

Then I called Earl and woke him up. I told him to keep an eye on my apartment all day long, that I had a visitor there I didn't want leaving. And I sure as hell didn't want anyone coming. Earl demanded to know who was there. Very quietly I told him. Earl started laughing. "You sly son of a bitch." He agreed to get over to my place within the hour and get more details later.

I made coffee and toast for breakfast. I apologized to Warren for not having more food in my place, but I promised I'd have someone deliver all kinds of food later this morning. I told him it would be someone from BRN, and he should not open the door without seeing a BRN identification card first. I left for the network only after I noticed Earl's car.

I made a pit stop at my office and gathered some of my notes from yesterday's meeting. Then I scurried down to Peter's office, scooping up Bart and Tim along the way.

"You won't believe who's staying at my apartment for the next couple days," I burbled.

"Well, it's not Edward Dunwoody," Tim Cullen said.

"Yes, it is," I said. "Only his real name is Warren Doones."

196

Looks of disbelief spread throughout Peter's office. I recounted the story of how he ended up staying with me. I told Peter we needed to send lots of food to my place, and that it had to be delivered by a BRN staffer with an ID card. I asked Bart if we were in any kind of trouble for housing a congressional witness. I told him Warren Doones had not been subpoenaed, only threatened with one. Bart seemed to think we were OK. And Tim Cullen knew exactly why we needed to send the intern to the Sheraton when I called.

"Dailey's going to make sure he checked in, right?"

I nodded. "But Warren doesn't expect Dailey to stop by." I also told them Earl was keeping an eye on my apartment, but we should put somebody inside. Tim suggested another news intern, Anne Seals. I said fine, as long as she can stay there all day with him.

Janine called the market and had them box up $50 worth of food and drinks. Anne Seals picked it up, dropped off a note from Peter to Earl telling him he could leave as soon as Anne was in, and went up to my apartment. She slid her BRN card underneath the door, and was greeted by Warren Doones, fully dressed in a dark blue suit and tie.

After Anne Seals reached my apartment to stay with Warren Doones, Earl went to the Sheraton. He slipped the manager $20 to keep everyone away from Dunwoody's room, and promised him another $30 if he kept track of when and who asked for Dunwoody. Within thirty minutes, the Sheraton manager called Earl. One of Leo Dailey's relatively young staffers inquired about Mr. Dunwoody, but was informed Dunwoody left detailed and specific instructions not to be disturbed by anyone. Earl instructed the manager to call whenever he had more information.

Tim Cullen directed his intern, Willie Houston, to stay in the room, not talk to anyone and call the network at 11 a.m. for further instructions. When he called, Cullen asked for his room number, told him we'd deliver food to him, and to keep his mouth shut. Willie, young and eager to please the network news director, said, "Yes, sir."

I went into the air studio around 11:30 that morning, needing some quiet time to finish prepping for Rico Tozzi. At 11:56, I looked up and saw Rico and his six guards walk toward the studio. Rico and his main guard entered, but I told him the guard had to wait outside. "Just you and me, Rico." Rico nodded, and his main guard left the studio.

The last thing I told Rico before we went on was, "Watch your fucking mouth, Rico. We're live coast-to-fucking-coast." Rico Tozzi grinned and nodded.

"Good afternoon, and welcome to the BRN Midday Conversation. I'm Michael Audray. Over the past few months, the nation's attention has been riveted on the personal scandal surrounding the President and Mrs. Roosevelt. Even as the events in Europe have become increasingly ugly, we are fixated on the details of the First Family's personal life. Congressman Leo Dailey, a freshman Republican from Montana, is chairing a House Committee investigation into the president's conduct. That drama reached all the way to the United States Supreme Court a few weeks ago, with a ruling that anyone who currently works inside the Roosevelt White House, or who did so in an earlier term, is protected by the president's executive privilege and cannot be compelled to testify. But Congressman Dailey, himself the subject of a personal life exposé, has refused to buckle. Indeed, he has stepped up the investigation, and this week his committee has begun hearing testimony from a number of different people with insights into the conduct of the First Family. One of the people called to testify in front of the Committee is Rico Tozzi. Mr. Tozzi is scheduled to testify tomorrow. But today, we'll spend the next hour with Rico Tozzi, as we learn who he is, what he does, and how he fits into this investigation. Thank you for joining us, Mr. Tozzi."

Rico leaned in toward the microphone and practically yelled, "Glad to be here, Michael."

"You can speak normally, Mr. Tozzi," I said, motioning with my hands to speak a little more softly. "Let's find out a little about you. Tell us where you're from and what you do."

Rico cleared his throat. "Well, Michael, it's like this. I was born in Detroit, raised there, went to Catholic school there, still live there. My mom and dad, God rest their souls, raised me and my brothers to always take care of ourselves, and to help other people when we could."

"How many brothers do you have?"

"Two, one older, one younger. Alphonse is my older brother and Don is my kid brother. Anyway, my dad worked hard his whole life, and my mom took care of us and ran the house."

"What did your dad do?"

"What did my dad do? Yeah, what did my dad do? That's a good question. I don't really know."

"You don't know what your dad did?"

"No."

"You really don't know what your dad did?"

Rico was getting hot. But at least he didn't swear. "No, I really do not know what my dad did. I was a kid, you know. I didn't pay attention to what he did."

"You said your dad passed. How old were you when he passed?"

"Me? I was, let me think, I was thirty."

"You were thirty when your dad passed and you don't know what he did for a living?"

"For the seventy millionth time, no."

"OK. But we've heard reports your father was a close associate of a number of top Midwest gangsters."

Rico pointed his finger at me. "My dad worked down by where the Ambassador Bridge is, between Detroit and Canada. He always came home smelling like fish. But I don't know what he did!"

"Alright, Mr. Tozzi. Let's move on. Where'd you go to school? What did you study?"

More calmly, Rico answered the questions. "I went to the University of Detroit, both high school and a little bit of college. My mom wanted me to be able to be a businessman, so I studied business and economics, things like that."

"Did your brothers go to school there, too?"

"Yeah, yeah. We all did. Only Don graduated from college, though. He's the real smart one in the family." Rico chuckled at his own expense.

"Do they still live in Detroit? What do they do? How do they earn their livings?"

"Alphonse, he moved on to Pittsburgh. He's got one of them Mary Carter Paint businesses, one of them franchises. He's been living there for a long time, I guess." Rico absent-mindedly began playing with a pencil in front of him. "And Don still lives in Detroit. He's a teacher. He teaches sixth grade at Our Lady of Sorrow Catholic school."

"And what about you? What does Rico Tozzi do for a living?"

"I own Tozzi's Bowling Alley on the East Side of Detroit."

"Tell me a little bit about it. Is it big?"

"Yeah, it's big. It's got forty lanes, and a restaurant and a bar inside it."

"How long have you owned it?"

"Fourteen years."

"Has the restaurant and bar always been in it?"

"Yeah, absolutely. It kind of goes with bowling, know what I mean?"

"I think I do. What took place inside the bar before 1933?"

Rico smiled and wagged his finger at me. "You're tricky, you are. I know what you're doing. Hey, we are an upstanding business. People of all ages come and bowl there. We got lots of kid leagues, women like to come and play, we got pool tables there. It's a nice place for the whole family."

"Sounds like a wonderful place, Mr. Tozzi. We're going to take a break, and when we return, we'll talk about why you think the FBI has been targeting you over the years. More with Rico Tozzi, when the BRN Midday Conversation continues."

I closed the microphones and took off my headset. "How'm I doing?" Rico asked. I told him fine, but we were going to ask some tough questions next, and he better be ready to answer.

Janine came in during the break and handed me a note from Peter. He got a call from Leo Dailey screaming about our interview with Rico Tozzi. Peter jotted that Dailey threatened him with contempt of Congress. He reminded me to get Rico to say he was appearing in front of the House Committee voluntarily, so we would have it in the public record we were not interfering with Congress in any manner.

When we got back from the break, I jumped right in. "Mr. Tozzi, you have been the subject of numerous investigations by local, state and federal authorities. Though you've never been arrested in connection with these investigations, authorities continue to believe that you are connected with large gambling operations, loan sharking, what is loosely called enforcement, and prostitution…"

"I've never done none of those things!"

"That's my question, Mr. Tozzi. Why do you think that in 1935, the Detroit Police Department raided your bowling alley in an effort to break up a large prostitution ring, only to find nothing?"

"I don't know. They're idiots."

"Then in 1937, the Michigan State Police went undercover and discovered a sophisticated bookmaking enterprise was operating out of the back room at Tozzi's Bowling Alley, only to discover absolutely nothing when they raided your establishment."

"They're idiots, too. There was nothing there."

"Later that year, 1937, and continuing through just two months ago, the FBI has consistently monitored your bowling alley. In reports released by J. Edgar Hoover…"

"You know what I think about him!" interrupted Rico Tozzi.

"...the FBI is convinced that the bulk of illegal, underworld racketeering in the Midwest takes root at Tozzi's Bowling Alley in Detroit..."

"That's a lie!" Rico snapped.

"...and that you are able to escape detection through a sophisticated network of informants and payoffs, thereby compounding the scope of your illegal activity."

"They're all a bunch of scum," Rico Tozzi growled. "They don't know nothing! The Federal Bureau of Idiots wouldn't know illegal activity from a breadbox. I'm just a regular businessman, trying my hardest to make a living, to make my mother proud, to live up to her dream of me being a businessman. If they think I'm such a crook, how come they can't find nothing? How come they can't prove nothing?"

"I don't know, Mr. Tozzi. Why can't they?"

"Because there's nothing to prove. They've been digging into me and my business for years, and they ain't found nothing! I wish somebody would show me where all this money and power is that I'm supposed to have."

"Where do you live, Mr. Tozzi?"

"Detroit. I already told you."

"But where in Detroit do you live? Don't you live in Grosse Pointe, a very nice, rather upscale part of the city?"

"Yeah, I live in Grosse Pointe. So what?"

"Your house has twenty-seven rooms, including six bathrooms and six bedrooms. You have a separate guest house, a four-car garage and an enclosed gazebo, all situated on six acres of prime city property."

"Yeah. What's your point, Audray?"

"I'm just wondering how a guy who owns one bowling alley makes that kind of money to be able to afford a house like that. How do you do it?"

Rico Tozzi leaned back in his chair and rubbed his fingers against his lips. He took his time answering, and I just let the question hang. "I invested wisely," he eventually said.

"What did you invest in?"

Again, Rico Tozzi leaned back and glowered at me. "Stocks," he said slowly, "and United States Saving Bonds, because that's the patriotic thing to do."

"Mr. Tozzi, if you're just a regular business guy, who's a patriotic American buying US Savings Bonds, why do you travel with six bodyguards?"

Up until this point, everything we talked about was covered yesterday in my office. But this question hadn't been.

"I don't," he said.

I was astounded. "Mr. Tozzi, I can see six bodyguards right outside our studio door. What do you mean you don't travel with six bodyguards?"

"I mean, sometimes I travel with ten."

I laughed out loud. "Alright, why do you travel with anywhere from six to ten bodyguards?"

"Because you never know when the FBI is going to do something really stupid, like try to shoot me. This is a dangerous world, and I want to be prepared."

"So you're telling me that you travel with armed bodyguards because you want to be protected from the FBI?"

"Yes."

"Hmmm," I muttered. "We'll take a break and be right back." I told Rico Tozzi to relax, that we only had a few minutes left. He was visibly relieved.

Peter motioned for me to step out of the studio for a minute, away from Tozzi's main bodyguard. He whispered Bart was on the phone right then with McKay, and Dailey had ordered the lunch recess to go until two o'clock. Peter smiled when he said Dailey was really pissed off. He told me to finish Tozzi.

I walked back in the studio for the last segment. "Mr. Tozzi, you're scheduled to testify tomorrow in front of the House Committee investigating the First Family's conduct. Do you know why you're testifying?"

"No, not really."

"You're testifying, and you don't really know why you're testifying?"

"That's right."

"Have you been subpoenaed to testify in front of the Committee?"

"No. I've never been served with a subpoena in my life."

"I just want to be clear, Mr. Tozzi. You are voluntarily testifying in front of the House Committee tomorrow morning."

"Yes, alright? They asked me to go. I'm going, and I'll answer whatever questions I get asked."

"What do you expect to be asked?"

"I expect that the congressmen will ask me questions about how a legitimate businessman like me, a lowly bowling alley owner, has been bullied by the FBI for years and years, even though they can't prove anything that I'm doing wrong."

"As I understand it, Mr. Tozzi, this Committee is investigating the president's conduct. How does the FBI investigating your business fall into that category?"

"It's like this, Michael." Rico Tozzi got very comfortable when he gave this answer. "Ever since my ancestors came over here from Italy and tried to make a life for ourselves, guys like Roosevelt have had it in for us. If your name is Capone or Pascucci or Corleone or Capogna or Tozzi, you've got cops checking you out. Now there's some bad guys among us, sure. But I'm not Al Capone. I run a bowling alley! I work my tookus off every day. I don't do nothing wrong, I go to church every Sunday, I help out around my neighborhood. But every day, I got the FBI in my face, wanting to see this or see that. They just threaten me everyday. And the way I see it, the FBI works for J. Edgar Hoover. But he takes his orders from Franklin D. Roosevelt. And I am one American who is sick and tired of being constantly bothered by the FBI. So, that's the part of the president's conduct I want to talk about."

Leo Dailey's strategy became as clear as Waterford crystal when I heard this answer. Leo was going to combine both the personal and professional conduct of the president to make his case that FDR was abusing the authority of the office. "Who contacted you to testify in front of the House Committee?"

"Congressman Leo Dailey."

"Were you surprised that he asked you to testify?"

"Yeah, a little bit."

"Do you know Congressman Dailey?"

"Yeah. We know each other."

"When did you first meet the Congressman?"

"Long before he was a congressman, let me tell you that!" Rico Tozzi laughed at his own remark. "I guess I met Leo in, I mean, Leo Dailey, in about 1931 or 1932. Something like that."

"Where'd you meet him?"

"We met in Milwaukee. We were both on business trips."

"Were you both meeting a man named Lou Martilotta?"

Rico Tozzi smiled and wagged his finger at me again. "Maybe. I don't really remember."

I rolled my eyes and kept going. "Do you know Congressman Dailey's wife, Jane?"

Rico Tozzi clearly enunciated each syllable of "Intimately."

"Really, Mr. Tozzi? Intimately? You know Jane Hall Dailey intimately?"

"Yes, I know Janie intimately. I hear you ask Clark Gable and Lana Turner and all those big stars questions like that, and I know what they mean. I don't know Lana Turner intimately, but I know Janie intimately." We both laughed at the sheer audacity of his remarks.

"Alright then." I tried to stop laughing. "I'll leave that one on the table for you, Mr. Tozzi. But how long have you known her?"

"Ah, jeez, at least as long as I've known Leo, I mean, the congressman."

"Have you ever contributed in any way to any of Leo Dailey's political campaigns? Money or volunteering your time or anything like that?"

"Yeah. I've tossed some money his way every time he's run for something."

"Why would a bowling alley owner in Detroit contribute money to a candidate running for office in Montana, Mr. Tozzi?"

"That's a good question." Tozzi hesitated and said, "I like him. I like his style. I like what he stands for. I like how he thinks about issues, like me being smacked around by the FBI. He thinks that's wrong, too. So I tossed him some dough. And there's nothing wrong with that," Tozzi pointedly remarked.

"So you gave him these campaign contributions - what, thousands of dollars?"

"Yeah, probably."

"So you gave Leo Dailey thousands of dollars in campaign contributions. Was there ever a quid pro quo?"

"A what? My father smelled like fish, but I don't know what a squid pro whatever is."

I chuckled at his feigned ignorance. I knew he knew. "You never thought that by giving Leo Dailey money to get elected he might turn around and help you sometime?"

"No, never. Nothing like that. He's a nice guy. And his wife!"

Again, I rolled my eyes, but didn't touch it. "We have only time for one more question. Mr. Tozzi, do you expect us to believe that a man who owns a single bowling alley in Detroit, lives in a twenty-seven-room house on six acres in Grosse Pointe, travels with anywhere between six and ten bodyguards, volunteers to testify in front of a Congressional committee without even really knowing what the testimony is expected to provide, contributes money to a relatively unknown Montana state politician for every election he's run in for the past ten years, and has admitted intimately knowing that congressman's wife, you expect us to believe you're really on the level?"

"What?" Rico Tozzi looked at me incredulously. "You got a problem with that?"

I wrapped it up and turned off the microphones. Tozzi stuck his hand out toward me. I shook his hand. "You're alright, Michael. That went pretty well, don't you think?"

"It was certainly memorable, Rico. I'm sure people have a much clearer picture now of who you are. By the way," I said, "I know your niece Sharon."

"Sharon?" He seemed puzzled. "You mean Don's girl? Little Sharon? How you know her?"

"She works in Washington, and we've met."

"Jesus, Sharon. God, I haven't seen her since she was just a little squirt."

Just then, Peter walked up. Rico greeted him with "Hey, Mr. Money!"

"You kept up your end of the deal, Mr. Tozzi," Peter said. "But now you're going to have to trust me. I'm not going to give you the money we discussed yet. I'll give it to you tomorrow, after you finish testifying in front of Leo's committee. Your appearance here created quite a stir in Congress, or at least in certain offices in Congress. I wouldn't want you to have to perjure yourself tomorrow if they ask you about money."

Rico Tozzi smiled. "That's pretty good thinking. Because you know, I don't want no trouble."

"Trust me," Peter said. "You'll have your money after your congressional appearance."

Rico Tozzi nodded. He didn't need the money, but a deal was a deal. He opted to trust Peter. He and his bodyguards left. By that time, word filtered back that Leo Dailey was using Rico Tozzi's BRN interview to his advantage. He was rewriting tomorrow's opening remarks to reference how Rico's network radio appearance underscored his sincerity and beliefs about the abuse of presidential power. Dailey was one of the few members of Congress who truly understood that an ideological point of view, even if completely unsubstantiated by facts, could be furthered by selectively addressing parts of the truth.

I left my office around 3 p.m. I still had to convince Warren Doones that appearing on my show prior to his congressional testimony was in the best interest of both him and the United States.

Suffice it to say I was not prepared for what I saw when I reached my apartment. News Intern Anne Seals was giving head in order to get ahead. She and Warren Doones, naked and completely oblivious to my entrance, were deep in the throes of passion in my bed. She was on top, sitting on his face, as his hard Republican member was buried deep in her mouth. The moans from both of them were steady and genuine, and it didn't look like this was the first time they'd done this today. Her skirt, blouse and bra were scattered around the living room, and her panties were hanging on my doorknob.

I poured myself a drink and sat down in my chair facing the bedroom. I couldn't see anything from that angle, but I could hear it all. Warren Doones stamina matched Anne Seals insatiability.

After about forty-five minutes, Anne Seals got up out of bed, wrapped his shirt around her and walked into the living room. "Hi, Michael," she said quietly and confidently. I'd seen her around the news department, knew her name, and actually found her quite attractive. She was about twenty-one, a senior at Georgetown, 5'3", slightly buxom with mid-back length blonde hair. As she walked past me toward the kitchen, she said, "I think you have the guest you want for tomorrow."

I followed her into the kitchen and tried to say something, anything. But this extremely self-assured, and dare I say, talented, young woman put me at ease.

"I didn't plan on any of this," she said. "I brought the food here and started putting it away. He came in to the kitchen and we started talking. I was fumbling around with your coffee pot - you really have to get a better percolator, Michael - and he helped me. We had some breakfast and I asked him what his part in all of this congressional stuff is. And he told me." She poured herself a glass of tap water, took a sip.

"And?" I begged.

"And what?" she wondered.

"What is his part in all of this?"

"He hasn't told you?" Anne Seals tried to stifle a laugh. "You were in a car for two hours with him, you put him up at your apartment, and you're trying to get him on your show, and you don't even know what his part in all this is?" She laughed again.

"Well," I ventured, "I'm not as good looking as you."

She chortled and shook her head. "Anyway, he told me what happened. See, he and his family were vacationing in Washington last year. They took a group tour of the White House, but at one point, Warren strayed from the group to poke his head in another room. He had a camera with him, and he wanted to take some pictures of rooms that the public doesn't get to see very often. He said he didn't see any guards or anything, so he walked down a hall and saw a door half-open. He poked his head in silently and saw a woman on her knees going down on FDR. He knows they didn't see him. He couldn't stop looking. Like I said, he had his camera with him, and he realized that no one would believe him without some kind of proof. So he took some pictures."

"He took pictures of FDR and this woman? Was it Lucy?" Anne shook her head. "No. I don't know who it is."

"It wasn't Lucy?" I was incredulous. This was getting more bizarre by the moment. "Didn't the flash bulbs get their attention?"

"Well, that's the thing," she said. "He had this new kind of camera and film that takes a picture using whatever light is around. He didn't use a flashbulb."

I was mesmerized. Here I was, standing in my own kitchen, with a nearly naked news intern telling me that the mystery witness in a congressional hearing, who is currently blissful and naked in my bedroom, has a photograph of the president enjoying the explorations of another woman, and he's going to testify to that.

"Where are the pictures?" I asked Anne.

"In your bedroom. He showed them to me."

"He showed them?"

"Yeah," she said. "That's when things got going. He said he'd never even heard about *that*."

"You mean…?"

"Yeah. Well, I told him it was exciting. One thing led to another, and…" Anne Seals took a breather and a sip of water. "I've got to tell you, Michael. He's pretty good. He catches on pretty quick." She was so matter-of-fact about the whole thing.

"What's he doing right now?"

"I think he's sleeping. I don't think he knows you're here. I thought I heard you come in, but I didn't care at that moment."

We just stood there for a minute, looking at each other. Eventually, we burst out laughing. Finally, I asked her what kind of a guy he is.

"He's never done anything like this before, I can tell you that," she said with a wicked smile. "He's been married twenty-three years, he's got kids, he's on the school board, that kind of thing. He's a pretty straight-laced guy. He's kind of cute."

I just stood there, shaking my head and smiling. Another minute passed, then I asked her how he came to Leo Dailey's attention.

"He'd been reading about it, and, actually, listening to your show. He felt that Roosevelt was doing a good job, even though he voted for Willkie. He thinks Hitler's got to be stopped, but he believes we need leaders who will truly lead by example. So, he wrote a letter to Dailey about a month ago and told him about these pictures."

"How many pictures are there?"

"Three. So Dailey called him up about ten days ago and asked him all kinds of questions. Then he said he wanted Warren to come to Washington to tell everybody about this. Warren didn't really want to, but Dailey said he'd subpoena him if he didn't cooperate. So, after talking it over with his wife, Warren said he'd be willing to come to Washington if his expenses would get covered. Dailey said that was a deal. And now he's in your bedroom." She took another drink of water.

"What's your sense: is he willing to do this?"

She considered her answer. "He's reluctantly willing, a little ambivalent, mostly about being in the spotlight himself. He offered to give the pictures to Dailey if he didn't have to testify. But Dailey said unless he came forth, people would assume the pictures were fake."

"But now, he's willing to go on the radio and tell his story to twenty million listeners?"

"Mm-hmm," she said with a twinkle in her eye, "Let's not forget who made him *come*." She touched my cheek and walked back into the bedroom.

She closed the door and told Warren she was going to take off. He was quite clearly uncomfortable with me being there at this moment, so I tried to diffuse his awkwardness. I poked my head in the room and said, "Hi, Warren. Anne tells me you're willing to talk about things on the radio tomorrow. That's great. Glad you made that decision. Take your time, get dressed. We'll figure out all the details. Don't worry about a thing. Really, don't worry."

About ten minutes later, Anne and Warren came out from my bedroom, fully clothed. Anne was amazingly calm and composed, while Warren seemed sheepish. "I'll come by around eight tomorrow morning and make sure you get to the network safely, Warren," she said as she lightly kissed him on the cheek. Then she just tossed off a "See you later, Michael," and she was out the door.

Warren Doones and I stood there, looking first at the door, then at each other. Eventually, he said, "I've never done anything like this before. You've got to believe me."

"Forget about it, Warren. You don't have to explain anything to me. And everything stays within these walls." I sized him up and asked, "Want a drink?" He nodded. I handed him a whiskey and water and invited him to sit down. We talked for quite a while about the photographs he had, how he kept quiet about them ("I didn't even tell my wife for the longest time," he said) and his personal crisis in coming forward with them.

"I'm not like you, Michael," he said. "I mean, I don't want to be famous. I ran for the school board, and that was really difficult. And I actually think President Roosevelt is doing a pretty good job. But if he's really been living this kind of double life, and his wife, too, and the kids know about it, well, maybe we do need to expose him. Maybe it'll help him be more honest with us Americans about everything, including the war." Then he spouted a Leo Dailey line. "It's hard to know if the war is really getting as bad as FDR says it is or if he's just telling us that to cover up what's going on in his personal life. I mean, does Roosevelt want us to get into the war to save Europe or save himself? I don't really know. But I have these pictures, and I finally thought somebody should know about them."

Warren got up and went into my bedroom and came back with two envelopes. "Here they are," he said, and handed one envelope to me.

I looked at the three explicit pictures Warren Doones had taken. I'd seen other ones with better angles, but there was no mistaking who was in them and what was going on. They were pictures of FDR and his secretary, Missy LeHand.

"I have another one in this envelope, too," Warren told me. I stretched out my hand, but Warren held tight. "This isn't of the president." He gingerly placed the envelope in my fingers.

I opened it up to see an outdoor picture of Eleanor and Lorena, locked in a clearly passionate kiss. "Where'd you get this one, Warren?"

"Two years ago, we were on another vacation at the Grand Canyon. It's not too far from Flagstaff, and we went there for a couple of days. We knew Mrs. Roosevelt was going to be making a speech there, so we thought maybe we'd see her. We got to this spot just down the road from where she was going to give her speech. My wife and kids went ahead to get a seat, and I stayed behind with my camera. I was thinking I could get a great shot of Eleanor Roosevelt with the Grand Canyon in the background. I saw her standing there talking with this other woman. I figured they were friends, the way they were talking, so I just pointed my camera at them. I'm standing maybe thirty yards away, and all of a sudden, they started kissing. I only took this one picture because I was so stunned. I'm sure they didn't see me, but when I left they were still kissing. I caught up with my family and told them we had to go. But my wife insisted we stay and listen to the First Lady. That whole time, I was in a fog. My wife asked me if I got the picture I wanted, and I said no. That's the truth. I didn't want this picture."

Warren seemed to melt in the chair. He sipped his drink and sat silently.

I gently asked him if Leo Dailey knew about this picture. Warren said no. Immediately, I knew if Warren revealed the existence of all four pictures on my show the next day, BRN would blow the doors off both the Oval Office and Congress. We would once again re-assert dominance over this story.

I made a good dinner for us, got Warren to start feeling better about himself and trust me even more. I put his mind at ease over the contradictory nature of why he was in Washington DC and what happened with Anne Seals.

Dressed exquisitely, Anne Seals sauntered in with a cheery Good Morning for both Warren and me at precisely eight o'clock Friday morning. Warren seemed glad to see her, although he had told me there would be "no further activity." Anne figured out how to get him out of my apartment and into the network without anybody noticing. She said she'd deliver Warren to my office by 11:30, and I believed her.

When I got to my office, I must have had fifty messages. Some of them were rivals with mock congratulations for my Rico Tozzi interview. Some were interview requests from newspapers and weekly magazines. A few were from people I didn't know. One was from Sharon Tozzi.

"Now are you convinced I don't know this guy?" She laughed when I called her at Senator Buckfield's office. "Honest to God, Michael, my dad *is* the smart one in that family. I called my dad during the interview and told him to listen, and he said he had no desire to hear what Rico was saying."

"It'll be interesting to hear what both Rico and Leo have to say today," I replied. "And I think you should listen today, too."

"Who's on, Michael?" I hesitated. "C'mon, Michael, who are you talking to today?"

"Warren Doones."

"No kidding! How'd you get him? What's he got?"

"Long story how I got him, Sharon. He's got pictures."

"Pictures! Of who?"

"You're just going to have to listen. I've got to go."

"I'm going to tell Buckfield."

"I know. See you."

Earl left a message regarding Edward Dunwoody. His hotel sources told him Dunwoody had five attempted visitors yesterday, but none got through.

Tim Cullen was on his way to the House Committee hearing. Peter stopped by to tell me both McKay and Kerse personally registered their belief our Rico Tozzi interview interfered with a congressional investigation. He laughed. "Wait'll they hear today!" He was grinning ear to ear.

About an hour later, Leo Dailey opened up the House Committee hearings for the day with a brief statement.

"Good morning. This Committee is searching for the truth regarding the conduct of the president of the United States and his wife and family. Most of the attention has been focused on his personal conduct. Today, though, we will look at the way the president uses and abuses the power at his disposal. Many of you may have heard a radio interview yesterday with our witness for the day, Mr. Rico Tozzi of Detroit, Michigan. While you may have heard what he had to say then, you haven't heard it all. We will detail the abuses the Federal Bureau of Investigation has rained down on a legitimate businessman. And you will be astounded at the end of the day. However, there is another story of FBI abuse with which I am even more familiar. It directly involves the president and me. Recently, I was summoned to meet the president in his office. I had never been alone in the Oval Office prior to this meeting. When I arrived, the president was sitting at his desk. He asked me to approach him, and when I did, he tossed an envelope at me. Inside the envelope were photographs the FBI took of my wife and me over the past year. The president directly threatened me, telling me to remember who was in charge, and that the FBI was watching. I told the president of the United States I was not scared of him. I have the truth on my side. I am more convinced than ever that if President Roosevelt would use the FBI to threaten my wife and me in a blatant attempt to shut down an investigation into his conduct, he would certainly use the FBI to investigate, harass and belittle legitimate business people he doesn't like. I am also convinced that by the end of this day, you, too, will be convinced of the president's abuse of power. As the world becomes an ever more dangerous place, we need to be assured, we need to be satisfied, we need to know that our leaders truly have the larger interests of the United States of America at heart, and not merely the retention of power. This kind of presidential abuse of authority undermines his credibility with the American people, the Congress of the United States, and other world leaders. I submit that when Franklin Roosevelt ignored tradition and ran for a third term as president, it was a tacit admission he is a power hungry individual, more concerned with his own fiefdom than his job. At this time, I call to the witness table Mr. Rico Tozzi."

As he said this, two people got up from their chairs in the gallery. Rico Tozzi headed toward the table. Jack Denif headed for the door.

Denif went straight to the White House, begging for a comment, any comment, from an official spokesman to the charges Leo Dailey had just leveled. Again, the official Roosevelt White House response was No Comment. The president himself was not available for comment, either.

Jack Denif then marched over to Vice President Henry Wallace's office, and again, begged for a comment. Wallace's office was even more tight-lipped than FDR's. So, Jack called John Nance Garner at his home in Texas. "Hell yes, we used the FBI to track people down," Garner said on-the-record. "What else are they good for? I mean, how do you think we got Capone? Luck? Welcome to the real world." Garner was on a roll. "Now, we wouldn't tell them to chase after some two-bit thug. This is the *Federal* Bureau of Investigation. It had to be big time before we'd get involved. But if you think we don't use the FBI to check on people who are running illegal operations, you're nuts. We do, and we do it everyday."

"Mr. Garner," Denif asked, "would you use the FBI to investigate a Republican congressional candidate from Montana, as Leo Dailey charged today?"

Garner, again on-the-record, replied, "I don't know the specifics of that case. I really don't. But as I understand it, Congressman Dailey has had some kind of past business dealings with Mr. Tozzi. It's quite possible that Mr. Dailey was photographed simply as part of the investigation into Mr. Tozzi's activities."

"So you're acknowledging, as the former vice president of the United States, that the FBI has been involved in an ongoing investigation of Rico Tozzi?"

"Yes. Absolutely. The guy's a gangster, a smart and crafty gangster, which is why we've never arrested him. But he's as crooked as one of these Texas sidewinders I see on my ranch all the time."

Jack Denif had his story. While everyone else focused on the House Committee's witnesses and bluster, Jack had John Nance Garner confirm the Roosevelt Administration used the FBI to investigate people it suspected of criminal activity. And that's the story he filed at noon.

Also at noon, Dailey recessed the House Committee for a two hour lunch and Warren Doones began his one-hour conversation with me.

Warren was remarkably comfortable with me. He was relaxed, at least as relaxed as a mechanical engineer could be under these circumstances. He had reached the conclusion that telling his story now, prior to testifying in Congress, was preferable. He felt more people would hear what he said, how he said it and the reasons he came forward.

Predictably, Leo Dailey hit the roof. He couldn't believe he'd been usurped two days in a row by BRN. He also couldn't understand how his star witness, for whom he had provided an alias and a hotel room, could slip through his staff's grasp and into mine. He called Peter Betz directly, screaming, "This is an egregious contempt of Congress. You haven't heard the last of this!"

Peter shrugged it off. He let Bart Johnson know, and Bart notified Peter he'd have a lawyer for Warren Doones before he left the studio.

Jack's Garner story resonated throughout official Washington, particularly his tag line. "As usual, the Roosevelt White House had No Comment." Dailey, McKay and Kerse were actually thrilled with this turn of events, and planned on addressing the report when recess was finished.

On the air, I guided Warren through the hour, starting with his background, his job and family, and how his vacations had led to his being in Washington to testify. Then he calmly and matter-of-factly revealed the existence of all four pictures, how he came to get them, and why he felt the need to bring them to the public's attention.

During a late break in the hour, I saw Bart Johnson standing outside the studio with Hunter Rose, the lawyer who had helped Lou Martilotta gain parole. I also noticed Willie Houston, our Edward Dunwoody fill-in, was back in the newsroom talking with Tim Cullen. Cullen had told Willie to quietly slip out of the hotel around 12:30 p.m. without checking out.

When the hour was over, I shook Warren's hand. "That was well done," I told him. "You're a good guy, Warren." Just then, Bart entered and introduced Hunter Rose to Warren Doones.

"You're going to need an attorney, Warren," Bart explained. "In my mind, there's no better attorney right now than Hunter Rose. I've arranged for you and Hunter to talk over all the details of the matter - how you got here, why you decided to speak with Michael today, that kind of thing - at a hotel in Silver Springs, Maryland. Hunter will stay with you overnight and sit with you at your Congressional hearing tomorrow. And don't worry about Hunter's legal fees. They're already taken care of."

Warren, looking once again like the forty-seven-year-old, Baptist-Church-going, school-board-member father of four that he was, thanked Bart and me, then left with Hunter. On the way out, he stopped to shake Anne Seals hand before disappearing into a waiting car.

September 16, 1941: Riza Khan is forced to abdicate the Persian throne. British and Soviet forces jointly occupy the country.

Chapter 26 – Lucy Testifies

Reaction to the concurrent events of Tozzi's testimony, Garner's FBI quotes, and my interview with Warren Doones was swift and ubiquitous. In the next day's Washington Post, B.W. Corkman wrote:

> If even half the allegations against the president are true, we have indeed crossed the boundary between politics as usual and an Imperial View of Power. Clearly the events across the Atlantic are worrisome. Even more worrisome, though, is a leader bogged down by personal problems compounded by political mistakes. Who is to say if the path Roosevelt has us on regarding the War In Europe is a response to international events or a response to embarrassing revelations? It spells trouble, no matter which way you look at it. Despite winning in a landslide only ten months ago, President Roosevelt is in deep political hot water. And it's getting deeper and hotter by the minute.

The Chicago Tribune published an editorial saying essentially the same thing. Roosevelt was quickly losing political capital and the ability to convince Congress of anything. He was badly wounded, the Tribune said, and ought to consider any number of things, starting with a press conference to address these allegations.

The Manchester Guardian, New Hampshire's biggest newspaper, called for a further investigation into the president's conduct especially as it related to the FBI.

> Even if Rico Tozzi is a gangster, as the FBI says he is, they have not been able to prove anything. Until and unless they can, they should stop harassing him. And the Roosevelt Administration

215

must stop the practice of using J. Edgar Hoover's finest to injure innocent American citizens.

The St. Louis Post-Dispatch delivered a stinging rebuke of...

...the president's use of the FBI to investigate a Congressional candidate who has never been accused of any wrongdoing. The irony that this candidate became a congressman who is leading the investigation into the Roosevelt Administration's abuses is not lost on this newspaper. We stand behind Congressman Dailey's calls for further investigation.

Leo Dailey read Corkman's entire column as his House Committee's opening statement that morning. He also repeated the Garner quotations, recounted highlights of Tozzi's testimony and promised a Warren Doones fireworks extravaganza. "However," Dailey said, "we will not be bound to finish our questioning in a one-hour period. Again, I submit to you that by the end of the day, you will be convinced our president and his family are morally bankrupt and have failed the test of leadership."

By this time, reporters were converging on the White House press room. FDR's press secretary, Steve Early, remained steadfast in his refusal to comment on "these scurrilous allegations," which was the first time they even included an adjective in their defense.

On Sunday, Fr. Charles Coughlin was in a full-blown frenzy over the "degenerate, deviant, demented, morally devoid, devil-inspired damnable activities of the president and his family. What came to light, through photographs provided by a good, God-fearing Baptist, is proof beyond a shadow of a doubt that the entire Roosevelt Family is beyond redemption. As a Christian nation, we must rise up, band together and demand that our house, our White House, be not sullied anymore, be once again a Pure White House, a White House that is pure and above reproach. We must demand that the people who live in our White House be able to lead both politically and morally, because without morals there can be no good politics. We must write our congressmen and senators and demand they take action against the president for this totally outrageous, morally repugnant and reprehensible lifestyle he lives. He cannot lead us anymore. He has abdicated any moral authority the office of the president afforded him. President Roosevelt is not our leader anymore!"

Coughlin implored his listeners to write and call their representatives and demand something be done "before it is too late, before this power-crazed man inserts boys in front of bullets in Europe to protect his skin in Washington."

On Monday, all the news coverage focused on the impending testimony of Lucy Mercer Rutherfurd. Reporters had camped near her New Jersey home ever since Dailey subpoenaed her. She hadn't left her home in more than a week, although she had a steady stream of visitors. Photographers climbed trees near her house, and at one point neighbors called police to remove some of the more annoying members of the press from private property.

Late Monday afternoon, Lucy Mercer Rutherfurd, wearing a long skirt, a coat and a head covering, was hurriedly escorted from her house to a waiting car that sped off toward the train station. When she arrived, she was greeted by an entirely different set of reporters and photographers, all of them screaming or popping flashbulbs in her face. Four very large men in black suits surrounded her as she entered the train uneventfully and unencumbered. She went directly to her private berth, while the four men stood guard.

Around eight o'clock that night, Lucy's train pulled into Union Station in DC. Again, a media phalanx did their best to get her to look their way or say anything, but she remained cocooned inside her four large men hive. Another waiting car took her directly to the Washington Hilton, where she entered through the security area and was quickly escorted to her room. The photographers and reporters battled for turf all night in front of the hotel, angling for the best view of her departure in the morning to Capitol Hill.

That day, Lucy again wore a long skirt, a coat and a head covering. Escorted by the four large men through the security area and into a waiting car, Lucy was delivered to the steps of the Capitol twenty minutes before her scheduled appearance in front of Leo Dailey's House Committee. She opened the door and stepped from the car.

The flashbulbs popped and the reporters converged, each shouting questions louder than the other. She took two steps away from the car and removed her head covering. The flashbulbs were popping at a record pace.

"Hey!" one of the reporters yelled. "That's Carole Lombard!"

Indeed it was Carole Lombard. The poomp-poomp-poomp of the flashbulbs came to a standstill, and the reporters barked, "What are you doing here? Where's Lucy? Where is she?"

Carole Lombard, the graceful movie star, wife of Clark Gable, considerate Democrat and friend of mine, smiled and answered all the questions at once. "I'm here as a private citizen to watch today's House Committee proceedings. I've just finished working on a film with Jack Benny called *To Be Or Not To Be*, which deals with the strength of the Poles in the face of the Nazi occupation. It's a serious subject, but we treat it comedically to help get our points across. And as for Mrs. Rutherfurd, I believe she arrived here around seven o'clock this morning."

All but one reporter fled into the Capitol. Matt Shafer of The Chicago Tribune remained behind. Shafer approached the now unguarded movie star, laughing. "How'd you do that?" he wanted to know.

Feigning ignorance, Carole Lombard replied, "Do what? You mean, making you all think I was somebody else?" He nodded. "Honey, I do that for a living."

"Touché," he said. "Seriously, Miss Lombard, how'd you fake us all out?"

"Mrs. Rutherfurd and I have mutual friends. They asked me to help out, and I said alright."

"Do you know Mrs. Rutherfurd?" Matt Shafer asked.

"I've never met her."

"Then," Shafer stumbled for words, "what? How?"

Carole Lombard gave him a Movie Star smile, and said, "I don't know all the details. But I believe that Mrs. Rutherfurd has been at her home in South Carolina for a couple weeks. She arrived in Washington on Sunday, I think, and came to the Capitol this morning around seven. That's really all I know." She smiled again, patted him on his arm, and walked up the steps of the Capitol.

Lucy Mercer Rutherfurd was already seated at the witness table, even though the proceedings had not yet started. With her was her long-time personal attorney, Ted Ferguson, who was reviewing notes and papers with her. She was quite attractive, stunning, really, the complete opposite of Eleanor. She seemed poised and ready for whatever the day would bring.

Leo Dailey opened the Committee hearings that morning with a very short statement.

"Today, our Committee investigating the conduct of the Roosevelt Administration will hear testimony from the only witness who refused to voluntarily cooperate with our request to appear. It was with great reluctance that this Committee issued a special Congressional subpoena, but in order to seek the truth we felt it was absolutely necessary. I understand that our witness today, Lucy Mercer Rutherfurd of Allamuchy,

New Jersey, would like to make a statement before our questions begin. Mrs. Rutherfurd."

Lucy Mercer Rutherfurd sat straight up at the witness table in front of a standing-room only crowd of reporters and what few supporters could get inside. Her voice clear and strong, she began her statement.

"Mr. Chairman, my name is Lucy Mercer Rutherfurd, and I am appearing here today as the direct result of a congressional subpoena. I am a law-abiding citizen who loves my country, and I am not the kind of person who would ignore the weight of the law surrounding such a subpoena. For months now, this nation has been regaled with stories, many of them completely unsubstantiated, about the private lives of some very public individuals, and in my case, a very private individual. I need only point to the crush of reporters and photographers following my every move over the past few weeks to underscore how events can be overblown and misidentified. Over one hundred reporters tried to take my photograph as I arrived this morning, only to find out the woman they were photographing was someone else. I actually arrived in Washington two days ago, and here at the Capitol two hours ago, and did not see one reporter. My point is that these stories, unprecedented in their invasiveness and quite clearly slanted toward the salacious, have led to a kind of paralysis of action. They have diverted the nation's attention from the real issues at hand, namely the expanding war in Europe, our responsibilities to help our allies, our adherence to newly enacted treaties, increasing domestic production and employment, providing benefits for our older citizens and good schools for our children, increasing our efforts at racial integration and being a beacon of hope to countries the world over. Furthermore," she continued, "these stories have irreparably damaged the lives and reputations of the people involved, both directly and indirectly. They have lowered the standards upon which we as a society base ourselves. Now, instead of talking about ideals and values and collective goals, we've been reduced to discussing in public the most private details imaginable. I cannot think of anything else that has harmed our Republic in the same way as these stories that have escalated in both number and scope this year. Society will crumble when good people do nothing. It is my belief that good people everywhere should reject this kind of titillation and privacy invasion to concentrate on what we as a nation can do together. In the past nine years, we have weathered the Depression and come out of it stronger than ever. That takes leadership. We have more people working today than ever before. That takes leadership. We have an electrification program that is connecting

219

rural America, providing untold benefits to millions of people. That takes leadership. And we are now living in a world whose European face is being rearranged by a small man with a small moustache, and he won't stop in Europe. It takes leadership, real leadership, to get through these dangerous times. We cannot be distracted from the real task at hand. We must not allow ourselves to become fixated with gossip and innuendo in any form. We must not give in to this kind of garbage can journalism." Lucy paused, looked up from her notes and directly at Leo Dailey. "Therefore, Mr. Chairman, I intend to assert my 5th Amendment rights as guaranteed by the Constitution of the United States for each and every question you or the Committee will ask today or in the future."

There was a palpable buzz among the crowd. Although not unexpected, her refusal to answer any questions was a risky political move. Anytime a witness invokes their 5th Amendment rights, the public tends to believe they're covering up something.

It did not deter Congressman Leo Dailey, however.

"Thank you, Mrs. Rutherfurd. That was a lovely statement. Did the president write it for you?"

At that very moment, the press corps realized Dailey had taken off the gloves and was going to brutally administer as much punishment as he could.

"I assert my 5th Amendment rights," she replied.

"Did the president's speech writers write it for you?"

"I assert my 5th Amendment rights."

Could you possibly have written that yourself?"

"I assert my 5th Amendment rights." Lucy was prepared to repeat this sentence all day, and repeat it with as much of an even tone in her voice as possible. She'd been counseled not to show any anger.

For each question Dailey asked, Lucy gave him the same answer all day. The questions never seemed to end.

"How did you come to meet Eleanor Roosevelt? How long did you work for her? When did you first meet Franklin Roosevelt? Did you ever work for Franklin Roosevelt? When was the first time you were alone with Franklin Roosevelt? When did you first begin an intimate relationship with Franklin Roosevelt? How long did you continue working for Eleanor Roosevelt once she discovered your affair with Franklin Roosevelt? When did you meet Winthrop Rutherfurd? How did you meet Winthrop Rutherfurd? When did you marry Winthrop Rutherfurd? How long did you live in South Carolina? Do you still have a home there? When did you move to New Jersey? While you were married to Winthrop Rutherfurd, how often did you contact Franklin Roosevelt? Did Winthrop Rutherfurd know about your love affair with Franklin Roosevelt? Did you ever have contact with Eleanor Roosevelt while you were married to Winthrop Rutherfurd?"

Lucy seemed to be keeping her cool, but the questions got tougher.

"Isn't it true you attended Franklin Roosevelt's inauguration as governor of New York as his personal guest? Isn't it true you sat in the front row? Isn't it true you spent the night at the Governor's Mansion in Albany that night? Isn't it true you attended Franklin Roosevelt's inauguration as president in 1933, again as his personal guest? Isn't it true you sat in the front row for that event, as well? Isn't it true you attended Franklin Roosevelt's inauguration as president in 1937, once again as his personal guest? Isn't it true you also sat in the front row at that event, and that you stayed overnight at the White House that night? Isn't it true you attended the inauguration of Franklin Roosevelt in January of this year as his personal guest? Isn't it true you spent the night at the White House that night as well?"

Lucy kept repeating her 5th Amendment assertion, biting her lip at times.

Dailey kept coming. "And isn't it true, Mrs. Rutherfurd, that at each of those government-sponsored occasions, you arrived at each of them in a limousine sent by Franklin Roosevelt to pick you up? A limousine bought and paid for with the tax dollars of hard-working Americans, a limousine that is supposed to be used for government employees, and government employees only?"

The press discerned a new Dailey twist: the specter of FDR abusing taxpayer money for his own personal gain, broadening of the scope of the Committee's investigation. It now included personal misconduct, abuse of power and abuse of government property.

Dailey continued, shifting ever so slightly in his seat. "Let's move on to another line of questioning, Mrs. Rutherfurd." Dailey shuffled some papers and decided to take advantage of her not answering questions by asking things simply to get them into the public record. "Do you know Marguerite LeHand? Wasn't Marguerite LeHand the personal secretary to President Roosevelt until she fell ill? Do you know if President Roosevelt had an intimate relationship with her?"

That brought an interruption from Lucy's attorney, Ted Ferguson. "Mr. Chairman," he interrupted, " we really don't see the relevance in this line of questioning. You're asking things that are completely out of the scope of Mrs. Rutherfurd's knowledge."

"Mr. Ferguson," Dailey shot back arrogantly, "neither you nor Mrs. Rutherfurd get to control the scope or determine the relevance of my questions. I will ask what I feel is necessary."

"For the record, Congressman," Ted Ferguson stated, "I object to this line of questioning." He muttered something to Lucy as he sat back in his seat.

"Mrs. Rutherfurd," Dailey began again, "do you know Grace Tully? Isn't Grace Tully the personal secretary to President Roosevelt now? Do you know if President Roosevelt had an intimate relationship with her?"

Ferguson again interrupted. "Congressman Dailey, this is completely out of order, and I object!"

"Frankly, Mr. Ferguson, I'm tired of your objections. If you interrupt one more time, I will hold you in contempt, and will ask the House guards to escort you out. That would leave Mrs. Rutherfurd all alone."

Ferguson took one last shot before sitting back in his seat. "This entire proceeding is out of order!" Once again, he muttered something to Lucy.

"Let's try this again, Mrs. Rutherfurd." Dailey cleared his throat and moved some more papers around. "Do you know Margaret Suckley? Are you aware that Margaret Suckley is the sixth cousin of President Roosevelt? Do you know if Franklin Roosevelt had an intimate relationship with her? Do you know Princess Martha of Norway? Do you know that she is the mother of three small children? Do you know if President Roosevelt recently had an intimate relationship with her?"

The press was really buzzing. Notebooks and pens were moving faster than ever before. Dailey was pulling out all the guns, all the rumors and innuendo he'd ever heard about FDR. He was getting it all on the record, and had a witness who refused to answer on the grounds that it may incriminate her.

"Let's try this," Dailey said. "Do you know Lorena Hickok? Do you know that Lorena Hickok and Eleanor Roosevelt have traded many letters over the years? Do you know that many of these letters are quite intimate in detail? Do you know that Eleanor Roosevelt and Lorena Hickok often travel together? Do you know that Eleanor Roosevelt and Lorena Hickok have often spent weekends together? Do you know if Eleanor Roosevelt and Lorena Hickok are lovers?"

Almost everyone in the room was slack-jawed at Dailey's ferocity. He was pounding and pounding and pounding, then delivered the knock-out punch.

"I have only one more question, Mrs. Rutherfurd." Dailey paused, looking straight at Lucy and not at any notes. "President Roosevelt is wheelchair-bound from polio that he contracted in the 1920s. Yet whenever he is seen in public, he's not in his wheelchair. He gives the appearance of being physically able to walk. My question, Mrs. Rutherfurd is this: Don't you think it is misleading, even lying, to the American people, and indeed the people of the world, for President Roosevelt to misrepresent his ability to walk? Don't you think that speaks to the larger issue of character? Don't you think that says loud and clear that President Roosevelt is a lying, devious, cheating character who will do anything at all to remain in power?" thundered Dailey.

Lucy meekly asserted her 5th Amendment rights. The assembled reporters looked for buckets and towels to mop up the blood.

Dailey sat back, done with his line of questioning. The other Committee members wanted no part of this. They declined to ask Lucy Mercer Rutherfurd any questions. She was excused from the witness table at 11:17 a.m., after having asserted her 5th Amendment rights 312 times in a little more than two hours. By three o'clock, every news network and newspaper was leading with Leo Dailey's bludgeoning of Lucy Mercer Rutherfurd. Even though many reporters in the room thought Dailey overplayed his hand, the fact she invoked the 5th only made her look bad in the public's eye.

The Carole Lombard gambit also backfired on FDR. Most people, both reporters and average citizens, believed only Roosevelt had the clout to pull off that kind of flim flam. Lombard herself was immune to the criticism. She was portrayed as merely helping a friend, not as the mastermind behind a concerted effort to deceive the public through the press.

Leo Dailey's final question, about FDR's paralysis, cut two ways. The press had known for years about Roosevelt's use of a wheelchair, but chose not to report it. But the public generally didn't know, and they agreed with Dailey that it underscored a pattern of deceit spanning his entire presidency. The public was quickly losing all belief in Franklin Roosevelt.

The afternoon press briefing was dominated by questions begging for a comment on Lucy's non-testimony to Dailey's attack. For the most part, Steve Early stuck to the information about the abdication of the Persian throne and the occupation by British and Soviet troops. Finally, after repeated "No comment" and "We're not discussing that," Early caved and made his first official statement on the day's political events.

"I can safely tell you that today the president was much busier dealing with real world problems than the private witch hunt of the minority party. This congressional attack is designed to inflict as much political damage to the president as possible. It is nothing more than a political attack. President Roosevelt will not be drawn into this mud pit. That's all," Early said as he left.

Privately, though, Early and FDR's other advisers were worried. Fr. Coughlin's Sunday tirade was turning into thousands of phone calls, telegrams and notes to each congressman and senator, most demanding FDR's hide. The leadership of both parties huddled to discuss where to go and what to do now that they were on this road to who-knows-where. Newspapers across the country were preparing editorials that smacked Leo Dailey around, but absolutely strafed Roosevelt. Mutual Radio pre-empted all its entertainment programs that night for a re-cap of the day's testimony, with comments from people across the country. By a 12-1 margin, people were absolutely disgusted with the things they'd learned about the President and Mrs. Roosevelt. Mutual reported, flatly, "The American people have lost trust in their elected leader. They simply don't believe him anymore."

A late evening press release sent by Dailey's office announced the House Committee was suspending further testimony until September 29th, with details at a 10 a.m. press conference on September 17th. All the networks rearranged their schedule in order to carry the press conference live.

Every heavyweight Washington reporter was there. Ellen Monroe, AP, front and center. Jack Denif, NBC, front left. Tim Cullen, BRN, next to Jack. The lead reporters for CBS, Mutual, The New York Times, The Washington Post, the Washington Herald, The Chicago Tribune, the Los Angeles Times, everyone. I stood in the back. But the real surprise attendee was Charles McNary.

Leo Dailey entered the overcrowded conference room flanked by McKay and Kerse, and accompanied by McNary, the Senate minority leader. Dailey had grown very confident in his role. He strutted with the cocksure demeanor of a gladiator who smelled victory, buoyed by the papers he was waving in his hand.

"I have here," he began, holding those papers high above his head, "the results of a poll conducted by the highly-respected Roper organization. This poll was conducted yesterday from their offices in five of the biggest cities in our country. Average Americans were asked what they knew about the current scandal enveloping the First Family and what they thought about them. 77% felt they knew enough about them to comment. Of those people who answered, 83% are disgusted with the reports of the Roosevelt family shenanigans. 91% are upset with what they've learned. 82% feel that the Roosevelt Family does not represent the values of the average, hard-working American. 88% feel the Roosevelts are morally vacant. 80% feel the president has lied and betrayed them. And, finally, 93% feel the president thinks he's above the law." Dailey set the paper down with a thump on the podium. *"93% of the American people believe President Roosevelt thinks he's above the law!"* Dailey emphasized. "And so do I!" he thundered. "Since yesterday's appearance and refusal to answer questions by *one* of the president's paramours," he pointedly continued, "the entire House and Senate have been inundated with hundreds of thousands of telegrams and phone calls and letters demanding action. Members of our Committee, along with Representative Martin McKay, the House minority leader and Representative Ken Kerse, the House minority whip, have met with members of the Senate, including the honorable Senator Charles McNary, the minority leader in the world's most deliberative body. We have heard the calls from the people, and we will heed the calls. I'll be happy to answer any and all questions, but before I do that, I'd like to turn the podium over to my distinguished party leaders from the House and the Senate."

Dailey made way for both McKay and McNary, and it was the senator who spoke first.

"Over the course of the past few months, the continuing revelations regarding the president's conduct have proven detrimental to the effective running of the government. The War in Europe is heating up, and we are getting dragged deeper in the bog. There is really not much question about that. The question now, however, becomes: Is our leader able to lead? Will the American people follow him, believe him, do what must be done, especially if he decides to send troops to battle? Can we be confident that the decisions being made in the White House are being made with our national security truly in mind? Or must we doubt the very intentions of the president? These are very large questions, and I don't ask them cavalierly. That is why I have met with Representative McKay and other party leaders. Today, we are announcing the formation of a bi-partisan committee from both the House and the Senate to continue the investigation into the president's professional conduct, his personal conduct, and the conduct of his family as it relates to official government duties. This kind of committee, bi-partisan and from both Houses of Congress, is unique in nature. But these are unique times.

This committee will convene beginning next Monday, September 22nd, and will supersede the House Committee that had been investigating the president's conduct. While the members of this committee are still being formulated, it will be bi-partisan, and it will have an equal number of members from both Houses. I can tell you that two of its members will be Representative McKay and myself."

McNary gave way to McKay, who declined to comment. Leo Dailey returned and asked for questions.

"Senator!" It was Ellen Monroe. "Senator, you ran as the Republican vice presidential candidate just last year, and were outspoken in your beliefs that President Roosevelt should not serve a third term and that the United States should remain on the sidelines of the War in Europe. How can we be sure that your intentions are pure? And what do you hope this bi-partisan committee will accomplish?"

"Those are good questions, Miss Monroe," Senator McNary began. "We hope this Committee will quickly reach the bottom of the investigation, find the truth, and make recommendations to both Houses of Congress. Additionally, we are willing to meet with the president to hear what he has to say. As you know, he's been silent on all this, which is quite out of character." He stepped back, but Ellen jumped at him again.

"What about the pure intentions part, Senator?"

"Oh, yes," McNary chuckled, "that. Well, let me tell you, I learned a great deal in the past national election. I learned that the British desperately want us to join the fight. And I learned that Franklin Roosevelt will do just about anything to remain in power."

Dailey quickly called for the next question, surprisingly from Tim Cullen.

"Congressman Dailey, you yourself have been the subject of a radio investigation into your background and personal life. That series…"

Dailey interrupted, "It's all twaddle!"

"…that series," Cullen continued, "revealed some pretty unseemly parts of your life that in many ways parallel the allegations against the president and his family. My question, sir, is this: Regardless of whether or not the accusations against you or the president are true, do you think it is a bigger issue for the president of the United States to be accused of infidelity than a member of Congress? And why?"

"Yes, I do," Dailey shot back. "For the simple reason I am not the president of the United States, and I don't have the authority to send boys into harms way. I'm just a hard-working rookie from Montana."

"Congressman McKay!' shouted Jack Denif. Dailey rolled his eyes, not wanting to hear anything from Denif, but it was too late. "Congressman, why did you decide to install a self-described hard working rookie from Montana as chairman of one of the most politically charged House Committee investigations in decades?"

It was a great question, clearly a Denif-question. No matter how McKay answered, Denif had probably two dozen follow-ups.

McKay squirmed. Although he was the House minority leader, he was much more comfortable working a room behind the scenes, cajoling his colleagues, counting votes, keeping track of the political score. But there was a reason he'd been in Congress for twenty-five years and had risen to the leadership role. He could verbally tap dance.

"It's true Congressman Dailey is new this year to Washington," McKay began, "but I've known about him for years. His reputation in Montana preceded him. His skill as a lawyer, I felt, would serve him well in this particular role. And I believed then, as I believe now, that because he is a freshman, he would be viewed as having no ax to grind, no agenda to carry out. He could and would be impartial and let the evidence take this investigation wherever it would lead. And I think he's done a good job."

Denif, as expected, pounced with a quick second question. "Are you saying, Congressman McKay, that Congressman Dailey's appointment as chairman of this Committee has nothing to do with the fact that each of you has received substantial campaign contributions over the years from Rico Tozzi?"

McNary's head swiveled quickly toward McKay. Indignantly, McKay replied, "His appointment as chairman of the Committee was based solely on his qualifications. And as a freshman, he had fewer committee assignments. Thereby he had more time. Furthermore, until this very moment, I had no idea that Mr. Tozzi had contributed to both of our campaigns. And may I remind you, Mr. Denif, that Mr. Tozzi has never been arrested or convicted of any crime, yet he has been harassed by the FBI over a number of years, an FBI who takes orders from President Roosevelt. It is no crime for Mr. Tozzi to donate money to any political candidate he chooses, and I resent the implication that his campaign contributions have influenced any decision I have ever made."

Leo called on Bill Denton from CBS. "Congressman Dailey, in her opening statement yesterday, Mrs. Rutherfurd indicated she would invoke her 5th Amendment rights to each question you would ask. In light of that, sir, why did you proceed to ask her 312 questions?"

"I thought she might change her mind," he replied to snickers among the assembled.

"Seriously?"

"Yes."

Denton followed up quickly. "Did it have anything to do with you wanting to make broad stroke accusations against the president and his family to place embarrassing political material into the permanent public record?"

Dailey, trying to control his quick temper, simply said, "No."

"In that same vein," interrupted Charles Parker of Mutual, "would all of you comment on what the president's press secretary said yesterday? That this is nothing more than a politically inspired attack - he used the phrase "witch hunt" - designed to undermine the president's political base."

Senator McNary stepped forward. "I speak for all of us assembled here this morning, and for the members of our bi-partisan committee, when I say that the President and the First Lady have brought whatever embarrassment they're feeling upon themselves. No one has made them do what they've done. People can discuss the personal aspect of it all, but I'm concerned mostly with the abuse of official authority that has become well documented. The questions that Congressman Dailey asked yesterday may be both embarrassing to the Roosevelts and be a part of the permanent public record. But those questions needed to be asked." He then waved his hands. "That's all the questions we'll take for today."

As they began to walk away from the podium, Ellen shouted a question. "Senator, is it true that Wendell Willkie had an affair during the campaign last year?"

Barely turning his head without stopping, McNary refused to even acknowledge the question.

I walked up to Ellen. "Wow. Where'd that come from?"

"Sons of bitches," she muttered. "They're all hypocrites. Everybody's fucking everybody."

September 19, 1941: German forces capture Kiev, killing 500,000
Russian troops, capturing 650,000 more. Germany lost 100,000 troops.
September 28, 1941: Averill Harriman meets Josef Stalin in Moscow.
The US extends its assistance to the Soviet Union through the Lend –Lease
Act.
October 2, 1941: Hitler orders the resumption of the attack on Moscow.

Chapter 27 – A Fireside Chat

By this time, all of FDR's advisers were panicking. Official Washington was consumed by this ever-growing scandal, with accusations of infidelity and abuse of authority swirling around both the Executive and Legislative branches of government. Ellen was right. Everybody was fucking everybody. And the public was becoming increasingly fed up with all of them.

Politically, FDR was in a real bind. He grasped his accusers had badly wounded him, but he needed their support to rally the country to enter the war. However, the conservative Democrats, the ones Roosevelt tried and failed to replace in the 1938 elections, were clearly siding with the Republicans. Despite the Democrats having a lopsided majority by number in both Houses, Roosevelt found himself having to count heads to find out who was still supporting him.

McNary held a very public meeting with Alben Barkley, the Democratic Senate majority leader, to discuss the Bi-Partisan Committee. Although Barkley would never desert FDR publicly, privately he confessed to McNary he was worried about FDR's continued viability.

Poll after poll showed the public becoming dissatisfied with the leadership in Washington, the tone of incivility and how that would affect our ability to react to world events. The polls also showed the public wanted the investigations to continue. They remained extremely interested in the story, and felt the reporting had, so far, been fair and well documented.

The White House continued to refuse comment on anything related to The Affairs of State. Instead, they released war updates and details of FDR meetings with auto industry leaders about rubber rationing.

In the midst of all this, Eleanor made a very public trip to the Midwest. This long-scheduled trip to promote reading and literacy at the Indianapolis Public Library was her first since many of the most damaging revelations came to light.

It was ugly. A massive and almost completely hostile crowd had gathered, carrying placards that read, "Where's Lorena?" and "Stay Away from our Children" and "Go Home to Hyde Park." Nearly 10,000 protesters, most of them organized and encouraged by the area's Catholic and Baptist churches, chanted, "One, two, three, four, we don't like you anymore. Five, six, seven, eight, go away and take your date!" The protesters blocked the entrances and exits of the library. The head of her Secret Service detail, Joseph Lash, told Eleanor he could not guarantee her safety. Eleanor Roosevelt left Indianapolis without ever reaching the library

It only made the scandal bigger and worse. The front pages of every newspaper carried the story of how the First Lady was booed out of town. The lead story on every newscast on every network was how the Heartland had lost its heart for Eleanor.

Editorial columns from Portland to Portland, from Seattle to Miami made mention of the Indiana throng who made the First Lady leave. The Washington Post's B.W. Corkman wrote three consecutive columns pointing out the country had now arrived at the same opinion of Eleanor he'd held since 1933.

The press corps relentlessly beat up Steven Early. They badgered for a comment about polls showing a sizable majority of Americans agreed with the Indianapolis protesters, and FDR's infidelities were worse than anyone else's because of his power and authority. Just like Leo Dailey posited.

On September 29th, impeachment was first discussed publicly. Matt Shafer of The Chicago Tribune quoted Martin McKay saying, "We have a Constitutional responsibility to look into all forms of redress against this president for the official misconduct we've uncovered, including, but not limited exclusively to, impeachment." On October 6th, McKay explained, preliminary hearings would be held to determine whether or not the full House should hear evidence of impeachable offenses. "This is an incredibly dangerous time in the world," McKay said. "We must have a leader in the White House who is not distracted by personal scandals and a perception of political maneuvering for every action or statement he makes."

FDR's advisers begged him to take off the gloves. Steven Early pleaded with him to make an official statement. After a couple hours of discussion, Roosevelt agreed to two things: a statement delivered by Early, and a Fireside Chat on Thursday, October 2nd.

But Vice President Henry Wallace was nowhere near this meeting. No one called him.

At the afternoon press briefing, Steven Early read the first official comment from Franklin Roosevelt about the scandal that was threatening his entire presidency. "I have stayed focused on my job throughout this growing political attack on my family and me. Three times, the American people have entrusted me with the responsibility to lead our great country through perilous times. I have never forgotten that trust, and I have never abused my authority through this office. What I have done is work very hard to ensure America is prosperous, that there are jobs for everyone, that we enjoy the benefits of today's technological advances, and that we remain a diligent partner to promote peace throughout the world. The accusations I have done anything that would rise to the level of an impeachable offense are ludicrous. I have never done anything that would remotely be construed as acting against the long-term national interests of the United States. While I cannot control the actions of the minority party in our House and Senate, or some rogue members of my own party, I can control what I say and do. I will no longer sit silently by and let these accusations fester. This Thursday, I will address the American people directly in a Fireside Chat beginning at eight o'clock Eastern Time. I will say what I have to say at that time, and then I hope we can move forward together, to work on the issues facing this country today."

Like the skilled orator he was, Franklin Roosevelt held the nation's rapt attention that October 2nd. In 25 minutes, he laid out the expanding War in Europe, our assistance to our allies, and why the United States must not remain on the sidelines. He related news of the advancing German forces toward Moscow, and the reasons for extending the Lend-Lease program to the Soviet Union. He spoke of his decision to reject a summit meeting with Japanese leaders unless they removed their troops from China first. He discussed his meetings with Winston Churchill, and his top aide's meetings with Josef Stalin. FDR sounded confident, intelligent and engaged. But people wanted to hear something else.

It wasn't until the final five minutes that he got to what everyone wanted to hear. "Over the past few months, a steady drumbeat of questions about my private life, the private life of my wife and children, and our use of the perquisites that come with this office have become topics of daily conversation in cities and villages all over this country. These questions, accusations, doctored pictures and revisionist memories all are serving to deflect from the real issues facing us. Adolph Hitler is the greatest threat to your everyday life and security. By his own admission, Hitler is trying to take over the world. I am determined he won't. This Hemisphere will stand together to defeat any invasion on our soil. I know many of you want me to comment on each and every scurrilous detail, but I find it beneath the dignity of this office to do so. There is, however, one aspect I would like to address." Roosevelt paused, the consummate politician using every means at his disposal. "In the early 1920s, I did contract polio, which has made it nearly impossible for me to walk. With help, with crutches and the love and support of my friends, family and staff, I get around as well as I can. I have never tried to hide, as such, the fact I use a wheelchair quite often. Members of the press have known about this for years, as have members of Congress and other world leaders. Until a few weeks ago, it didn't seem to matter to anyone. I have sought to turn my affliction into a positive benefit for all who see me. That is, if I can overcome this disease, and do the job you've entrusted me to do, then anyone can. Anyone in America can do anything they want, if they put their minds to it. Over the past nine years, together, you and I have re-built this nation from the ground up. Let us not lose sight of where we were nine years ago. Let us not lose sight of where we are today. And let us not lose sight of where we should be in the next few months and the next few years. Thank you for listening. Good night."

A lifetime in the political arena had honed FDR's skills at assessing the mood of the country. But all of a sudden, it seemed he'd gone tone deaf.

This Fireside Chat, expected to truly address The Affairs of State, instead was a re-hash of previously released Nazi and Fascist alarm sounding. What people wanted to hear him say - that the accusations were false, or they were true but trumped up, or they were true and he was sorry - he didn't say. The only admission he made was that he used a wheelchair. That admission only backfired. People didn't care he was a polio victim. They cared he had misled them.

In short, the American public had heard enough from Roosevelt. Overwhelmingly, two sentiments emerged after October 2nd: Hitler was indeed a menace that needed to be stopped; and Roosevelt, despite all his guidance, vision and brilliance over the past decade, needed to step aside in order for the country to defeat Hitlerism. The public was unwilling to go to war under the orders of a president they no longer trusted.

Within forty-eight hours, it was apparent to FDR and his inner circle he had badly miscalculated what the public wanted to hear. Instead of a president angry enough to fight his political opponents, he gave them a president who refused to even acknowledge the stories. Instead of a president who denied the very basis of the stories, he gave them credence by ignoring them. And instead of blasting his former vice president by name, he did not even recognize his existence.

The public yearned for him to be Joe Louis, the undisputed heavyweight champ. What he gave them was the broken record of a Bum of the Month.

Over the weekend, his advisers discussed all the possible ramifications. They suggested another Fireside Chat, but rejected that idea as being too little, too late, now simply too calculated. They discussed a press conference with all the networks to answer any and all of the questions, but FDR refused for two reasons. One, he honestly felt it was beneath the dignity of the office. And two, some of the stories were true, some were not, and he wasn't going to confirm or deny them, or embarrass anyone. They settled on private meetings with the Leaders of the House and the Senate.

On Sunday afternoon, October 5th, Alben Barkley, Charles McNary, Sam Rayburn and Martin McKay came to the White House. Accompanied by his advisers, FDR led the meeting. Quickly getting to the point, Roosevelt wanted to know how badly damaged the leadership thought he was. Quickly answering, all four men told him he was quite severely wounded.

Rayburn summed up the House Democrats. Many of them had never forgiven Roosevelt for his meddling in the 1938 mid-term elections, his treatment of John Nance Garner (who remained a darling among the House), his New Deal alphabet soup of social programs, his disdain for the legislative process and his expansionist foreign policy. Rayburn told FDR there were twenty Democrats who would vote against him on everything, and upwards of a hundred who were leaning against him now. He also said each House member was getting swamped with telegrams and phone calls condemning the president.

McKay told Roosevelt bluntly there was not one Republican who could support him now for any piece of legislation, including increased military action in the Atlantic. They certainly wouldn't support him during this scandal.

McNary told him the Senate Republicans were slightly different. Though they were largely isolationists, they understood the threat Hitler posed and the need for governmental continuity. But they, too, were getting thousands of phone calls and telegrams running nearly 20-1 against the president. McNary told FDR it's difficult to ignore the people you're supposed to be representing.

It fell to Barkley to deliver the crushing blow. He told Roosevelt he wasn't sure he could deliver enough Democrats to pass any legislation or referendum that would wind up on the Senate floor. The conservative Democrats, outraged at the revelations, had bonded with all the Republicans. It was a combination of personal beliefs and political expediency that made this a particularly tough coalition. Known for his fiery oratory, the Senate majority leader from Kentucky told FDR, "The mood is against you."

The meeting continued. FDR shared more intelligence briefings he'd recently received, unveiled new statistics on increased manufacturing production, and revealed the latest unemployment figures. He argued these are the important things, not scandalous details about his private life. The leadership sat there uncomfortably.

FDR asked the leadership of both parties to go slow, to let the story burn itself out. Eventually, Roosevelt suggested, people will grow tired of this sideshow and begin again to worry about their very existence.

Barkley stood up and solemnly said, "Mr. President, you don't seem to understand. People are worried about their existence. They're worried about the existence of their sons, going into war and not coming home. And they are rapidly concluding they don't trust you. You've lied to them. That's how they feel. And Eleanor. And Anna. But mostly you." Barkley paused, looked around at the others in the room. "You have some very big decisions to make, Mr. President. For your sake, and the country's sake, I hope there are no more shockers."

The leadership began to leave. Barkley turned once more to Roosevelt and asked, "Where's Henry?" FDR said he hadn't invited him to this meeting. "Well, from now on," Barkley said, "he damn well better be here."

Chapter 28 – Rebecca Jeanette

On Monday, October 6th, the Bi-Partisan House & Senate Committee met for the first time. All relatively somber, they posed for pictures before entering the conference room. In the middle were the two Senate Party leaders, Alben Barkley and Charles McNary. On Barkley's left were Sam Rayburn, Oklahoma Congressman Jay White, and, in a move that created a small ripple of attention, Senator Paul Buckfield. To McNary's right were Ken Kerse, Leo Dailey and the real surprise of the group, Michigan Senator Arthur Vandenberg.

All the Democrats on this Committee were staunch Roosevelt supporters, but none more so than Buckfield. As the ranking member on the Senate Foreign Relations Committee, Buckfield also was privy to high-level information the War in Europe. Barkley and Rayburn lobbied hard to get McNary to agree to Buckfield, arguing that Buckfield's knowledge and experience in foreign affairs was necessary to counterbalance whatever political hardball would be played. McNary came around, but only after Barkley and Rayburn acquiesced to Vandenberg's inclusion. They also agreed to hearings behind closed doors, out of the glare of the press.

Those eight officials took no questions while they posed for pictures. The lines were already divided into the Get Roosevelt and Lay Off Roosevelt camps. The somber pictures and their collective silence underscored the ambiguous nature of their task.

What FDR wanted was for them to meet in private, give the appearance of impartially investigating whatever they wanted to, and allow the story to blow over. But Kerse, Dailey and Vandenberg had decidedly dissimilar ideas.

About the same time they began their meeting, the BRN switchboard put a call through to my office from a woman named Rebecca Jeanette. She said she lived in New Jersey and listened to me everyday. She heard my interview with Warren Doones and was appalled at what she heard about the Roosevelts. Rebecca Jeanette said after she heard that interview, she decided to go look at some home movies she took when FDR visited her area of New Jersey one afternoon in 1938. She said she went to where the presidential train was parked, hoping to catch a glimpse of Roosevelt. No one was getting off the train, but after a while, a large car with the seal of the president on the side drove up next to the train. She pointed her camera at the car, and instead of Roosevelt, she said she saw a woman get out of the car and enter the train. She waited for another hour, but no one else came or went, so she went home and made dinner. After dinner, she went back to the depot and noticed the presidential train was still there. It was starting to get dark, but she saw this same woman leave the train and climb back into the presidential car. She didn't think anything about it, until she heard Warren Doones on my show. But now, she said, after she looked at it again, she's pretty sure the woman was Lucy Mercer Rutherfurd. She called me because she wondered what she should do, if she should call anybody or tell anybody, or just forget it. I told her to sit tight, and I'd call her back in just a little bit.

I gathered Bart for a quick meeting in Peter's office. I relayed Rebecca Jeanette's story and told them I'd like to bring her and the home movie down to DC to determine its authenticity. They agreed.

I called her back, told her we'd pay for her train and hotel expenses, but she had to bring the home movie. If we were satisfied with its legitimacy, she could be a guest on my show. She said OK, and I told her Janine would make the arrangements.

Then I briefed Earl and asked him to do a background check on Rebecca Jeanette.

When I got off the air that day, I walked back to my office. Earl was sitting in my chair with his feet up on my desk, smoking a cigarette and looking as rumpled as ever. He was reading the Washington Herald and heard me come in, but he didn't even bother to put the paper down.

"Redskins are playing the Packers this weekend," he announced. "Who's going to win, Michael?"

"I don't know. Redskins."

"Nah! Not a chance. The Packers are going to cream 'em!" He took his feet off my desk and set down the paper. "Got the info you want on that Rebecca Jeanette woman." He just looked at me.

"OK," I said. "What is it?"

He pulled out a notebook from his jacket's side pocket. He kept flipping through the pages, taking his time to tell me.

"Who are you?" I laughingly wondered. "Sam Spade? What do you have?"

He blew cigarette smoke through his nose. "Rebecca Jeanette is thirty. Moved to New Jersey with her family when she was ten. Works at a pharmacy. Does some community theater. Never been arrested. She's a widow. Her husband died in '37, choked on some food. One kid, a daughter who's five. But here's the interesting part." He paused and did his Sam Spade thing again. "Her dad's sister is Mary Beth Keefer's mother. Rebecca Jeanette and Mary Beth Keefer are first cousins."

"You're making that part up, Sam."

"The hell I am," Earl boomed.

I sat down in the guest chair, Earl still in my seat. Then he went on. "On September 30th, Rebecca Jeanette deposited $5000 in cash into her bank account, bringing her overall balance to $5079.12. And she bought a new car, a Mercury. Paid cash for that, too." He started rifling through my drawers. "You got a drink in here?"

"Uh, no, no I don't, Earl. I'm sure Peter does."

Earl shrugged his shoulders and sat back in my chair again. "Sounds to me like Rebecca Jeanette has some explaining to do. I'd look pretty closely at whatever movie she brings in." He stood up and excused himself as he headed toward Peter's office.

I walked down to Bart's office and gave him the update. I proposed it was more beneficial to us to help Rebecca Jeanette through whatever tawdry scheme she was almost surely involved in. He saw the merits in that argument, and said he'd make sure she had some representation at our first meeting.

At 4:30 p.m. Tuesday, Janine picked up Rebecca Jeanette at Union Station and delivered her to the BRN Conference Room a little after five. I introduced myself, and the assembled throng. "Rebecca Jeanette, this is Peter Betz, the president of the Betz Radio Network. Bart Johnson, lead corporate counsel for BRN. You already know Janine. And this is Hunter Rose. He's an outside attorney that we've brought here on your behalf."

She looked puzzled at that introduction. Then Bart said, "Miss Jeanette, we felt that, due to the nature of your story, you may need some legal representation. We didn't know if you already had an attorney. If you do, Mr. Rose will stay here only for this meeting, but if you don't have a lawyer, Mr. Rose has agreed to represent you. We've filled him in on all the aspects of the story as we know it."

"I don't have a lawyer," Rebecca Jeanette said. "I never even thought about one. And I don't think I can afford one. Do you really think I need one?"

We all said yes. Hunter Rose then sat down next to her and said, "I'd be happy to represent you *pro bono*, Miss Jeanette. Mr. Johnson has been kind enough to refer other clients to me, and I would be pleased to offer my services to you for the privilege of being part of this story."

"Well, alright," she said. "This is all so, so, so out of my everyday world." She looked validly baffled.

"Did you bring the movie with you?" I asked. She said yes, and handed it to Janine, who threaded it on the projector. "Rebecca, may I call you Rebecca?" She nodded. "Please tell us what you told me on the phone yesterday."

She reiterated her story, telling the same tale with slightly more details. The train was there, it parked on the tracks for hours, a woman drove up in a presidential car, stayed for hours, left when it was nearly dark, and was driven away in that same presidential car. She filled in the details about how far she lived from the train station, how many other people were there, why she had her camera, where she was standing and how long she waited. She said she went back after dinner because "it's not very often you get a chance to see a president. I wanted to see him in person."

The movie showed a crowd of about fifty people lining the platform. As the train arrived and parked on the tracks, the camera moved toward the caboose, where the president would be expected to depart or talk to the crowd. The next sequence showed a large black car with the presidential seal arriving behind two motorcycle policemen. A woman departed from the rear passenger side, and walked unescorted into the president's caboose.

"What year is this?" I asked.

""This is three summers ago. 1938," she said.

I scribbled a note to Bart, who read it and passed it on to Hunter Rose. The next sequence is much darker, as night is beginning to fall. The woman leaves the caboose, enters the rear passenger door and is driven away. The camera follows the car for a moment before turning back toward the train. The lights in the presidential caboose are turned off, and after a few more seconds the film ends.

We all sat quietly for half a minute, until finally I slowly said, "Well. Would you like something to drink? Water? Coca-Cola? Scotch?" Everyone but Rebecca Jeanette snickered. She declined, but I gave her a glass of water anyway.

"Rebecca," I began, "here's the problem. We know that about a week ago you deposited five grand into your bank account and bought a brand new Mercury. We know that you're Mary Beth Keefer's first cousin. Now that's circumstantial and there might be explanations, including mere coincidence." She looked uncomfortable beyond words. "But I guess the first question I'd like you to answer is: how can a home movie from 1938 feature a 1940 Lincoln?"

"Ohhhh," she sighed, as she slumped in her chair.

Hunter Rose leaned in closely. "Would you like me to represent you?" She nodded. "Can we have the room for a little bit?" he asked us.

"No, no, that's OK," she said. "Let me just tell all of you right now." She took a big drink of water and began her story.

"First of all, I honestly do listen to you every day, Michael. I think you do a really good job, and I really did hear your interview with Warren Doones. But you know that movie's not mine. You do know it's not mine, don't you?" She seemed alarmed. Turning to Hunter Rose, she said, "What kind of trouble am I in?"

"Maybe nothing, maybe a lot. Just tell us your story, Miss Jeanette."

Rebecca Jeanette took another deep breath. "Right after your interview with Warren Doones, Mary Beth showed up at my house out of the blue. I hadn't seen her in years, maybe fifteen years. I asked her what she was doing in New Jersey, and she told me she was on vacation and decided to stop in. I live with my daughter - I'm a widow - and I asked her if she'd like to stay for a day or two. She said she'd like that. That night, after my daughter went to bed, Mary Beth told me she had a business deal for me. It was an easy way to make some money, she said, and I need every penny. So I listened." She took another sip of water.

"She told me she had a home movie back in Montana that showed Lucy Rutherfurd and Roosevelt on a train together. I asked her where she got it, and at first she said she always had it. I didn't believe her, and eventually that night she told me she got it from Jane. She said..."

"Jane?" I interrupted.

"Jane Dailey. You know, Leo Dailey's wife." We all looked at each other, then asked her to continue.

"Anyway, Mary Beth said Jane knew about her and Leo long before that NBC report a few weeks back. Jane had been staying in Montana since that report, Mary Beth said..."

"Do you know Jane Dailey?"

"No. No, I don't. But Mary Beth said Jane wanted to help Leo, and Jane felt sure Mary Beth wanted to help him, too. I've known about Mary Beth and Leo ever since they were in college together. I mean, whenever I'd get a letter from Mary Beth, she'd always write about Leo doing this or Leo doing that or Leo going here. She never got over him, and I figured they stayed in touch. So it didn't surprise me when Mary Beth said she was doing something that could help Leo over this bad publicity, and maybe help his career. I asked her what she wanted me to do. She told me she wanted me to call you and tell you I had taken this movie and try to get on your show and tell everyone about it. I told her I didn't think I could do that. Then she said she knew I liked to act in the community theater, which I do. I was in a play just last year. I wasn't too bad. She said, just think that it's a character I'm playing, just a role. I still wasn't sure. But then she said she'd give me $7000. Well, I've never seen $7000, and I've got my daughter to take care of all by myself, and I needed some new clothes and a car. I thought about it for a day or two, and just before she left, I said OK. I said I'd do it, but I wanted to see the money before I did anything." She took another deep breath, sipped some more water.

"A couple days later, I came home from work - I work at a pharmacy. Most of the time I'm making chocolate sodas and pouring coffee for people. So, I got home, and there's this guy who pulls into my driveway even before I reached my front door."

"Did you know this guy?"

"No, hadn't ever seen him before. But he was a nice enough looking fella, well dressed. He walked about and asked me if I was Rebecca Jeanette, and I said yes. Then he hands me a package and said, 'This is from Mary Beth.' Then he left. I went inside and opened it up, and I saw that movie that I brought you and $7000."

"Was there a note?"

"No, just the movie and the money. I sat down, and I have to be honest, I kept thinking about all that money. I thought that if I could just do this one thing, my daughter could have a better life than what was lined up for her. I mean, money won't bring her daddy, my husband, back, but it's better than scraping by from what I make at the pharmacy. So that night, I wrote her a letter and told her I got the package and I'd follow through when I heard back from her. She telephoned me the day she got the letter, and then I called you yesterday. And here I am today." She looked off into the distance and said, "You know, I don't even have a projector. I've never even seen that movie until right now."

She took another deep breath, and wondered, "What's going to happen to me now?"

Hunter Rose huddled with Peter, Bart and me for a few minutes while Janine sat with Rebecca. We agreed that, if her story checked out, we'd be better off dealing with this privately rather than on-the-air. We also didn't want anything to happen to Rebecca Jeanette, who seemed like a decent enough person.

We asked her to stay our guest in Washington for a few days while we looked into her story. We wished her no ill will, and Hunter Rose promised to look out for her. She seemed relieved. Janine took her to The Knapp.

Peter called Earl immediately to have his Montana sources report what Mary Beth Keefer and Jane Hall Dailey had been doing. Then, as only Peter could do, he phoned McNary and Barkley. He insisted they bring the entire Bi-Partisan Committee to BRN that night for an extremely important and necessarily secret meeting. They agreed to have everyone there at 8:00.

Earl called around seven and confirmed Rebecca Jeanette's story. According to his sources, who still had a tap on Mary Beth's phone, there were a number of calls between Mary Beth Keefer and Jane Dailey around the time Rebecca Jeanette said. Moreover, Jane had been spotted in Helena with Rico Tozzi shortly after his testimony in Washington, but there weren't any photos.

Peter got really pissed why the hell we didn't know this before. Earl explained, "They were just on the look-out for phone calls between Mary Beth and Leo. And there aren't any. None, since late August."

By eight o'clock, the entire Committee had assembled in our conference room. After Peter introduced Bart, Hunter and me, he set the table. He told them we had come into possession of a short home movie that purported to show FDR and Lucy in 1938, but we believed the movie was a hoax. However, because of the nature and origin of the hoax, Peter felt it necessary to share this information with the Committee.

As he showed the movie, Peter continued talking, pointing out the entrance of the woman in the car and the much later departure. When it was over, Peter reminded the Committee this was ostensibly 1938, but the car in the film was a 1940 Lincoln.

"OK, Peter," said Alben Barkley. "I'll bite. Why the hell did you bring us here to show us something that's so obviously fake?"

Peter Betz turned to Hunter Rose. "I think you should answer that."

Hunter Rose, seated in the middle of the long conference table, looked across directly at Leo Dailey. "Nice to see you again, Congressman. We met a few weeks ago when Warren Doones testified." Dailey nodded, said he remembered. "My client is the one who brought this movie in to the

Betz Radio Network. When it was discovered this was a not legitimate film, my client retained my services. And she told me the story of how this movie arrived here. We have investigated those details, and they hold up. I have no reason to doubt my client, nor does anyone at BRN." Looking directly at Leo Dailey, Hunter Rose said, "My client is Rebecca Jeanette, the first cousin of Mary Beth Keefer of Montana. Miss Jeanette told me she was approached by Miss Keefer with a business proposition." Hunter Rose shifted his gaze to the other Committee members. "Basically, Miss Jeanette would receive $7000 if she would deliver this footage to this network and claim it as a legitimate home movie. Furthermore, Miss Jeanette claims, with independent substantiation, that Miss Keefer was originally approached with this business plan by Jane Hall Dailey…"

"Jesus Christ!" Leo gasped. The other committee members audibly groaned.

"…by Jane Dailey, who then supplied $15,000 to Miss Keefer, $7000 of which went to my client." Hunter Rose paused for a moment. "We have reason to believe, although we cannot yet confirm this, that the $15,000 came from Rico Tozzi, that Mrs. Dailey acted as the first intermediary, and Miss Keefer as the direct contact with my client."

Paul Buckfield summed it up for the Committee. "Jesus Christ, Leo. What the hell are you doing?"

"I don't know anything about this goddamn thing! I swear to God, I have no clue what he's talking about." Leo's protestations actually seemed genuine.

Peter Betz rose from his seat and walked to the head of the table. "We have no interest in either broadcasting this information, or prosecuting this woman. We have no intention of turning her into the police or the FBI, at this time. We are, however, very concerned about the implications this brings to your committee. We suggest you take care of this matter amongst yourselves in a timely manner. But know that we will be watching what you do even more closely than before."

We had Leverage.

With the skill acquired through years of conducting high powered meetings, Peter waved his hands to signal the meeting was over. They all rose as one and began filing out.

Leo Dailey looked right at Hunter Rose. "I swear to God, I don't have one goddamn clue about any of this."

October 8, 1941: Secretary of State Cordell Hull demands Japan withdraw troops from China before any diplomatic agreement can be reached with the US.
October 9, 1941: FDR seeks revision of 1939 Neutrality Act to arm merchant ships.
October 15, 1941: FDR tells Churchill: "Japan situation definitely worse. I think they are headed north."
October 16, 1941: Tojo becomes Japanese Prime Minister.
October 17, 1941:- US destroyer "Kearny" torpedoed and damaged with 11 killed inside Security Zone.
October 19, 1941 - U.S. freighter "Lehigh" sunk in South Atlantic.

Chapter 29 – The Vandenberg GOP Plan

I t was impossible to miss the story, the headline in nearly every major newspaper on October 8, 1941.

VANDENBERG QUESTIONS FDR's RELEVANCE
By Ellen Monroe, Associated Press

Washington - The biggest surprise of the formation of the Bi-Partisan Committee Investigating the President was the inclusion of Senator Arthur Vandenberg. The Michigan Republican, long a vocal critic of President Roosevelt, and one of the Republicans who ran for the presidential nomination last year, was not expected to be one of the three GOP members appointed by Senate minority leader Charles McNary. His mere presence could spell continued trouble for the president.
The make-up of this committee seemed to be already cast. McNary and his Senate counterpoint, Majority Leader Alben Barkley, would co-chair. Barkley was expected to appoint Speaker of the House Sam Rayburn and Representative Jay White from Oklahoma. White, an extremely able criminal attorney prior to entering the House in 1930, has a reputation amongst his peers

as a no-nonsense legislator who reveres the Constitution and is able to deconstruct the most complex issues to a basic common denominator.

McNary was expected to name Representatives Ken Kerse, the minority whip, and Leo Dailey, the Montana freshman who had been chairing the House Committee Investigating the President.

Then the horse-trading began.

Both McNary and Barkley wanted heavyweights in their camps, senators who commanded the respect of their peers and the public. Barkley insisted on the inclusion of Senator Paul Buckfield, the ranking member on the Foreign Relations Committee. Buckfield, a friend and supporter of Franklin Roosevelt since his days as Assistant Navy Secretary in the early 1920s, is also widely regarded as an expert on global issues due to his immersion in foreign affairs since his election to the Senate in 1926.

But in order to include Buckfield, the Democrats had to agree to McNary's demand. Arthur Vandenberg, the articulate former editor of the Grand Rapids Herald and a long-time critic of almost every policy proposed or followed by President Roosevelt, was the price the majority leader had to accept.

After hours of debate this past Sunday evening, Barkley and McNary agreed on the elected officials who would look into this growing scandal. At 11:00 p.m. Sunday night, Barkley and McNary called each, including Buckfield and Vandenberg, and told them to be at the Committee room at 9:00 a.m. Monday morning.

In an exclusive interview, Senator Vandenberg answered questions about the scandal surrounding the First Family, the direction our country is heading, his latest thoughts on our foreign policy, and his suggestions for the next immediate steps.

"I was actually asleep when Sen. McNary called Sunday night," Senator Vandenberg said. "But I was only too happy to serve not just my Party's Leader, but the nation as a whole."

Vandenberg sees this nation "at a crossroads right now. We have documented evidence that the war in Europe is expanding to other arenas. We have a president who is doing everything he can to get us into that fight. But we are saddled with a president who right now is battling to retain his mere credibility with the American people and the Congress. His every move is being scrutinized, as it should be."

Speaking calmly and forcefully, using his hands to punctuate his words in the air, Senator Vandenberg again explained his long-held position. "The war in Europe is not our fight. Outside of the Great War, the United States historically has stayed out of the conflicts that have enveloped other nations. Their fight, their struggle, is heroic and necessary. But it is not our fight. Nor should it be. I have seen no reason to believe that the United States of America should become directly involved in a land, sea and air battle in Europe." Pausing for emphasis, he added, "If the United States is directly attacked on American soil, which I highly doubt will happen, then and only then should we become involved. But I repeat: this fight is not our fight."

Responding to criticism that his isolationism is at odds with the mood of the American people, Senator Vandenberg pointed out, "A recent Roper Poll showed that while a majority of people support our helping Britain and France, nearly 70% of the people do not want us to directly enter this conflict." The senator added, "The American people have bought a bill of goods sold by one of the greatest salesmen ever to occupy 1600 Pennsylvania Avenue." He went on to say, "Since this scandal involving the First Family came to light, the president has gone out of his way to increase defense production, provide material and support to Britain and others, put our Navy and cargo ships in harm's way, and met with other world leaders all in an attempt to change the subject away from him and his policies. President Roosevelt is, in my estimation, using scare tactics to bamboozle the American public into believing we must enter a war 3000 miles away. I believe it's nothing more than a diversionary tactic of a man who is demonstrably proven to be a power-hungry megalomaniac."

The Man from Michigan continued without even being asked a question. "It is almost irrelevant if the allegations against Franklin and Eleanor Roosevelt are true. If they are, it is shocking, disgraceful, immoral and beneath contempt. My point, however, is not to pass judgment on the way the First Family lives their lives. My point is that the scandal has made it nearly impossible for the president to conduct the duties of his office without both the public and the Congress wondering if what he's telling us is true, or if it is just another story designed to deflect attention away from his personal problems."

When Vandenberg was asked why he ran for president, he reflexively responded. "George Washington set the standard by which future presidents should be measured. He made it a point to retire after two terms in office, clearly signaling that this country should have fresh leadership at least every eight years. President Roosevelt has completely overstepped the historical powers of the presidency from the day he took office in March 1933. He believes, quite wrongly, that the federal government is a panacea for American workers. He believes the alphabet soup approach to these costly make-work schemes are the only things that can save the American people and our economy. He has proposed and tried to implement program after program that have been ruled unconstitutional, from the National Recovery Act to the Agricultural Adjustment Act, even, I would submit, the Works Project Administration. He has decided to tax the wealthy to feed the poor, which is a ridiculous concept. Beyond all that," he said, slowing his speech pattern down for effect, "President Roosevelt has shown a blatant disregard for the historical patterns of the presidency as laid down by George Washington. When he ran for a third term, he was basically telling the American people that he was the only one who could steer the ship of state through rough waters. Poppycock!"

Despite his deeply-held and often-stated views, Senator Vandenberg is optimistic that a truly bi-partisan recommendation will come from the Committee Investigating The President.

"Again, let me state, I am not going to pass judgment on the way the president chooses to live his private life. If it's true, I find it wrong, and I find it personally distasteful. My concern is for the country. And I believe that our president, President Franklin Delano Roosevelt, is badly wounded politically."

Punching the air with both his index fingers, Vandenberg said he's not sure FDR can recover. "I am not naïve. The winds of war are out there. But those winds have not come to our door. Yet our leader wants to go to where the winds are. He has put himself in a position where every move he makes will be doubted and challenged by the public and the Congress. That is a recipe for disaster. If he loves this country, as I believe he does, even though I disagree with him on everything, then he must make some hard decisions about what is the best path for this country to take, both now and for the future. If he is not careful, the decision will be made for him."

Pressed to explain exactly what he meant by that statement, Senator Arthur Vandenberg, often called the de facto leader of the Republicans, declined to expound. "I'll leave it right there," he said. "But the president will know what I mean."

Ellen's article laid bare the Republican strategy. McNary demanded Vandenberg be included on the Committee so they could pummel the president to death. The Democrats, including the usually crafty Barkley, were sideswiped. They never saw it coming. They believed the Committee would be truly bipartisan and statesmanlike, not merely populated with an equal number of opposing political party members. Barkley knew almost immediately there was going to be no way out.

McNary, Vandenberg and Kerse fanned out among all the radio networks and major newspapers, granting interviews and spouting many of the same lines Vandenberg used in Ellen's interview. Leo Dailey was put on the sidelines. Dailey had served their purpose. They had used him. They had let him believe he was driving the investigation. In actuality, they had set him up. He had been the front man, unaware that McKay, Kerse and McNary had been watching his every move and pulling his strings. In football terms, he had carried the ball within sight of the goal line. Now they brought in the bruising fullbacks to score.

Over the next two weeks, the Republicans, energized by the political hay they were making and led by a coalition of failed national candidates and isolationists, commissioned polls that tracked the Roosevelts' approval ratings. The questions were about the president's believability, trustworthiness, his leadership skills, truthfulness and ability to conduct a war. Each poll, conducted by the Market Analysis Group, showed a rapid deterioration in trust. They also showed that if war was necessary, Americans weren't sure if they could believe everything FDR said. The Republican leadership trumpeted the results of each poll to any and every radio network and newspaper.

The Democrats, flat-footed and outflanked, burdened by a leader who had remained silent too long on The Affairs of State, commissioned their own polls. Although the questions were posed differently, the results were largely the same. Almost overnight, particularly after Arthur Vandenberg's articulate shredding, the president had lost the confidence of the American electorate. The Democrats also talked to all the radio networks and major newspapers, but never released their own poll results. They had a serious political dilemma on their hands.

Over the previous week and a half, FDR's approval ratings had plummeted to 18%. The polls showed a majority of Americans believed Roosevelt could guide the country through war, but they bought the idea that increased war talk was merely a political maneuver designed to deflect attention from the First Family's problems. McNary and Vandenberg had reached their own conclusions about how best to utilize this scandal to their party's advantage. In a late night closed door meeting on Friday, October 17th, they presented their arguments to the House and Senate Republicans and worked the room seeking unanimous support. They knew if they kept up the attacks on Roosevelt's character, even while denying they were talking about his private life, they would undermine both public and Democratic support for any of his initiatives. If they could oust Roosevelt now, they argued, they could wrestle control of both houses of Congress and the White House in 1944.

McNary and Vandenberg had two separate, but not mutually exclusive, visions of what could happen. McNary had a more worldly view, knew the dangers Hitler posed, and believed the United States might have to get into the war eventually. Vandenberg remained a rabid isolationist, determined to keep the US from escalating a European turf battle into another world war. Both men viewed Henry Wallace as controllable in the short term and beatable in the long term. They believed that with Wallace as president, he would be forced to work more closely with the Republicans in the House and the Senate, particularly when it came to entering the war.

They'd also done the math. If all the Republicans voted as one, unanimously in both chambers, they could pick up enough conservative Democrats who'd had enough of FDR to render his presidency irrelevant. They also knew the Democratic leadership could count, too.

Their plan was to let the press know that Articles of Impeachment were going to be drafted. The articles would point to FDR's abuse of power, specifically related to his use of the FBI to harass individuals, the use of the IRS to investigate American citizens for no apparent reason, the use of government property for private gain, overstepping presidential authority by ignoring the Neutrality Act and expanding the Lend-Lease program to the Soviet Union without express Congressional consent and conduct unbecoming a president.

This was a balancing act worthy of the Wallendas. The Republicans didn't want to be perceived as unnecessarily adding to the president's political trouble, but they wanted to put themselves in their best electoral position since the Hoover Years.

Though they had already drafted the Articles of Impeachment, the Republican leadership didn't plan to actually convene an Impeachment panel. They would leak the articles to the press and circulate them throughout Congress. McNary, convinced the Democrats would be terrified at the prospect of a long, drawn-out partisan impeachment battle while war loomed, thought Barkley would count heads and implore FDR to resign. He was absolutely sure they would not choose a constitutional slugfest, not after looking at their own polls.

For his part, Vandenberg was satisfied this plan, however partisan it seemed, was the best way to keep the US out of the war. He was anxious to be the main spokesman to articulate these ideas publicly.

By the time that Friday night meeting was over, the Republicans had all signed on to the plan. In the end, they felt there was very little risk. If the Democrats successfully fought the Impeachment Articles draft, the Republicans could say they were circulated by a small group of disgruntled party members. If the Democrats were not able to defend the articles effectively, the Republicans were in good shape to control legislation. No matter what happened, FDR would be neutralized.

A series of smaller meetings took place that weekend, each led by either McNary, Vandenberg, McKay or Kerse. The goal was to ensure that whoever spoke to any radio network, radio station, newspaper or magazine, said the same thing, with the same language and the same intonations. After more than a decade of being in the proverbial desert, the Republicans found an oasis. They wanted to make sure they didn't squander it.

On Monday morning, October 20th, they began executing their plan. McNary granted interviews to Time Magazine, The New York Times and NBC. Kerse was on Mutual, then sat down with The Chicago Tribune. McKay was interviewed first by CBS, then UPI, The Washington Times and the Los Angeles Times. Hamilton Fish, the most strident of the isolationists in the House, spoke with WBAL Radio in Baltimore, the Charlotte Observer and the Atlanta Constitution.

Vandenberg sat down for an extensive interview with his former newspaper, the Grand Rapids Herald, before he joined me on the air. It was the first time he'd been a guest on my show, and Ellen had tipped me off to how charming and articulate he was. He came as billed. The entire show was a recapitulation of everything he had told Ellen, which was the script all other Republicans were following. To my question regarding the politics behind this concerted move, he replied, "What may look political to some is really nothing more than our patriotic duty. Are we to stand by and say nothing, do nothing, while this immensely distracted president gets us so deeply involved in a shooting war? Are we to believe that he's not playing politics? No, the stakes are too high for us to ignore what the American people are saying. It is not just our right as the opposition party. It is our duty."

FDR's advisers were sick. No matter what poll they looked at, no matter what news report they heard, no matter what article they read, the news was ominous for Roosevelt. They were also immensely concerned that FDR seemed not to grasp the depth of the problem. He was convinced that the story of his character would blow over once the US was forced to enter the war. He believed the American public knew the imminent danger posed by continued inaction to Hitler's aggression. He refused to acknowledge or respond to the concerted attack underway by the Republicans.

On Thursday, October 23rd, Alben Barkley and Sam Rayburn met with other Democratic leaders to gauge the mood among the party members and their constituents. It was dark and foreboding. Nothing was getting accomplished in Congress. All anyone could talk about were the Articles of Impeachment, the consistently awful polls, and Roosevelt's growing detachment from it all.

The Democrats had mounted their own media offensive, talking to all the same radio networks and newspapers as the GOP. However, their stories and defense were not as unified as the Republicans, which only served to create more unrest throughout the country. It also didn't help that nearly every southern Democrat, and many conservative northern Democrats, were spouting the McNary/Vandenberg lines.

The next day, The Chicago Tribune wrote an editorial that called on FDR to resign. "Whether or not the Republican-written impeachment issues actually become Articles of Impeachment to be voted on by the House and Senate, it is clear that President Roosevelt's influence has dwindled dramatically. As the news from across the Atlantic becomes ever-more worrisome, the thought of a protracted constitutional battle at this time of crisis is something this country cannot abide. Some may argue the GOP is merely using this tactic as leverage to gain further congressional influence. Others may argue the president brought this problem on himself. Whatever the case, we believe it is in the best interest of this country if the president were to remove himself from the political discussion and allow the Constitution to work the way the Founders intended. Unless he does, we foresee a contentious debate that will ultimately divert our attention from the larger menace in this world. As a newspaper, we have disagreed with President Roosevelt many times during the course of his tenure. We have also supported him when we felt he needed it. After much debate, it is our conclusion that President Roosevelt should resign, and he should do it before a real constitutional crisis rises."

The Democrats were glum. The Republicans were giddy.

FDR was not amused.

Barkley and Rayburn went to the White House on Sunday, October 26th. They met privately with FDR and his press secretary, Steve Early, for more than two hours. The president kept providing fresh details of the war, including information provided by the British Secret Service. Roosevelt told them he was planning to give a speech the next day to share the details of what he knew. Barkley and Rayburn, though sympathetic and interested, kept returning to the daunting political realities. It didn't matter, they told him, that our boats were being fired upon. It didn't matter that the Germans were within twenty miles of Moscow. What did matter is that he could no longer make his case to the American people. What's worse, he could no longer make his case to Congress. Worst of all, he had lost the support of more than two-thirds of each house. He couldn't get anything passed. His pleas were falling on deaf ears. And if the Republicans were able to actually get impeachment articles prepared and entered, there was no guarantee he could survive what was sure to be a long, bruising, ugly, divisive battle.

Franklin Roosevelt lit a cigarette and had a drink. He told Barkley and Rayburn he understood. He asked them to do what they could in the coming week. But he told them to come back the following Sunday.

October 30, 1941: US-Panama tanker "Salinas" torpedoed and damaged.
October 31, 1941: US destroyer Reuben James sunk inside the Security Zone. 115 killed.
November 1, 1941: Japanese Combined Fleet changes radio code.

Chapter 30 – The End Game

On Monday, October 27ᵗʰ, Roosevelt went ahead as scheduled with what he called his Navy Day speech. All the radio networks carried it live that night, and the nation listened with great anticipation.

Five months ago tonight I proclaimed to the American people the existence of a state of unlimited emergency. Since then much has happened. Our Army and Navy are temporarily in Iceland in the defense of the Western Hemisphere. Hitler has attacked shipping in areas close to the Americas in the North and South Atlantic. Many American-owned merchant ships have been sunk on the high seas. One American destroyer was attacked on September 4. Another destroyer was attacked and hit on October 17. Eleven brave and loyal men of our Navy were killed by the Nazis. We have wished to avoid shooting. But the shooting has started. And history has recorded who fired the first shot. In the long run, however, all that will matter is who fired the last shot....

...I have in my possession a secret map made in Germany by Hitler's government, by the planners of the new world order. It is a map of South America and a part of Central America, as Hitler proposes to reorganize it. Today in this area there are fourteen separate countries. The geographical experts of Berlin, however, have ruthlessly obliterated all existing boundary lines; and have divided South America into five vassal states, bringing the whole continent under their domination. And they have also arranged it that the territory of one of these new puppet states includes the Republic of Panama and our great life line, the Panama Canal. That is his plan. It will never go into effect....

...These grim truths, which I have told you of the present and future plans of Hitlerism will, of course, be hotly denied tonight and tomorrow in the controlled press and radio of the Axis Powers. And some Americans, not many, will continue to insist that Hitler's plans need not worry us and that we should not concern ourselves with anything that goes on beyond rifle shot of our own shores.

The protestations of these American citizens, few in number, will, as usual, be paraded with applause through the Axis press and radio during the next few days in an effort to convince the world that the majority of Americans are opposed to their duly chosen Government and in reality are only waiting to jump on Hitler's band wagon when it comes this way.

The motive of such Americans is not the point at issue. The fact is that Nazi propaganda continues in desperation to seize upon such isolated statements as proof of American disunity....

...Furthermore, the House of Representatives has already voted to amend part of the Neutrality Act of 1937, today outmoded by force of violent circumstances. The Senate Committee on Foreign Relations has also recommended elimination of other hamstringing provisions in that act. That is the course of honesty and of realism....

...Ours has been a story of vigorous challenges which have been accepted and overcome, challenges of uncharted seas, of wild forests and desert plains, of raging floods and withering drought, of foreign tyrants and domestic strife, of staggering problems, social, economic, and physical; and we have come out of them the most powerful Nation, and the freest, in all of history.

Today in the face of this newest and greatest challenge of them all we Americans have cleared our decks and taken our battle stations. We stand ready in the defense of our Nation and the faith of our fathers to do what God has given us the power to see as our full duty.

I listened to the speech in the BRN Conference Room with Peter, Bart, Tim Cullen, and, of all people, Earl Mercia. It was a good speech, vintage Roosevelt, convincing and presidential, forceful and compelling. Tim went back to the newsroom to call the House and Senate members for comment. Peter, Bart and Earl all had a drink. I used the conference room phone and called Sharon Tozzi.

"What did Buckfield think of the speech?" She didn't respond. "Sharon, can you hear me? What did Buckfield think of the speech?" I knew she could hear me, because I could hear her clearing her throat. "Sharon! What's up?"

She hemmed and hawed, stammered, stopped and started. Then she said, "You didn't hear this from me."

"OK."

Again, she paused for what seemed like a minute. "The map's a fake."

"What map?"

"The map Roosevelt said Hitler made showing how South America was already divided up. The British Secret Service made that map to show what Hitler might do. It's a fake."

"Are you sure?"

Sharon got stronger and adamant. "Look, goddammit, I'm not corroborating anything for you. You're going to have to get this verified somewhere else. If you run with this based on what I've said, we'll deny it forever." Then she took a deep breath. "The senator's sick about this. He doesn't want to talk right now."

By this time, Peter, Bart and Earl were all looking at me. "How does he know this?"

"Off-the record, Michael."

"Off-the-record, Sharon."

"He was in the meeting when the British Secret Service presented the map to show the weak spots in South America's defense, and how Hitler might divide it up. But they made it up."

"So he lied about it in the speech."

Sharon again paused for a few moments. "Your words, not mine."

"Alright," I said quietly. "We'll look into it, and keep you out of it. Promise."

I hung up and let everyone know what I had just found out.

Peter was the most surprised. "Jesus Christ! What's he thinking? I mean, that kind of a map is easy to verify. What the hell's he doing?"

"He's hanging on for dear life," Bart said with a professorial tone.

I ran down to the newsroom and told Tim Cullen what I'd learned, but that it was all off-the-record. We needed verification and comment from the highest placed sources. We both worked the phones for the next hour.

Even at that time of night, most of the House and Senate heavyweights were in their offices. Most of them, both Democrats and Republicans, gave us a "No Comment" immediately, either because they didn't know anything about the fake map, or because they wanted to confer with each other to see what the unified line was going to be. When we called them back, some that night and some in the morning, there was a very obvious division of response.

The Democrats backed every word President Roosevelt said. To a man, they all said they believed Hitler was indeed planning to take over the world, and it fit his personality to draw up this kind of map. The Democratic leadership, who were privy to the highest-level war information, said they had seen the map and had no reason to doubt its authenticity.

The Republicans, led by both McNary and Vandenberg, pounced on this. They demanded the president show the map to the press and the world and allow independent verification of its authenticity, or fall prey to the charge that, even if Hitler is planning to divide South America as purported, FDR was clearly using a scare tactic to remain in power, to defuse the political maelstrom surrounding him, and that this underscored his thirst to remain president at all cost - even lying to the American people.

The British Ambassador to the United States had no comment other than to say, "The map speaks for itself." No other British official at any level had any comment.

Reporters besieged Steve Early, FDR's press secretary, demanding comment from the president.

Early stated, "If you focus on the map of Central and South America, you miss the larger point of what the president was saying. Hitler is not going to be satisfied with overrunning Europe, Asia and Africa. Soon enough, he will want the Americas. And if he overruns South America, then captures the Panama Canal, there is every reason to believe he will eventually launch an attack on the United States. The president is adamant that that will not happen. To focus on the veracity of a map we obtained through our military intelligence sources, to question the president's veracity, is beyond the bounds of journalistic necessity. It is dangerous."

Pressed, though, for a response to the charge that FDR made it up in order to maintain hold on power through scare tactics, Early blew up. "Stop it! You see the blood in the water, and you're all vultures. The president is talking about real blood, the blood of potentially countless citizens from all the countries in North, Central and South America. And all you want to talk about is the political nature of some goddamned map."

Shouting, some reporter asked Early if he had seen the map.

"I'm just the press secretary," he said. "I'm not involved in high level military intelligence meetings."

Most of the stories written and broadcast featured a lead that FDR did not deny the map was a fake. He did not confirm its authenticity, or where he got it, or how it was obtained, or when it was drawn up, but he also did not deny it.

The fallout was enormous. The broad-spectrum public reaction was belief and disgust. Americans believed the threat Hitler posed, they believed Hitler was capable of attacking the Americas, but they were disgusted the president would lie to them, especially when he didn't need to.

On October 29th, Barkley and Rayburn led a contingent of nearly thirty Democrats, which included Buckfield, into a private meeting with Roosevelt in his upstairs White House office. Henry Wallace was not there. He was at that moment presiding as president of the Senate.

For nearly three hours, they pulled no punches with the man who had led them out of the Great Depression, which, ironically, began on that date twelve years earlier. Their message was clear: Franklin Roosevelt had been so badly damaged over the past ten months that he was not going to be able to withstand this fake map disaster. They had counted heads in both houses of Congress, and these thirty people were all that was left on his side. They were the only thirty left who believed FDR enough to be willing to fight whatever came up against him in Congress.

Buckfield painfully explained two points to Roosevelt. One, these thirty had plenty of parliamentary tricks in their bag to fight off any Congressional censure or impeachment for a while, but would be eventually out-voted. Two, the fight would be a monumental distraction in the Congress, in the nation, and in the world at a time when we could least afford distraction.

Franklin Delano Roosevelt, a twenty-eight-year veteran on the national and international stage, knew he was done. He told the assembled Democrats that he'd need a week to wrap things up, to talk with Churchill, DeGaulle, other world leaders, and with his military commanders. He'd also need that time to bring Henry Wallace up to speed.

Over the next week, there was a funereal atmosphere surrounding the White House. FDR rarely came out of his office. He cancelled his regular press briefings. He made no public statements, which fueled rumors about personal decisions related to the political turmoil surrounding his presidency.

The news from the battlefront was not very good, but the White House merely put out press releases. No domestic policy legislation was even discussed. Eleanor hadn't written her newspaper column in nearly six weeks. The Republican leadership did not let up. Day after day, all the GOP leaders took to the air and print to decry FDR, his failed moral leadership, his lying and his desire to hang on to power at all costs. The Democrats were muted in their response, mainly because they were so completely outnumbered.

On Thursday afternoon, November 6th, Steve Early told the assembled White House press corps that the president would make a speech from his office at four o'clock tomorrow afternoon. He took no questions.

Chapter 31 – The FDR Meeting

That Thursday night, I was in Peter's office. We were working late, trying to find out any details about FDR's upcoming address. Janine came in around seven, and said simply, "There are Secret Service agents here for you."

We looked, and standing behind Janine were four Secret Service agents. "The president would like to see both of you. Now."

Peter and I grabbed our suit coats, straightened our ties and went with the agents. They took us directly to Grace Tully, FDR's personal secretary. She announced our arrival.

"Please! Come in!" Roosevelt bellowed, blowing smoke as he spoke. "Don't worry about me. I'm just an old man in a wheelchair." Then he laughed.

His wheelchair was near the window, and he motioned to us to sit on the couch. He wheeled over and offered us a drink. Peter had a Scotch. I declined. I felt a bit out of my element.

"How are you, Peter?" Roosevelt seemed jovial, which was not the emotion either one of us expected. "I don't think we've seen each other in six months or so."

"Actually, Mr. President, I was here in late January. You sent for me then, too."

"That was January? My. Time flies, time flies." FDR lit another cigarette. "So, how are things at the Betz Radio Network, Peter?"

"They're going exceptionally well, thank you. We've had a lot of news to cover lately." Peter said this with the knowing needle that only people who have known each other for more than twenty years can use.

"I'm glad to know I can still be of service to the economy," FDR laughed.

I was astounded. I had never before been this alone with the president, and I certainly didn't expect Roosevelt to be in this mood. But then he turned to me.

"And I'm glad you're here, too, Mr. Audray."

"It's my pleasure, Mr. President."

"You know, Mr. Audray, that was a helluva question you asked that started all of this." He just looked at me, took a drag on his cigarette. "I've always wondered. What made you ask that question?"

Peter started to say he told me to ask, but FDR cut him off. "I'd like to hear what Mr. Audray has to say."

"Well, sir," I began. My mouth was dry, my heart was racing 1000 beats a minute, my head felt like it was going to explode. "We did our research on the subject, and I felt it was a legitimate issue."

"A legitimate issue? Really?" His demeanor changed immediately. "Let me show you what a legitimate issue really is." He clamped down on his cigarette holder, wheeled over to his desk, and grabbed some photos and some papers. He wheeled over to me and handed them to me. "These are legitimate issues." I glanced at them. "Go ahead," he said. "Take your time. Look at them closely."

I shared them with Peter, first the photos. There were pictures of Jews being rounded up into Nazi death trains, pictures of the concentration camps I'd heard about, pictures of women and children slaughtered on the streets of Poland and Norway, pictures of the dead and maimed in London, Nazis surrounding the Eiffel Tower, of thousands dead on the Russian Front. Then there were pictures of families living in squalor in what looked like West Virginia and Texas, of farmers standing in a field killed by drought and lack of irrigation, of a mob lynching in Georgia.

I began to skim the papers. They seemed to be military intelligence reports unknown and unreported by any news organization. They discussed Nazi troop movements, stolen Nazi plans, Japanese codes and naval build-up, the danger of Tojo and the paranoid irrationality of Mussolini.

After a few minutes, Franklin Roosevelt said to me, "These are legitimate issues. Hitler is going to try to take over the world." His voice rising, he said, "At the same time, we've got people in this country who can't eat, can't find a job, can't farm because there's no water, and can't move simply because they're a different color." Then he thundered, "*These are legitimate issues!*"

Peter and I sat there quietly. Eventually FDR said, "You can't use any of that. That's all top-secret, and if any of that comes out, I'll know where it came from. For now, those pictures and that information stays in this room."

Peter stared at his Scotch. I reminded myself to keep breathing.

Roosevelt lit yet another cigarette, poured himself another drink. Setting it down on the table in front of him, he looked at us and announced, "I'm going to resign tomorrow." Cocking his head and drifting off a little, he began talking.

"A lot of what has come out about me - and Eleanor - is true. I'm very attracted to women. Despite my condition, they seem to be attracted to me. And to my wife. I was not aware that my wife was attracted to other women until after she found out about Lucy in 1918. But Eleanor is a woman of substance, a good woman with a great mind. We made a deal to make the best of our lives and allow each other to seek happiness the way we needed to. In return, we'd support each other, because we knew that together we could accomplish a great deal more than we could individually. Some people would call this a marriage of convenience. I'd call it a marriage." He paused, took a sip, and continued. "I never tried to hide how I felt about Lucy. She's a remarkable woman. And we did stay in touch over the years, but it wasn't until Winthrop died that I got back together with her. There were a few other women along the way, but Lucy is special. And as for Eleanor, well, she met Lorena when we were campaigning in '32, and they made each other happy. All I ever told her was to be discreet, and to the best of my knowledge, she was. Our kids, they're grown now. They knew something was going on, but they also knew that Eleanor and I both loved them. My children are wonderful people." He paused again, flicked the ash off his cigarette. "My political mistake was not sensing, not realizing that the nature of the media and press coverage has changed. Especially with your new network, Peter. By God, we twisted Garner's nuts that first day, didn't we?" He laughed, as did Peter. It wasn't until right then that I realized John Nance Garner was right. Peter insisted I ask Garner that first question my first day because he had gotten the question from his friend, Franklin Roosevelt.

"Yeah, we got him," Peter said. "And he stormed out, just like you said he would." They both laughed.

"See that closet over there?" FDR pointed to a small door near one of the exit doors. "Harding used to go in that closet and screw Nan Britton. Christ, he got her pregnant before he ran for president. And she was barely out of high school. Didn't hear about that, did you?"

I shook my head no.

"It's true, though. He was a crooked son of a bitch. You know about Carrie Phillips, don't you?"

Again, I shook my head no.

"Carrie Phillips was another woman Harding had an affair with. Lasted about fifteen years. She was a German sympathizer and she tried to blackmail Harding to vote against declaring war on Germany. So when he's running for president, what do you think the Republicans did?"

I shrugged my shoulders. Peter rolled his eyes, because he knew what was coming.

"They paid her $20,000 up front, sent her and her husband on a trip to Japan, and agreed to send her money every month if she'd just keep quiet about it." FDR leaned back in his chair. "Jesus, I still can't believe Cox and I lost to that asshole." He took a breath. "Grover Cleveland, you know about Grover Cleveland?"

"What about him?" I asked.

"First time he's running for president, it comes out that he's got an illegitimate kid. He wins anyway. Then he marries the gorgeous young daughter of one of his best friends. The guy's treated like a hero! She did more for his image than anything. Did you know I met Cleveland when I was a kid?"

Again, I shook my head no.

"Yeah, I was about ten. He told me never to become president." He chuckled under his breath. "I should've listened." FDR lit another cigarette. "And Grant, hell, Grant was a drunk. And Wilson had a stroke, and his wife ran the country. So much for the vice president!" FDR laughed again.

He dragged on his cigarette and his eyes drifted off again. "I never tried to hide the fact I had polio, not really. All the press guys knew it. They just never reported it. It didn't stop me from doing what I had to do, even before I became governor of New York. I didn't think it mattered, not really. But I didn't even think about how news gets reported these days. I thought I could continue to control the agenda, if I stayed on task and showed everyone I was doing the job I was elected to do, these questions about my personal life would go away. You know, I could put up with all the bullshit that was said about me. And Eleanor was pretty good at deflecting it, too. But when Anna got dragged through the mud...." His voice trailed off.

He sat quietly for a moment or two, as did we. When he spoke again, he spoke softly.

"I never lied to anyone. I don't feel like I lied to anyone. I didn't respond to these kind of questions, and that was my problem. But I just don't think you, or anybody else in radio or the press, has any right to ask anybody about their personal life. If we're doing something criminal, like Harding, great, go after us. But we all have to have a sphere of privacy."

Then he chuckled a little and said, "The map of South America… Buckfield told me I oversold it. I didn't need to say it was a secret German map. I could have just said we came into possession of a map that showed how Hitler proposed dividing South America. So that was my mistake, too.

"But it's not that big of a mistake. On top of everything else, though, it pushed me over." He crushed out his cigarette and blew smoke through his nose. It made him look like a tired, old dragon.

"The Japanese are going to attack us soon. I don't know exactly where or when, but it's coming. And when it does, remember that I told you this tonight. It's coming. But now…" he shook his head back and forth a number of times, "…now you've got Wallace. God help him. God help this country." He lit another cigarette. "Henry's a smart guy, but he doesn't have a clue how to do this job. He's going to need all the help he can get."

He picked his drink up off the table and sipped it. He looked at me. "It's the Law of Unintended Consequences, Mr. Audray. You asked a question thinking you'd get a big story. Well, you did get a big story. The biggest. But it snowballed and threw this country into turmoil at a time when we can least afford internal strife. And that's why I'm leaving." He took one last hearty gulp of his Scotch. "I'm going back to Hyde Park and will try to help from there." He turned his wheelchair and faced the window. "Thanks for coming."

"Thank you, Mr. President," we both said. Then Peter said, "I'm sorry, Franklin." Keeping his back to us, Roosevelt just waved his arm in the air.

As we reached the door, Roosevelt turned around.

"Do me a favor," he said. "What I told you here, tonight, in this room? It stays in here forever. Do that much for me."

Peter and I both nodded.

"Alright," I said. "I promise."

November 7, 1941: 387 British bombers attack sites on the North Sea and in Berlin.

Chapter 32 - Resignation

We walked back to BRN from the White House. It was chilly, but we needed the air. We didn't talk. When we reached the network, I followed Peter into his office. He pulled out a bottle of Scotch, and we both got drunk. I don't think we said five words all night.

I fell asleep on his couch. He passed out in his desk chair. We were in rough shape when Janine came in at 7:30 a.m. She made some coffee, sent out for some food, and asked if there was anything we needed. Peter told her to keep people away from him, at least for a while.

I had to do a show yet. Luckily, Tim Cullen was going to be my sole guest that day. When we found out FDR was planning to make an announcement, we decided to go over the entire chronology of The Affairs of State during my program. So at least I didn't have to do much preparation.

The day was really a blur. Around 10:30 a.m., I started feeling human. I must have talked with 200 people that day, but I don't remember any of them. Except Ellen. I called and told her FDR was resigning, but made her swear to embargo it until after his speech. She promised. Ellen Monroe was the only person I told about the nature of the speech. But I didn't even tell her about my White House meeting.

It felt like the entire nation stopped at four o'clock to listen once more to President Franklin Delano Roosevelt.

"My fellow Americans. For the past nine years, you and I have traveled many roads together. You chose me to lead this country out of the Great Depression because you believed in my ideas, my vision. We began quickly, instituting many new laws in our first hundred days that led directly to more jobs, more money, a healthier economy, and a happier nation. It didn't take too long, because we were all working together. We made real progress.

"Then in 1936, you chose me to again lead this country. We electrified the nation, bringing the progress of electricity to every corner of our land. We created more jobs, built more roads and bridges and dams. We began to feel even better about ourselves. We became strong enough to look at our own shortcomings - in racial relations, in education, in farming and other sectors of our economy - because we knew that together we are stronger than we are separately.

"Two years ago, our nation awoke to a growing menace in Europe. Adolph Hitler began a systematic and premeditated attack on his neighbors to his north, south, east and west. His goal is nothing less than ruling the world. As Americans, we debated what this really meant to us, if it really was a situation that demanded our attention. The answer we decided is: yes, we must do everything we can to help our allies.

"Because of the uncertain and dangerous road facing this country, I decided to run for another term as your president. Once again, you chose me to lead this country through uncertain times.

"However, during this calendar year, I have been unwilling to respond to certain questions that have dealt with my personal life, and the personal lives of my wife, Eleanor, and our children. I believed that answering those questions would only dignify them, give them substance and credence, make it easier for more questions like that to be posed at any given moment. I believed that if I did the job you elected me to do, if I paid attention to the events around the world and throughout our country, you would quickly tire of the salacious and scurrilous stories circulated throughout radio, newspapers and magazines. I believed that you would grow weary of the unnecessary and unwanted intrusion into not just my private life, but the intrusion into our collective national best interest.

"Throughout this time, no one has ever accused me of breaking any laws, of doing anything illegal or even remotely considered against the long-term national interest. Yes, there have been charges that I overstepped my authority as president when it came to using government automobiles, but that is just trumped-up hokum. No credible accusation has ever been made stating that I or any member of my family has broken any law.

"Rather, the damaging stories have centered on my personal life, the personal life of the First Lady, and, most regrettably, our children. I have not dignified those stories with a detail by detail response, and I will not now. I will not ever. I long ago realized that in politics, people will pretty much make up their own minds, regardless of the facts.

"But I do have enough experience to tell me that I no longer have the political strength necessary to lead this great country through what I am sure are going to be incredibly challenging times. I have made mistakes in my life, and one of the biggest was underestimating my political opponents and the power of the press.

"Last year, I chose Henry Wallace to be my vice president. I believed then, as I believe now, that if anything was to happen to me, Henry Wallace would be an able and capable leader, a fine president. I hand-picked Henry Wallace for that very reason. He is a smart man who has been involved in high-level discussions for many, many years.

"Make no mistake. The road that lies in the immediate future for the United States is extremely difficult and perilous. Hitler has us in his sights, as does Tojo. Our brothers in Great Britain are putting up the most gallant fight in world history to beat back the advance of the Nazis. We must be willing to step up and shoulder the load with them, because that is in our own self-interest.

"I have concluded, however, that the national self-interest is paramount at this critical point in our history. The Founding Fathers, in their wisdom, put into place the smooth order of leadership succession, to insure that no matter what was happening in the world, there would be no vacuum of leadership here.

"I state categorically, at this moment, I broke no laws, gained nothing personally, and poured every ounce of my energy every waking moment into leading this country, the greatest nation in the world. It is abhorrent to me to admit to any charge that I know is fallacious. But I also know that if I fight these charges with the same gusto with which I intend to fight the war in Europe, it will become an even larger national distraction, perhaps even undermining our national will and efforts to defeat Hitlerism.

"It has been my great honor and distinct pleasure to serve as your president these past nine years. But the larger goal, the goal of keeping our country vibrant and free, able to help our allies whenever and wherever they need it, to be a beacon of democracy for the entire world, is larger than one man. This country will survive everything. But I am convinced, absolutely convinced, that this country cannot be distracted for even one moment from the task of defeating Hitler.

"Therefore, I have decided to resign as your president, effective at 5 p.m. today. Vice President Henry Wallace will be sworn in at that time, in this office.

"Thank you. God Bless You. And Godspeed."

November 13, 1941: The Neutrality Act officially amended.
December 7, 1941: Japan attacks Pearl Harbor.
December 8, 1941: Britain declares War on Japan.
December 8, 1941: Nazis begin gassing Jews at Concentration Camps.
December 8, 1941: Japanese troops invade The Philippines and Malaya,
attack Hong Kong, bomb Guam, destroy a substantial part of the American
air force on the ground at Clark Field Navy Base in Manila.
December 11, 1941: Germany and Italy declare War on the United
States, sign military agreement with Japan.
December 13, 1941: Bulgaria, Romania and Hungary declare War on
the United States.
December 22, 1941: Japanese troops land on Midway and Wake Island.
December 22, 1941: Churchill meets with Wallace in Washington, DC.
December 24, 1941: The United States declares War on Germany and
Japan and the rest of the Axis countries.

Chapter 33 – Wallace's War

Henry Wallace was sworn in as the president of the United States at 5:01 p.m. on Friday, November 7, 1941, in the Blue Room of the White House by Chief Justice Harlan Fiske Stone in front of about twenty people. He immediately addressed the nation in a short and embarrassingly poor speech, thanking Franklin Roosevelt for his years of service to the country, imploring the nation to continue the fight against Hitler, pledging to do his best to avoid direct involvement in the war, and asking for the prayers of the country.

World wide reaction to FDR's resignation was stunned disbelief. DeGaulle called it "the most disheartening news since Paris fell." Winston Churchill said he was "disgusted at the fact Americans seem more interested in what Franklin Roosevelt may have done with another woman than what Adolph Hitler is doing to the world." Stalin just wanted to make sure there would be no interruption in supplies and materials. There was no official comment from Berlin.

President Wallace had to deal with the people he least liked - his colleagues in the House and Senate. While he could more easily get away with dismissing them while he was secretary of agriculture, he couldn't as vice president and certainly not as president. He was, however, politically tone deaf. One of his first acts as vice president had been to close down Cactus Jack Garner's Bureau of Education, the private bar Garner ran to inspire colloquy and congeniality. And just months before his ascension to the Oval Office, Wallace and Louisiana Senator Allen Ellender had a friendly boxing match for charity. Wallace knocked him out.

Wallace had always been interested in foreign policy, even as secretary of agriculture. He believed, rightly, that democracy would be more easily achieved in developing nations if people had enough in their bellies. He was very global in that regard. And in 1940, FDR sent him to the inauguration of Mexican President Manuel Avila Camacho. Wallace delivered a speech in Spanish that earned him high marks on both sides of the border.

Unfortunately, Camacho was the leader of Mexico, not Britain. Wallace and Churchill never warmed up to each other. They had met many times, and their styles - Wallace was spiritual and mystical, Churchill earthy and pragmatic - were polar opposites. Privately, Churchill worried mightily about the leadership abilities of Henry Wallace. At one time, FDR and Churchill were speaking about Charles DeGaulle, who was living in London while leading the Free French movement. FDR said DeGaulle thought he was Joan of Arc. Churchill agreed, but bemoaned that "my bloody bishops won't let me burn him at the stake."

With Wallace on the scene, Churchill felt surrounded by "intemperate and ill-suited boobs." When Churchill replaced Neville Chamberlain as Prime Minister, both British and Americans rejoiced over a leader who understood the danger and was poised to address it. When FDR resigned, though, Churchill felt as if the United States had a leader who may understand the danger but was unable to deal with it.

It wasn't that Wallace was an appeaser or an isolationist. Rather, he believed battles and wars could be won with diplomacy and negotiations. Regrettably, Wallace had neither the skill for diplomacy nor the patience for negotiations. Just a month into the Wallace presidency, the Japanese attacked Pearl Harbor. The next day, Churchill's Britain declared War on Japan. Wallace, in a radio address, vowed to "re-double my efforts to reach a negotiated settlement of grievances with Prime Minister Tojo." It wasn't until Churchill arrived in Washington December 22nd that Wallace became convinced the US had to enter the War. By that time, both

Germany and Italy had declared War on the United States, the Japanese invaded the Philippines and destroyed a substantial number of Air Force planes sitting on the ground in Manila. The Japanese had also invaded Hong Kong and Malaysia, bombed Guam, and landed on Midway and Wake Islands in the Pacific. Wallace's repeated attempts to negotiate with Tojo were rebuffed. It began to dawn on the new president that Japan didn't want to talk. Churchill pulled no punches on his trip to the White House. He told Wallace that unless the US declared war soon there would be very little point. On Christmas Eve, President Henry Wallace sought and received a Declaration of War on the Axis Powers in a unanimous resolution from both Houses of Congress. When he addressed the nation that night, Winston Churchill was literally at his side.

But his international diplomatic deficiencies were soon on display domestically. He ignored pleas from his advisers to work more closely with the Congressional leaders, who were aching to cooperate. Rather than marshalling an effective leadership style Wallace was soon perceived as taking orders from Churchill. Wallace remained hopeful that continued negotiations would bring about a quicker end to the fighting, and reached out through various channels to the Axis leaders. He ignored advice from Secretary of State Cordell Hull, his other Cabinet members, the leaders of both Houses and, to his everlasting embarrassment, Churchill. It wasn't until Josef Stalin sent a telegram to Henry Wallace in February 1942 that Wallace realized talk was futile. The telegram read: "You want to talk with the Axis Leaders. I intend to kill those sons of bitches."

The most surprising change in American leadership, though, came from Arthur Vandenberg. The most vocal Senate isolationist had quickly and dramatically altered his views. Because the United States had been directly attacked, Vandenberg declared, we must defend ourselves, for our present and our future. All the remaining isolationists, including the outspoken and outlandish Congressman Hamilton Fish, embraced this position.

The Republicans managed to galvanize public support. The Wallace Honeymoon ended with the Pearl Harbor attacks, and his lack of immediate action served as a political springboard for the GOP. They tread a fine line between politicizing the war for their own gain, and patriotic opposition to Wallace's lack of leadership. The race for 1944 was well underway in early 1942.

Where FDR had been able to inspire the citizenry to make his alphabet soup programs work, Wallace couldn't. His droning speech pattern made it nearly impossible to feel any rhythm or cadence to his emotional appeals. When he formed the War Production Board in January 1942 to increase production of airplanes, tanks, guns, ammunition and other military necessities, a collective yawn fell over the country.

Wallace also had trouble reigning in his military commanders. In February, he had to choose between Dwight Eisenhower and George Patton to head the War Plans Division. He chose the head-strong Patton, who was more suited for combat than office work. Patton was frustrated with what he saw as Wallace's inability to take quick decisive action. It reached a boiling point just two months later when Patton ignored a direct presidential order and established a Desert Training Center for the First Armored Division in California. Instead of firing Patton, Wallace said nothing. Behind the scenes, FDR tried to give advice to Wallace. But of all his closest confidants, the ones Wallace chose to listen to convinced him FDR was poison politically, and the new president virtually ignored the former. It didn't matter, though. On March 3, 1942, Franklin Delano Roosevelt died of a massive heart attack at his home in Hyde Park, New York.

Those first six months of 1942 the US focused efforts in the Pacific. Fighting from behind since the Pearl Harbor attack, the US forces began to have some success against the Japanese Navy and Air Force. However Wallace continually second-guessed the Admiral of the Navy, Charles Nimitz, opting almost always to wait until nearly too late to launch an attack or a counter-attack.

In August, Churchill flew to Moscow for a meeting with Stalin. Wallace was pointedly not even invited. Though he tried publicly to put a good face on it, Wallace was embarrassed by the snub. His political enemies, now growing bolder every day, pounced on this as yet another example of how we might defeat Hitler but still come out a loser.

From August through October, Republicans took every opportunity to pummel Wallace for every conceivable gaffe. It showed at the polls on November 3, 1942. For the first time in more than a quarter century, the Republicans wrestled control of both houses of Congress in the mid-term elections.

Even though Churchill thought Wallace too idealistic for the job, he didn't want to "have to break in another president." He invited Wallace to meet him in Casablanca in January 1943. At the conference, they agreed to concentrate on an even more aggressive defense in the Atlantic. The battle for the Pacific was still raging, but Wallace believed he could effectively maintain two simultaneous fronts.

Despite everything Wallace lacked, the Allies were making progress in the War. The Central Command in London, under the direction of General George Montgomery, took advantage of Hitler's massive ego and tactical errors. They planned the war and its strategies and told Wallace what to do. The Russians, under Stalin, were slowly demoralizing the German army through its sheer tenacity and insane stubbornness along the Eastern Front. By the end of 1943, there were glimmers of hope, but a long path still remained.

The US economy was doing pretty well by this time. The War Production Board Wallace initiated was paying dividends both at home and abroad. Wallace was able to maintain a high manufacturing and distribution level of war materials, and the US really was The Arsenal of Democracy that FDR envisioned.

Shortly before the conventions began the official 1944 election season, the Allies attempted an invasion and re-capturing of France. Under orders from President Wallace to launch the attack, the Allied invasion was not as successful as had been hoped. General Douglas MacArthur led the multi-national military operation in June 1944. The plan was to surprise the Nazis at their most vulnerable point along the French coast and re-take Paris, then move east toward Germany. But the Axis powers found out and mounted a spirited defense. The Battle of France slowed down the pace and shifted the focus of the War for months.

Wallace was vulnerable within the Democratic Party and from the Republicans. Alben Barkley and Paul Buckfield seriously considered a Democratic challenge to Wallace. Ultimately, they decided that a divisive intra-party battle would almost ensure a Republican victory in 1944. Barkley and Buckfield backed away, and convinced their supporters to campaign for Henry Wallace.

The Republicans had no shortage of capable and eager candidates. Wendell Willkie clearly wanted to run again, but his expedient 1940 conversion to the Republican Party, followed by his ex-officio ambassador work for FDR, rendered him a Party Pariah. Arthur Vandenberg, Charles McNary and Ohio's Robert Taft all became presidential candidates. But they were once more going to be usurped by a Dark Horse.

Thomas Dewey became the governor of New York in 1942 following a high-profile stint as a Special Prosecutor and District Attorney who took on the racketeers. Dewey had succeeded in arresting and convicting a number of high-profile mobsters, including Lucky Luciano, and rode that into national prominence.

Although he had only been a statewide elected official for two years, Dewey threw his hat into the presidential sweepstakes. For the second straight convention, the Republicans nominated an unlikely candidate, but a candidate they felt had the absolute best chance of defeating Henry Wallace. Dewey proved enormously popular, promising to do to Hitler what he had done to the National Syndicate of Crime. During the campaign, Dewey used the power of his governor's office to show how tough he was. Louis Lepke Buchalter, the leader of Murder Incorporated, a gang of mobsters so ruthless they'd indiscriminately kill both their rivals and their underlings, was in Sing Sing staring his execution date in the face. Dewey had convicted Lepke, as he was called, in 1940, after he was tricked into surrendering to J. Edgar Hoover. Lepke contacted Governor Dewey looking for a commutation of his death sentence in exchange for information about the hierarchy of the Mob.

In a highly-publicized meeting, Dewey met with Lepke, promising nothing in advance. Lepke told Dewey that Sidney Hillman, a top advisor to FDR and later to Henry Wallace, was actually a member of the National Syndicate of Crime. Lepke had the proof to back it up.

Dewey took the information, made it public, and challenged Henry Wallace to "rid himself of the influence of organized crime in his inner circle." Then, Dewey refused to commute Lepke's death sentence, and he was electrocuted as scheduled.

Although the popular vote was close, the Electoral College overwhelmingly went for Thomas Dewey. Henry Wallace carried all the Midwest farm states with lower population and fewer electoral votes, while Dewey carried all the major states in all the regions of the country.

As President, Tom Dewey took charge of the War. Forging a close tie with Churchill, they devised strategies to end the War. Churchill told Dewey about The Manhattan Project, the development of a nuclear bomb. Wallace had put the kibosh on the project, proclaiming it too evil to contemplate. Although Wallace understood the necessity for the theoretical knowledge of the bomb, he refused to OK its development past theory. Dewey immediately gave the green light.

Dewey and Churchill met with Stalin in Yalta in 1945. Dewey, to Churchill's utter astonishment and apoplexy, shared detailed information about the Manhattan Project with Stalin. Despite Churchill's assessment of Wallace's leadership skills, he preferred him to Stalin. He knew Stalin was a ruthless murderer who wouldn't remain friendly with the Allies after the War. Wallace and Churchill agreed never to share the Nuclear Secrets with Stalin. Dewey didn't know that, or didn't care to know that. Dewey was enamored of his tough-guy image, and only wanted to determine where and how the Russians and the Americans could help each other. By February of 1946, the Nazis were retreating toward their original border. Mussolini was captured by the British Secret Service in May 1946, and in a brilliant PR move, President Dewey negotiated to have Mussolini incarcerated at Alcatraz. He stayed there until his War Crimes trial began in late 1947.

The end of the War in Europe came rather quickly. The Allies liberated all the concentration camps in early June 1946. The Allies completely surrounded Berlin in late June, and though all the German troops had surrendered their weapons, Hitler was not yet captured. On July 1, 1946, Russian troops broke through Hitler's fortress and captured him alive. In a previously worked out agreement amongst the Allies, whichever force captured Hitler would take jurisdiction and custody. The Russian troops took Hitler to Auschwitz. Stalin planned to oversee his speedy execution.

Stalin arrived at Auschwitz on July 3, 1946. With a bevy of international photographers and military filmmakers on hand, Adolph Hitler was brought into the courtyard at Auschwitz at 1 p.m. Handcuffed to a pole, he faced a Russian firing squad. Stalin, however, had another idea. He ordered his troops to put down their weapons. Stalin walked over to Hitler and unlocked his handcuffs. Hitler, surprised, stood there. Josef Stalin reached into his jacket, pulled out a .45 caliber automatic, and put a bullet through Hitler's head. Then he ordered the photographers and the filmmakers to take as many pictures as they wanted, as long as they distributed them to the world.

The picture of the slain Hitler touched off a round of global celebrating as never before seen. The Japanese, weary of the war and suffering both low morale and a decimated military, surrendered unconditionally on July 5, 1946.

Chapter 34 – The Presidents

The end of the War was a short-lived victory for Thomas Dewey, though. In October 1946, Lucky Luciano was paroled. In interviews immediately after his parole, Luciano said that Dewey had been "on the take" since his days as a New York District Attorney. Luciano claimed, and had some written documentation to back it up, that he had paid Dewey $90,000 during the 1944 presidential campaign in return for his freedom. Luciano also revealed that Dewey was a major stockholder in Mary Carter Paints, the company that backed the building of a casino in the Bahamas run by notorious Mob figure Meyer Lansky. Coincidentally, a Mary Carter Paints franchise was owned and operated in Pittsburgh by Rico Tozzi's brother, Alphonse. Dewey tried to shrug it off, but the stain remained.

That paved the way for Senator Paul Buckfield to defeat Dewey in the 1948 election. The country, tired of nearly twenty years of Depression and War, yearned for a period of peace. Buckfield, an expert in foreign affairs and a highly respected domestic policy wonk, led the country through its first few years of relative calm. He knew he could deal with the intractable demands and continued expansionist thoughts of Josef Stalin, and worked toward an open dialog between the two countries, despite our post-war differences.

The relative peace, fueled by the massive re-building the Allies were funding throughout Europe, lasted quite a long time. A military crisis in Korea was averted when he sent Secretary of State Arthur Vandenberg - a brilliant appointment by Buckfield, who recognized Vandenberg's conversion from isolationism to internationalism was heartfelt - to Seoul to negotiate the settlement of differences between Communist North Korea and democratic South Korea.

As president, Buckfield put racial relations and education at the top of his agenda. A huge baseball fan, Buckfield realized the importance of the Cleveland Indians breaking the color barrier in 1950 with the signing of Larry Doby. He felt the time was right in the United States to accelerate societal integration. It stalled, however, when Paul Buckfield died on

September 19, 1951. His vice president, Adlai Stevenson, finished his term.

Stevenson's first year as president was mostly a caretaker time period. With an election on the horizon, Stevenson wanted to maintain an even keel. When Stevenson ran in 1952, he needed to fill the vice presidential slot. The Republicans had nominated young California Senator Richard Nixon, who chose Wisconsin Senator Joe McCarthy as his running mate. Stevenson knew he needed someone who would bring a wealth of life experience to the position, and who was already highly respected. He chose Dwight Eisenhower, who had established his credentials during the War.

Stevenson and Eisenhower won in both 1952 and 1956. Then in 1960, Eisenhower was the Democratic nominee for president, easily beating Henry Cabot Lodge. The Old General, as he was called, oversaw the development of the Space Agency, and set a national goal of landing an astronaut on the moon by 1975. In '64, Eisenhower ran again, this time easily defeating Arizona Senator Barry Goldwater. Eisenhower retired in 1968, and the Democrats had groomed no one to replace him. Richard Nixon was once again the Republican nominee, and this time he won.

Nixon had cut his teeth as a virulent anti-Communist, and had not changed any of his views over the years. Nixon was obsessed that the Chinese and, to a lesser extent, the Soviet Union, would utilize their population advantage to force feed Communist doctrine on the world. He set into motion a plan to launch a pre-emptive invasion of China and a regime change in Peking. Nixon believed once a friendly government was in place in China, democracy would follow and spread to the Soviet Union.

But the American people were not interested in another foreign war. They were more interested in rockets ships and astronauts. When little known Alabama Governor George Wallace began to articulate those emotions, he quickly captured both the 1972 Democratic nomination and the presidency.

George Wallace was the antithetical Paul Buckfield. A racist to his core, Wallace managed to ride a wave of populism and "plain talk," as he called it, all the way to the White House. Under the glare of the national press and international spotlight, his White Supremacist views became transparent. Only ten months into his term, George Wallace was gunned down in New Orleans by Huey Newton, the leader of an organization called the Black Panthers.

Wallace's vice president, Lyndon LaRouche, was no less of a White Supremacist than Wallace. But as president, LaRouche employed a more moderate tone of voice, even though the policies he endorsed were abhorrent to most Americans.

The Democrats were in a quandary. They didn't want to renominate LaRouche in '76, but were boxed in by some shrewd political maneuvers LaRouche accomplished. He was able to squash the primary challenges mounted by Georgia Governor Jimmy Carter and Arizona Congressman Morris Udall. However, once he secured the nomination, the party leaders refused to mount a campaign for LaRouche. The Democratic leadership let it be known to anybody who listened that LaRouche had hijacked the Party. They repudiated LaRouche every chance they had.

That set up the Republicans in 1976. Ronald Reagan, whom I had interviewed years earlier and who told me he had no interest in politics, ran for the nomination against the House minority leader Gerald Ford of Michigan. It was largely assumed that whoever secured the nomination would win the presidency. It was a bruising primary battle, but in the end, Gerald Ford captured enough delegates to ensure a first-ballot nomination.

Ford and his vice president, Jacob Javits, served two terms. Ford chose Javits, it must be noted, for two reasons. One, he was a powerful and respected New York Senator. And two, he was Jewish. Not only would it help the Republicans grab the Jewish vote, it provided a name and a face for LaRouche's virulent anti-Semitism and White Supremacist viewpoints. Javits endured an unbelievable barrage of slurs during that first campaign, but he knew it would only help the country in the long run. He was right.

1984 ushered in the Kennedy Era. For over two decades, John and Robert Kennedy were the US Senators from Massachusetts, the only brothers in American history to simultaneously represent their state as Senators. They had charisma, vision, the ability to articulate, and a wicked sense of humor. Everyone assumed that at one point John Kennedy would run for president. Timing never presented itself, until 1984. That's when he decided he was too old to do it. But Robert Kennedy, Bobby as he was known, was only fifty-nine. He ran, he won, and he presided over the greatest economic boom of the 20th Century.

Bobby Kennedy had the good fortune of becoming president when personal computers were taking off. He understood the good they could do for people, for companies, for governments and for economies around the world. He articulated the need to invest in computer technology, and by the time he was running for re-election in 1988, the Dow Jones Industrial Average was over 15,000. By the end of his term in January 1993, the Dow had topped 22,000, unemployment nationally was at 1.3%, and the average American income was $41,000.

In 1992, Bobby Kennedy campaigned tirelessly for his heir apparent. Kennedy never made any secret of the fact that when he retired, he wanted his vice president, George McGovern, to retire with him. Throughout his second term, Kennedy scoured the Democratic Party for someone to follow him. He found the man he wanted in Little Rock. Arkansas Governor Bill Clinton was The Man.

The '92 election really underscored the different directions the two national parties had taken. The Democrats were the party of Progressive Thinking, Prosperity and Imagination. The Republicans, epitomized by their presidential nominee Pat Buchanan, were the Party of Moral Elitism, Relativism, and Societal Braking. Clinton and his vice president, Al Gore, thrashed Buchanan and his running mate Phyllis Schlafly, and faced no real opposition in 1996.

Bill Clinton was the 12th man to be president of the United States during my career at the Betz Radio Network. But my name has forever been linked with the first, Franklin Delano Roosevelt.

Chapter 35 – Epilogue

The people involved in The Affairs of State remained in the headlines in one fashion or another for years to come.

FDR died in 1942, but Eleanor lived until 1961. She and Lorena, who died penniless in 1968, remained close, but they never admitted publicly that theirs was a love affair. They maintained an air of private decorum for the rest of their lives.

Lucy Mercer Rutherfurd spent the remaining years of her life at her estate in Allamuchy, New Jersey. She never granted any interviews. Her only public statements on The Affairs of State were the 312 times she invoked the 5th Amendment in September 1941. She passed in 1955.

Charles McNary remained in the Senate until his sudden death in 1944. It was only years after his death that his fingerprints were found all over the rudder that forced FDR's resignation. It was his plan, ably aided and abetted by Arthur Vandenberg, Martin McKay and Ken Kerse that provided the media strategy the Republicans used throughout 1941.

Martin McKay, who had benefited from some of Rico Tozzi's largesse, told McNary about Leo Dailey shortly after the 1940 election. McNary suggested, and McKay concurred, that Dailey be made the Doberman to attack FDR. They knew that Dailey's ego would allow him to believe he was driving the investigation, when the truth was he was their Fall Guy if necessary. Kerse went along with the plan from the beginning, and Vandenberg signed on when it looked as if the Republicans were getting somewhere with their tactics.

It took years for Leo Dailey to recover from his smackdown by the Republican leadership. Though he had been carefully set up to take whatever fall was necessary, the GOP Leaders hadn't counted on such an obviously deceitful gambit as The Lucy On The Train Movie. They quickly used it to their advantage. As he told me years later at a Washington cocktail party, "They shot me in the nuts and wanted me to bleed to death. But I didn't." It turned out he really didn't know anything about The Lucy On The Train movie. His wife, Jane, had thought it all up. Ever the power-hungry of the two, she contacted Rico Tozzi with her plan, and he provided the money. She arranged everything else. When Leo found out, he initiated divorce proceedings. The divorce and his subsequent re-marriage to Mary Beth Keefer hindered him politically until after the 1952 Election. That's when the old guard leadership changed - McKay, Kerse and Vandenberg all died within three months of each other in 1951 - allowing him to re-enter with experience, vigor, style and media savvy. Leo Dailey became House minority leader in early 1953, then a United States Senator in 1956. He remained in the Senate until his retirement in 1988 at age eighty-three.

After her divorce, Jane Hall Dailey moved to Chicago and became a Windy City Socialite, often squired about town by Thomas Marety, the editor of The Chicago Tribune. Marety died under mysterious circumstances in 1957, leaving the bulk of his two-million dollar estate to Jane Hall Dailey, as she still called herself. She drowned off the coast of Aruba in 1966.

Rico Tozzi was shot to death in the office of his bowling alley in Detroit in 1944. The autopsy revealed that he had been shot sixty-three times. No one was ever charged with his murder.

Sharon Tozzi continued to make American history, becoming the first woman White House Chief of Staff when Paul Buckfield became president in 1948. When he died in 1951, she became an author. She had two best-sellers, *Buckfield* and *The Rising Woman in Washington*. We remained friends, eventually enjoying each other's company at large Washington parties. But she held me responsible for the entire Affairs of State, and we never again were as close as we were when we first arrived in Washington in the late '30s. Sharon married well, had three children, and was a doting grandmother when she died in 1995.

Lou Martilotta stayed on the straight and narrow. He settled in the Baltimore area, and became the Head of Hospitality for the Washington Redskins beginning in 1943. He held that position - and truth be told, provided tickets to me regularly - until his retirement in 1958. He died in 1963.

Warren Doones faded into obscurity, becoming the answer to trivia questions. He and his wife remained in Arizona for the rest of their lives.

Carole Lombard, the terrific actress who helped Lucy Mercer Rutherfurd, died on January 16, 1942, in a plane crash in the Nevada desert. She was returning to her home in Los Angeles after traveling the country selling War Bonds. It sent her husband, Clark Gable, into a deep depression. Over time, he pulled out of it, and made a string of hit movies until his death from a heart attack in 1960.

Bart Johnson remained the BRN Corporate Counsel until he retired in 1954. Right after FDR resigned, though, Bart brought in Hunter Rose as Assistant Corporate Counsel. Hunter Rose succeeded Bart Johnson and stayed in that capacity until 1980. Bart died in 1963, Hunter in 1984.

BRN News Director Tim Cullen remained with the network until 1966, when he left to become the Executive Editor of the PBS Nightly News with Charles Collingwood. He retired in 1990, and is, at this time, quite ill.

Peter Betz remained the Chairman and CEO of the Betz Radio Network until he retired at seventy-seven in 1952. He retained the title of Chairman Emeritus, and hired Pat Weaver away from NBC to become BRN's new chairman and CEO. Peter would come into the office about twice a week, but mostly just dabbled and shot the breeze with everyone. He really did step away from the day-to-day operation of the network, which retained its #1 Network position until the late '70s. Peter was found slumped in his office chair, with a glass of Scotch in one hand and The Washington Post in the other on August 31, 1964. He was eighty-nine.

Peter's loyal and trusted Gal Friday, the incomparable Janine Hart, worked with Peter throughout his semi-retirement. She retained her office and her stature, working only when Peter worked. When he passed, she officially retired from BRN. She bought a nice ocean-view house in Boca Raton with the $500,000 Peter bequeathed her in his will. In her life she married and divorced twice, had three children, and enjoyed her last years traveling to visit her grandkids. Janine was seventy-eight when she passed quietly in 1990.

When Pat Weaver joined BRN, he was finally, finally able to spirit away Jack Denif from NBC. Jack and I had become the best of friends over the years, and we would good-naturedly try to get the other to jump networks. But Weaver offered Jack the chance to do investigative stories from an anchor desk, and sweetened the offer with a boatload of money. Jack joined BRN in the summer of 1953, and stayed until he was diagnosed with lung cancer in 1968. He was seventy-four when he passed in 1970.

Earl Mercia made the most of his affiliation with The Affairs of State. In the spring of 1942, I was interviewing the producer/director Preston Sturges about his latest movie, *The Palm Beach Story.* Earl came by after the show and pigeonholed Sturges with ideas for movies and lots of inside information about how Washington really worked. Sturges saw The Affairs of State as an absurd societal farce and invited Earl out to Hollywood. In his own ingratiating style, Earl struck a three-picture deal as a writer and technical consultant. Those three movies, *Snapshot*, *Leverage* and *The Monument* dealt with different aspects of the Franklin-Eleanor story. Fictionalized, of course, and comically absurd.

Earl was able to parlay that into becoming an actual producer, able to make the pictures he wanted. His shining moment came on April 22, 1957, when he accepted the Oscar for Best Picture of 1956, *Marooned in Montreal*. I had to bring him on as a guest, and I asked him on the air how he went from being a private investigator to an Oscar-winning Hollywood Producer.

"Leverage."

"The movie?" I asked.

"No," he said, smiling broadly. We both laughed heartily, because I knew exactly what he meant.

Despite our rocky beginning, Earl and I grew to respect each other's talents. Although we were never close, I considered him a true friend, and we stayed in touch throughout the decades. Earl died of a stroke in 1966. He was sixty-three.

And then there was Ellen Monroe. Ellen and I fell deeply and completely in love during 1941. A few months after FDR resigned, we took a ten-day vacation to Florida. We talked about getting married, having kids, how that would impact each of our careers and lives, where we would live and what we really wanted. We returned to DC energized and happier than we'd ever been. Although we hadn't set a date, we considered ourselves engaged.

Friday, February 27, 1942 was a cold and blustery day in DC. Ellen was hustling back to her office at the AP headquarters when she darted out in front of a Chevy. To this day, I've never quite understood if she didn't see the car, or if the driver didn't see her, or if the driver saw her but couldn't stop. She was only twenty-six.

Ellen Monroe was the best damn reporter I ever knew in my life. She got the big story, protected her sources, and wrote magical, lyrical prose on deadline. As close as we were, and we were very close, she refused to tell me how she came to possess all those letters from Lorena. We'll never know.

Following her death, I submersed myself in work. For the next ten years I didn't even come up for air. Then I met a woman, Diana Burnham, who changed my life. Within a year of our first date, we were married. In fact, Jack was my Best Man. Diana and I had twin girls in 1955. They are the greatest joys of my life.

We were happily married for thirty-eight years, until Diana developed cancer. After she passed, the girls looked after me, making sure I stayed busy and focused.

That's what I did, stayed busy and focused. I am proud of what I believe is a record of continuous on-air service with one network. I appeared on the Betz Radio Network five days a week for sixty-one years. I don't think that record will ever be surpassed.

The radio industry has certainly changed in that time. Beyond the fact that there's television and cable and satellite and the Internet, people still listen to the radio wherever they go. I survived the three different times BRN was sold, most recently to Disney. I like to think I survived strictly because of my talent, but deep down I know it's because I had a smart lawyer who wrote an ironclad contract for me.

The fact you're reading this means I'm dead. That lawyer who negotiated my BRN contract also negotiated my deal for this book. The one item I absolutely insisted on was that this book not be released until after my death.

I had some strong points, and some weak ones. But I wasn't very good at keeping secrets or promises.

Except one.

I promised Franklin Delano Roosevelt that I wouldn't reveal any of the details of my Oval Office meeting with him the night before he resigned. I promised him the conversation would remain with me forever. But we're all gone now. So I guess it's not breaking a promise. And I thought you should hear it from me.

OTHER BOOKS AVAILABLE FROM TWENTY FIRST CENTURY PUBLISHERS

RAMONA

How did a little girl come to be abandoned in the orange scented square of the Andalusian City of Seville? Find out, when the course of her life is resumed at age seventeen.

Ramona catches the mood of Europe in transition, as Ramona, brought up in a quiet village in southern Spain, moves into the cosmopolitan world. Her strange background holds a mystery, revealed as the novel develops, but then events take on a different hue as a new perspective emerges. But that is not all, and reality seems to bend further, but does it?

From a novel within a novel, we move on to ... well, let's not say. Read it, and the author challenges you to predict each step of the unfolding plot, and just when it defies belief, read on – you will believe.

Ramona by Johnny John Heinz
ISBN: 1-904433-01-4

MEANS TO AN END

Enter the world of money laundering, financial manipulation and greed, where a shadowy Middle Eastern organisation takes on a major corporation in the US. As the action shifts through exotic locations, who wins out in the end? Certainly, the author's first hand experience of international finance lends a chilling credibility to the plot.

As well as being a compelling work of fiction this book offers, in a style accessible to the layman, a financial insider's insight into the financial and moral crisis, which broke in the early millennium, in the top echelons of corporate America.

Means to an End by Johnny John Heinz
ISBN: 1-84375-008-2

THE SIGNATURE OF A VOICE

The Signature of a Voice is a cat-and-mouse-game between a violent trio, led by a psychopathic killer, and a police officer on suspension. Move and countermove in this chess game is planned and enacted. The reader, in the position of god, knows who is guilty and who plans what, but just as in chess, the opponents' plans thwart one another. The outcomes twist and turn to the final curtain fall.

There is a sense of suspense but also anger as the system seems to be working against those who are fighting on the side of right, while the perpetrators of vicious crimes seem able to operate freely and choose to do what they wish. They choose the route of ultra-violence to stay ahead of the law in an otherwise tranquil community: they plan and execute, in all senses of the word. Is it possible to triumph over this ruthlessness?

The Signature of a Voice by Johnny John Heinz
ISBN: 1-904433-00-6

TARNISHED COPPER

Tarnished Copper takes us into the arcane world of commodity trading. Against this murky background, no deal is what it seems, no agreement what it appears to be. The characters cheat and deceive each other, all in the name of grabbing their own advantage. Hiro Yamagazi, from his base in Tokyo, is the biggest trader of them all. But does he run his own destiny, or is he just jumping when Phil Harris pulls the strings? Can Jamie Edwards keep his addictions under control? And what will be the outcome of the duel between the hedge fund manager Jason Serck, and brash, devious, high-spending Mack McKee? And then one of them goes too far: life and death enters the traders' world........

Geoff Sambrook is ideally placed to take the reader into this world. He's been at the heart of the world's copper trading for over twenty years, and has seen the games - and the traders - come and go. With his ability to draw characters, and his knack of making the reader understand this strange world, he's created an explosive best-selling financial thriller. Read it and learn how this part of the City really works.

Tarnished Copper by Geoffrey Sambrook
ISBN 1-904433-02-2

OVER A BARREL

From the moment you land at Heathrow on page one the plot grips you. Ed Burke, an American oil tycoon, jets through the world's financial centres and the Middle East to set up deals, but where does this lead him? Are his premonitions on the safety of his daughter Louise in Saudi Arabia well founded? Who are his hidden opponents? Is his corporate lawyer Nicole with him or against him?

As the plot unfolds his company is put into play in the tangle of events surrounding the 1990 invasion of Kuwait. Even his private life is drawn into the morass.

In this novel Peter depicts the grim machinations of political and commercial life, but the human spirit shines through. This is a thriller that will hold you to the last page.

Over a Barrel by Peter Driver
ISBN 1-904433-03-0

THE BLOWS OF FATE

It is a crisp clear day in Sofia and three young friends are starting out in life, buoyant with their hopes, aspirations, loves. But this is not to be, as post war Eastern Europe comes under the grip of its brutal communist regime. Driven from their homes and deprived of their basic rights, the three friends determine to escape ... but one of them cannot seize that moment. It may seem that life cannot become worse for the families who are ostracised and trapped in their own country, but the path of hopelessness descends to the concentration camps and unimaginable brutality.

For those who escape there is the struggle to survive, tempered by the kindness they encounter along their way. We see how talent and determination can win through. Yet, though they may have escaped those terrible years in Bulgaria, they can never escape their personal loss of family, homeland, friends and love that may have been.

While life is very difficult for the three friends, they do not forget each other. After forty years of separation, they meet. For each one fate has prepared a surprise....

Can beauty, art and love eclipse the manmade horrors of this world? You will think they can, as Antoinette Clair brings out the beautiful things in life, so that the poignancy of her novel reaches into the toughest of us, and moves to tears.

This is a tale of beauty, music and a grand love, but it is also expressive of the sad recurring tale of Europe's recent history.

The Blows of Fate by Antoinette Clair
ISBN 1-904433-04-9

THE GORE EXPERIMENT

William Gore is not a mad scientist: he is a dedicated medical researcher working on G.L.X.-14, an AIDS serum. He is on the brink of a major breakthrough and seeks to force the pace, spurred on by his knowledge of the suffering to be spared, if he is right, and the millions of lives of AIDS victims to be saved. But as things begin to go askew, how far dare he go? What level of risk is warranted? What, and who, is he prepared to sacrifice? The answers become worse than you can imagine as William Gore treads a path to horror.

The Gore Experiment may be fiction, but it addresses real issues in the world of experimental vaccines, disease-busting drugs and genetic engineering. Is science unknowingly exposing us to risk through overconfidence in ever narrowing fields of expertise, ignorant of ramifications? Or is the red tape of bureaucracy signing the death warrants of the terminally sick? Well, William Gore at least is confident. He is convinced of what he must do. Should he do it?

This is not a book for the faint-hearted. H.Jay Scheuermann adds a new high-tech dimension to the traditions of vampires, Jekylls and Hydes as William Gore paves his own road to hell. But there is a twist....

The Gore Experiment by H. Jay Scheuermann
ISBN 1-904433-05-7

CASEY'S REVENGE

Is this the best of all possible worlds? Well, almost, or so Casey Forbes thinks. She is a college professor with bbb successful career and good friends; boyfriend trouble in the past, perhaps, but who hasn't? And her prospects are excellent.

But no woman can expect to descend into the real life nightmare, that envelopes Casey ... out of nowhere.

Mary Charles's heroine is forced to confront the darkest side of human nature and the most bestial of acts committed by man. Yet it is the strength of will, the trauma inflicted on Casey's personality and the resourcefulness of the female psyche that Mary Charles explores in this novel. What does it take to survive overwhelming adversity and does Casey have it?

Many dream of revenge but wonder if they have within themselves the capacity to carry it out. Can Casey? And is the price going to be too high?

Read this thriller and one thing is certain: don't ever let this happen to you.

Casey's Revenge by Mary Charles
ISBN 1-90443-06-5

SABRA'S SOUL

From the heart of the California rock music scene comes this story of much more than just love and betrayal.

Does Sabra know who she is? She thinks she is a loving mother and a trusting wife, but her husband Logan, a powerful figure in rock music, seems consumed by commitments to his latest band, 23 Mystique. Sabra begins to feel that something is missing, to feel a yearning for something more. Is she too trusting and too slow to spot Logan's lapses in behaviour?

When Sabra meets the pop idol of her sub-teen daughters, things begin to change. She can't believe the attraction growing in her for this youthful figure, her junior by several years.

Lisa Reed paints a picture of virtue and vice in this tale of love, lust, betrayal and drug-induced psychosis, set amidst the glitter of the rock scene. It is not fate that leads these people on but their own actions. Can they help it and where does it lead?

Who better than Lisa Reed, with her access to the centre of rock, to weave this tense plot as it descends from the social whirl into the deadly serious. If you are a successful rock star, this is a book for you, and if not ... well, read on and dream.

Health warning: this book contains salacious sex scenes demanded by its setting.

Sabra's Soul by Lisa Reed
ISBN 1-90443307-3

FACE BLIND

From the pen of Raymond Benson, author of the acclaimed original James Bond continuation novels (Zero Minus Ten, The Facts of Death, High Time to Kill, DoubleShot, Never Dream of Dying, and The Man With the Red Tattoo) and the novel Evil Hours, comes a new and edgy noir thriller.

Imagine a world where you don't recognize the human face. That's Hannah's condition - prosopagnosia, or "face blindness" - when the brain center that recognizes faces is inoperable. The onset of the condition occurred when she was attacked and nearly raped by an unknown assailant in the inner lobby of her New York City apartment building. And now she thinks he's back, and not just in her dreams.

When she also attracts the attention of a psychopathic predator and becomes the unwitting target of a Mafia drug ring, the scene is set for a thrill ride of mistaken identity, cat-and-mouse pursuit, and murder.

Face Blind is a twisting, turning tale of suspense in which every character has a dark side. The novel will keep the reader surprised and intrigued until the final violent catharsis.

Face Blind by Raymond Benson
ISBN 1-904433-10-3

CUPID AND THE SILENT GODDESS

The painting Allegory with Venus and Cupid has long fascinated visitors to London's National Gallery, as well as the millions more who have seen it reproduced in books. It is one of the most beautiful paintings of the nude ever made.

In 1544, Duke Cosimo de' Medici of Florence commissioned the artist Bronzino to create the painting to be sent as a diplomatic gift to King François I of France.

As well as the academic mystery of what the strange figures in the painting represent, there is the human mystery: who were the models in the Florence of 1544 who posed for the gods and strange figures?

Alan Fisk's Cupid and the Silent Goddess imagines how the creation of this painting might have touched the lives of everyone who was involved with it: Bronzino's apprentice Giuseppe, the mute and mysterious Angelina who is forced to model for Venus, the brutal sculptor Baccio Bandinelli and his son, and the good-hearted nun Sister Benedicta and her friend the old English priest Father Fleccia, both secret practitioners of alchemy.

As the painting takes shape, it causes episodes of fear and cruelty, but the ending lies perhaps in the gift of Venus.

'A witty and entertaining romp set in the seedy world of Italian Renaissance artists.' Award-winning historical novelist Elizabeth Chadwick. (The Falcons of Montabard, The Winter Mantle).

'Alan Fisk, in his book Cupid and the Silent Goddess, captures the atmosphere of sixteenth-century Florence and the world of the artists excellently. This is a fascinating imaginative reconstruction of the events during the painting of Allegory with Venus and Cupid.' Marina Oliver, author of many historical novels and of Writing Historical Fiction.

Cupid and the Silent Goddess by Alan Fisk
ISBN 1-904433-08-4

TALES FROM THE LONG BAR

Nostalgia may not be what it used be, but do you ever get the feeling that the future's not worth holding your breath for either?

Do you remember the double-edged sword that was 'having a proper job' and struggling within the coils of the multiheaded monster that was 'the organisation'?

Are you fed up with forever having to hit the ground running, working dafter not smarter - and always being in a rush trying to dress down on Fridays?

Do you miss not having a career, a pension plan or even the occasional long lunch with colleagues and friends?

For anyone who knows what's what (but can't do much about it), Tales from the Long Bar should prove entebrtaining. If it doesn't, it will at least reassure you that you are not alone.

Londoner Saif Rahman spent half his life working in the City before going on to pursue opportunities elsewhere. A linguist by training, Saif is a historian by inclination.

Tale from the Long Bar by Saif Rahman
ISBN 1-904433-10-X

COUSINS OF COLOR

Luzon, Philippines, 1899. Immersed in the chaos and brutality of America's first overseas war of conquest and occupation, Private David Fagen has a decision to make - forsake his country or surrender his soul. The result: A young black man in search of respect and inclusion turns his back on Old Glory - and is hailed a hero of the Filipino fight for independence.

Negro blood is just as good as a white man's when spilled in defense of the American Way, or so Fagen believed. But this time his country seeks not justice but empire. Pandemonium rules Fagen's world, Anarchy the High Sheriff, and he knows every time he pulls the trigger, he helps enslave the people he came to liberate.

Not just an account of an extraordinary black solider caught in the grip of fate and circumstance, Cousins *of Color* tells the story of Fagen's love for the beautiful and mysterious guerilla fighter, Clarita Socorro, and his sympathy for her people's struggle for freedom. *Cousins* also chronicles Colonel Fredrick Funston's monomaniacal pursuit of victory at any cost and his daredevil mission to capture Emilio Aguinaldo, the leader of the Philippine revolution. Other characters include the dangerously unstable, Captain Baston, particularly cruel in his treatment of prisoners, and Sergeant Warren Rivers, the father Fagen never had.

Himself a Vietnam combat veteran, author William Schroder hurtles us through the harsh realities of this tropical jungle war and provides powerful insight into the dreams and aspirations of human souls corrupted and debased by that violent clash of cultures and national wills. Based on actual events, David Fagen's pursuit of truth and moral purpose in the Philippine Campaign brings focus to America's continuing obsession with conquest and racism and provides insight into many of today's prevailing sentiments.

Cousins of Color by William Schroder
Hardcover - ISBN 1-904433-13-8
Paperback - ISBN 1-904433-11-1

EVIL HOURS

"My mother was murdered when I was six years old." Shannon has become used to giving this explanation when getting to know new arrivals in the small West Texas town of Limite. She has never hidden the truth about her mother, but she is haunted by the unresolved circumstances surrounding her mother's murder and the deaths of a series of other women around the same time. It is when she sets about uncovering the truth, with the help of an investigator, that the true depravity of Limite's underbelly begins to emerge.

The very ordinariness of the small town lends a chill to *Evil Hours*, as revelations from a murky past begin to form a pattern; but much worse they begin to cast their shadow over the present.

As Shannon delves behind the curtain of silence raised by the prominent citizens of Limite, she finds herself caught up in a sequence of events that mirror those of the previous generation…and the past and the present merge into a chilling web of evil.

In *Evil Hours* Raymond Benson revisits his roots and brings to life the intrigue of a small West Texas Town. Benson is the author of the original James Bond continuation novels: *The Man With the Red Tattoo*; *Never Dream of Dying*; *DoubleShot*; *High Time to Kill*; *The Facts of Death*; and *Zero Minus Ten*. He has recently released a thriller set in New York, *Face Blind*.

Evil Hours by Raymond Benson
ISBN 1-904433-12-X

PAINT ME AS I AM

What unique attribute dwells within the creative individual? Is it a flaw in the unconscious psyche that gives rise to talent, influencing artists to fashion the product of their imagination into tangible form, just as the grain of sand gives rise to the precious pearl? Or is it more?

To the world around him, Jerrod Young appears to be a typical, mature art student. He certainly has talent as a painter, but hidden within the darkest corners of his mind are unsavory secrets, and a different man that nobody knows.

H. Jay Scheuermann, author of The Gore Experiment, gives us another great psychological thriller, delivering a chilling look inside the psyche of a man whose deepest thoughts begin to assume control over his actions. The needs of the darkness within him seem to grow with each atrocity, his ever-increasing confidence fueling an inexorable force for evil.

Hell is not a place, but a state of mind, a state of being: it exists within each of us. We like to believe we can control it, but the cruel alternative is that our choices have already been made for us. Jerrod has accepted his truth, and is resolved to serve his inner demon.

Special Agent Jackie Jonas has been given her first assignment, a case that may mark the beginning and the end of her FBI career, as it leads her into a web of violence and deception, with each new clue ensnaring the lives of the ones she loves....

This gripping story brings to life the awful truth that the Jerrod Young's of this world do, in fact, exist. It could be one of your co-workers, the person behind you in the supermarket checkout line, or even the person next door. Can you tell? Are you willing to stake your life on it?

Paint Me As I Am by H. Jay Scheuermann
ISBN 1-904433-14-6

EMBER'S FLAME

"He could focus on her intelligent conversations and the way her aqua blue eyes lit up when they were amused and turned almost gray when they were sad. It was easier to admire the strength she carried in her soul and the light she carried in her walk. Now, seeing her in five inch heels and hot pants..."

Ember Ty is majoring in journalism. Graced with stunning looks, she finances her studies by dancing in a strip club. She has a hot boyfriend in a rock band, a future writing about the music world, and yes, she's working hard to achieve it.

But it all starts to go wrong. There is a predator on the loose, and Ember is sucked into a nightmare that none of us would care to dream, let alone live.

Vulnerable and threatened, Ember is drawn into a love triangle that might never have been, with the man she is to marry and the man she knows she can never have.

Ember's Flame by Lisa Reed
ISBN 1-904433-15-4

THE RELUCTANT CORPSE

"Stewart Douglas could not, under any circumstances, be considered your average human being. He'd always been a fan of agony as long, of course, as it wasn't his own." Well, Stewart is the local mortician, and maybe he has a less than healthy interest in the job. Every community has its secrets, and Savannah, Georgia, is no exception. The questions are: exactly what are those secrets, and who do they belong to?

Mary Charles introduces us to a community of characters, and although we do see the mortician at work, everything is comfortably tranquil, or so it seems. But strange things are afoot. Who can you trust? It may be best to let things rest, but events have their own momentum.

There is a foray into the antique art market, which gives the plot a subtle twist, and as the sinister undertone begins to take on real menace, you will be unable to put down this exciting suspense novel.

"Set within the confines of Savannah and Southeast Georgia, The Reluctant Corpse confronts the reader with frightening images lurking just behind closed doors and stately homes. Well written and enjoyable." William C. Harris Jr. (Savannah best-selling author of Delirium of the Brave and No Enemy But Time).

The Reluctant Corpse by Mary Charles
ISBN 1-904433-16-2

SINCERE MALE SEEKS LOVE AND SOMEONE TO WASH HIS UNDERPANTS

Colin Fisher is long-divorced with two grown-up children and an ageing mother in care. He is not getting any younger. Perhaps it is time to get married again. There are hordes of mature, nubile, attractive, solvent (hopefully) women out there, and marriage would provide regular sex and companionship, and someone to take care of the tedious domestic details that can make a man late for his golf and tennis matches. All Colin needs to do is smarten up a bit, get out more and select the lucky woman from amongst the numerous postulants. What could be easier?

Christopher Wood had adapted various personae to write over fifty books, ranging from high adventure to saucy picaresque. He has also written the screenplays for fourteen movies, including two of the most successful James Bond films ever: The Spy Who Loved Me and Moonraker. When not writing, he makes wine at his home in France.

Sincere male seeks love and somone to wash his underpants by
Christopher Wood
ISBN 1-904433-18-9

GUY DE CARNAC: DESCENT

The character from the Dr Who New Adventure, Sanctuary, and the audio drama, The Quality Of Mercy, returns in a full-length novel.

Set in 1303, young Templar Knight Guy de Carnac begins a long and life-changing journey when everything he holds dear is torn apart into mayhem and intrigue between the French crown and the Papacy.

Guy de Carnac: Descent by David McIntee
ISBN 1-904433-19-7

Please visit our website to learn more about our authors and their books. We welcome your feedback by e-mail

www.twentyfirstcenturypublishers.com

Printed in the United States
23023LVS00002B/382-387

9 781904 433170